PRAISE FOR
THE GREAT INDIAN NOVEL

"A wickedly funny satire, sparing no one, not even Mahatma Gandhi . . . Just thinking about it makes me want to go back and reread it."
—Fareed Zakaria, *New York Times Book Review*

"A richly complex work of imaginative flight and scholarly depth. *The Great Indian Novel* combines historical fact with daily marvels."
—Louise Erdrich

"A hot-minded, century-striding tale of modern Indian shenanigans . . . Reads fast and randy, like a miniseries that won't quit. . . . It should entertain everyone."
—*Washington Post Book World*

"An outrageous feast, spilling over with myths, rhymes, tales of ancient treachery and wisdom and tales of modern foolishness and heroism . . . Wildly original."
—*Chicago Tribune*

"A great Indian novel . . . An exhilarating experience."
—*Village Voice*

"A tour de force of considerable brilliance."
—*Times Literary Supplement*

"Enormously successful . . . This is indeed a great Indian novel."
—*Newsday*

"An entertaining tour de force."
—*Sunday Times* (London)

THE GREAT INDIAN NOVEL

SHASHI THAROOR

THE
GREAT INDIAN
NOVEL

ARCADE PUBLISHING • NEW YORK

Arcade Publishing books may be purchased in bulk at special discounts for sales promotion, corporate gifts, fund-raising, or educational purposes. Special editions can also be created to specifications. For details, contact the Special Sales Department, Arcade Publishing, 307 West 36th Street, 11th Floor, New York, NY 10018 or info@skyhorsepublishing.com.

Arcade Publishing® is a registered trademark of Skyhorse Publishing, Inc.®, a Delaware corporation.

Visit our website at www.arcadepub.com.

10 9 8 7 6 5 4 3 2

Library of Congress Cataloging-in-Publication Data is available on file.

ISBN: 978-1-61145-318-8

Printed in the United States of America

for
my sons
Ishan and Kanishk
and
for our own
Tilottama

ABOUT THE TITLE

A hasty note of disclaimer is due to those readers who may feel, justifiably, that the work that follows is neither great, nor authentically Indian, nor even much of a novel. *The Great Indian Novel* takes its title not from the author's estimate of its contents but in deference to its primary source of inspiration, the ancient epic the *Mahabharata*. In Sanskrit, *Maha* means great and *Bharata* means India.

The *Mahabharata* has not only influenced the literature, art, sculpture and painting of India but it has also moulded the very character of the Indian people. Characters from the Great Epic . . . are still household words [which] stand for domestic or public virtues or vices . . . In India a philosophical or even political controversy can hardly be found that has no reference to the thought of the *Mahabharata*.

C. R. Deshpande, *Transmission of the Mahabharata Tradition*

The essential *Mahabharata* is whatever is relevant to us in the second half of the twentieth century. No epic, no work of art, is sacred by itself; if it does not have meaning for me now, it is nothing, it is dead.

P. Lal, *The Mahabharata of Vyasa*

Our past and present and future problems are much more crowded than we expect . . . I think in India, some stories should be kept alive by literature. Writers experience another view of history, what's going on, another understanding of 'progress' . . . Literature must refresh memory.

Gunter Grass, speaking in Bombay

CONTENTS

The Great Indian Family

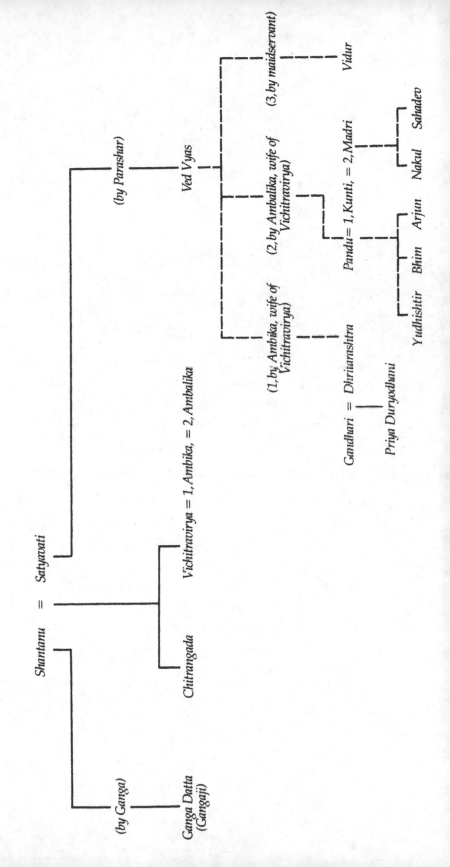

ॐ

What follows is the tale of Vyasa,
  great Vyasa, deserver of respect;
a tale told and retold,
  that people will never cease telling;
a source of wisdom
  in the sky, the earth, and the lower world;
a tale the twice-born know:
  a tale for the learned,
skilful in style, varied in metres,
  devoted to dialogue human and divine.

    P. Lal
    The Mahabharata of Vyasa

THE FIRST BOOK:
THE TWICE-BORN TALE

They tell me India is an underdeveloped country. They attend seminars, appear on television, even come to see me, creasing their eight-hundred-rupee suits and clutching their moulded plastic briefcases, to announce in tones of infinite understanding that India has yet to develop. Stuff and nonsense, of course. These are the kind of fellows who couldn't tell their *kundalini* from a decomposing earthworm, and I don't hesitate to tell them so. I tell them they have no knowledge of history and even less of their own heritage. I tell them that if they would only read the *Mahabharata* and the *Ramayana*, study the Golden Ages of the Mauryas and the Guptas and even of those Muslim chaps the Mughals, they would realize that India is not an underdeveloped country but a highly developed one in an advanced state of decay. They laugh at me pityingly and shift from one foot to the other, unable to conceal their impatience, and I tell them that, in fact, everything in India is over-developed, particularly the social structure, the bureaucracy, the political process, the financial system, the university network and, for that matter, the women. Cantankerous old man, I hear them thinking, as they make their several exits. And, of course, there is no party-ticket for me any more, no place for me in their legislative confabulations. Not even a ceremonial governorship. I am finished, a man who lives in the past, a dog who has had his day. I shall not enter the twenty-first century with them.

But I do not finish so easily. Indeed, I have scarcely begun. 'I have a great deal to say,' I told my old friend Brahm, 'and if these fellows won't hear it, well, I intend to find myself a larger audience. The only thing is that the old hand doesn't quite behave itself any more, tends to shake a bit, like a ballot-paper in a defecting M P's grasp, so could you get me someone I could dictate it to, an amanuensis?'

Brahm looked a little doubtful at first, and said, 'You know, V.V., you have a bit of a reputation for being difficult to work with. You remember what happened to the last poor girl I sent you? Came back in tears and handed in her resignation, saying she didn't want to hear of the Apsara Agency again. I can't afford another one of those incidents, and what's all this about a book, anyway? You ought to be leaning back on those bolsters and enjoying a quiet retirement, letting these other fellows run about for you, reaping the adulation of a good life well spent. After all, what are laurels for but to rest on?'

I fairly bit his head off, I can tell you. 'So, you think I'm not up to this, do you?' I demanded. 'Dammit, what I am about to dictate is the definitive memoir of my life and times, and you know what a life and times mine have been. Brahm, in my epic I shall tell of past, present and future, of existence and passing, of efflorescence and decay, of death and rebirth; of what is, of what was, of what should have been. Don't talk to me of some weepy woman whose shorthand trips over her fingernails; give me a man, one of your best, somebody with the constitution and the brains to cope with what I have to offer.'

And Brahm said, 'Hmm, well, if you insist, I have a chap in mind who's almost as demanding as you, but who can handle the most complex assignments. Humour him and you won't be disappointed.'

So, the next day the chap appeared, the amanuensis. Name of Ganapathi, South Indian, I suppose, with a big nose and shrewd, intelligent eyes. Through which he is staring owlishly at me as I dictate these words. Brahm was right about his being demanding. He listened to me quietly when I told him that his task would be no less than transcribing the Song of Modern India in my prose, then proceeded to lay down an outrageous condition. 'I'll do it,' he said, without batting an eyelid, 'provided you work to my pace. I shall reside with you, and as long as I'm ready, you must not pause in your dictation.'

Something about him, elephantine tread, broad forehead and all, impressed me. I agreed. And he was back in the afternoon, dragging his enormous trunk behind him, laden with enough to last him a year with me, I have no doubt. But I hadn't given in without a thought. I made my own condition: that he had to understand every word of what I said before he took it down. And I was not relying merely on my ability to articulate my memories and thoughts at a length and with a complexity which would give him pause. I knew that whenever he took a break to fill that substantial belly, or even went around the corner for a leak, I could gain time by speaking into my little Japanese tape-recorder. So you see, Ganapathi, young man, it's not just insults and personal remarks you'll have to cope with. It's modern technology as well.

Yes, yes, put it all down. Every word I say. We're not writing a piddling Western thriller here. This is my story, the story of Ved Vyas, eighty-eight years old and full of irrelevancies, but it could become nothing less than the Great Indian Novel.

I suppose I must begin with myself. I was born with the century, a bastard, but a bastard in a fine tradition, the offspring of a fisherwoman seduced by a travelling sage. Primitive transport system or not, our Brahmins got about a lot in those days, and they didn't need any hotel bookings then. Any householder was honoured by a visit from a holy man with a sacred thread and no luggage but his learning. He would be offered his host's hospitality, his food, his bed and often, because they were a lot more understanding then, his daughter as well. And the Brahmin would partake of the offerings, the shelter, the rice, the couch, the girl, and move on, sometimes leaving more than his slippers behind. India is littered with the progeny of these twice-born travelling salesmen of salvation, and I am proud to be one of them.

But fisherfolk weren't often their style, so the fact of her seduction says something for my mother Satyavati. She was on the river that day, the wet fold of her thin cotton sari flung over one shoulder, its hem riding up her thigh, the odour of perspiration mixing with that of the fish she was heaving into her boat, when a passing sage, Parashar, caught a glimpse of her. He was transfixed, he later told me, by the boldness of her beauty, which transcended any considerations of olfactory inconvenience. 'Lovely lady,' he said in his best manner, 'take my love', and coming from a Brahmin, especially one as distinguished as he was, that was an offer no woman could refuse.

But my mother wasn't wanton or foolish, and she had no desire to become known as either. 'There are people watching from both sides of the river,' she replied, 'so how can I give myself to you?'

The Brahmin was no novice in the art of seduction, though; he had spotted a little deserted island some way up the river, whose interior was screened by a thick copse of trees. He motioned her to paddle towards it, and swam to it himself in a few swift, strong strokes.

Satyavati followed, blushing. She had no intention of resisting the sage: a mist around the island, already curtained by the trees, dispelled her modest hesitation. (When she told me the story she claimed Parashar had caused a magic cloud to settle on the island to keep off prying eyes, which I took as evidence of understandable female hyperbole.) Obedience was, of course, a duty, and no maiden wished to invite a saintly curse upon her head. But Satyavati was no fool, and she understood that for an unmarried virgin, there was still a difference between bedding a persuasive Brahmin on her own and being offered to one by her father — which was hardly likely to happen, since sages did not stop at fisherfolk's huts and Parashar could not be expected,

with one of her caste, to go through a form of marriage that would sanctify
their coupling. 'I've never done this before,' she breathed. 'I'm still a virgin
and my father will be furious if I cease to be one. If you take me, what will
become of me? How can I show my face amongst my people again? Who will
marry me? Please help me,' she added, fluttering her eyelashes to convey that
though her flesh was willing, her spirit was not weak enough.

Parashar smiled in both desire and reassurance. 'Don't worry,' he said,
'virginity isn't irretrievable. I'll make sure that no one will doubt your
virginity even after you yield to me. That's nothing to be afraid of.'

And his ardour stifled further conversation.

Even men of the world — and few in this category can equal one who is
above this world — feel tenderly for those they have loved. So, afterwards,
lying by her side, Parashar asked Satyavati when she had had her time of
month. And when he had heard her answer, he did not attempt to evade his
responsibility. 'There will be a child born of our union,' he said simply, 'but I
will keep my word and ensure that your normal life as a daughter of your
people will not be disturbed.'

Refusing to let her panic, Parashar led Satyavati to her father's hut, where
he was received with due deference. 'Your daughter, whom I have met by the
river today, has a spark of grace in her,' he intoned sententiously. 'With your
permission, I wish her to accompany me for a short period as my maid, so that
I may instruct her in higher learning. I shall, of course, return her to you when
she is of marriageable age.'

'How can I be sure that no harm will come to her?' asked the startled father,
who was no village innocent either.

'You know of me in these parts,' Parashar responded haughtily. 'Your
daughter will return to you within one year, and she will return a virgin. You
have my word.'

It was not often that a fisherman, even a head fisherman, which is what
Satyavati's father was, challenged the word of a Brahmin. He bowed his head
and bade his daughter farewell.

Satyavati fared well. Parashar took her far away from the region before her
pregnancy began to show. I was born in an old midwife's home in the forest.

'We must name the child Dvaipayana, one created on an island,' said
Satyavati rather sentimentally to my father. He nodded, but it wasn't a name
that ever seemed likely to stick. 'Women,' he said to me once, years later,
shaking his head in amused tolerance. 'Imagine, a name like that for the son of
a wandering Brahmin in British India. No, Ved Vyas is much easier. I've
always wanted a son named Ved Vyas.' And so Ved Vyas it was and, since I
was a somewhat diminutive fellow, V.V. I became.

After less than a month's suckling, I was taken away from my mother, who had to begin her journey home. My father had taught her several lessons from the ancient texts, including one or two related to the inscrutabilities of virginity. Upon her return, to quell the rumours in the village, her father had Satyavati examined by the senior midwife. Her hymen was pronounced intact.

Brahmins knew a great deal in those days.

3

It was just as well, for Satyavati the fish-odorous was destined to become the wife of a king. Yes, we had kings in those days, four hundred and thirty-five of them, luxuriating in titles such as Maharaja and Nawab that only airline ads and cricket captains sport any more. The British propped them up and told them what to do, or more often what not to do, but they were real kings for all that, with palaces and principalities and twenty-one-gun salutes; well, at least some of them had twenty-one guns, but the number of cannonballs wasted on you descended in order of importance and the man who was entranced by my mother was, I think, only a fourteen- or even an eleven-gunner. His name was Shantanu and he had had a rather unfortunate marriage in the past to an exquisite Maharani who suffered seven successive miscarriages and disappeared when her eighth pregnancy produced a son.

There were all sorts of stories circulating about the ex-queen, one saying that she was in fact enamoured of Shantanu's father, the old King Pritapa, and had married the son instead, as a sort of substitute; others casting doubt on her pedigree and claiming that Shantanu had picked her up on the banks of the Ganga; another suggesting that they had what would today be called an 'open marriage' which left her free to lead her own life; still others, whispered, that the seven children had died not entirely natural deaths and that the Maharani was not altogether normal. Whatever the truth of the rumours – and there was always enough evidence to suggest that none of them was wholly unfounded – there was no doubting that Shantanu had seemed very happy with his wife until she abruptly left him.

Years later, inexplicably, the now middle-aged king returned from a trip to the river bank with a handsome lad named Ganga Datta, announced that he was his lost son, and made him heir-apparent; and though this was a position which normally required the approval of the British Resident, it was clear that the young man possessed in abundant measure the qualities and the breeding required for the office of crown prince, and the Maharaja's apparently eccentric nomination was never challenged. Not, that is, until my mother entered the scene.

She was in the woods on the river bank when Shantanu came across her. He was struck first by the unique fragrance that wafted from her, a Brahmin-taught concoction of wood herbs and attars that had superseded the fishy emanations of pre-Parashar days, and he was smitten as my father had been. Kings have fewer social inhibitions than Brahmins, and Shantanu did not hesitate to walk into the head fisherman's hut and demand his daughter's hand in marriage.

'Certainly, Your Majesty, it would be an honour,' my maternal grandfather replied, 'but I am afraid I must pose one condition. Tell me you agree and I will be happy to give you my daughter.'

'I don't make promises in advance,' the Maharaja replied, somewhat put out. 'What exactly do you want?'

The fisherman's tone stiffened. 'I may not be able to find my Satyavati a better husband than you, but at least there would be no doubt that her children would inherit whatever her husband had to offer. Can you promise her the same, Your Majesty – that her son, and no one else, will be your heir?'

Of course, Shantanu, with the illustrious Ganga Datta sitting in his capital, could do nothing of the kind, and he returned to his palace a despondent man. Either because he couldn't conceal his emotions or (more probably) because he didn't want to, it became evident to everyone in or around the royal court that the Maharaja was quite colossally lovesick. He shunned company, snubbed the bewhiskered British Resident on two separate occasions, and once failed to show up at his morning *darshan*. It was all getting to be too much for the young Crown Prince, who finally decided to get the full story out of his father.

'Love? Don't be silly, lad,' Shantanu responded to his son's typically direct query. 'I'll tell you what the matter is. I'm worried about the future. You're my only son. Don't get me wrong, you mean more to me than a hundred sons, but the fact remains that you're the only one. What if something should happen to you? Of course we take all due precautions, but you know what an uncertain business life is these days. I mean, it's not even as if one has to be struck by lightning or something. The damned Resident has already run over three people in that infernal new wheeled contraption of his. Now, I'm not saying that that could happen to you, but one never knows, does one? I certainly hope you'll live long and add several branches to the family tree, but you know, they used to say when I was a child that having one son was like having no son. Something happens and sut! the British swoop in and take over your kingdom claiming the lack of a legitimate heir. They still haven't stopped muttering about the way I brought you in from, as they think, nowhere. So what happens if you pick a fight with someone, or get shot hunting with some incompetent visiting Angrez? The end of a long line, that's what. Do you understand why I'm so preoccupied these days?'

'Yes, I see,' replied Ganga Datta, who was certain he wasn't seeing enough. 'It's posterity you're worried about.'

'Naturally,' said Shantanu. 'You don't think I'd worry about myself, do you?'

Of course that was precisely what Ganga Datta did think, and probably what the ageing Maharaja had hoped he'd think, for the Crown Prince was not one to let matters drop. Kings, he well knew, did not travel to forests alone; there were drivers and aides to witness the most solitary of royal recreations. So a few inquiries about the Maharaja's recent excursion rapidly led the young man to the truth, and to the hut of the head fisherman.

Ganga Datta didn't travel alone either. In later years he would be accompanied by a non-violent army of *satyagrahis*, so that the third-class train carriages he always insisted on travelling in were filled with the elegantly sacrificing élite of his followers, rather than the sweat-stained poor, but on this occasion it was a band of ministers and courtiers he took with him to see Satyavati's father. Ganga D. would always have a penchant for making his most dramatic gestures before a sizeable audience. One day he was even to die in front of a crowd.

'So that's what you want,' he said to the fisherman, 'that's all? Well, you listen to me. I hereby vow, in terms that no one before me has ever equalled and no one after me will ever match, that if you let your daughter marry my father, her son shall succeed as king.'

'Look, it's all very well for you to say so,' said the fisherman uneasily, warily eyeing the ceremonial weaponry the semicircle of visitors was carrying. 'I'm sure you mean every word you say and that you'll do everything to keep your vow, but it's not really much of a promise, is it? I mean, you may renounce the throne and all that, but your children may have other ideas, surely. And you can't oblige them to honour *your* vow.' His guests bristled, so he added hastily, 'Forgive me, huzoor, I don't mean to cause any offence. It's just that I'm a father too, and you know what children can be like.'

'I don't, actually,' Ganga Datta replied mildly. 'But I have made a vow, and I'll ensure it's fulfilled. I've just renounced my claim to the throne. Now, in front of all these nobles of the realm, I swear never to have children. I shall not marry, I shall desist from women, so your daughter's offspring need never fear a challenge from mine.' He looked around him in satisfaction at the horror-struck faces of those present. 'I know what you're thinking – you're wondering how I can hope to get to Heaven without producing sons on this earth. Well, you needn't worry. That's one renunciation I don't intend to make. I intend to get to Heaven all right – *without* any sons to lift me there.'

The head fisherman could scarcely believe how the discussion had gone. 'Satyavati,' he called out in joy. 'The king can have her,' he added superfluously. 'And I shall be grandfather to a maharaja,' he was heard mumbling under his breath.

The wind soughed in the trees, signalling the approach of the monsoon rains, rustling the garments of the consternated courtiers. A stray gust showered petals on to Ganga Datta's proud head. He shook them off. 'We'd better be going,' he announced.

One of the courtiers stooped to pick up the fallen flowers. 'It's an omen,' he said. 'The heavens admire your courage, Ganga Datta! From now on you should be known as Bhishma, the One Who has Taken a Terrible Vow.'

'Ganga is much easier to pronounce,' the ex-Crown Prince said. 'And I'm sure you know much more about omens than I do, but I think this one means we shall get very wet if we don't start our return journey immediately.'

Back at the palace, where the news had preceded him, Ganga was greeted with relief and admiration by his father and king. 'That was a fine thing to do, my son,' Shantanu said, unable to conceal his pleasure. 'A far, far better thing than I could ever have done. I don't know about this celibacy stuff, but I'm sure it'll do you a lot of good in the long run. I'll tell you something, my son: I've simply no doubt at all that it'll give you longevity. You will not die unless and until you really want to die.'

'Thanks awfully, father,' said Ganga Datta. 'But right now I think we'd better start trying to get this arrangement past the Resident-Sahib.'

4

'Wholly unsuitable,' the British Resident said, when he heard of Satyavati. 'A fisherman's daughter for a maharaja's wife! It would bring the entire British Empire into disrepute.'

'Not really, sir, just the Indian part of it,' replied Ganga Datta calmly. 'And I cannot help wondering if the alternatives might not be worse.'

'Alternatives? Worse? Don't be absurd, young man. You're the alternative, and I don't see what's wrong with you, except for some missing details in your . . . ahem . . . past.'

'Then perhaps I should start filling in some of those missing details,' Ganga replied, lowering his voice.

There is no record of the resulting conversation, but courtiers at the door swore they heard the words 'South Africa', 'defiance of British laws', 'arrest', 'jail' and 'expulsion' rising in startled sibilance at various times. At the end of the discussion, Ganga Datta stood disinherited as crown prince, and Shantanu's strange alliance with Satyavati received the official approval of His (till lately Her) Majesty's Government.

That was not, of course, the end of the strange game of consequences set in train by the wooded wanderings of my malodorous mother. The name 'G. Datta' was struck off imperial invitation lists, and a shiny soup-and-fish was shortly placed on a nationalist bonfire. One day Ganga Datta would abandon his robes for a loincloth, and acquire fame, quite simply, as 'Gangaji'.

But that is another story, eh, Ganapathi? And one we shall come to in due course. Never fear, you can dip your twitching nose into that slice of our history too. But let us tidy up some genealogy first.

 5

Satyavati gave Shantanu what he wanted – a good time and two more sons. With our national taste for names of staggering simplicity, they were called Chitrangada and Vichitravirya, but my dismayed readers need not set about learning these by heart because my two better-born brothers do not figure largely in the story that follows. Chitrangada was clever and courageous but had all too brief a stint on his father's throne before succumbing to the ills of this world. The younger Vichitravirya succeeded him, with Gangaji as his regent and my now-widowed mother offering advice from behind the brocade curtain.

When the time came for Vichitravirya to be married, Gangaji, with the enthusiasm of the abstinent, decided to arrange the banns with not one but three ladies of rank, the daughters of a distant princeling. The sisters were known to be sufficiently well-endowed, in every sense of the term, for their father to be able to stay in his palace and entertain aspirants for their hands. None the less, it came as a surprise when Ganga announced his intention of visiting the Raja on his half-brother's behalf.

He had been immersing himself increasingly in the great works of the past and the present, reading the *vedas* and Tolstoy with equal involvement, studying the immutable laws of Manu and the eccentric philosophy of Ruskin, and yet contriving to attend, as he had to, to the affairs of state. His manner had grown increasingly other-worldly while his conversational obligations remained entirely mundane, and he would often startle his audiences with pronouncements which led them to wonder in which century he was living at any given moment. But one subject about which there was no dispute was his celibacy, which he was widely acknowledged to have maintained. His increasing absorbtion with religious philosophy and his continuing sexual forbearance led a local wit to compose a briefly popular ditty:

> 'Old Gangaji too
> is a good Hindu
> for to violate a cow
> would negate his vow.'

So Ganga's unexpected interest in the marital fortunes of his ward stimulated some curiosity, and his decision to embark on a trigamous mission of bride-procurement aroused intense speculation at court. Hindus were not wedded to monogamy in those days, indeed that barbarism would come only after Independence, so the idea of nuptial variety was not in itself outrageous; but when Gangaji, with his balding pate and oval glasses, entered the hall where the Raja had arranged to receive eligible suitors for each of his daughters and indicated he had come for all three, there was some unpleasant ribaldry.

'So much for Bhishma, the terrible-vowed,' said a loud voice, to a chorus of mocking laughter. 'It turns out to have been a really terrible vow, after all.'

'Perhaps someone slipped a copy of the *Kama Sutra* into a volume of the *vedas*,' suggested another, amidst general tittering.

'O Gangaji, have you come for bedding well or wedding bell?' demanded an anonymous English-educated humorist in the crowd.

Ganga, who had approached the girls' father, blinked, hitched his dhoti up his thinning legs and spoke in a voice that was meant to carry as much to the derisive blue-blooded throng as to the Raja.

'We are a land of traditions,' he declared, 'traditions with which even the British have not dared to tamper. In our heritage there are many ways in which a girl can be given away. Our ancient texts tell us that a daughter may be presented, finely adorned and laden with dowry, to an invited guest; or exchanged for an appropriate number of cows; or allowed to choose her own mate in a *swayamvara* ceremony. In practice, there are people who use money, those who demand clothes, or houses or land; men who seek the girl's preference, others who drag or drug her into compliance, yet others who seek the approbation of her parents. In olden times girls were given to Brahmins as gifts, to assist them in the performance of their rites and rituals. But in all our sacred books the greatest praise attaches to the marriage of a girl seized by force from a royal assembly. I lay claim to this praise. I am taking these girls with me whether you like it or not. Just try and stop me.'

He looked from the Raja to the throng through his thin-rimmed glasses, and the famous gaze that would one day disarm the British, disarmed them — literally, for the girls emerged from behind the lattice-work screens, where they had been examining the contenders unseen, and trooped silently behind him, as if hypnotized. The protests of the assembled princes choked back in their throats; hands raised in anger dropped uselessly to their sides; and the royal doorkeepers moved soundlessly aside for the strange procession to pass.

It seemed a deceptively simple victory for Ganga, and indeed it marked the beginning of his reputation for triumph without violence. But it did not pass entirely smoothly. One man, the Raja Salva of Saubal, a Cambridge blue at fencing and among the more modern of this feudal aristocracy, somehow found the power to give chase. As Ganga's stately Rolls receded into the distance, Salva charged out of the palace, bellowing for his car, and was soon at the wheel of an angrily revved up customized Hispano-Suiza.

If Ganga saw his pursuer, it seemed to make little difference, for his immense car rolled comfortably on, undisturbed by any sudden acceleration. Salva's modern charger, the Saubal crest emblazoned proudly on the sleek panel of its doors, roared after its quarry, quickly narrowing the distance.

Before long they drew abreast on the country road. 'Stop!' screamed Salva. 'Stop, you damned kidnapper, you!' Sharply twisting his steering-wheel, he forced the other vehicle to brake sharply. As the cars shuddered to a halt Salva flung open his door to leap out.

Then it all happened very suddenly. No one heard anything above the screeching of tyres, but Ganga's hand appeared briefly through a half-open window and Salva staggered back, his Hispano-Suiza collapsing beneath him as the air whooshed out of its tyres. The Rolls drove quietly off, engine purring complacently as the Raja of Saubal shook an impotent fist at its retreating end.

'So tiresome, these hotheads,' was all Ganga said, as he sank back in his seat and wiped his brow.

6

Vichitravirya took one look at the women his regent had brought back for him and slobbered his gratitude over his half-brother. But one day, when all the arrangements had been made in consultation with his – my – mother Satyavati, the invitations printed and a date chosen that accorded with the preferences of the astrologers and (just as important) of the British Resident, the eldest of the three girls, Amba, entered Ganga's study and closed the door.

'What do you think you are doing, girl?' the saintly Regent asked, snapping shut a treatise on the importance of enemas in attaining spiritual purity. ('The way to a man's soul is through his bowels,' he would later intone to the mystification of all who heard him.) 'Don't you know that I have taken a vow to abjure women? And that besides, you are pledged to another man?'

'I haven't come . . . for that,' Amba said in some confusion. (Ever since his vow Ganga had developed something of an obsession with his celibacy, even if he was the only one who feared it to be constantly under threat.) 'But about the other thing.'

'What other thing?' asked Ganga in some alarm, his wide reading and complete inexperience combining vividly in his imagination.

'About being promised to another man,' Amba said, retreating towards the door.

'Ah,' said Gangaji, reassured. 'Well, have no fear, my dear, you can come closer and confide all your anxieties to your uncle Ganga. What seems to be the problem?'

The little princess twisted one hand nervously in the other, looking at her bangled wrists rather than at the kindly elder across the room. 'I . . . I had already given myself, in my heart, to Raja Salva, and he was going to marry me. We had even told Daddy, and he was going to . . . to . . . announce it on that day, when . . . when . . .' She stopped, in confusion and distress.

'So that's why he followed us,' said the other-worldly sage with dawning comprehension. 'Well, you must stop worrying, my dear. Go back to your room and pack. You shall go to your Raja on the next train.'

For Gangaji's sake I wish that were the end of this particular story, but it isn't. And don't look at me like that, young Ganapathi. I know this is a digression – but my life, indeed this world, is nothing more than a series of digressions. So you can cut out the disapproving looks and take this down. That's what you're here for. Right, now, where were we? That's right, in a special royal compartment on the rail track to Saubal, with the lovely Amba heading back to her lover on the next train, as Ganga had promised.

If Gangaji had thought that all that was required now was to reprint the wedding invitations with one less name on the cast of characters, he was sadly mistaken. For when Amba arrived at Saubal she found that her Romeo had stepped off the balcony.

'That decrepit eccentric has beaten, humiliated, disgraced me in public. He carried you away as I lay sprawling on the wreck of my car. You've spent God knows how many nights in his damned palace. And now you expect me to forget all that and take you back as my wife?' Salva's Cambridge-stiffened upper lip trembled as he turned away from her. 'I'm having your carriage put back on the return train. Go to Ganga and do what he wishes. We're through.'

And so, a tear-stained face gazed out through the bars of the small-windowed carriage at the light cast by the full moon on the barren countryside, as the train trundled imperviously back to Ganga's capital of Hastinapur.

'You must be joking, Ganga-*bhai*, I can't marry her now,' expostulated Vichitravirya, ripping the flesh off a breast of quail with his wine-stained teeth. 'The girl's given herself to another man. It was hardly my idea to have her shuttling to and from Saubal by public transport, in full view of the whole world. But it's done: everyone knows about her disgrace by now.' He took a quick swallow. 'You can't expect me, Vichitravirya of Hastinapur, son of Maharaja Shantanu and Maharani Satyavati, soon to be king in my own right and member of the Chamber of Princes, to accept the return of soiled goods like some Porbandar *baniya* merchant. You can't be serious, Ganga-*bhai*.' He rolled his eyes in horror at his half-brother and clapped loudly for an attendant. 'Bring on the nautch-girls,' he called out.

'Then you must marry me yourself,' said the despairing Amba when Ganga had confessed the failure of his intercession with the headstrong princeling. 'You're the one who's responsible for all this. You've ruined my life, now the least you can do is to save me from eternal disgrace and spinsterhood.'

Gangaji blinked in disbelief. 'That's one thing I cannot do,' he replied firmly. 'I cannot break my vow, however sorry I may feel for you, my dear.'

'Damn your vow,' she cried in distress. 'What about me? No one will marry me now, you know that. My life's finished – all because of you.'

'You know, I wouldn't be so upset if I were you,' replied Gangaji calmly. 'A life of celibacy is a life of great richness. You ought to try it, my dear. It will make you very happy. I am sure you will find it deeply spiritually uplifting.'

'You smug, narcissistic bastard, you!' Amba screamed, hot tears running down her face. 'Be like you, with your enemas and your loincloths? Never!' And she ran out of the room, slamming the door shut on the startled sage.

She tried herself after that, imploring first Vichitravirya, then Salva again, equally in vain. When six years of persistence failed to bring any nuptial rewards, she forgot all but her searing hatred for her well-intentioned abductor, and began to look in earnest for someone who would kill him. By then, however, Gangaji's fame had spread beyond the boundaries of Hastinapur, and no assassin in the whole of India was willing to accept her contract. It was then that she would resolve to do it herself . . .

 *7*

But I am, as Ganapathi indicates by the furrow on his ponderous brow, getting ahead of my story. Amba's revenge on Gangaji, the extraordinary lengths to which she went to obtain it, and the violence she was prepared to inflict upon herself, are still many years away. We had paused with Vichitravirya committing bigamy, bigamy inspired by Gangaji and sanctioned by religion, tradition, law and the British authorities. Another instance of Ganga's failure to judge the real world of flawed men, for his debauched half-brother needed no greater incentive to indulgence than this temple-throbbing choice of nocturnal companions. Ambika and Ambalika were each enough for any king, with ripe rounded breasts to weigh upon a man and skins of burnished gold to set him alight, bodies long enough to envelop a monarch and full hips to invite him into them; together, they drove Vichitravirya into a fatally priapic state. Yes, it was terminal concupiscence he died of, though some called it consumption and a variety of quick and quack remedies were proposed in vain around his sickbed. He turned in his sceptre just seven years into his reign, in what the British Resident, in his letter of condolence, was to describe as the 'prime of life', and he died childless, thus giving me a chance to re-enter the story.

When kings died without heirs in the days of the Raj, the consequences could be calamitous. Whereas in the past the royal house could simply have adopted a male child to continue the family's hold on the throne, this was not quite as easy under the British, who had a tendency to declare the throne vacant and annex the territory for themselves. (We even fought a little war over the principle in 1857 — but the British won, and annexed a few more kingdoms.) Satyavati, whose desire to see her offspring on the throne had deprived Gangaji of more than a crown, turned to him anxiously.

'It's entirely in your hands,' she pointed out. 'If the British want, they can take over Hastinapur. But one thing can stop them — if we tell them one of the queens was pregnant at the time of Vichitravirya's death, and that his legitimate heir is on his way into this world. Oh, Ganga, my son's wives are still lovely and young; they can produce the heirs we need. Do your duty as a brother, as the son of my husband, and take Ambika and Ambalika to bed.' She saw his expression. 'Oh God, you're going to tell me about your vow, aren't you, Ganga? You took it, after all, for me. Now I'm asking you to ignore it, for the sake of the family — for your father's dynasty.'

'But I can't, Mother,' said Ganga piously. 'A vow is a vow. I'd rather give up my position, this kingdom, the world itself, than break my promise.'

'But no one need know,' Satyavati remonstrated, adding, after a moment's hesitation, 'except the girls themselves.'

'That's bad enough,' Ganga replied, 'and it doesn't matter whether someone knows or not. What's essential is to remain true to one's principles. My vow has never been so sorely tested, but I'm sorry, Mother, I won't give in to untruth for any reason.' (He tried not to sound pompous while saying this, and nearly succeeded.) 'But don't despair, the idea's still a good one, and I'm not the only person who can fulfil it. Don't forget that we have a long tradition of Brahmins coming to the rescue of barren Kshatriyas. It may have fallen somewhat into disuse in recent years, but it could be useful again today.'

'Dvaipayana!' she exclaimed. 'Of course – my son Ved Vyas! I hadn't thought about him. If he's anything like his father, he can certainly do the job.'

And indeed I could. We Brahmin sons never deny our mothers, and we never fail to rise to these occasions. I rose. I came.

Permit an old man a moment's indulgence in nostalgia. The palace at Hastinapur was a great edifice in those days, a cream-and-pink tribute to the marriage of Western architecture and Eastern tastes. High-ceilinged rooms and airy passages supported by enormous rounded columns stretched ever onwards across a vast expanse of mosaic and marble. In the dusty courtyard beyond the front portico stood a solitary sedan, ready for any royal whim, its moustachioed chauffeur dozing at the wheel. The other vehicles lay in garages beyond, below the servants' quarters where the washing hung gaily out to dry against walls of red brick – saris, dhotis, and, above all, the tell-tale uniforms of the numerous liveried attendants, brass buttons gleaming in the sunlight. The estate was all that was visible, lush lawns and flowered footpaths; the visitor was made conscious of a sense of spaciousness, that evidence of privilege in an overcrowded land. Inside, the cool marble, the sweeping stairways, the large halls, the furniture that seemed to have been bought to become antique, imposed rather than captivated. But one could walk through the mansion at peace with oneself, hearing only the soft padding of the servants' bare feet, the tinkle of feminine laughter from the zenana, and the chirping melodies of the birds in the garden, being wafted indoors by the gentle afternoon breeze. And sometimes, when my ageing but still exquisite mother forgot herself, another noise could be heard, the high, tinny sound of a gramophone, Hastinapur's only one, scratching out an incongruous waltz as a lonely head swayed silently in tune with the music.

At night there was stillness where once there was sound, and new sounds emerged where silence had reigned during the day. Raucous laughter from behind closed doors broadcast the young king's pleasure: a fat madam musician played the harmonium while singing of romance through betel-stained lips, and lissom nautch-girls clashed their jingling *payal*s with each assertive stamp of their hennaed heels. And Vichitravirya threw his head back in delight, flinging gold and silver coins, sometimes a jewel or a necklace, at the hired houri's feet, or after a particularly heady mixture of music and ambrosia, tucking his reward into her low-bent cleavage as she pouted her gratitude. Then there followed all the frolic, and all the futility, of intoxication, which ended, eventually, in my princely half-brother's death.

It was to this place that I went, and it was here that my mother told me anxiously why she had sent for me. 'Of course I'll help, Mother,' I assured her, 'provided my royal sisters-in-law are willing. For they have never seen me, and after a lifetime, even a short one, spent as a wandering Brahmin sage and preacher of sedition, I am not a pretty sight.'

My mother took in my sweat-stained *kurta*, my face burned black with constant exposure to the sun, the cracked heels of my much-walked feet, and the livid scar from a recent political encounter with the lathi-wielders of the Raj. 'I see what you mean,' she said. 'But Ganga will take care of them.'

Between them, my mother and Ganga obtained the widows' acquiescence – the issue of dynastic succession is, as every television viewer today knows, a powerful aphrodisiac. A few discreet inquiries and my father's training enabled me to calculate the exact day required for the production of offspring. At the appointed moment Ambika, freshly bathed and richly adorned, was laid out on a canopied bed, and I duly entered the room, and her. But she was so appalled by the sight of her ravisher that she closed her eyes tightly throughout what one might have called, until the Americans confused the issue, the act of congress. Ambalika was more willing, but as afraid, and turned white with fear at my approach. The result, I warned my mother as I went to her to take my leave, was that the products of our union might be born blind and pale, respectively. So, on my last night Satyavati sent Ambika to me again, in the hope of doing better. But Ambika had had enough, and sent me a substitute, a maidservant of hers, bedecked in her mistress' finery. By the time I discovered the deception it was too late, and a most agreeable deception it had proven, too. But I had made my plans to leave the next morning, and I slipped out as quietly and unobtrusively as I had come, leaving the secret of my visit locked in three wombs.

From Ambika emerged Dhritarashtra, blind, heir to the Hastinapur throne; from Ambalika, Pandu the pale, his brother; from the servant girl, Vidur the wise, one day counsellor to kings. Of all these I remained the unacknowledged father. Yes, Ganapathi, this is confession time.

THE SECOND BOOK:

THE DUEL WITH THE CROWN

8

Are you with me so far, Ganapathi? Got everything? I suppose you must have, or you couldn't have taken it down, could you? Under our agreement, I mean.

But you must keep me in check, Ganapathi. I must learn to control my own excesses of phrase. It is all very well, at this stage of my life and career, to let myself go and unleash a few choice and pithy epithets I have been storing up for the purpose. But that would fly in the face of what has now become the Indian autobiographical tradition, laid down by a succession of eminent bald-heads from Rajaji to Chagla. The principle is simple: the more cantankerous the old man and the more controversial his memoirs, the more rigidly conventional is his writing. Look at Nirad Chaudhuri, who wrote his *Autobiography of an Unknown Indian* on that basis and promptly ceased to live up to its title. It is not a principle that these memoirs of a forgotten Indian can afford to abandon.

Right, Ganapathi? So, we've got the genealogies out of the way, my progeny are littering the palace at Hastinapur, and good old Ganga Datta is still safely ensconced as regent. No, on second thoughts, you'd better cut out that adverb, Ganapathi. 'Safely' wouldn't be entirely accurate. A new British Resident, successor of the bewhiskered automobilist, is in place and is far from sure he likes what is going on.

Picture the situation for yourself. Gangaji, the man in charge of Hastinapur for all practical purposes, thin as a papaya plant, already balder then than I am today, peering at you through round-rimmed glasses that gave him the look of a startled owl. And the rest of his appearance was hardly what you would call prepossessing. He had by then burned his soup-and-fish and given away the elegant suits copied for him from the best British magazines by the court master-tailor; but to make matters worse, he was now beginning to shed part or most of even his traditional robes on all but state occasions. People were for ever barging into his study unexpectedly and finding him in nothing but a loincloth. 'Excuse me, I was just preparing myself an enema,' he would say, with a feeble smile, as if that explained everything. In fact, as you can well imagine, it only added to the confusion.

But it was not just the Regent's personal eccentricities that were causing alarm at the Resident's residence across the hill from the palace. Word was beginning to get around of Gangaji's radical, indeed one might say, dangerous, ideas about the world around him.

'He's renounced sex, of course, but we knew that already,' the new representative of the King-Emperor said to his equerry one evening on his verandah, as one of my men hung from a branch above and listened. (We 'itinerant seditious fakirs,' as that ignorant windbag Winston Churchill once called us, had to have our sources, you understand. Not all of them were happy with the ash-smearing requirement, but they and I learned more wandering about with a staff and a bowl under the British than I did after becoming a minister in independent India.) 'Problem is, he's now going further. Preaching a lot of damn nonsense about equality and justice and what have you. And you tell me he cleans his own toilet, instead of letting his damn *bhisti* do it.'

'*Jamadar*, Sir Richard,' the aide, a thin young man with a white pinched face, said, coughing politely. 'A *bhisti* is only a water-carrier.'

'Really?' The Resident seemed surprised. 'Thought those were called *lotas*.'

'They are, sir.' The equerry coughed even more loudly this time. '*Lotas* are those little pots you carry water in, I mean *they* carry water in, Sir Richard, whereas . . .'

'A *bhisti* is the kind they have to balance on their heads, I suppose,' Sir Richard said. 'Damn complicated language, this Hindustani. Different words for everything.'

'Yes, sir . . . I mean, no, sir,' began the equerry, doubly unhappy about his own choice of words. He wanted to explain that a *bhisti* was a person, not a container. 'What I mean is . . .'

'And different genders, too,' Sir Richard went on. 'I mean, is there any good reason why a table should be feminine and a bed masculine? D'you think it has to do with what you do on them?'

'Well, no, sir, not exactly.' The young man began his reply cautiously, unsure whether the question required one. 'It's really a matter of word-endings, you see, sir, and . . .'

'Ah, boy,' said the Resident, cutting him in full flow, as a white-haired and white-shirted bearer padded in on bare feet, tray in hand. 'About time, eh?'

It was the convivial hour. The sun had begun its precipitous descent into the unknown, and the distant sky was flaming orange, like saffron scattered on a heaving sea. In the gathering gloom the insects came into their own, buzzing, chirping, biting at the blotchy paleness of colonial flesh. This was when English minds turned to thoughts of drink. Twilight never lasts long in

India, but its advent was like opening time at the pubs our rulers had left behind. The shadows fell and spirits rose; the sharp odour of quinine tonic, invented by lonely planters to drown and justify their solitary gins, mingled with the scent of frangipani from their leafy, insect-ridden gardens, and the soothing clink of ice against glass was only disturbed by the occasional slap of a frustrated palm against a reddening spot just vacated by an anglovorous mosquito.

'Boy, whisky *lao*. *Chhota* whisky, *burra* water, understand? What will you have, Heaslop?'

'A weak whisky will suit me very well, too, Sir Richard.'

'Right. Two whiskies, *do* whisky, boy. And a big jug of water, understand. Not a little *lota*, eh? Bring it in a *bhisti*. *Bhisti men lao*.' He smiled in satisfaction at the bearer, who gave him an astonished look before bowing and salaaming his way backwards out of the room.

'Er . . . if I might point out, sir –'

'Nothing to it, really,' Sir Richard continued. 'These native languages don't really have much to them, you know. And it's not as if you have to write poetry in them. A few crucial words, sufficient English for ballast, and you're sailing smoothly. In fact,' his voice became confidential, 'I even have a couple of tricks up my sleeve.' He leaned towards the young man, his eyes, mouth and face all round in concentration. '"There was a banned crow,"' he intoned sonorously. '"There was a cold day." Not bad, eh? I learned those on the boat. Sounds like perfect Urdu, I'm told.' He paused and frowned. 'The devil of it is remembering which one means, "close the door," and which one will get someone to open it. Well, never mind,' he said, as his companion opened his mouth in diffident helpfulness. 'We're not here for a language lesson. I was speaking about this damn regent we have here. What d'you make of him, eh?'

'Well, sir, he's very able, there's no question about that,' Heaslop responded slowly. 'And the people seem to hold him in some regard.'

'They would, wouldn't they, with all the ideas he puts into their head. All this nonsense about equality, and toilet-cleaning. I understand he's suggesting that caste distinctions ought to be done away with. We've always believed they were the foundation of Indian society, haven't we? And now a chap comes along out of nowhere, scion of the ruling caste, and says Untouchables are just as good as he is. How does he propose to put that little idea into practice, d'you know?'

'He seems to believe in the force of moral authority, sir. He cleans his own toilet to show that there is nothing inherently shameful about the task, which, as you know, is normally performed by Untouchables.' Sir Richard produced a sound which might have been prompted by a winged assault on his ear, or then again by Heaslop's implied enthusiasm for Ganga's stand. The young man continued, carefully moderating his tone. 'He seems to think that by getting down to their level, he will make them more acceptable to the people at large. Untouchability is no longer legal in Hastinapur, but he knows it's still impossible for a cobbler to get into the main temple. So he makes it a point of inviting an Untouchable, or a "Child of God", as he calls them, to his room for a meal every week. As you can imagine, sir, this gets talked about.'

'Favourably?'

'I'd say public opinion is divided in about equal parts of admiration and resentment, sir. The latter mainly from the upper castes, of course.'

'Of course. And how do they take all this at the palace? Regent or no Regent, there must be many who don't agree with his ideas. Cleaning his own toilet, indeed.'

'Absolutely, sir. We have heard that he tried to get the royal widows to clean their own bathrooms, sir, and they burst into tears. Or threw him out of the zenana. Or both.' The equerry cleared his throat. 'Old inhibitions die hard, sir. Our information is that the reason he entertains the Untouchables in his own room is that there were too many objections to their eating in any of the palace dining-rooms. And the attendant who serves them has strict instructions to destroy the plates afterwards, so that no one else need risk eating off them.'

'Hmm. What about us?'

'Er . . . us?'

'Yes, Heaslop, us.'

The equerry looked nonplussed. 'No, sir, I don't think they destroy the plates *we're* served on. But I haven't really checked. Would you like me to?'

'No, Heaslop.' The Resident's asperity was sharpened by the buzzing around his ears and his increasing desire for a drink. 'I meant, what does he think about us? The British Raj; the King-Emperor. Is he loyal, or a damn traitor, or what?'

'I don't know, sir.' The equerry shifted his weight in the cane chair. 'He's not an easy man to place, really. As you know, Sir Richard, there was a time when he was rather well regarded by us. Among the king's most loyal subjects, in fact. He was a regular at receptions here. Even arranged a major contribution to the Ambulance Association, sir, during the last war. But of late, he has been known to say things about *swaraj*, you know, sir, self-rule. And about pan-Indian nationalism. No one seems to know what started him off on that track. They say he reads widely.'

'Basic truth about the colonies, Heaslop. Any time there's trouble, you can put it down to books. Too many of the wrong ideas getting into the heads of the wrong sorts of people. If ever the Empire comes to ruin, Heaslop, mark my words, the British publisher will be to blame.'

Heaslop seemed about to comment on this insight, then thought better of it. The Resident reached for his glass and realized he still didn't have one. 'Boy!' he called out.

There was no answer. Sir Richard furrowed his florid brow. 'And this Ganga Din, or whatever they call him,' he snapped. 'How does he comport himself? Has he been giving us any trouble? That's a rather important position to leave someone of his stripe in, isn't it? Perhaps I should be doing something about it.'

'The Regent has always behaved very correctly, Sir Richard. In fact,' Heaslop licked a nervous lip, 'I believe he was our candidate for the throne once. Your predecessor was rather sorry when things took a different turn, at the time of the late Maharaja's second marriage. But it would seem it was Ganga Datta who wanted it that way.'

'I've seen the files,' the Resident nodded. 'What on earth has happened to our drinks? Boy! Boy!'

The elderly bearer, dusty and panting, responded at last to the summons. 'Sahib, I coming, sahib,' he stated, somewhat unnecessarily.

'What the devil's taking you so long? Where's our whisky?'

'I bring instantly, sahib,' the bearer assured him. 'I am looking for *bhisti* all this time, as sahib wanted. I now found, sahib. With great difficulty. I bring him in, sahib?'

'Of course you can bring the water in,' Sir Richard said crossly. A choking sound emanated from the equerry beside him.

The bearer clapped his hands. A grimy figure in a dirty undershirt and dirtier loincloth entered the verandah, carrying a black oilskin bag from one end of which water dripped relentlessly on to the tiled floor.

'*Bhisti*, sahib,' the bearer proudly announced, like a conjuror pointing to a rabbit he has just produced out of an improbably small hat.

'What the devil . . .?' The Resident seemed apoplectic.

Heaslop groaned.

 *9*

Back to my offspring, eh, Ganapathi? Can't neglect the little blighters, because this is really their story, you know. Dhritarashtra, Pandu and Vidur: ah, how their names still conjure up all the memories of the glory of Hastinapur at that time. Their births seemed a signal for the state's resurgence. Prosperity bloomed around the palace, Ganapathi: the harvests produced nothing short of bumper crops, the wheat gave off the scent of jasmine, and the women laughed as they worked in the fields. There were no droughts, Ganapathi, no floods either; the rains came, at just the right times, when the farmers had sowed their seeds and said their prayers, and never for longer than they were welcome. Fruit ripened in the sunshine, flowers blossomed in the gentle breeze; the birds chirped gaily as they built their nests in the shade, and aimed their droppings only at passing Englishwomen. The very cows produced a milk no *doodhwala* could bear to water. The towns and the city of Hastinapur overflowed with businessmen and shopkeepers, coolies and workmen, travelling seers and travelling salesmen. Yes, Ganapathi, the glory of those days drives me to verse:

> With the birth of the boys
> Flowed all the joys
> Of the kingdom of Hastinapur;
> The flags were unfurled
> All was well with the world
> From the richest right down to the poor.

(Not too good, hanh, Ganapathi? If you'd grimace a little less, though, it might get better.)

> The harvests were good
> There was plenty of food
> The land gave a bountiful yield;
> The rains came in time
> To wash off the grime
> And to ripen the wheat in the field.

> The man at the plough
> And the bird on the bough
> Both sang of their peace and content;
> The fruit in the trees
> Flowers, sunshine and breeze
> Were all on happiness intent.

(Well, you try and do better, Ganapathi. On second thoughts, don't – you might succeed, and this is *my* memoir.)

The city was crowded
All fears were unfounded
There were money and goods in the shops;
  And although the Taj
  Was still ruled by the Raj
The glory of Ind came out tops.

The citizens worked hard
(And won the praise of this bard)
There was never, at all, any crime;
  The piping hot curries
  Removed all our worries
And prosperity reigned all the time.

Yes, the birth of the boys
Was the best of God's ploys
To fulfil our great people's karma;
  Under their regent (a sage)
  There reigned a Golden Age –
The turn of the Wheel of Dharma.

It was, indeed, Gangaji who brought up my sons – as if, I must admit, they were his own children. Though the Regent was getting more and more ascetic in his ways, he spared no extravagance in giving the boys the best education, material comforts and personal opportunities. Each developed, in his own way, into an outstanding prospect, a princely asset to Hastinapur.

Dhritarashtra was a fine-looking young fellow, slim, of aquiline nose and aristocratic bearing. His blindness was, of course, a severe handicap, but he learned early to act as if it did not matter. As a child he found education in India a harrowing experience, which was, no doubt, why he was in due course sent to Eton. The British public school system fitted the young man to a T (the finest Darjeeling, which he obtained every month from Fortnum and Mason and brewed several times a day in a silver pot engraved with the Hastinapur crest). He quickly acquired two dozen suits, a different pair of shoes for each day of the week, a formidable vocabulary and the vaguely abstracted manner of the over-educated. With these assets he was admitted to King's College, Cambridge (there being no Prince's); unable to join in the punting and the carousing, he devoted himself to developing another kind of vision and became, successively, a formidable debater, a Bachelor of Arts and a Fabian Socialist. I have often wondered what might have happened had he been able to see the world around him as the rest of us can. Might India's history have been different today?

Pandu – ah, Pandu the pale, whose mother had turned white upon seeing me – Pandu never lacked in strength or courage. (Nor, unlike his half-brother, in eyesight, though he did take to wearing curious little roundish glasses that gave him the appearance of a Bengali teacher or a Japanese admiral.) What Pandu never had much of was judgement – or, as some of his admirers prefer to see it, luck. He too could have enjoyed the English education Dhritarashtra revelled in, but he did not even complete the Indian version of it. After insisting, with more pride than judgement, on pursuing his studies in India rather than in England, he was expelled from one of the country's best colleges for striking a teacher, an Englishman, who had called Indians 'dogs'. Yes, we Indians do have a number of dog-like characteristics, such as wagging our tails at white men carrying sticks, and our bark is usually worse than our bite. But Pandu could not resist showing his Professor Kipling one attribute of the species that most of us, including the distinguished academic, had overlooked – teeth. It was a pattern of conduct that was to last all his life.

Finally, for ever bringing up the rear (for reasons of ancestry and nothing else), came my son Vidur Dharmaputra. In intellectual gifts and administrative ability he outshone his two brothers, but knowing from the very beginning that unlike them he had no claim on a kingly throne, he developed a sense of modesty and self-effacement that would enhance his effectiveness in his chosen profession. For Vidur became that most valuable and underrated of creatures, the bureaucrat. He did brilliantly in his examination, stood First Class First throughout and, along with many of the country's finest minds, applied for entry into the Indian Civil Service.

Queen Victoria had thrown the doors of the ICS open to 'natives' immediately after the 1857 revolt (which the British preferred to call a 'mutiny'). No one was quite sure how far Britannia meant to waive the rules, but two Indians, both Bengalis, did achieve the miraculous distinction of entry – Satyendra Nath Tagore and Surendra Nath Banerjee. Indian exhilaration soon turned to resignation, however, when Banerjee was drummed out of the service a few years later, on a series of trumped-up charges. From the early years of our century, though, things began to change. When Vidur applied, there were more Indians being admitted to the civil service, adding their supposedly baser mettle to the 'steel frame' of the Raj. Vidur topped the written examinations to the ICS, in which one's name did not figure on the test paper; in the interview, regrettably, the same degree of anonymity did not prevail, and he found himself rapidly downgraded, but not so far as to miss selection altogether. So he joined the ICS's emerging administrative alloy, and before long was a rising star in the States Department, which looked after the princely states – among them Hastinapur.

You see, Ganapathi, this old man's seed was not wasted, after all, eh? Whatever people might think. Pass me that handkerchief, will you? My eyes are misting on me.

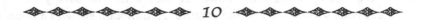 *10*

But we must get back to our story. Where were we, Ganapathi? Ah, yes – my sons. When the three young men reached marriageable age, Gangaji summoned them to his study.

'You are the hope of Hastinapur,' he said sagely. 'I have brought you up to carry on our noble line, and when you assume the responsibilities of rulers, I wish to be free to pursue other interests. But I cannot give up the regency and retreat to an ashram without first assuring not just your accession but the succession to yourselves as well. (One can never be too sure.) I have been making discreet inquiries, and I have identified three suitable ladies, of impeccable descent and highly praised beauty, with whom I intend to arrange your marriages. What do you have to say to this?'

It was Vidur who spoke first; Vidur could always be relied upon to take his cue and to say the right thing at the right time. 'You have been both a father and a mother to us, Gangaji,' he said dutifully. 'You have brought us up to follow your instructions in all matters. The *shastras* say that the word of a guru is law to his disciples. Why should it be any different now? If you want us to marry these ladies of your choice, it would be an honour as well as a duty to obey you.'

Pandu gave his low-born brother an expressive look, as indeed Dhritarashtra might have, had he been able. But both remained silent, particularly since Gangaji had seized upon Vidur's answer with barely concealed satisfaction and was already detailing his plans.

'For you, Dhritarashtra, the eldest, I have found a girl from a very good family of Allahabad. She is called Gandhari, and I am told she has lustrous black eyes. Not,' he added hastily, 'that that matters, of course. No, the main attraction of this lovely lady, from our point of view, is that she hails from a most productive line. Her mother had nine children, and her grandmother seventeen. There is a story in the family that Gandhari has obtained the boon of Lord Shiva to have no less than a hundred sons.' Seeing that Dhritarashtra appeared somewhat underwhelmed by the prospect, Gangaji spoke in a sterner tone of voice. 'You can never be too careful with these British, my son. They have had their designs on Hastinapur for years.'

'Whatever you say, Bhishma,' Dhritarashtra replied, deliberately using the name that recalled Gangaji's terrible vow of celibacy. The older man looked at him sharply, but Dhritarashtra remained expressionless behind his dark glasses.

'For you, Pandu, I propose Kunti Yadav,' Gangaji went on, noting with pleasure the young man's sharp intake of breath, for the beauty of Miss Yadav was widely known across the country. And though she was a princess only by adoption, many a more important raja might not have been averse to grafting her branch on to their family tree, were it not for the faint whiff of scandal that clung to her name.

'I'm delighted, of course,' Pandu said, looking even paler than usual. 'But, Gangaji —'

'Say no more.' The saintly loincloth-clad figure raised his hand. 'I know what you are about to ask. And I have, of course, made inquiries.' He settled his rimless glasses more firmly on the bridge of his nose and opened a red-ribboned folder. 'Miss Kunti Yadav has, despite her unquestioned beauty and the good name of her adoptive family, received no, repeat no, offers of marriage to date. The reason: it appears that there may have been, ah . . . a certain indiscretion in her past.'

Gangaji looked up at the perspiring Pandu, who was visibly hanging on his every word, his eyes roving restlessly from his uncle to the open dossier before him. 'It seems,' he went on, 'that Miss Yadav might have conducted a brief and entirely unwise liaison with a certain Hyperion Helios, a foreign visitor at her father's palace. From what I have been able to ascertain and divine, it would seem that Mr Helios was a very charming and wealthy man of the world, who radiated an immense presence and warmth, and it is easy to imagine how an impressionable and inexperienced young maiden could be taken in by the blandishments of this plausible stranger. No one knows what exactly transpired between them, but it does appear that Mr Helios was ordered summarily out of the palace by his host, and,' Gangaji looked up at the anxious Pandu, 'that Miss Yadav went into near-total seclusion for several months. Some people draw conclusions from all this that are not flattering to the young lady. For myself, having reviewed all the elements of the case, I cannot see that much blame attaches to the Princess Kunti. If we were all to be punished for ever for the errors of our youth, the world would be a particularly gloomy place. Certainly, there has been no suggestion of the slightest misconduct since by the lady, but our princely marriage-makers have unforgiving hearts. I believe we in Hastinapur have a somewhat more generous spirit. Will you accept her, Pandu?'

'If you, sire, are willing to admit her into our home, I shall be only too happy to follow suit,' Pandu replied, somewhat formally.

'Then it is settled,' Gangaji said, closing his file. 'But I do not wish your reputation to suffer as a result of my, ah . . . progressive ideas. Lest it be said that you are in any way inferior to those who have so far disdained the hand of Kunti Yadav, I have resolved upon a second marriage for you as well, of a princess not as glamorous, perhaps, but completely irreproachable.' Seeing Pandu's raised eyebrow and flushed face, the old celibate allowed himself a chuckle. 'The British have put an end to our practice of burning widows on their husbands' funeral pyres, but they have not interfered very much with our other customs. Whom you marry, how old you are, how much you pay, or how many you wed, are issues they have sensibly refused to touch upon. So I have found a very good second wife for you, Pandu. She is Madri, sister of the Maharaja of Shalya. The Shalya royal house has a rather peculiar tradition of requiring a dowry from the prospective bridegroom rather than the other way around, and their womenfolk have the reputation of being somewhat self-willed, but I am willing to overlook both these factors if you are, Pandu.'

'Oh, I am, Gangaji, I am,' Pandu responded fervently.

'Good,' said the Regent. 'I shall visit Shalya myself to arrange it.' He turned at last to the youngest (youngest, that is, by a few days, but in royal households every minute counts. It is one of the miracles of monarchy that no king has ever started parenthood with twins, but you can take my word for it, Ganapathi, that if he had, the second one out of the womb would never have been allowed to forget his place for an instant. And Vidur, don't forget, was not in contention for a princess's hand: Ambika's deception and my indiscriminate concupiscence had ensured that.) 'As for you, Vidur, I have identified a young lady whose circumstances perfectly match yours. The Raja Devaka, no mean prince, had a low-caste wife, who gave him a most elegant and lissom daughter, Devaki. She may not be of the highest rank, but she was educated at the Loreto Convent and is fluent in English, which can only be an asset in your work.'

'I am satisfied,' said Vidur humbly.

The sage heaved a deep sigh.

'Well, there it is then, at last,' he said. 'Once these marriages are all arranged, I shall turn over the kingdom to Dhritarashtra and Pandu, knowing too that Vidur is at the States Department, keeping an eye on Hastinapur. And I shall be able to devote myself to broader pursuits.'

'What will you do, sire?' asked Vidur politely.

'Many things, my son,' replied the terrible-vowed elder. 'I shall pursue the Truth, in all its manifestations, including the political and, indeed, the sexual. I shall seek to perfect myself, a process I began many years ago, in this very palace. And I shall seek freedom.'

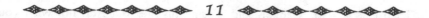 *11*

How shall I tell it, Ganapathi? It is such a long story, an epic in itself, and we have so much else to describe. Shall I tell of the strange weapon of disobedience, which Ganga, with all his experience of insisting upon obedience and obtaining it toward himself, developed into an arm of moral war against the foreigner? Shall I sing the praises of the mysterious ammunition of truth-force; the strength of unarmed slogan-chanting demonstrators falling defenceless under the hail of police lathis; the power of wave after wave of *khadi*-clad men and women, arms and voices raised, marching handcuffed to their imprisonment? Shall I speak, Ganapathi, and shall you write, of the victory of nonviolence over the organized violence of the state; the triumph of bare feet over hobnailed boots; the defeat of legislation by the awesome strength of silence?

I see, Ganapathi, that you have no advice to offer me. You wish, as usual, to sit back, with your ponderous brow glowering in concentration, that long nose of yours coiling itself around my ideas, and to let me choose my own thoughts, my own words. Well, I suppose you are right. It is, after all, my story, the story of Ved Vyas, doddering and decrepit though you may think I am, and yet it is also the story of India, your country and mine. Go ahead, Ganapathi, sit back. I shall tell you all.

What a life Gangaji led, and how much we know of it, for in the end he spared us no detail of it, did he, not a single thought or fear or dream went unrecorded, not one hope or lie or enema. It was all there in his writings; in the impossibly small print of his autobiography; in the inky mess of his weekly rag; in those countless letters I wonder how he found the time to write, to disciples, critics, government officials; in those conversations he conducted (sometimes, on his days of silence, by writing with a pencil-stub on the backs of envelopes) with every prospective biographer or journalist. Yes, he told us everything, Gangaji, from those gaps in his early years that the British had been so worried about, to the celibate experiments of his later life, when he got all those young women to take off their clothes and lie beside him to test the strength of his adherence to that terrible vow. He told us everything, Ganapathi, yet how little we remember, how little we understand, how little we care.

Do you remember the centenary of his birth, Ganapathi? The nation paid obeisance to his memory; speeches were delivered with tireless verbosity, exhibitions organized, seminars held, all on the subject of his eventful life. They discussed the meaning of his vegetarianism, its profound philosophical implications, though I know that it was simply that he didn't want to sink his teeth into any corpse, and you can't make that into much of a philosophy, can you? They talked about his views on subjects he knew nothing about, from solar energy to foreign relations, though I know he thought foreign relations were what you acquired if you married abroad. They even pulled out the rusting wood-and-iron spinning wheels he wanted everyone to use to spin *khadi* instead of having to buy British textiles, and they all weaved symbolic centimetres of homespun. Yet I know the entire purpose of the wheel was not symbolic, but down-to-earth and practical: it was meant to make what you South Indians call *mundus*, not metaphors. And so they celebrated a hundredth birthday he might have lived to see, had not husbandless Amba, after so many austerities, exacted her grotesque revenge.

We Indians cannot resist obliging the young to carry our burdens for us, as you well know, Ganapathi, shouldering mine. So they asked the educational institutions, the schools and colleges, to mark the centenary as well, with more speeches, more scholarly forums, but also parades and marches and essay contests for the little scrubbed children who had inherited the freedom Gangaji had fought so hard to achieve.

And what did they find, Ganapathi? They found that the legatees knew little of their spiritual and political benefactor; that despite lessons in school textbooks, despite all the ritual hypocrisies of politicians and leader-writers, the message had not sunk into the little brains of the lucubrating brats. 'Gangaji is important because he was the father of our Prime Minister,' wrote one ten-year-old with a greater sense of relevance than accuracy. 'Gangaji was an old saint who lived many years ago and looked after cows,' suggested another. 'Gangaji was a character in the *Mahabharata*,' noted a third. 'He was so poor he did not have enough clothes to wear.'

Of course, it is easy, Ganapathi, to get schoolchildren to come up with howlers, especially those whose minds are being filled in the bastard educational institutions the British sired on us, but the innocent ignorance of those Indian schoolboys pointed to a larger truth. It was only two decades after Gangaji's death, but they were already unable to relate him to their lives. He might as well have been a character from the *Mahabharata*, Ganapathi, so completely had they consigned him to the mists and myths of historical legend.

Let us be honest: Gangaji was the kind of person it is more convenient to forget. The principles he stood for and the way in which he asserted them were always easier to admire than to follow. While he was alive, he was impossible to ignore; once he had gone, he was impossible to imitate.

When he spoke of his intentions to his three young wards, trembling tensely before him at the brink of adulthood, he was not lying or posturing. It was, indeed, Truth that he was after – spell that with a capital T, Ganapathi, Truth. Truth was his cardinal principle, the standard by which he tested every action and utterance. No dictionary imbues the word with the depth of meaning Gangaji gave it. His truth emerged from his convictions: it meant not only what was accurate, but what was just and therefore right. Truth could not be obtained by 'untruthful', or unjust, or violent means. You can well understand why Dhritarashtra and Pandu, in their different ways, found themselves unable to live up to his precepts even in his own lifetime.

But his was not just an idealistic denial of reality either. Some of the English have a nasty habit of describing his philosophy as one of 'passive resistance'. Nonsense: there was nothing passive about his resistance. Gangaji's truth required activism, not passivity. If you believed in truth and cared enough to obtain it, Ganga affirmed, you had to be prepared actively to suffer for it. It was essential to accept punishment willingly in order to demonstrate the strength of one's convictions.

That is where Ganga spoke for the genius of a nation; we Indians have a great talent for deriving positives from negatives. Non-violence, non-cooperation, non-alignment, all mean more, much more, than the concepts they negate. 'V.V.,' he said to me once, as I sat on the floor by his side and watched him assiduously spin what he would wear around his waist the next day, 'one must vindicate the Truth not by the infliction of suffering on the opponent, but on oneself.' In fact he said not 'oneself' but 'one's self', which tells you how carefully he weighed his concepts, and his words.

I still remember the first of the great incidents associated, if now so forgettably, with Gangaji. He had ceased to be Regent and was living in a simple house built on a river bank, which he called an ashram and the British Resident – who now refused to use 'native' words where perfectly adequate English substitutes were available – referred to as 'that commune'. He lived there with a small number of followers of all castes, even his Children of God whom he discovered to be as distressingly human as their touchable counterparts, and he lived the simple life he had always sought but failed to attain at the palace – which is to say that he wrote and spun and read and received visitors who had heard of his radical ideas and of his willingness to live up to them. One day, just after the midday meal, a simple vegetarian offering concluding with the sole luxury that he permitted himself – a bunch of dates procured for him at the town market many miles away – a man came to the ashram and fell at his feet.

We were all sitting on the verandah – yes, Ganapathi, I was there on one of my visits – and it was a scorching day, with the heat rising off the dry earth and shimmering against the sky, the kind of day when one is grateful to be in an ashram rather than on the road. It was then that a peasant, his slippers and clothes stained with the dust of his journey, his lips cracking with dryness, entered, called Gangaji's name, staggered towards him and fell prostrate.

At first we thought it might simply be a rather dramatic gesture of obeisance – you know how we Indians can be – but when Ganga tried to lift the man up by his shoulders it was clear his collapse had to do with more than courtesy. He had lost consciousness. After he had been revived with a splash of water he told us, in a hoarse whisper, of the heat and the exhaustion of his long walk. He had come over a hundred miles on foot, and he had not eaten for three days.

We gave him something to chew and swallow, and the peasant, Rajkumar, told us his story. He was from a remote district on Hastinapur's border with British India, but on the British side of the frontier. He wanted Gangaji to come with him to see the terrible condition of his fellow peasants and do something to convince the British to change things.

'Why me?' Ganga asked, not unreasonably. 'I have no official position any more in Hastinapur. I can pull no strings for you.'

'We have heard you believe in justice for rich and poor, twice-born and low-caste alike,' the peasant said simply. 'Help us.'

He was reluctant, but the peasant's persistence moved him and in the end Ganga went to Rajkumar's impoverished district. And what he saw there changed him, and the country, beyond measure.

 12

I was there, Ganapathi. I was there, crowding with him into the third-class railway carriage which was all he would agree to travel in, jostling past the sweat-stained workers with their pathetic yet precious bundles containing all they possessed in the world, the flat-nosed, wide-breasted women with rings through their nostrils, the red-shirted porters with their numbered brass armbands bearing steel trunks on their cloth-swathed heads, the water-vendors shouting 'Hindu pani! Mussulman pani!' into our ears, for in those days even water had a religion, indeed probably had a caste too, braving the ear-splitting shrieks of the hawkers, of the passengers, of the relatives who had come to bid them goodbye, of the beggars who were cashing in on the travellers' last-minute anxiety to appease the gods with charity, and finally of the guards' whistles. Yes, Ganapathi, I was there, propelling the half-naked crusader into the compartment as our iron-wheeled, rust-headed, steam-spouting *vahana* clanged and wheezed into life and heaved us noisily forward into history.

Motihari was like so many other districts in India – large, dry, full of ragged humans eking out a living from land which had seen too many pitiful scratchings on its unyielding surface. There was starvation in Motihari, not just because the land did not produce enough for its tillers to eat, but because it could not, under the colonialists' laws, be entirely devoted to keeping them alive. Three tenths of every man's land had to be consecrated to indigo, since the British needed cash-crops more than they needed wheat. This might not have been so bad had there been some profit to be had from it, but there was none. For the indigo had to be sold to British planters at a fixed price – fixed, that is, by the buyer.

Ganga saw the situation with eyes that, for all his idealism, had too long been accustomed to the palace of Hastinapur. He saw men whose fatigue burrowed into their eyes and made hollows of their cheeks. He saw women dressed day after day in the same dirty sari because they did not possess a second one to change into while they washed the first. He saw children without food, books or toys, snot-nosed little creatures whose distended bellies mocked the emptiness within. And he went to the Planters' Club and saw the English and Scots in their dinner-jackets and ballroom gowns, their laughter tinkling through the notes of the club piano as waiters bearing overladen trays circled their flower-bedecked tables.

He saw all this from outside, for the dark Christian hall-porter who guarded the club's racial character denied him entry. He stood on the steps of the clubhouse for a long while, his eyes burning through the plate-glass windows of the dining-room, until a uniformed watchman came out, took him by the arm and asked him brusquely to move on. I expected Ganga to react sharply, to push the man away or at least to remove the other's grip on his arm, but I had again underestimated him. He simply looked at the offender: one look was enough; the watchman dropped his hand, instantly ashamed, eyes downcast, and Ganga walked quietly down the steps. The next morning he announced his protest campaign.

And what a campaign it was, Ganapathi. It is in the history books now, and today's equivalents of the snot-nosed brats of Motihari have to study it for their examinations on the nationalist movement. But what can the dull black-on-white of their textbooks tell them of the heady excitement of those days? Of walking through the parched fields to the huts of the poorest men, to listen to their sufferings and tell them of their hopes; of holding public hearings in the villages, where peasants could come forth and speak for the first time of the iniquity of their lives, to people who would do something about it; of openly defying the indigo laws, as Ganga himself wrenched free the first indigo plant and sowed a symbolic fistful of grain in its stead.

Even we who were with him then were conscious of the dawn of a new epoch. Students left their classes in the city colleges to flock to Gangaji's side; small-town lawyers abandoned the security of their regular fees at the assizes to volunteer for the cause; journalists left the empty debating halls of the nominated council chambers to discover the real heart of the new politics. A nation was rising, with a small, balding, semi-clad saint at its head.

Imagine it for yourself, Ganapathi. Frail, bespectacled Gangaji defying the might of the British Empire, going from village to village proclaiming the right of people to live rather than grow dye. I can see him in my mind's eye even now, setting out on a rutted rural road on the back of a gently swaying elephant – for elephants were as common a means of transport in Motihari as bullock-carts elsewhere – looking for all the world as comfortable as he would in the back of the Hastinapur Rolls, as he leads our motley procession in our quest for justice. It is hot, but there is a spasmodic warm breeze, touching the brow like a puff of breath from a dying dragon. From his makeshift howdah Ganga smiles at passing peasants, at the farmers bent over their ploughs, even at the horse-carriage that trundles up to overtake him, with its frantically waving figure in the back flagging him down. Ganga's elephant rumbles to a halt; the man in the carriage alights and thrusts a piece of paper at the ex-Regent, who bends myopically to look at it before sliding awkwardly down the side of his mount. For it is a message from the district police, banning him from proceeding further on his journey and directing him to report to the police station.

Panic? Fear? There is none of it; Ganga smiles even more broadly from the back of the returning carriage and we follow him cheerfully, bolstered by the courage of his convictions.

Gangaji enters the police *thana* with us milling behind him. The man in uniform does not seem pleased, either with us or with the piece of paper in front of him.

'It is my duty,' he says, taking in the appearance and attire of the former Regent of Hastinapur with scarcely concealed disbelief, 'to serve notice on you to desist from any further activities in this area and to leave Motihari by the next train.'

'And it is my duty,' responds Ganga equably, 'to tell you that I do not propose to comply with your notice. I have no intention of leaving the district until my inquiry is finished.'

'Inquiry?' asks the astonished policeman. 'What inquiry?'

'My inquiry into the social and economic conditions of the people of Motihari,' replies Ganga, 'which you have so inconveniently interrupted this morning.'

Ah, Ganapathi, the glorious cheek of it! Ganga is committed to trial, and you cannot imagine the crowds outside the courthouse as he appears, bowing and smiling and waving folded hands at his public. He is a star — hairless, bony, enema-taking, toilet-cleaning Ganga, with his terrible vow of celibacy and his habit of arranging other people's marriages, is a star!

The trial opens, the crowd shouting slogans outside, the heat even more oppressive inside the courtroom than under the midday sun. The police, standing restlessly to attention outside the courthouse gate, some helmeted in the heat and mounted on riot-control horses, cannot take it any longer. Their commander, a red-faced young officer from the Cotswolds, orders them to charge the peaceful but noisy protestors. They wade in, iron-shod hooves and steel-tipped staves flailing. The crowd does not resist, does not stampede, does not flee. Ganga has told us how to behave, and there are volunteers amidst the crowd to ensure we maintain the discipline that he has taught us. So we stand, and the blows rain down upon us, on our shoulders, our bodies, our heads, but we take them unflinchingly; blood flows but we stand there; bones break but we stand there; lathis make the dull sound of wood pulping flesh and still we stand there, till the policemen and their young red-faced officer, red now on his hands and in his eyes as well, red flowing in his heart and down his conscience, realize that something is happening they have never faced before . . .

You think I'm simply exaggerating, don't you, Ganapathi? The hyperbole of the old, the heroism of the nostalgic, that's what you think it is. You can't know, you with your ration-cards and your black markets and the cynical materialism of your generation, what it was like in those days, what it felt like to discover a cause, to belong to a crusade, to *believe*. But I can, don't you see. I can lean here on these damned lumpy bolsters and look at your disbelieving porcine eyes and *be* there, outside the courtroom at Motihari as the lathis fall and the men stand proud and upright for their dignity, while inside — surprise, surprise — the prosecution asks for an adjournment. Yes, the prosecution, Ganapathi, it is the government pleader, sweating all over his brief, who stumbles towards the bench and asks for the trial to be postponed . . .

But, hello — what's this? The accused will have none of it! The magistrate is on the verge of acquiescing in the request when Gangaji calls out from the dock: 'There is no need to postpone the hearing, my Lord. I wish to plead guilty.'

Consternation in the court! There is a hubbub of voices, the magistrate bangs his ineffectual gavel. Gangaji is speaking again; a silence descends as people strain to hear his reedy voice. 'My Lord, I have, indeed, disobeyed the order to leave Motihari. I wish simply to read a brief statement on my own behalf, and then I am willing to accept whatever sentence you may wish to impose on me.'

The magistrate looks wildly around him for a minute, as if hoping for guidance, either divine or official; but none is forthcoming. 'You may proceed,' he says at last to the defendant, for he does not know what else to say.

Gangaji smiles beatifically, pushes his glasses further back up his nose, and withdraws from the folds of his loincloth a crumpled piece of paper covered in spiky cramped writing, which he proceeds to smooth out against the railing of the dock. 'My statement,' he says simply to the magistrate, then holds it closely up to his face and proceeds to read aloud.

'I have entered the district,' he says, and the silence is absolute as every ear strains to catch his words, 'in order to perform a humanitarian service in response to a request from the peasants of Motihari, who feel they are not being treated fairly by the administration, which defends the interests of the indigo planters. I could not render any useful service to the community without first studying the problem, which is precisely what I have been attempting to do. I should, in the circumstances, have expected the help of the local administration and the planters in my endeavours for the common good, but regrettably this has not been forthcoming.' The magistrate's eyes are practically popping out at this piece of mild-mannered effrontery, but Ganga goes obliviously on. 'I am here in the public interest, and do not believe that my presence can pose any danger to the peace of the district. I can claim, indeed, to have considerable experience in matters of governance, albeit in another capacity.' Ganga's tone is modest, but his reference is clear. The judge shifts uncomfortably in his seat. The air inside the courtroom is as still as in a cave, and the punkah-wallah squatting on the floor with his hand on the rope of the fan is too absorbed to remember to pull it.

'As a law-abiding citizen' − and here Gangaji looks innocently up at the near-apoplectic judge − 'my first instinct, upon receiving an instruction from the authorities to cease my activities, would normally have been to obey. However, this instinct clashed with a higher instinct, to respect my obligation to the people of Motihari whom I am here to serve. Between obedience to the law and obedience to my conscience I can only choose the latter. I am perfectly prepared, however, to face the consequences of my choice and to submit without protest to any punishment you may impose.'

This time it is our turn, the turn of his supporters and followers, to gaze at him in dismayed concern. The prospect of glorious defiance was one thing, the thought of our Gangaji submitting to the full rigours of the law quite another. Unlike its post-Independence variant, with its bribable wardens and clubbable guards, the British prison in India was not a place anyone would have liked to know from the inside.

'In the interests of justice and of the cause I am here to serve,' Gangaji continues, 'I refuse to obey the order to leave Motihari' – a pause, while he looks directly at the magistrate – 'and willingly accept the penalty for my act. I wish, however, through this statement, to reiterate that my disobedience emerges not from any lack of respect for lawful authority, but in obedience to a higher law, the law of duty.'

There is silence, Ganapathi, pin-drop silence. Gangaji folds his sheet of paper and puts it away amidst the folds of his scanty garment. He speaks again to the magistrate. 'I have made my statement. You no longer need to postpone the hearing.'

The magistrate opens his mouth to speak, but no words come out. He looks helplessly at the government pleader, who is by now completely soaked in his own sweat, and in a kind of despair at his complacent defendant. At last the judge clears his throat; his voice emerges, a strained croak: 'I shall postpone judgment,' he announces, with a bang of his gavel. 'The court is adjourned.'

There are cheers from the assembled throng as the meaning of that decision becomes clear: the magistrate does not know what to do!

We carry Ganga out on our bloodied shoulders. The horses draw back, neighing; the soldiers withdraw, shamed by the savagery of their success; the fallen stagger to their feet; and our hero, hearing the adulation of the crowd, borne aloft on a crescendo of hope, our hero weeps as he sees how his principles have been upheld by the defenceless.

Ah, Ganapathi, what we could not have achieved in those days! The magistrate was right not to want to proceed, for when reports of what had happened reached the provincial capital, immediate instructions came from the Lieutenant-Governor to drop all the charges. Not only that: the local administration was ordered to assist Gangaji fully with his inquiry. Can you imagine that? The *satyagrahi* comes to a district, clamours for justice, refuses an order to leave, makes his defiance public, and so shames the oppressors that they actually cooperate with him in exposing their own misdeeds. What a technique it was, Ganapathi!

For it worked – that was the beauty of it – it worked to redress the basic problem. After the interviews with the peasants, the hearing conducted with the actual participation of district officialdom, and the submission of sworn statements, the Lieutenant-Governor appointed Gangaji to an official inquiry committee which unanimously – unanimously, can you imagine? – recommended the abolition of the system which lay at the root of the injustice. The planters were ordered to pay compensation to the poor peasants they had exploited; the rule requiring indigo to be planted was rescinded: Gangaji's disobedience had won. Yes, Ganapathi, the tale of the Motihari peasants had a happy ending.

That was the wonder of Gangaji. What he did in Motihari he and his followers reproduced in a hundred little towns and villages across India. Naturally, he did not always receive the same degree of cooperation from the authorities. As his methods became better known Ganga encountered more resistance; he found magistrates less easily intimidated and provincial Governors less compliant. On such occasions he went unprotestingly to jail, invariably shaming his captors into an early release.

All this was not just morally right, Ganapathi; as I cannot stress enough, it worked. Where sporadic terrorism and moderate constitutionalism had both proved ineffective, Ganga took the issue of freedom to the people as one of simple right and wrong – law versus conscience – and gave them a method to which the British had no response. By abstaining from violence he wrested the moral advantage. By breaking the law non-violently he showed up the injustice of the law. By accepting the punishments the law imposed on him he confronted the colonialists with their own brutalization. And when faced with some transcendent injustice, whether in jail or outside, some wrong that his normal methods could not right, he did not abandon non-violence but directed it against himself.

Yes, against himself, Ganapathi. Gangaji would startle us all with his demonstration of the lengths to which he was prepared to go in defence of what he considered to be right. How, you may well ask, and I shall tell you. But not just yet, my impatient amanuensis. As the Bengalis say when offered cod, we still have other fish to fry.

THE THIRD BOOK:
THE RAINS CAME

13

'That's the last bloody straw,' the British Resident said. He was pacing up and down his verandah, a nervous Heaslop flapping at his heels. 'Indigo inquiry, indeed. I'll crucify the bastard for this.'

'Yes, sir,' the equerry said unhappily. 'Er . . . if I may . . . *how*, sir?'

'How?' Sir Richard half-turned in his stride, as if unable to comprehend the question. 'What do you mean, how?'

'Er . . . I mean, how, sir? How will you, er, crucify him?'

'Well, I don't intend to nail him to a cross in the middle of the village bazaar, if that's what you're asking,' the Resident snapped. 'Don't be daft, Heaslop.'

'Yes, sir, I mean, no, sir,' the aide stuttered. 'I mean, I didn't mean that, sir.'

'Well, what did you mean?'

Sir Richard's asperity invariably made the young man more nervous. 'I mean that when I asked you *how*, I didn't really mean *how*, you know, physically, sir. When I said *how* I meant sort of *what*, you know, *what* exactly you meant when you meant to, er, crucify him . . . sir,' Heaslop ended a little lamely.

The Resident stopped, turned around, and stared at him incredulously. 'What on earth are you going on about, Heaslop?'

'Nothing, sir,' replied the hapless Heaslop, backing away. He was beginning to wish himself back on the North-West Frontier, being shot at by the Waziris. At least there he knew when to duck.

'Well, then don't,' Sir Richard advised him firmly. 'There's nothing as irritating when I'm trying to think as hearing you go on about nothing. Sit down, will you, and pour yourself a stiff drink.' He gestured at a trolley laden with bottles and siphons which now stood permanently on the verandah.

Heaslop sat gingerly on a lumpily cushioned cane-chair and busied himself with a bottle. Sir Richard continued to pace, his white sideburns, in need of a trim, quivering with the strength of his emotion. 'This man has publicly confronted, indeed humiliated, the Raj. Which means for all practical purposes the King-Emperor. Whom I represent. Which means he has humiliated *me*.'

'Er . . . I wouldn't take it so personally, sir,' Heaslop began.

'Shut up, Heaslop, will you, there's a good fellow,' came the reply from the Resident, whose round red cheeks gave him the appearance of a superannuated cherub, albeit one whose wings have been trod upon by a careless Jehovah. 'When I want your opinion I'll ask for it.'

The equerry subsided into a sulky silence.

'He has humiliated me,' his superior went on. 'And he has made matters worse by drawing attention to his former position here, which means I shall be unwelcome in every planters' club from here to Bettiah.' He glowered pinkly at the enormity of the privation. 'Never in the entire history of my family in India has such a thing happened to any of us. Not even to my brother David, who spends his time drawing pictures of animals.'

He stopped in front of the young man, who was drinking deeply from a tall glass. 'I must do something about this rabble-rouser,' he muttered. 'Presuming to usurp the legitimate functions of the district administration! Standing half-naked before a representative of His Majesty and inviting him, daring him, to pronounce sentence on his open defiance of the law! Serving on so-called "inquiry committees" and depriving honest planters of their livelihood! There has to be an end to this nonsense.'

Heaslop opened his mouth in habitual response, then thought better of it.

'Things are bad enough already,' Sir Richard went on. 'We have native lawyers declaiming against our rule in every legislative forum, even when they have been nominated to their seats for the most part as presumed Empire loyalists. We have had a nasty little boycott of British goods, with fine Lancashire cotton being thrown on to bonfires. We have even had bombs being flung by that Bengali terrorist, Aurobindo, and his ilk. But all these were, in the end, limited actions of limited impact. Ganga Datta shows every sign of being different.'

'In what way, sir?' Despite himself, Heaslop was intrigued.

'The man challenges the very rules of the game,' the Resident barked. 'Paradoxically, by using them for his own purposes. He knows the law well, and invites, even seeks, its sanction by deliberately – deliberately, mind you – violating it in the name of a higher truth. Twaddle, of course. But dangerous twaddle, Heaslop. He appeals to ordinary people in a way the chaps in the pin-stripe suits in the Viceroy's Council simply can't. In Motihari they flocked to him, irrespective of caste or religion. Untouchables, Muslims, Banias all rubbing shoulders in his campaign, Heaslop! And he stands before them in his bed-sheet, revelling in their adulation.'

Heaslop remained studiously mute. 'You know what the fellow dared to say when the President of the Planters' Club commented on the inappropriateness of his attire?' Sir Richard rummaged in his pockets and pulled out a newspaper clipping. '"Mine is a dress,"' he quoted in mounting indignation, '"which is best suited to the Indian climate and which, for its simplicity, art and cheapness, is not to be beaten on the face of the earth. Above all, it meets hygienic requirements far better than European attire. Had it not been for a false pride and equally false notions of prestige, Englishmen here would long ago have adopted the Indian costume." I ask you! Your precious Mr Ganga Datta would have the Viceroy in a loincloth, Heaslop. What on earth is that sound you are making?'

For Heaslop, overcome by the image of Lord Chelmsford's sturdy calves bared in Delhi's Durbar Hall, was spluttering helplessly into his glass.

'Drastic measures are called for, Heaslop,' Sir Richard continued, unamused. 'I'm convinced of that. This fellow must be taught a lesson.'

'How, sir?' Heaslop asked, in spite of himself.

The Resident looked at him sharply. 'That's precisely what I'm trying to give some thought to, Heaslop.' He lowered his tone. 'We've capitulated too often already. Think of that terrible mistake over the partition of Bengal. We carve up the state for our administrative convenience, these so-called nationalists yell and scream blue murder, and what do we do? We give in, and erase the lines we've drawn as if that were all there was to it. That could be fatal, Heaslop, fatal. Once you start taking orders back you stop being able to issue them. Mark my words.' He stopped pacing, and turned directly to his aide. 'What action can we take? It must be something I can do, or recommend to the States Department, something in keeping with the gravity of his conduct. If he were still Regent I'd have his hide for a carpet. But I suppose it's too late for that now.'

'Yes, sir,' Heaslop agreed reflectively. 'Unless . . .'

'Yes?' Sir Richard pounced eagerly.

'Unless it isn't really too late,' Heaslop said slowly. 'I have an idea that, if it's a question of our competence to act against him, we might be able to, er, catch him on a technicality.'

'Go on,' the Resident breathed.

'You see, when Ganga Datta handed over the reign, I mean the reins, of Hastinapur to the princes Dhritarashtra and Pandu and retired to his ashram, he was obliged under the law to notify us formally that he had ceased to be Regent,' Heaslop explained carefully. 'But he was probably so busy organizing the marriages of his young charges as soon as they'd come of age, that he quite simply forgot.'

'Forgot?'

'Well, it happens, sir. In the ordinary course we'd hardly pay much attention to it. Many of the princely states are less than conscientious about observing the fine print of their relations with us. Indians simply haven't developed, ah . . . our sense of ritual.'

Sir Richard looked at him suspiciously. Heaslop did not blink. 'But doesn't the court at Hastinapur employ an Englishman as a sort of secretary, to attend to this sort of thing?'

'Well, yes, there is Forster, sir, Maurice Forster, just down from Cambridge, I believe. But he seems to, ah, prefer tutoring young boys to performing his more routine secretarial duties. I have the impression he doesn't take many initiatives, sir. Never quite managed to get the hang of what India's all about. Considers it all a mystery and a muddle, or so he keeps saying. He waits to do what he is told, and I suspect that if the business of the notification didn't occur to the Regent, it wouldn't have occurred to poor Forster, either.'

'Hmm.' The Resident's round features softened with hope. 'And what exactly does this permit me to do, Heaslop?'

'Well, sir.' Heaslop sat up, choosing his words carefully. 'If we haven't been notified that Ganga Datta has ceased to be Regent, then technically, as far as we're concerned, he still is. I mean, despite any other evidence to the contrary, we're entitled to consider him to be in full exercise of the powers of Regent until we have been formally notified otherwise. Do you see, sir?'

'Yes, yes, man, go on.'

'Well, sir, if he's still Regent —'

'He has no business going about preaching sedition outside the borders of the state.' Sir Richard finished the sentence gleefully. 'Conduct unbecoming of a native ruler. I like it, Heaslop, I like it.'

'There's only one thing, sir,' the equerry added in a slightly less confident tone of voice.

'Yes?' The fear of bathos added octaves to the Resident's timbre. 'Don't tell me you've overlooked something, Heaslop.'

'No, sir. It's just that what he did, sir, in Motihari, wasn't exactly criminal, sir. The case was withdrawn. On the direct orders of the Lieutenant-Governor of the state. And then he was invited to join the official inquiry committee. It might be going too far, sir, for us to proceed against him for something Delhi doesn't consider seditious.'

'Piffle, Heaslop, piffle.' Sir Richard's tone was firm. 'That case wouldn't have been withdrawn if the indigo market weren't already in the doldrums. Your nationalist hero simply provided a good excuse to withdraw a regulation that wasn't needed any more, and earn the goodwill of some of these babus.' Sir Richard glowered at the thought. 'And don't make the mistake of assuming that Delhi thinks with one mind on a question like this. Not a bit of it. For every Lieutenant-Governor Scott with a soft spot for the uppity natives, there are ten on the Viceroy's staff who believe in putting them in their place. Besides, Paul Scott and his ilk can't tie our hands on a matter concerning the princely states. It's simply none of their damn business.'

'If you say so, sir.' Heaslop tried to keep the anxiety he felt out of his voice. He was beginning to feel like Pandora after casually opening the box. 'What exactly do you propose to do, sir? I mean, there isn't much point in demanding his ouster as Regent, is there, when we know perfectly well he isn't Regent any more?'

'Ouster? Who in damnation spoke about demanding his ouster, Heaslop?'

'Well, you said, sir, I mean no one, sir, but you did say that if he were still Regent you would —'

'Have his hide for a carpet.' Sir Richard recalled his metaphor. 'I'm not foolish enough to ask for his dismissal from functions he no longer exercises, Heaslop. It's not a symbolic victory I'm looking for. I want to teach Mr Datta, and any others like him, a lesson they'll never forget.'

'May I ask how, sir?' Heaslop's voice was faint.

'You may indeed, Heaslop, and I will answer you in one word,' Sir Richard replied, rubbing his hands in anticipatory satisfaction. 'Annexation.'

 14

'I'm not sure I want a *hundred* sons,' Dhritarashtra said to his bride. 'But I'd be happy to have half a dozen or so.'

They were reclining on an enormous swing, the size of a sofa, which hung from the ceiling of their royal bedroom. The unseeing prince lay on his side, propped up against a bolster, his head supported partly by an elbow and partly by Gandhari's sari-draped lap. His new princess, playing idly with strands of his already thinning hair, did not smile at his words, nor did she look at him. Gandhari the Grim, as this frail, dark beauty was already being called in the servants' quarters, could not, for her eyes were completely covered by a blindfold of the purest silk.

'You shall have a son,' she said softly, 'who shall be strong and brave, a leader of men. And he shall see well enough and far enough for both of us.'

Her husband sighed. 'Dearest Gandhari,' he whispered, his free hand reaching for her face and feeling the satin bandage around it. 'Why must you do this to yourself?'

'I have already told you,' she replied, decisively moving his hand away. 'Your world is mine, and I do not wish to see more of it than you do. It is not fitting that a wife should possess anything more than her husband does.'

A fragrance of the attar of roses wafted slowly down to him as she spoke. It was one of the signs by which he could tell her from any other presence in a room, that and the silvery tinkle of the *payals* at her ankle. 'How often must I tell you that you would be more useful to me the way you are?' Dhritarashtra asked sadly.

He never ceased to marvel at the strength of this woman's resolve. For a young girl, embarking on adulthood and marriage, to vow never to see the world again! What it must have meant to her to make this sacrifice, to blot out the world to conform to an idea of matrimony even fiercer and more intense than that handed down over the generations. What was it that drove her to this extreme act of self-denial? Not just tradition, for even the tradition of the dutiful wife, the Sati Savitri of myth and legend, did not demand so much. Not love, for she had never set eyes on Dhritarashtra before; nor admiration, for the days of his greatness still lay ahead. No, it was some mysterious inner force that led this young girl to will herself into blindness, to give up the glory of the sunlight and the flowers, to renounce the blazing splendour of the *gulmohar*s or the gathering thunderclouds of the monsoons, to have to judge a sari by its feel rather than its colour, a space by its sound rather than its size, a man by his words rather than his looks. It was a sacrifice few, let alone this delicate wisp of a woman, would be thought capable of making.

'Useful? It is not a wife's role to be *useful*.' Gandhari tossed her determined head. 'If that is all you want, you can hire any number of assistants, secretaries, readers and scribes, cooks and servants and even women of pleasure. As I am sure you have done whenever you have felt the need.' She ran her fingers through his hair to remove any hint of offence. 'No, my lord, a *dharampatni* is not expected to be useful. Her duty is to share the life of her husband, its joys and triumphs and sorrows, to be by his side at all times, and to give him sons.' A note of steely wistfulness crept into her voice. 'A hundred sons.'

Dhritarashtra had never known a woman like this in England. He tried to inject a note of playfulness into the conversation. 'Not a hundred. That would be exhausting.'

His quiet wife did not laugh. This was not a subject on which she entertained levity. 'Who knows? That is what the astrologer has foretold. It would take a long time, to produce a hundred sons.'

'And so it would.' Dhritarashtra the sceptic, with his Cambridge-taught disbelief that the stars could be read any more accurately than the tea leaves he constantly brewed, chuckled, and reached for his wife. This time his hands touched a different fabric, and felt a responsive warmth beneath. 'So what are we waiting for?'

His fingers tickled her and at last she laughed too. The swing rocked with their love, at first slowly, then with accelerating rhythm, casting moving shadows on the walls that neither could see.

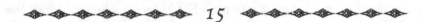 15

Behave yourself, Ganapathi. What do you mean, how could I know? You don't expect me to spell out everything, do you? I just know, that's all. I know a great many things that people don't know I know, and that should be good enough for you, young man.

Meanwhile, as they say in those illustrated rags which I suppose are all your generation reads these days, Pandu was having the time of his life with his two wives. The scandal-burdened Kunti was every bit as delectable as her reputation suggested, and the steatomammate Madri, if less symmetrically proportioned, more than made up for this with the inventiveness of her love-making. Pandu was always something of a physical soul, if you get my meaning, and he revelled in the delights of bigamy, taking due care to ensure that his pleasures were not prematurely interrupted by pregnancy.

It was, of course, too good to last. That, Ganapathi, is one of the unwritten laws of life that I have observed in the course of a long innings at the karmic crease. It is just when you are seeing the ball well and timing the fours off the sweet of the bat that the unplayable shooter comes along and bowls you. And it is because we instinctively understand this that we Hindus take defeat so well. We appreciate philosophically that the chap up there, the Great Cosmic Umpire, has a highly developed sense of the perverse.

Didn't think I knew much about cricket, did you? As I told you, Ganapathi, I know a great deal about a great deal. Like India herself, I am at home in hovels and palaces, Ganapathi, I trundle in bullock-carts and propel myself into space, I read the *vedas* and quote the laws of cricket. I move, my large young man, to the strains of a morning raga in perfect evening dress.

But we were talking about something else — you mustn't let me get distracted, Ganapathi, or you will be here for ever. Was it not the profound inscrutability of Providence I was on about? It was? More or less? Well, in Pandu's case it manifested itself quite early. He was in bed one day with both his consorts, attempting something quite unspeakably imaginative, when an indescribable pain shot through his chest and upper arm and held his very being in its grip. He fell back, unable to mouth the words to convey his torture, and for a brief moment his companions thought their ministrations had brought him to a height of ecstasy they had never seen before. But a quick look lower down convinced them something quite different was the matter. They frantically screamed for help.

'Massive coronary thrombosis,' said Dr Kimindama, as Pandu lay paler than ever under the oxygen tent. 'Or in plain Hindustani, a whopping great heart attack. He's lucky to be alive. If it weren't for the prompt call,' he added, looking with appreciation at the two not-quite-shevelled ladies beside the bed, 'I'm not sure we could have saved him.'

Pandu recovered; his big heart rode the blow and knit itself together. But when he was ready to resume a normal life the doctor took him aside and gave him the terrible news.

'I'm afraid,' Dr Kimindama said, 'that in your case there is one prohibition I must absolutely enjoin upon you. The circumstances of your attack and the present condition of your heart make it imperative that you completely, and I mean completely, give up the pleasures of the flesh.'

'You mean I have to stop eating meat?' Pandu asked.

The doctor sighed at the failure of his euphemism. 'I mean you have to stop having sex,' he translated bluntly. 'Your heart is simply no longer able to withstand the strain of sexual intercourse. If you want to live, Your Highness, you must abstain from any kind of erotic activity.'

Pandu sat heavily back on his bed. 'That's how bad it is, doctor?' he asked hollowly.

'That's how bad it is,' the doctor confirmed. 'Your next orgasm will be your last.'

Think of it, Ganapathi! To be married to two of the most delightful companions that could have been conjured from Adam's rib, and yet to be denied, like an over-cautious chess-player, the pleasures of mating! Such was the lot of my pale son Pandu, and it could have been the ruin of a lesser man. But the blood of Ved Vyas ran in his veins, don't you forget that, Ganapathi, and he resolutely turned his back on his misfortune, and his wives. His putative father had died of his lust, and Pandu had no desire to conform to the pattern.

'This is a signal,' he explained to his grief-stricken spouses. 'I must pull up my socks, turn over a new leaf and make something of my life, if I am ever to acquire salvation. Sex and worldly desires only tie a man down. I am determined to roll up my sleeves and put my nose to the grindstone, not forgetting to gird my loins while I am about it. I shall practise self-restraint and yoga, and devote myself to good causes. Oh, yes, and I shall be sleeping alone from now on.'

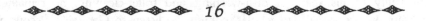 *16*

It was a time of great grief and much sorrow
When Pandu rose up from the dead;
For starting today (not tomorrow)
He must renounce the joys of the bed.

The medic didn't give him an option
Except 'tween this world and the next;
To live (and avoid any ruption)
He just had to give up sex.

To young Pandu, as you can imagine
It came as a painful wrench;
He could enjoy life's great pageant
But he couldn't lay hands on a wench.

To his wives, two lovely ladies,
He could offer no more than a kiss;
They might as well have lived in Hades
For all the hope they could have of bliss.

Yes, after those nights full of pleasure –
Full of baiting and biting and laughter –
They would now have only the leisure
To contemplate the hereafter.

Good deeds! was now the motto
Of the rest of their lives on this earth;
No frolic, no getting blotto,
No foreplay, no unseemly mirth;

No, nothing but an ascetic's toga
And the quest of the good and the right:
A regular session of yoga
And a guru to show him the light.

> Thus Pandu abandoned the pastime
> Of expending in women his lust;
> He shrugged passion off for the last time
> And set off to strive for the just.

And where else could he go, Ganapathi, but to his uncle Ganga, now ensconced in his ashram on the river bank? Of course, Pandu the so-recent sybarite was not about to enrol straight away in the commune and take cheerfully to his share of dish-washing and toilet-cleaning; he remained initially an occasional day-scholar, coming to listen to Gangaji's discourses when he could, then returning to the comforts and — for he was still the younger brother of a blind maharaja — the responsibilities of the palace.

This was about the time of Motihari, just after, in fact, and the ashram was already beginning to attract its fair share of hangers-on. You know the song, Ganapathi:

> groupies with rupees and large solar topis,
> bakers and fakers and enema-takers,
> journalists who promoted his cause with their pen,
> these were among his favourite men!

Pandu joined this motley crowd at Gangaji's feet, listening to his ideas and marvelling at the disciples' devotion to him. He learned of politics and Gangan philosophy:

> of opposing caste
> unto the last
> (for Sudras are human, too)
> of meditation
> and sanitation
> (and cleaning out the loo).
>
> He learned to pray
> the simple way
> (for Ganga taught him how)
> to help the weak
> turn the other cheek
> (and always protect the cow).

Soon he sounded more
like his mentor
(than any other *chela*)
Spoke Ganga's words
ate Ganga's curds
and became even paler.

He brooked no debate
on being celibate
(a trait that's Sagittarian).
His passionate defence
of abstinence
turned others vegetarian.

Poetry, Ganapathi, but it's not enough to sing of the transformation of Pandu
under Ganga's tutelage. No, one must turn to prose, the prose of the
Bharatiya Vidya Bhavan biographies and the school textbooks. How about
this, O long-nosed one? In discourse his speech became erudite, his tone
measured. In debate he thought high and aimed low. He became adept at
religion, generous in philanthropy and calm in continence. No? You don't
like it? Well, take it down anyway. We must move on: Pandu has begun
quoting the *shastras* at unlikely moments, applying the most arcane of our
ancient concepts to the circumstances of everyday life, and we must not leave
these unrecorded.

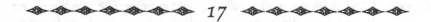 *17*

Where shall we rejoin Pandu? He began, you see, to enliven his conversation
with legend and fable – a myth, he thought, was as good as a smile – and his
moral tales would curl the pages of the *Kama Sutra*. Shall we intrude upon him
as he tells his red-eared Madri of lustful Vrihaspati, who forced his attentions
upon his pregnant sister-in-law Mamta, and found his ejaculation blocked by
the embryonic feet of his yet-to-be-born nephew? Or of the Brahmin youth
who turned himself into a deer to enjoy the freedom to fornicate in the forest,
until he was felled by a sharp-shooting prince on a solitary hunt? Or should
we, instead, eavesdrop on our pale protagonist as he pontificates on the
virtues of celibacy to his ever-sighing mate Kunti?

'But sons I must have,' said Pandu one day, after a close reading of the holy
books. In addition to Gangaji he had been spending some time with his

grandmother Satyavati and with, need I say it, me, and we all had, as well you know by now, Ganapathi, fairly flexible ideas on the subject. Flexible, but sanctified by scripture, as Pandu explained to his doe-eyed wife Kunti:

'I have learned to live without sex, as Gangaji has done for so much longer, but I cannot, like him, hope for salvation in the next life without a son. His is a life of exceptional merit and purity and good works; he need never spill his seed, yet a thousand sons will step forward to light his funeral pyre. I am not so fortunate, Kunti. No ritual, no sacrifice, no offering, no vow will help me attain the moksha that is denied the sonless man.'

He gazed at his wife with sorrowful eyes – no, Ganapathi, make that with eyes full of sorrow – and spoke in the firm voice of a preceptor, detached from the subject of his discourse. 'I have talked to our elders and read the scriptures, and they tell me there are twelve kinds of sons a man can have. Six of these may become his heirs: the son born to him in the normal course from his lawfully wedded wife; the son conceived by his wife from the seed of a good man acting without ignoble motive; the son similarly conceived, but from a man paid for this service; the posthumous son; the son born of a virgin mother; and finally, the son of an unchaste woman.'

Kunti listened speechlessly, with widening eyes. Her learned husband went remorselessly on. 'The six who cannot become his heirs are: the son given by another; the adopted son; the son chosen at random from among orphans; the son born from a wife already pregnant at marriage; the son of a brother; and the son of a wife from a low caste. Since I need an heir it is clear that I cannot adopt a son; you must give me one.'

Kunti looked at him with what the poet – and don't ask me which poet, Ganapathi, just write the poet – called a wild surmise. She was beginning to get his drift, and she was not sure she liked the way his wind was blowing.

'I cannot, as you know, give myself a son through you. I do not know how to go about obtaining the services of a surrogate father. But I leave it to you, Kunti. Find a man who is either my equal or my superior, and get yourself pregnant by him.'

Kunti raised a hand to her mouth in horror. 'Don't ask me to do this,' she pleaded. 'Ever since we met I have remained completely faithful to you. You know people have already gossiped about me before we were married. Don't give them an excuse to start again, my darling. Besides, I know we can have children together. Couldn't we, whatever that doctor might say? If we're really careful?'

'No, we can't,' Pandu replied, 'and you know I simply can't afford to take the chance. Look, Kunti, it's very good of you to want to stay faithful to me and I appreciate it, really I do. But you've got to realize that for a good Hindu it is far more important to have a son, indeed to have a few sons, than to put a chastity belt on his wife.'

Kunti, still shocked – for you know the conservatism of our Indian women, Ganapathi, they are for ever clinging to the traditions of the last century and ignoring those of the last millennium – waited for the inevitable exegesis from the *shastras*. It was not long in coming. Pandu readjusted his lotus position, tucking his feet more comfortably under his haunches, and went on in high-sounding tones. 'You know, if you read our scriptures you will realize that there was a time when Indian women were free to make love with whomever they wished, without being considered immoral. There were even rules about it: the sages decreed that a married woman must sleep with her husband during her fertile period, but was free to take her pleasure elsewhere the rest of the time. In Kerala, the men of the Nair community only learn that their wives are free to receive them by seeing if another man's slippers aren't outside her door. Our present concept of morality isn't really Hindu at all; it is a legacy both of the Muslim invasion and of the superimposition of Victorian prudery on a people already puritanized by purdah. One man married to one woman, both remaining faithful to each other, is a relatively new idea, which does not enjoy the traditional sanction of custom. (Which is why I myself have had no qualms about taking two wives.) So I really don't mind you sleeping with another man to give me a son. It may seem funny to you, but the deeper I steep myself in our traditions, the more liberal I become.'

He could see she was not yet convinced. 'Look, I'll tell you something that might even shock you, but which, in fact, is in full accordance with our divine scriptures and ancient traditions. It's a closely guarded family secret that even I learned only when I became a man. Vichitravirya, my mother's husband, isn't really my father. Nor Dhritarashtra's, for that matter. Our mothers slept with their husband's half-brother, Ved Vyas, when their husband died, to ensure he would be graced with heirs.' Pandu saw that this story, at last, had sunk in. 'So you see? You'd just be following a family tradition. You've always done as I asked you to – so go and find yourself a good Brahmin and give me a son.'

Kunti's resistance melted at last. 'The truth is,' she began, 'I don't really know how to tell you this, but I already *have* a son.'

'What?' It was Pandu's turn to register offended astonishment. 'You? Have a son? By whom? When? And how could you talk so glibly of having been faithful to me?'

'Please don't be angry, my dear husband,' Kunti implored. 'I only mentioned it because you brought up the subject this way. And I *have* been faithful to you. My son was born before we even met, before your family asked for my hand for you.'

Comprehension dawned on a paling Pandu. 'Hyperion Helios,' he said through gritted teeth. 'The travelling magnate. So the scandal-mongers were right after all.'

Kunti hung her beautiful head in acknowledgement.

'And where is your son today?'

'I don't know,' Kunti admitted miserably. 'I was so ashamed when he was born – though I shouldn't have been, for he was a lovely little boy, his golden skin glowing like the sun – that I put him in a small reed basket and floated him down the river.'

'Down the river?'

'Down the river.'

'Then there isn't much point in talking about him, is there?' Pandu asked a little cruelly.

'Someone must have found him,' Kunti said defiantly. 'I'm sure he is still alive. And I know I'll recognize him the moment I see him again. His colour – it's so extraordinary I'm sure no one else in these parts would have anything like it. And then there's his birthmark – a bright little half-moon right in the centre of his forehead. There's no way he could have got rid of that.' She turned to Pandu. 'If you want a son, I know we can find him,' she pleaded. 'Let us have inquiries made in the area.'

A wind blew, Ganapathi, at those words, stirring up leaves, dust, shadows, clothing; eyelashes flickered in disturbed hope; an age sighed. 'I'm sorry,' Pandu replied. 'It's no use. A son born to you before we were even married, even if he were found, how can he be an heir of mine? No, you will simply have to find someone else, Kunti.' A hard edge entered his voice. 'And it shouldn't be all that difficult for you. After all, you do have the experience.'

Kunti seemed about to say something; then her face assumed a set expression. 'As you wish, my husband,' she said. 'You shall have your son.'

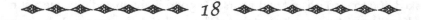 *18*

I remember, Ganapathi, I still remember the night our late Leader was born. It was a monsoon night, and the rain lashed down upon us, while a howling wind tore branches off trees and ripped roofs off shacks, turned our pathetic parasols inside out and drove the water into our homes. I entered the palace dripping, handed the shambles of my umbrella to the bowing servitor and mounted the stairs towards the women's quarters. A female attendant came out of Gandhari's room just as I reached the landing. Something about her expression led me to fear the worst. I asked her quietly, 'How is she?'

'Still in labour, sir.'

I nodded, both troubled and relieved. Still in labour: but it had been twenty-four hours already, time enough for me to receive the news and make my way through the mounting rage of the storm to the palace. And still she lay there; Gandhari the Grim lay there and sweated and suffered. I had a vision of that small, frail, delicately proportioned body stretched out and arched in the most grotesque of contortions, as a hundred lustily bawling sons fought their way out of her half-open womb . . .

And then, from behind Gandhari's closed door just down the corridor, there emerged a single, long, wailing sound. We both stood transfixed. It was a baby's cry and yet it was more than that; it was a rare, sharp, high-pitched cry like that of a donkey in heat, and as it echoed around the house a sound started up outside as if in response, a weird, animal moan, and then the sounds grew, as donkeys brayed in the distance, mares neighed in their pens, jackals howled in the forests, and through the cacophony we heard the beating of wings at the windows, the caw-caw-cawing of a cackle of crows, and penetrating through the shadows, the piercing shriek of the hooded vultures circling above the palace of Hastinapur.

'What was that, sire?' the woman servant asked, fear writ large on her face.

'Dhritarashtra's heir has been born,' I said.

I was right. For when the doctor emerged from Gandhari's room he was ashen with the strain. It had been the most difficult delivery of his life, he said, and it had taken a terrible toll on the brave young mother. She had survived, but she could never have children again. This one child would be her only offspring.

'A boy, of course?' Dhritarashtra, anxiously leaning on a cane, his dapper features strained with anticipation, asked the doctor. For weeks the midwives had said that all the signs pointed to a male heir: the shape of Gandhari's breasts in the eighth month, the sling of her uterus in the ninth. 'How is he?'

'A girl,' the doctor said shortly. 'And she's very well.'

The cane slipped with a clatter from Dhritarashtra's hand. A servant bent to pick it up and the new father leaned against the wall, breathing heavily.

I slipped quietly into the room and shut the door behind me. 'It is I, my child,' I said. 'I have come a long way to congratulate you.'

'A girl!' Gandhari's head was sunk into her pillow and the beads of perspiration had yet to dry on her face. She had refused to take off her blindfold even to see her own infant, and it clung wetly to her closed eyelids. Her customary grimness was accentuated by a startling pallor, as if all the blood had been drained out of her in the delivery. 'Is that all I shall have to show, Uncle, for the hundred sons you once promised me?'

I looked at her, pity overwhelming the admiration I had always felt for this spirited woman. I felt the exhaustion of that long wet night, the fatigue of that long hard birth; and my mind is still haunted by the image of poor grim Gandhari, head sunk into the pillow because she had failed to create the son her husband needed. History, Ganapathi, is full of savage ironies.

'Your daughter, Gandhari,' I said, taking her hand in mine, 'will be equal to a thousand sons. This I promise you.'

I could not see into those closed eyes; I knew she did not believe me. Nor would she have believed what destiny had in store for her painfully wrought child. Gandhari would not live to know it, but her sombre-eyed daughter, Priya Duryodhani, would grow up one day to rule all India.

THE FOURTH BOOK:
A RAJ QUARTET

19

The news of the annexation of Hastinapur by the British Raj was announced by a brusque communiqué one morning. There was none of the subtle build-up one might have expected, Ganapathi; no carefully planted stories in the press about official concern at the goings-on in the palace, no simulated editorial outrage about the degree of political misbehaviour being tolerated from a sitting Regent, not even the wide bureaucratic circulation of proposals, notes and minutes that Vidur, now a junior functionary in the States Department, might have seen and tried to do something about. No, Ganapathi, none of the niceties this time, none of the fabled British gentlemanliness and let-me-take-your-glasses-off-your-face-before-I-punch-you-in-the-nose; no sir, John Bull had seen red and was snorting at the charge. One day Hastinapur was just another princely state, with its flag and its crest and its eleven-gun salute; the next morning it was part of the British Presidency of Marabar, with its cannon spiked, its token frontier-post dismantled and the Union Jack flying outside Gandhari's bedroom window.

Sir Richard, former Resident of Hastinapur, now Special Representative of the Viceroy in charge of Integration, and a hot favourite to succeed the retiring Governor of Marabar himself, breakfasted well that morning on eggs and kedgeree, and his belly rumbled in satisfaction. He had just wiped his mouth with a damask napkin when an agitated Heaslop burst in.

'Come in, Heaslop, come in,' said Sir Richard expansively if unnecessarily, for the equerry was already within sneezing distance of the pepper-pot. 'Tea?'

'No, thank you, sir. I'm sorry to barge in like this, sir, but I'm afraid the situation is beginning to look very ugly. Your intervention may be required.'

'What on earth are you on about, man? Sit down, sit down and tell me all about it.' Sir Richard reached for the teapot, a frown creasing his pink forehead. 'Are you sure you won't have some tea?'

'Absolutely sure, sir. The people of Hastinapur haven't reacted very well to the news of the annexation, sir. Ever since this morning's radio broadcast they have been pouring out on the streets, sir, milling about, listening to street-corner speakers denouncing the imperialist yoke. The shops are all closed, children aren't going to school nor their parents to work, and the atmosphere in the city centre and the *maidan* is, to say the least, disturbing.'

Sir Richard sipped elegantly, but two of his chins were quivering. 'Any violence?'

'A little. Some window-panes of English businesses smashed, stones thrown, that sort of thing. Not many targets hereabouts to aim at, of course, in a princely state. It's not as if this were British India, with assorted symbols of the Raj to set fire to. A crowd did try to march toward the residency, but the police stopped them at the bottom of the road.' Heaslop hesitated. 'My own car took a couple of knocks, sir, as I tried to get through. Stone smashed the windscreen.'

'Good Lord, man! Are you hurt?'

'Not a scratch, sir.' Heaslop seemed not to know whether to look relieved or disappointed. 'But the driver's cut up rather badly. He says he's all right, but I think we need to get him to the hospital.'

'Well, go ahead, Heaslop. What are you waiting for?'

'There's one more thing, sir. Word is going round that Ganga Datta will address a mass rally on the annexation this afternoon, sir. At the Bibigarh Gardens. People are flocking to the spot from all over the state, sir, hours before the Regent, that is, the ex-Regent, is supposed to arrive.'

'Ganga Datta? At the Bibigarh Gardens? Are you sure?'

'As sure as we can be of anything in these circumstances, sir.'

Sir Richard harrumphed. 'We've got to stop them, Heaslop.'

'Yes, sir, I thought you might want to consider that, sir, that's why I'm here. I'm afraid we might not be able to block off the roads to the gardens, though. The police are quite ineffectual, and I wouldn't be too sure of their loyalties either, in the circumstances.'

'What would you advise, Heaslop?'

'Well, sir, I wonder if we don't stand to lose more by trying to stop a rally we can't effectively prevent from taking place.'

'Yes?'

'So my idea would be a sort of strategic retreat, sir. Let them go ahead with their rally, let off steam.'

'You mean, do nothing?'

'In a manner of speaking, yes, sir. But then passions would subside. Once they've had their chance to listen to a few speeches and shout a few slogans, they'll go back to their normal lives soon enough.'

'Stuff and nonsense, Heaslop. Once they've listened to a few speeches from the likes of Ganga Datta and his treacherous ilk, there's no telling what they might do. Burn down the residency, like as not. No, this rally of theirs has to be stopped. But you're right about the police. They won't be able to do it.'

'That's what I thought, sir,' Heaslop said unhappily. 'Not much we can do, then.'

'Oh yes, there is,' Sir Richard retorted decisively. 'There's only one thing for it, Heaslop. Get me Colonel Rudyard at the cantonment. This situation calls for the army.'

 *20*

The Bibigarh Gardens were no great masterpiece of landscaping, Ganapathi, but they were the only thing in Hastinapur that could pass for a public park. The plural came from the fact that Bibigarh was not so much one garden as a succession of them, separated by high walls and hedges into little plots of varying sizes. The enclosures permitted the municipal authorities the mild conceit of creating differing effects in each garden: a little rectangular pool surrounded by a paved walkway in one, fountains and rose-beds in another, a small open park for children in a third. There was even a ladies' park in which women in and out of purdah could ride or take the air, free from the prying eyes of male intruders; here the hedge was particularly high and thick. The gardens were connected to each other and to the main road only by narrow gates, which normally were quite wide enough for the decorous entrances and exits of pram-pushing ayahs and strolling wooers. On this day, however, they were to prove hopelessly inadequate.

One of the gardens, a moderately large open space entirely surrounded by a high brick wall, was used — when it was not taken over by the local teenagers for impromptu games of cricket — as a sort of traditional open-air theatre-cum-Speakers' Corner. It was the customary venue (since the *maidan* was too big) for the few public meetings anyone in Hastinapur bothered to hold. These were usually *mushairas* featuring local poetic talent or folk-theatre on a rudimentary stage, neither of which ever attracted more than a few hundred people. It was the mere fact of having staged such functions that gave the Bibigarh Gardens their credentials for this more momentous occasion.

When news spread of a possible address by Gangaji on the day of the state's annexation, Bibigarh seemed the logical place to drift towards. Soon the garden was full, Ganapathi; not of a few hundred, not of a thousand, but of ten thousand people, men, women, even some children, squeezed un-complainingly against each other, waiting with the patience instilled in them over timeless centuries.

When Colonel Rudyard of the Fifth Baluch arrived at the spot with a detachment, it did not take him long to assess the scene. He saw the crowd of fathers, mothers, brothers, sisters, sons, daughters, standing, sitting, talking, expectant but not restless, as a milling mob. He also saw very clearly – more clearly than God allows the rest of us to see – what he had to do. He ordered his men to take up positions on the high ground all round the enclosure, just behind the brick walls.

It is possible that his instructions had been less than precise. Perhaps he was under the assumption that the people of Hastinapur had already been ordered not to assemble for any purpose and that these were, therefore, defiant trouble-makers. Perhaps all he had was a barked command from Sir Richard, telling him to put an end to an unlawful assembly, and his own military mind devised the best means of implementing the instruction. Or perhaps he just acted in the way dictated by the simple logic of colonialism, under which the rules of humanity applied only to the rulers, for the rulers were people and the people were objects. Objects to be controlled, disciplined, kept in their place and taught lessons like so many animals: yes, the civilizing mission upon which Rudyard and his tribe were embarked made savages of all of us, and all of them.

Whatever it may be, Ganapathi – and who are we, all these decades later, to speculate on what went on inside the mind of a man we never knew and will never understand – Colonel Rudyard asked his men to level their rifles at the crowd barely 150 yards away and fire.

There was no warning, no megaphone reminder of the illegality of their congregation, no instruction to leave peacefully: nothing. Rudyard did not even command his men to fire into the air, or at the feet of their targets. They fired, at his orders, into the chests and the faces and the wombs of the unarmed, unsuspecting crowd.

Historians have dubbed this event the Hastinapur Massacre. How labels lie. A massacre connotes the heat and fire of slaughter, the butchery by bloodthirsty fighters of an outgunned opposition. There was nothing of this at the Bibigarh Gardens that day. Rudyard's soldiers were lined up calmly, almost routinely; they were neither disoriented nor threatened by the crowd; it was just another day's work, but one unlike any other. They loaded and fired their rifles coldly, clinically, without haste or passion or sweat or anger, resting their weapons against the tops of the brick walls so thoughtfully built in Shantanu's enlightened reign and emptying their magazines into the human beings before them with trained precision. I have often wondered whether they heard the screams of the crowd, Ganapathi, whether they noticed the blood, and the anguished wails of the women, and the stampeding of the trampling feet as panic-stricken villagers sought to get away from the sudden hail of death raining remorselessly down upon them. Did they hear the cries of the babies being crushed underfoot as dying men beat their mangled limbs against each other to get through those tragically narrow gateways? I cannot believe they did, Ganapathi, I prefer not to believe it, and so I think of the Bibigarh Gardens Massacre as a frozen tableau from a silent film, black and white and mute, an Indian *Guernica*.

The soldiers fired just 1600 bullets that day, Ganapathi. It was so mechanical, so precise; they used up only the rounds they were allocated, nothing was thrown away, no additional supplies sent for. Just 1600 bullets into the unarmed throng, and when they had finished, oh, perhaps ten minutes later, 379 people lay dead, Ganapathi, and 1,137 lay injured, many grotesquely maimed. When Rudyard was given the figures later he expressed satisfaction with his men. 'Only 84 bullets wasted,' he said. 'Not bad.'

Even those figures were, of course, British ones; in the eyes of many of us the real toll could never be known, for in the telling many more bled their lives into the ground than the British and the press and the official Commission of Inquiry ever acknowledged. Who knows, Ganapathi, perhaps each of Rudyard's bullets sent more than one soul to another world, just as they did the Raj's claims to justice and decency.

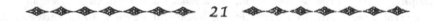 *21*

Gangaji came later, at the appointed hour of his address, and when he saw what had happened he doubled over in pain and was sick into an ornamental fountain. He stumbled among the bodies, hearing the cries of the injured and the moans of the dying, and he kept croaking to himself in Sanskrit. I was there, Ganapathi, and I caught the words, '*Vinasha kale, viparita buddhi*' – our equivalent of the Greek proverb: 'Whom the gods wish to destroy, they first make mad'.

It was Gangaji's strength to see meaning in the most mindless and perverse of human actions, and this time he was both wrong and right. He was wrong because the Massacre was no act of insane frenzy but a conscious, deliberate imposition of colonial will; yet he was right, because it was sheer folly on the part of the British to have allowed it to happen. It was not, Ganapathi, don't get me wrong, it was not as if the British were going around every day of the week shooting Indians in enclosed gardens. Nor was Rudyard particularly evil in himself; his was merely the evil of the unimaginative, the cruelty of the literal-minded, the brutality of the direct. And because he was not evil in himself he came to symbolize the evil of the system on whose behalf, and in whose defence, he was acting. It was not Rudyard who had to be condemned, not even his actions, but the system that permitted his actions to occur. In allowing Indians to realize this lay the true madness of the Hastinapur Massacre. It became a symbol of the worst of what colonialism could come to mean. And by letting it happen, the British crossed that point of no return that exists only in the minds of men, that point which, in any unequal relationship, a master and a subject learn equally to respect.

At the time this was perhaps not so evident. The incident left the population in a state of shock; if you think it provoked a further violent reaction, you would be wrong, Ganapathi, for no father of a family willingly puts himself in the firing-line if he knows what bullets can do to him. After Bibigarh everyone knew, and the people subsided into subordination.

Gangaji told me later that the Massacre confirmed for him the wisdom of the principles of non-violence he had preached and made us practise at Motihari. 'There is no point,' he said candidly, 'in choosing a method at which your opponent is bound to be superior. We must fight with those weapons that are stronger than theirs – the weapons of morality and Truth.' Put like that it might sound a little woolly-headed, I know, Ganapathi, but don't forget it had worked at Motihari. The hope that it might work again elsewhere, and the knowledge that nothing else could defeat the might of the Empire on which the sun never set, were what made us flock to Gangaji. In a very real sense Hastinapur gave him the leadership of the national movement.

And what of Colonel Rudyard, the great British hero of Bibigarh? His superiors in Whitehall were embarrassed by his effectiveness: there is such a thing, after all, as being too efficient. Rudyard was prematurely retired, though on a full pension. Not that he needed it; for across the length and breadth of the Raj, in planters' clubs and Empire associations, at ladies' tea parties and cantonment socials, funds were raised in tribute by patriotic pink-skins outraged by the slight to a man who had so magnificently done his duty and put the insolent natives in their place. The collections, put together and presented to the departing Colonel at a moving ceremony attended by the best and the whitest, amounted to a quarter of a million pounds, yes, Ganapathi, 250,000, two and a half lakhs of pounds sterling, which even at today's depreciated exchange rate is forty lakhs of rupees, an amount it would take the President of India thirty-five years to earn. It took Rudyard less than thirty-five minutes, much less. The gift, which his government did not tax, brought him more than £160 per Indian dead or wounded; as one pillar of the Establishment was heard to murmur when the figures were announced, 'I didn't think a native was worth as much as that.'

In some ways this gesture did even more than the Massacre itself to make any prospect of Indian reconciliation to British rule impossible. It convinced Gangaji, who derived his morals as much from the teachings of Christianity as from any other source, that the Raj was not just evil, but satanic. The Massacre and its reward made Indians of us all, Ganapathi. It turned loyalists into nationalists and constitutionalists into revolutionaries, led a Nobel Prize-winning poet to return his knighthood — and achieved Gangaji's absolute conversion to the cause of freedom. He now saw freedom as indivisible from Truth, and he never wavered again in his commitment to ridding India of the evil Empire. There was to be no compromise, no pussyfooting, no sellout on the way. He would think of the phrase only years later, but his message to the British from then on was clear: Quit India.

Rudyard retired to a country home in England. I wonder whether he was ever troubled by the knowledge of how much he was reviled and hated in the country he had just left. Or by the fact that so many hotheaded young men had sworn, at public meetings, in innumerable temples and mosques and *gurudwaras*, to exact revenge for his deed in blood. I like to think that Rudyard spent many a sleepless night agonizing if a stray shadow on the blind was of an assassin, starting at each unexpected sound in fear that it might be his personal messenger from Yama. But I am not sure he did, Ganapathi, because he knew, just as Ganga did, the limitations of our people in the domain of violence. The young men who swore undying revenge did not know how to go about exacting it, or even where. Only two of them finally had the intelligence and the resources to cross the seas in quest of their quarry. And when they got to Blighty, and made inquiries about an old India hand with an unsavoury Hastinapur connection, they found their man and, with great éclat and much gore, blew him to pieces.

Do not rejoice, Ganapathi, for it was not Rudyard whose brains they spattered over High Street, Kensington. No, not Rudyard, but a simple case of mistaken identity; to a sturdy Punjabi one British name is much like another, the people they questioned were themselves easily confused, and it was not Rudyard, but Kipling they killed. Yes, Kipling, the same Professor Kipling who had been careless enough to allude to the canine qualities of the Indian people, and who, for that indiscretion, had already been struck by my pale, my rash son Pandu. It makes you wonder, does it not, Ganapathi, about the inscrutability of Providence, the sense of justice of our Divinity. Our two young men went proudly to the gallows, a nationalist slogan choking on their lips as the noose tightened, blissfully unaware that they had won their martyrdom for killing the wrong man. Or perhaps he was not the wrong man: perhaps Fate had intended all along that Kipling be punished for his contempt;

perhaps the Great Magistrate had decreed that the sentence of death fall not on the man who had ordered his soldiers to fire on an unarmed assembly but on he who had so vilely insulted an entire nation. It does not matter, Ganapathi; in the eyes of history all that matters is that we finally had our revenge.

 22

So that is how my family entered politics, Ganapathi. Gangaji was more or less already in it, of course, since his crusade for justice had brought him smack up against the injustice of foreign rule, but now Dhritarashtra, with his dark glasses and white cane, and Pandu, whom celibacy had driven to fat, joined the cause full-time.

Vidur, too, might have joined; indeed, he wished to. He came down from Delhi the day after the annexation and the Bibigarh Massacre, and informed Gangaji and his brothers that he had resigned from the Service.

'What?' exclaimed Dhritarashtra. 'Resigned?'

'Good thing,' said Pandu. 'Well done, Vidur. You shouldn't have joined the bastards in the first place.'

'Withdraw it at once,' Gangaji said.

Vidur blinked in astonishment. 'I beg your pardon, Uncle?' he asked, for he was a polite young man.

'Withdraw it,' Gangaji said tersely. 'At once.'

'Withdraw my resignation? But I can't possibly do that.'

'Why not? Have they already accepted it?'

'No,' Vidur admitted, 'they haven't even seen it yet. I've put my letter of resignation in the Under-Secretary's in-tray, and he'll find it when he comes in on Monday morning.'

'No, he won't,' said Dhritarashtra, who was quick on the uptake, 'because you'll go back to Delhi immediately and take it out of his in-tray before he sees it.'

'But why?' Vidur asked despairingly. 'You can't seriously want me to serve this alien government, a government that has done *this* to our people!'

'Whether it is the government you will be serving or the people whom they have harmed is only a matter of opinion,' said Ganga sententiously. 'Explain it to him, Dhritarashtra.'

'Don't you see, Vidur?' asked Dhritarashtra, who, despite his blindness (or perhaps because of it), revelled in optical allusions. 'We need you there. If

we're going to fight the Raj effectively we shall need our own friends and
allies within the structure. And if we win,' he added, his voice acquiring that
dreamy quality that women in Bloomsbury had found irresistible during his
student days, 'we shall still need able and experienced Indians to run India for
us.'

And so Vidur reluctantly stayed on in the ICS and, because he had many
of his father's good qualities, rose with remarkable rapidity up the rungs of
the States Department. His princely upbringing at Hastinapur had given him
the knack of dealing with Indian royalty. He understood their whims and
wants, indulged their eccentricities and interpreted them sympathetically to
the British. In time he became a trusted intermediary between the pink
masters and their increasingly assertive brown subjects.

But we must put Vidur aside for a moment, Ganapathi, to look more
carefully at Gangaji and his two princely disciples as they, in turn, rose to the
peak of the nationalist movement.

Dhritarashtra's disappointment with fatherhood and the failing health of his
grim wife drove him wholeheartedly into politics. Here he surprised everyone
with his flair for the task. He had the blind man's gift of seeing the world not
as it was, but as he wanted it to be. Even better, he was able to convince
everyone around him that his vision was superior to theirs. In a short while he
was, despite his handicap, a leading light of the Kaurava Party, drafting its
press releases and official communications to the government, formulating its
positions on foreign affairs, and establishing himself as the party's most
articulate and attractive spokesman on just about anything on which Canta-
brigian Fabianism had given him an opinion.

Gangaji, the party's political and spiritual mentor, made no secret of his
preference for the slim and confident young man. Pandu, in the circumstances,
took it all rather well. He saw the world very differently from his blind half-
brother. His recent brush with the angels of death and his subsequent
immersion in the scriptures had made him more of a traditionalist than the
idealistic Dhritarashtra, and the solidity of his appearance testified to one
whose feet were staunchly planted on terra firma. Not for Pandu the flights of
fancy of his sightless sibling, nor, for that matter, the ideological flirtations,
the passionate convictions, the grand sweeping gestures of principle that
became the hallmarks of Dhritarashtra's political style. Pandu believed in
taking stock of reality, preferably with a clenched fist and eyes in the back of
one's head. He balanced an hour of meditation with an hour of martial arts.
'Of course I believe in non-violence,' he would explain. 'But I want to be
prepared just in case non-violence doesn't believe in *me*.'

His duties as the party's chief organizer were indirectly responsible for his political differences with Dhritarashtra. The process of building up a party-structure and a cadre committed to run it in the teeth of colonial hostility convinced him that discipline and organization were far greater virtues than ideals and doctrines. It was the classic distortion, Ganapathi, to which our late Leader would herself one day fall prey, the elevation of means over ends, of methods over aspirations. As long as Gangaji was there he shrewdly harnessed the divergent skills of my two sons to the common cause. But when his grip began to slip . . .

But you see, I am getting ahead of my story again, Ganapathi. You mustn't let me. I haven't yet told you about Kunti, Pandu's faithfully infidelious wife, and how she fulfilled her husband's extraordinary request for progeny. For it was not only Gandhari the Grim who assured India's next generation of leadership by her exertions in labour. After all, Ganapathi, as you well know, we were to develop a pluralist system, so a plurality of leaders had to be born to run it.

Stop looking so lascivious, young man. I have no intention of offering you a ringside seat by Kunti's bed. Facts, that is all I intend to record, facts and names. This is history, do not forget, not pornography.

In fact, if you must know, Pandu helped choose the genetic mix his sons would inherit. Kunti's first post-marital lover (yes, first, there were others, but I shall come to that in a moment) was the youngest Indian judge of the High Court; let us refer to him only as Dharma, so as not to wound certain sensibilities, though those who know who I am speaking about will be left in no doubt as to his real identity. Dharma was learned, distinguished, good-looking in the way that only men become when they start greying at the temples, and of a highly respectable family. A man of principle, he agonized over his adultery, but found himself agonizing even more when Kunti abandoned him abruptly – as soon, in fact (though he was not to know this) as her pregnancy was confirmed.

A son was born of their union, a weak-chinned, gentle boy with a broad forehead, whom they decided to name Yudhishtir. Pandu swears that, meditating while Kunti was in the final stages of labour, he heard a voice from the heavens proclaiming that the lad would grow up to be renowned for his truthfulness and virtue. But I have always suspected that Pandu had simply been reading a biography of George Washington too late into the night and dreamt the whole thing.

When Yudhishtir was born Hastinapur was still in the family's hands and Pandu was persuaded of the need for more – what shall I call it? – 'offspring insurance' to make the succession secure. But he did not want Kunti striking up too long an association with Dharma, and the lady herself was attracted by the idea of variety. (Few women, Ganapathi, fail to be excited by the thought of producing children from different men; it is the ultimate assertion of their creative power. Fortunately for mankind, however, or perhaps unfortunately, fewer still have the courage to put their fantasy into practice.) This time her privileged nocturnal companion was a military man, Major Vayu, of the soon-to-be-disbanded Hastinapur Palace Guard.

Vayu was a large, strong, blustery character, full of drive and energy but mercurial in temperament. He breezed into Kunti's life and out of it, his ardour more gusty than gutsy, leaving in her the seed of Pandu's second son, Bhim. Bhim the Brave, he came to be called in the servants' quarters, but also, among the exhausted ayahs, Bhim the Heavy, for his was a muscular babyhood. His narrow forehead, close-set eyes and joined eyebrows made it clear that he would never share his older brother's intellectual attainments nor inherit any part of his mother's looks; but it was also clear that in strength he would have few equals. The doctor delivering him fractured a wrist before deciding upon a Caesarian; Kunti gave up nursing him when she found herself unable to rise after a minute's suckling; a cot of iron had to be manufactured for him after he had demolished two wooden cribs with a lusty kick of his foot; and a succession of bruised ayahs had finally to be replaced by a male attendant, a former Hastinapur all-in wrestling champion. The last of the ayahs resigned after an incident she never ceased talking about: apparently she had accidentally dropped the unbearably heavy infant on to a rock in the garden and had watched in horror as the stone crumbled into dust. This time the voice from the heavens only said one word, Ganapathi: 'Ouch.'

But Pandu, absentee landlord of his wife's womb, was still not content; he wanted a son who would combine the brain of Yudhishtir with the brawn of Bhim. He went deeper and deeper into yoga and meditation, mastered the heaven-pleasing *asana* of standing motionless on one leg from dawn till dusk, asked Kunti to conserve her energies for an entire year (which, with Bhim on the premises, she was only too happy to do) and prayed for such a son. Finally, when he judged the moment to be right, he invited the revered Brahmin divine, Devendra Yogi, to partake of the pleasures of his wife's bed. The godlike yogi's expertise made the experience rewarding for Kunti in more ways than one. And thus, Ganapathi, was born Arjun, Arjun of lissom figure and sinewy muscle, Arjun of sharp mind and keen eye, Arjun of fine face and fleet foot. Oh, all right, I know I'm getting carried away again, but the boy deserves it, Ganapathi. The voice from the heavens proclaimed that Pandu's third son would be beloved of both Vishnu, the Preserver, and Shiva, the Destroyer. And this time Kunti heard the voice too, as she lay drained upon the delivery bed; the rishis on the Himalayan mountain-slopes heard it; the workers in the factories looked up from the clanging wheels of their machinery and heard it; and I, I paused in the midst of a stirring speech of sedition to a village panchayat and heard it. And Ganapathi, oh, Ganapathi, it filled us all with joy.

I think it was the startling discovery of celestial interest in her maternity that finally prompted Kunti to call a halt to her amatory experiments. Pandu, she was alarmed to note, was even prouder of his sons than he might have been had he personally fathered them, and he was speaking speculatively of a fourth candidate to cuckold him when Kunti put her pretty foot down. 'It's all very well for you,' she said bluntly, 'but you're not the one who has to grow, and swell, and become heavy, and retch into the sink in the morning, and give up *biryanis* and wine and swings because they make you sick, and suffer the pain- and the heaving and the agony of a thousand hot fingers pulling out your insides.' Kunti shuddered. She had become an elegant woman of the world; as she spoke she inserted a Turkish cigarette into an ebony holder and waited, but Pandu disapprovingly refrained from lighting it for her. 'I don't think even your sages would demand more of me.'

Pandu was on the verge of drawing himself up self-righteously when Kunti drove home the clincher. 'I've been doing some reading of the *shastras* myself,' she said tellingly, 'and I find that the views you quoted aren't the only ones on the subject. As far as I can tell, the scriptures say a woman who gives herself to five men is unclean and one who has slept with six is a whore. You haven't overlooked that, by any means, have you, my lord?'

Pandu opened his mouth as if to speak, then shut it with a sigh. 'All right, have it your way,' he said.

He might have been a great deal more insistent had it not been that Madri, his inventive second wife, had already come to him with a gentle admonition. 'I don't mean to thound as if I'm complaining or anything,' the large-hearted princess lisped, 'but it does seem as if you think much more of Kunti, who was only an adopted daughter of a mahawaja, anyway. I mean I'm not comparing or anything, but I *am* a real pwinceth and I *do* think you might want to have an heir thwough me too.'

Pandu had initially fobbed her off with gentle words of love and protestations about his reluctance to sully her chastity (which were all quite true, for Pandu did not relish the prospect of being cuckolded by *both* his wives) but following Kunti's rebellion he changed his mind. 'All right, Madri,' he told his heavy-breasted helpmeet. 'But just one affair, that's all, or my name will be the laughing-stock of Hastinapur.'

'Oh, *thank* you, my poor dear Pandu,' Madri gushed, her conspicuous cleavage wobbling in excitement. (Pandu felt a twinge and looked away.) 'Just one affair, I pwomise.'

Madri did indeed confine herself to just one affair, as promised. But she was nothing if not imaginative: she seduced a pair of identical, and inseparable, twins. Since Ashvin and Ashwin did everything together, Madri had the double satisfaction of adhering to her promise and enjoying its violation. The result of her efforts was also doubly gratifying: not one, but two sons. Pandu, rejecting Lav and Kush, the names of the legendary Ramayana twins, as too predictable, called Madri's boys Nakul and Sahadev.

'Oh, aren't you pleased, Pandu dear?' Madri beamed over the twins' cradle. 'Twinth! Now the nasty Bwitish can't do *anything* to the succession. Or do you think, Pandu, do you think,' – and here her little round eyes gleamed at the pwospect – 'that just to be safe, I should try once more? Just once?'

'Don't you dare let her,' warned Kunti when she heard of the request. 'She'll produce triplets next, and then where will I be? Don't forget that I *am* your first wife, after all. Ever since she came into the house this Madri has been trying to steal a march on me. Scheming woman.'

And there, Ganapathi, as you can well imagine, we had the makings of a first-rate family drama, with steamy romance and hot flushing jealousy. But it was all cut short by the one event that made the entire issue of heir-conditioning redundant: the annexation of Hastinapur.

THE FIFTH BOOK:

THE POWERS OF SILENCE

23

Right, Ganapathi, so have I caught up with myself? Filled you in on the rapidly expanding cast of characters? I don't imagine this is particularly easy for you, is it, with so many dramatis personae to keep abreast of, so many destinies to pursue. But then what we're talking about is the story of an entire nation, Ganapathi, a nation of 800 million people (and God knows how many more it has gone up by while I have been talking to you). It could have been a lot worse.

Let me see now. There is still so much to say about Gangaji. There is *always* so much to say about Gangaji. Even if I am, God knows, no hagiographer, I mustn't fail him entirely in this memoir. I have no intention of tracing every detail of his career here, you can take my word for it. Too many others have done that already, in print, ether and celluloid, for me to want to join the queue. But I did promise, didn't I, days ago, to tell you how Gangaji directed his non-violence against himself, how he first startled us by demonstrating the lengths to which he was prepared to go in defence of what he considered right. I shall now proceed, to your undoubted dismay, Ganapathi, to keep that promise.

It happened during an agitation Gangaji supported, not long after Motihari. But this time, instead of rural indigo-growing peasants, he was helping suburban jute-factory workers at Budge Budge, outside Calcutta. Jute, the fibre of the *Corchorus capsularis* (and, lest anyone accuse me of painting an incomplete picture, also of the *Corchorus olitorus*) plants of Bengal, was perhaps India's greatest contribution to the prosperity of Scotland. It was grown in the swamps of East Bengal and shipped off in vast quantities to Dundee, where it was turned into sacks, mats and bags and shipped right back to be sold at a vast profit to, among others, the Bengalis who had picked the plant in the first place. This pleasant little arrangement — fields in Bengal, factories in Scotland — might have gone on indefinitely were it not for Kaiser Wilhelm II, to whom all Bengalis owe a major debt of gratitude. He marched into Belgium and started World War I; the war quintupled the demand for jute because Europeans needed it to make sandbags with, to buffer their trenches and barricade their streets; and since it was quicker, and cheaper, and safer to process the jute near where it was grown, Bengal acquired a jute industry. The factories were built at last on Indian soil, and the area round Dundee finally began giving way to the environs of Dum Dum.

But if geography ensured an Indian triumph, history and economics kept the spoils in British hands. The factories were owned and managed by the sons of Scotland rather than the brethren of Bengal. And as Gangaji found, the indigenes who pulled the levers and moved the mechanical looms were paid the proverbial pittance (*their* proverb, Ganapathi, *our* pittance) which barely permitted them to eke out a living amidst the filth and stench of their slum dwellings.

It is a long story, Ganapathi, and I do not intend to recount it all here, so you can stop yawning that cavernous yawn of yours and concentrate on what I am telling you. Briefly, then, simplifying the issues at the risk of offending the historians and the jute-wallahs and the processional trade unionists and the professional apologists, what happened was this. Somebody else – an enlightened woman, an Englishwoman, in fact, indeed the sister of one of the jute-mill owners – had won a remarkable benefit for the workers during an epidemic that had swept through the slums after a particularly heavy monsoon. Sarah Moore, for this was her name, had persuaded her brother and his fellow employers to offer the workers a bonus for coming to work during the epidemic; and the bonus was a significant one, amounting to nearly 80 per cent of their normal salaries. It took the plague to earn them a decent wage, but when they got it the workers braved death and disease to work for it.

When the epidemic passed, the mill owners decided to withdraw the bonus, arguing that it had served its purpose. But the workers, led by their widowed English spokeswoman, claimed they could not continue to live without the bonus, and asked for a wage rise, if not of 80 per cent, then of 50 per cent. The employers refused, and declared a lock-out.

When Gangaji arrived in Budge Budge he found a situation verging on the desperate. The locked-out workers were, of course, being paid nothing at all. Their families were starving. I need not describe to you, Ganapathi, child of an Indian city as you undoubtedly are, the sights which met Ganga's eyes: the foetid slums; the dirt and the despair and the disrepair; the children playing in rancid drains; the little hovels without electricity or water in which human beings lived several to a square yard. This is now the classic picture of India, is it not, and French cinematographers take time off from filming the unclad forms of their women in order to focus with loving pity on the unclad forms of our children. They could have done this earlier too, they and their pen-wielding equivalents of an earlier day, but somehow all the foreign observers then could only bring themselves to write about the glories of the British Empire. Not of the Indian weavers whose thumbs the British had cut off in order to protect the machines of Lancashire; not of the Indian peasants whose lands had been signed over to zamindars who would guarantee the colonists the social peace they needed to run the country; and not of the destitution and hunger to which these policies reduced Indians. Indulge an old man's rage, Ganapathi, and write this down: the British killed the Indian artisan, they created the Indian 'landless labourer', they exported our full-employment and they invented our poverty.

It is difficult for you, living now with the evidence of that poverty around you, taking it for granted as a fact of life, to conceive of an India that was not poor, not unjust, not wretched. But that was how India was before the British came, or why would they have come? Do you think the merchants and adventurers and traders of the East India Company would have first sailed to a land of poverty and misery? No, Ganapathi, they came to an India that was fabulously rich and prosperous, they came in search of wealth and profit, and they took what they could take, leaving Indians to wallow in their leavings. Ganga knew, when he trod through the slush and the shit of the factory-workers' slums, that this had not existed before the British came, and that its existence was a negation of the idea of Truth in which he so passionately believed.

There is something particularly soul-destroying about urban squalor. The poverty of Motihari was set, after all, against the lush splendour of the sub-Himalayan countryside, the sun-dappled greens and golds isolating the misery as something temporal, something separate, something apart. But Budge Budge was different: in a city-slum Nature provides no soothing contrast to offset the man-made horror. In those narrow, airless alleys it is impossible to escape from the pervasive wretchedness. Gangaji, master of Hastinapur, veteran of Motihari, saw this for the first time, and for hours afterwards he could not speak.

Yet what touched him the most was not the abject poverty, Ganapathi, no, not even the near-empty tin plates at which the children scratched at supper-time, but the look of utter hopelessness on the faces of the locked-out workers. That was the closest to nothingness Ganga had seen: no money, no food, no clothes, no work, no salary, no future – no reason, in short, to live – and it moved and frightened him as nothing else had.

Ganga went with the idealistic Mrs Moore to speak to her brother and the other mill owners, or those among them who consented to meet him. They made an odd pair: the determined, strong-jawed, big-boned English-woman and the slight, balding, frail Indian sage, striding out to bargain for a cause that need not have been either's. It was a pairing that would raise eyebrows and hackles for years to come.

'I don't see what you have to do with the problem, Mr Datta,' Montague Rowlatt said heavily when they accosted him in his cool, high-ceilinged office. 'It involves a dispute between my employees and myself in which I have no need for a third party, not even one who may happen to be related to me.' He cast a meaningful look at his sister, who remained determinedly unperturbed. 'However, since you ask, I don't mind telling you that my partner, Morley, and I have been discussing the matter. We have jointly decided, together with our fellow mill owners, to make a fair offer to the workers. Not their ridiculous 80 per cent, of course, and certainly not 50 per cent, but the considerably generous figure of 20 per cent.'

'Twenty per cent!' It was Sarah Moore who had risen to her feet, eyes blazing. 'That's no sort of offer, Montague, and you know it. Come, Mr Datta. It seems we shall have to take this matter further.'

Ganga, bemused, gathered up the folds of his loincloth and walked out behind the Englishwoman. And he resolved to take up the workers' cause.

 24

But first, Gangaji had to make the cause his own. He called a meeting of the workers under a peepul tree on the banks of the Hooghly, where the river wends its brackish way past Budge Budge to the bay. And when he asked them whether they would be willing to follow his guidance in their struggle, to seek justice through his methods and never to deviate from the path of Truth, they responded with a full-throated 'yes'.

'Very well,' Gangaji said in that bookish way of his. 'The first thing we shall do is to reformulate our demands. You, through Sarah-behn here' – yes, Ganapathi, *behn*, for Ganga had already made her, in cheerful disregard of ethnicity, appearance and colonial history, his sister – 'have asked for a 50 per cent increase in wages. Your employers offer 20 per cent. Since in pursuit of Truth we must seek no unfair advantage over our adversary, I have decided we shall now ask for 35 per cent. It is a just figure, the mill owners can afford to pay it, it is better than what you have – and it splits the difference.'

This time the roar of approval from the crowd was somewhat more muted. But the workers, having accepted Gangaji's leadership, accepted his reformulation of their demand. The struggle was on.

And Ganga waged it in his own peculiar way. This time there were no depositions to take, no travels to undertake, no elephants to be overtaken. Instead he trudged through the slum dwellings every morning, holding a hand here, soothing a brow there. Then he rested, his shrinking frame lost under the covers of the enormous four-poster bed Sarah Moore had given him in a room at her home. Every afternoon, at precisely five o'clock, he arrived in Mrs Moore's Overland roadster at the peepul tree. A crowd would already have gathered for this ritual, and the Englishwoman's liveried chauffeur would have to toot-toot his way through the throng to the foot of the tree, his professional dead-pan expression betraying no hint of what he thought of his unusual errand. Ganga and his English 'sister' – a word that soon came to connote friend, hostess, protector and disciple all in one – would then alight. Ganga, a shawl sometimes draped over his bony shoulders to shield him from the Bengali winter, his glasses perched on his nose, would proceed to speak to the crowd.

It almost did not matter what he said, for he rarely raised his voice to harangue them and the words never carried to the farthest ranks of his audience. It is doubtful many would have understood him if they had. But it was as if, in simply being there and attempting to communicate with them, he was transmitting a message more powerful than words. His presence carried its own impulses to the people assembled before him, a wave of strength, and inspiration, and conviction, that sustained the workers in their hungry defiance.

I see that furrow on your brow again, Ganapathi. You think that this is not at all like the Ganga we know and have spoken about, the Ganga of the third-class railway carriages and the experiments in self-denial. But what can I say, young man, except that it is the truth? You would have expected him to make his home amongst the squalor of the slum, but Ganga stayed amidst the comforts of colonial civilization; you would have expected him to walk to the peepul (spell that any way you like, Ganapathi, the idea's the same), but instead he drove in a white woman's car. And yet neither prevented him from preaching to the workers about the importance of holding out for their just demands, even if they had to starve in order to do so.

This went on for days, Ganapathi, indeed for over two weeks, and Ganga made his speeches, and the workers got hungrier and more desperate, and the employers resolutely refused to heed the name of their town – they did not budge. God knows how long this might have gone on, and whether at the end of it all we might have had a worthwhile story to tell. But Fate has a habit of intervening at just the right moment to resolve these crises, to drop an apple on a sleeping head, to turn an aimless drift into a surging tide. Great discoveries, Ganapathi, are often the result of making the wrong mistake at the right time. Ask Columbus.

It happened when the mill owners, deciding that their employees had now reached the point of least resistance, announced that they were ending the lock-out: the factory gates were now open to any worker who was willing to accept the 20 per cent. Ganga responded at his five o'clock meeting that if the owners' lock-out was over, the workers' strike had begun. They would not, he declared, return to their machines until the 35 per cent had been granted. His announcement was greeted by some straggling cheers, and large areas of silence. The rumbling in the workers' stomachs had begun to drown out the defiance in their voices.

It was not that they had been less than fully committed in their stead-fastness. No, Ganapathi, they had held out, heeding Gangaji's daily exhorta-tions. And in the crude songs they had improvised after his speeches, in the chanting cadences of their processions back from the peepul tree to their hovels, they had given voice to their courage and their determination:

> I dreamt I saw Paradise last night
> Where every man was free;
> Where workers sang, and toiled, and prayed
> At the feet of Gangaji,
> At the feet of Gangaji.
>
> And Gangaji said, 'This bliss is yours
> 'Cause you held out till the end;
> For you stood with courage in your hearts
> And stoutly refused to bend –
> And stoutly refused to bend.'
>
> Yes, we shall win, brothers and friends,
> We shall win by staying true
> To our cause, our faith, our firm belief
> That God will give us our due,
> That God will give us our due.

Simple lyrics, Ganapathi, simply sung by the ragged band, with words they improvised each evening to reflect the most important theme of Gangaji's latest speech. They were often out of tune, God knows, but never out of step with that inner harmony that comes when it is the heart that sings and not just the tongue. But few things can test the human spirit as sorely as the needs of the human flesh. When the employers threw open the gates of the factories and offered to take the starving workers back, the workers' defiance trembled on the brink of collapse.

Ganga understood clearly that if even a few of his charges went back to the factory his cause – their cause – would fail, and the weeks of obduracy that had kept their stomachs empty would be in vain. So he added a practical step to his exhortations: he moved the timing of his daily meeting under the peepul tree from 5 p.m. to 7.30 a.m., the precise moment when the factory whistle would blow and the gates swing open to welcome the workers reporting for duty.

This was a bold gesture: the factory gates were situated directly across the road from the river bank upon which Ganga's peepul stood. He was confronting his followers with the source of their own temptation and teaching them to reject it as evil.

It worked the first day. The whistle blew, the immense gates clanged open; a florid foreman in khaki shorts came to the entrance and looked expectantly at the assembled workers. The temptation strained their faces, but Gangaji's crowd held: no worker was going to walk in through those inviting gates in full view of his comrades. It was a sort of primitive picket-line, I suppose, but it was far from certain that, in those pre-union days, the picket would hold. Ganga represented the wise, disinterested leadership the workers had yearned for, but his disinterest was also its own disqualification. By asserting his moral principles, by upholding abstract canons of Truth and justice, he was laying nothing more than his beliefs on the line. While they were, if their starvation continued, laying down their lives.

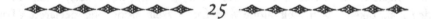 25

Late that afternoon, after the first 7.30 meeting, one of Ganga's volunteers — all right, Ganapathi, you can see through my attempt at reportage, it was me — was visiting a bustee, a slum settlement, to help keep up the morale of the workers and their families. But their sullen looks, their half-mumbled responses from averted faces, made it clear that the workers had begun to lose faith in what Ganga was trying to do. And then suddenly one man, cradling his sick infant daughter on his lap, burst out in bitter recrimination: 'It is all right for Gangaji to tell us not to give in. After all, what does it cost him? He eats fine food off Moore-memsahib's plates and travels by a car that is worth many years' wages.'

The words struck home, Ganapathi. Secure in his own sincerity, Gangaji had not thought that the depth of his commitment would ever be questioned. I hastened back to Moore-memsahib's house to tell Gangaji what one man had said and others undoubtedly thought.

Even I did not know how he would react to the charge. You or I,

Ganapathi, we might simply have ignored it, or sought, perhaps, to explain ourselves to the workers, and either course would have led ultimately to the loss of credibility that costs so many leaders their authority. A modern politician might have sought to address the source of the workers' discontent and tried to find food for their families from wealthy donors; but Gangaji had already refused many offers of help from rich Indians, on the grounds that the workers had to fight their own battles. ('If they win despite starving, it will be a far truer triumph than a victory built on the charity of strangers,' he declared to me. Yes, Ganapathi, Gangaji could be tough, tough to the point of callousness.) And finally, there was, of course, the possibility – though from what I knew of Gangaji it was the slenderest of possibilities – that he might just abandon his entire crusade on the grounds that his followers were not worthy of him.

Any of these responses would have been possible for another man. But Gangaji reacted in a way that reflected and defined his uniqueness.

'From this moment onwards,' he announced in a tone that reminded me of that other terrible vow he had taken, 'I shall not eat or drink, or travel by any vehicle, until the workers' just demands have been met.'

Neither eat nor drink! We were thunderstruck. 'Ganga,' I protested, 'you cannot do this to yourself. We all need you – the workers need you.'

But Ganga refused to be moved by any entreaties. Sarah-behn, myself, other volunteers, all offered to substitute themselves for him; but not only did he turn us down, he refused even to let us join him in his fast. 'This is my decision, taken by myself alone and for myself alone,' he declared. 'The workers have looked to me so far as their leader, and now that they are wavering it is I as their leader who must stand firm.' And then, in that mild tone of voice by which he instantly disarmed his listeners, he added the famous words, the immortal words that now etch his place in every book of quotations: 'Fasting,' he said, 'is my business.'

Fasting is my business. How many ways those words can be read, Ganapathi. *Fasting* is my business; fasting is *my* business; fasting is my *business*; even (why not?) fasting *is* my business. And even those who actually heard him utter the words cannot agree on where the Great Man had placed his emphasis. It does not matter. Perhaps, in some mysterious way, he conveyed all four meanings, and many nuances beyond, in his delivery of that classic phrase. Today it has passed into history, a slogan, a caption, worn by over-use, cheapened by imitation. Yet, once the words were out of his mouth, Gangaji himself never used them again.

The next morning he arose before dawn to walk the eight miles from Sarah-behn's comfortable residence to the peepul tree by the factory. He needed a stick now, but it was a prop more in the theatrical sense than in the physical. Of course, we all accompanied him, and as the strange procession headed past the workers' hutments, children ran out to find out what was happening and conveyed the news to their fathers. 'Gangaji has taken a vow,' the word passed from lip to sibilant lip, 'Bhishma has taken a vow.' By 7.25, when he reached the tree, a crowd had assembled around it larger than any that had greeted him so far in his daily meetings.

'Brothers and sisters,' Ganga said, joining his palms in a respectful *namaste*, 'I know I have demanded great sacrifices from you. Some of you may have begun to feel that you cannot continue, that the battle is too unequal. Yet I have asked you to be strong, for he who gives in now not only admits his weakness but weakens the strength of the others. Some of you may ask why you should heed my advice when all I am offering is my words. To them, and to all of you, I swear this solemn oath: not to eat or drink again, or travel by any means other than my own feet, until you have returned to work with a 35 per cent increase in wages.'

A great collective sigh escaped the lips of the crowd, like the first puff of a restive volcano; then a silence descended upon the throng as every man and woman near enough strained to catch Gangaji's next words.

'I have told you often in the past that our cause was worth dying for. Those were not just words, my friends; I believe in them. Today I declare to you all that if the Truth does not prevail, if justice is denied, I am prepared to die.'

The volcano rumbled, Ganapathi. It burst forth in a warm, molten gush of human lava, as man after man rose to his feet to shout his gratitude and his reverence for the Great Teacher. Praise mingled with prayers, shouts with slogans, until Ganga, seated in his usual mild-mannered and bespectacled way under the tree, seemed borne aloft on a cloud of adulation. In the confusion a brocaded Muslim weaver in a brilliant red fez leapt up and pulled out a knife. It appeared that what he was saying was that he was prepared to die immediately for the cause, if need be; but some undoubtedly thought he was threatening to finish off the English exploiters, and a great clamour rose up in support of his gesture. Clearly, Ganga's philosophy had not been fully understood, but he had achieved his objective.

At last the rest of India began to sit up and take notice of what Ganga was doing in the obscure Bengal town of Budge Budge. Indian nationalism had generated its share of agitators, boycotters and bonfire-stokers; its leaders had resorted to legal texts, holy sacraments and bombs; but no one had ever before tried to starve himself to death. Curiosity was aroused on a national scale, and opinion was inevitably divided. Radical students signalled their support by setting fire to university mess-halls, though some may merely have taken this as a reflection on the cooking. The eminent Scotswoman who headed the Indo-Irish Home Rule League cabled Ganga urging him not to waste his life on so trivial a cause as low wages. The leading English newspaper of the Bengal Presidency devoted three inches to the affair on an inside page, just beneath its Nature Notebook. A pleasant American professor came by the peepul tree to ask Ganga whether he had always resented his father.

The Scottish mill owners were apoplectic. 'For God's sake tell him not to be silly, Sarah,' Montague pleaded with his estranged sister. 'This is childish. Like a little girl denied a lollipop, threatening to hold her breath until she turns blue. And it's not even any of his damn business! This is between us and our workers. What's *his* bloody life got to do with it, anyway?'

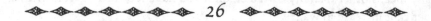 26

'Blackmail,' Sarah-behn said to Gangaji, stooped low over his books under the peepul tree. 'That's what they're calling it at the Mill Owners' Association. Blackmail.'

'They are wrong, my sister.' Ganga's voice was hoarse with thirst, enfeebled by hunger, but it emerged, Ganapathi, with spirit. 'My fast has nothing to do with their decision. I am not fasting to make them change their mind. *That* would be blackmail, and that would be wrong. Of what use would it be if the mill owners agreed to pay 35 per cent merely to save my life? They would not be acting in accordance with the Truth, or because they believe the workers' cause is just. That would be a hollow victory. No, Sarah-behn, I am fasting to strengthen the workers' resolve, to show them how firmly they must hold their beliefs if they expect them to triumph. My fast demonstrates my conviction, that is all. It is not meant to be a threat to anyone, certainly not to your brothers, the mill owners. Tell them so, Sarah-behn.'

She tried to tell them so. Sarah understood Ganga intuitively. It was one of the odder mysteries of Indian history that the person who most quickly got on to Ganga's instinctive wavelength was not one of us from Hastinapur, who had all found his eccentricities so difficult, but this English bourgeoise with the complexion of an under-ripe beetroot.

She understood him partially because she had come to understand something of the Indian tradition as it was lived in the hovels and shacks of the Indian poor and the lower-middle class, that section of the people whom Indian nationalism had so completely ignored until Ganga came and gave them their place in the sun. In the homes of the lowly factory clerks, whose wives she had taken the trouble to visit at times of distress or celebration, Sarah had come to admire the Indian capacity for altruistic self-denial. You know, Ganapathi, how Indians starve on certain days of the week, deny themselves their favourite foods, eliminate essentials from their diets, all to accumulate moral rather than physical credit. Where a Western woman misses a meal in the interest of her figure, her Indian sister dedicates her starvation to a cause, usually a male one. (Her husband or son, of course, never responds in kind: he manifests his appreciation of her sacrifice by enjoying a larger helping of her cooking.)

Sarah saw Ganga's act in this context, and understood it as an act of affirmation rather than of blackmail. But her brother and his friends in the Mill Owners' Association were no more capable of thinking in those terms than of converting to Hinduism. And they did not want to listen to her.

With each passing day Ganga weakened. His thinness, remarkable even in his later Hastinapur days, verged painfully on the ridiculous; his features sagged, until all that could be discerned under the stubble was the existence of skin beneath the staring, listless eyes. The visitors came in larger numbers, their concern for his health meriting larger and larger headlines in the papers. The crowds swelling outside his makeshift shelter were increasingly more angry than curious. The nervous jute-mill owners sent for a doctor, who took Gangaji's feeble pulse and declared that his condition was seriously deteriorating. If something was not done soon, he would be beyond recall, and Indian nationalism would have its first non-violent martyr.

We who maintained the unceasing vigil of those days and nights can never forget them, Ganapathi. We begged and pleaded with him to listen to us, to call off his suicidal action, to drink something, to accept a compromise. He was adamant: his fast would continue until the workers had their 35 per cent. After a while he simply stopped responding to our requests, turning his face away in silence if any of us ever raised the issue. I will admit, Ganapathi, that on the tenth day we had almost given up. I shall not forget an accidental glimpse of Sarah-behn leaving his side that evening, her strong face swollen, awash with tears.

At last the British authorities decided to take matters into their own hands. The consequences of inaction were too awful to contemplate. A terse message went to the Mill Owners' Association of Budge Budge from the Governor of Bengal: 'Give in.'

'Thirty-five per cent!' Sarah-behn yelled, her pale cheeks reddening in excitement as she brandished a piece of paper, a paper of peace, in Ganga's face. 'You've won!'

'No, my dear sister,' the weak voice croaked in response, as a faint smile battled through his exhaustion. Gangaji's hands spread out in a gesture that took in the delirious, screaming throng which had held out with him. '*They have won.*'

A glass of orange juice was brought to him, and he bowed his head while Sarah-behn held it out for him to sip. As the lukewarm droplets soaked into his parched gullet, the crowd burst into an ecstatic roar, as if the bobbing of his Adam's apple was the first sight of a lifebuoy to a dangerously listing raft. The oranges that season were sour, Ganapathi, but the taste of victory, and survival, was deliciously sweet.

 27

You can imagine the relief we all felt that day, Ganapathi, and the sense of triumph. Years later, in that candid autobiography of his, Ganga wrote that the moment of his sudden decision to embark on a fast was a 'holy' one for him. The inspiration, he says, came in a blinding flash; he just *knew* that this was what he had to do to pass his personal ordeal by fire. The workers had sworn to follow and be guided by him; he had to fast to prevent them from breaking their promise. And when he announced it, Ganga writes, it changed the course of his struggle immediately and for ever. 'The meeting, which had been hitherto unresponsive, came to life as if by a miracle,' was, I think, the way he put it. It was he who brought it to life, of course, and he who brought life to it. *His* life.

And yet, Ganapathi, what a small triumph this momentous first fast achieved. Thirty-five per cent? Yes, but 35 per cent for just *one day*. For that was the formula the wily British government had worked out for the mill owners. Ganga had said he would fast until the workers could go back to work with a 35 per cent increase; ergo, under the settlement, the workers could go back to work with a 35 per cent increase – but they could not *keep* that increase beyond the first day. For Day Two, it was 20 per cent, and for every subsequent day until the government's arbitrator announced his verdict: 27.5 per cent. You have to admire the ingeniousness of that formula, Ganapathi. The 35 per cent ended Ganga's fast and the workers' strike; the 20 per cent ensured that the mill owners did not have to concede defeat, which might have encouraged other workers to contemplate strikes; and the 27.5 per cent appeared to be fair to both sides while giving the arbitrator the most obvious figure for his solution. The workers of Budge Budge, who had started off wanting 80 per cent, had come down to 50 per cent and then reconciled themselves to claiming 35 per cent, finally had to settle for 27.5 per cent. Ganga's sense of justice, which had led him to 'split the difference' between the two original positions, served only to reduce the ultimate settlement when the arbitrator split the new difference as well. Moral politics, Ganapathi, is not always good mathematics.

But the fine print did not seem to bother the workers as they sang and danced in celebration of their victory. Ganga was thanked, prostrated to and garlanded profusely. His humble volunteers were fêted with coconut milk and river fish. Somebody produced a special gift for Sarah-behn, a cream-coloured Shantipuri cotton sari with a narrow black border. She accepted it with tears flowing down her strong face: it meant that she was now one of us. She wore it that very evening, and was never again seen in the skirts of her Caucasian past.

How do I explain to you, Ganapathi, what that first fast meant to Gangaji, to all of us? It was such a spontaneous, unplanned event, with minimal organization and — as we must, in the light of the 27.5 per cent, admit — marginal results. But it shone for us as a beacon of hope and strength in the darkness of our subjugation. It was an affirmation of purpose, of spirit, of faith. What happened at Budge Budge confirmed the force of the non-violent revolution that Gangaji had launched.

In fasting, in directing the strength of his convictions against himself, Gangaji taught us to resist injustice with arms that no one could take away from us. Gangaji's use of the fast made our very weakness a weapon. It captured the imagination of India in a way that no speech, no prayer, no bomb had ever done. In time, Gangaji's fasts slowed the heartbeat of the nation; hungry students pushed their plates away knowing the Great Teacher was not eating; entire villages refused to touch a flame to their wicks in order to share the darkness with him. On that first occasion interest was limited, and had to be won. Gangaji won it, and with it the attention — and the devotion — of the country. He had realized that the best way to bring his principles to life was, paradoxically, by being prepared to die for them.

In that realization lay the ultimate strength of the national movement. Gangaji's willingness to sacrifice his life set the tone for the other sacrifices that were, eventually, to make freedom possible — by making the price the British would have had to pay to stay on not worth paying.

Fasts, Ganapathi, have never worked half as well anywhere else as they have in India. Only Indians could have devised a method of political bargaining based on the threat of harm to yourself rather than to your opponent. Inevitably, of course, like all our country's other great innovations, fasts too have been shamefully abused. As a weapon, fasts are effective only when the target of your action values your life more than his convictions – or at least feels that society as a whole does. So they were ideally suited to a non-violent, upright national leader like Gangaji. But when used by lesser mortals with considerably less claim to the moral high ground and no great record of devotion to principle, fasts are just another insidious form of blackmail, abused and over-used in our agitation-ridden land.

It might have been worse, though. If more politicians, Ganapathi, had the courage to fast in the face of what they saw as transcendent wrong, Indian governments might have found it impossible to govern. But too many would-be fasters proclaim their self-denial and then retreat to surreptitious meals behind the curtain, which makes their demands easier to resist since there is no likelihood of their doing any real harm to themselves.

But that is not the worst of it, Ganapathi. What more bathetic legacy could there be to Ganga, who risked his life for 27.5 per cent, than that fasts have suffered the ultimate Indian fate of being reduced to the symbolic? What could be more absurd than the widely practised 'relay fast' of today's politicians, where different people take it in turns to miss their meals in public? Since no one starves for long enough to create any problems for himself or others, the entire point of Gangaji's original idea is lost. All we are left with is the drama without the sacrifice – and isn't that a metaphor for Indian politics today?

THE SIXTH BOOK:
FORBIDDEN FRUIT

28

To leave Gangaji aside for a moment – though that, as you can see, Ganapathi, is never easy; you see how he keeps taking over our story – let us return to his wards, the newly political, newly parental princelings of Hastinapur. They have not featured in the episodes I have recounted so far from Gangaji's career, for the simple reason that they were not there at the time, though to say so would probably be considered heretical by the numerous devotees of each today. Our contemporary hagiographers would have us believe that Dhritarashtra, with his dark glasses and his white stick, was everywhere by Gangaji's side in the struggle for Independence, and that – until he disagreed with his mentor – so was Pandu. Well, Ganapathi, you can take it from me that they were not, for most of the crucial events in Gangaji's life and career were those in which he acted alone, resolving the dictates of his hyperactive conscience within, and by, himself.

Not that his followers, our later leaders, were entirely idle at the time. After all, Independence was not won by a series of isolated incidents but by the constant, unremitting actions of thousands, indeed hundreds of thousands, of men and women across the land. We tend, Ganapathi, to look back on history as if it were a stage play, with scene building upon scene, our hero moving from one action to the next in his remorseless stride to the climax. Yet life is never like that. If life were a play the noises offstage, and for that matter the sounds of the audience, would drown out the lines of the principal actors. That, of course, would make for a rather poor tale; and so the recounting of history is only the order we artificially impose upon life to permit its lessons to be more clearly understood.

So it is, Ganapathi, that in this memoir we light up one corner of our collective past at a time, focus on one man's actions, one village's passion, one colonel's duty, but all the while life is going on elsewhere, Ganapathi: as the shots ring out in the Bibigarh Gardens babies are being born, nationalists are being thrown into prison, husbands are quarrelling with wives, petitions are being filed in courtrooms, stones are being flung at policemen, and diligent young Indian students are sailing to London to sit for the examinations that will permit them to rule their own people in the name of an alien king. It is no different for the protagonists of our story, the little band of individuals and families selected from the swirling mists of an old man's memory to represent a past in which others too have played a significant but unrecalled part. Time did not stand still for them as Ganga plodded through Motihari or starved to such good purpose in Budge Budge. No, Ganapathi, our friends too lived and breathed and thought and worked and prayed and (except for Pandu) copulated the while, their endeavours unrecorded in these words you have so laboriously transcribed. History marched on, leaving only a few footprints on our pages. Of its deep imprints on other sands, you do not know because I do not choose to wash in the waters that have swept them away.

In other words, Ganapathi, as our story unfolded on your notes and my little cassettes, Pandu and Dhritarashtra were working busily in Hastinapur, in Bombay, in Delhi, to organize and promote, respectively, the institution that would one day propel Gangaji's vision into a tangible nationhood — the Kaurava Party.

At first their paths did not diverge. Indeed, were it not for Dhritarashtra's unfortunate affliction, I might have said that they invariably saw eye to eye. Till my blue-blooded scions entered the fray in Gangaji's wake, the Kaurava Party had been a distinguished but remarkably ineffective forum for the rhetorical articulation of Anglophile dissatisfaction with the English. Brown-skinned Victorian gentlemen, often in three-piece suits with watch-chains strung fashionably across their waistcoats (bad enough for cultural, climatic and aesthetic reasons, but to make matters worse, Ganapathi, this was decades before the advent of air-conditioning) declaimed in the language of that ignorant imperialist, Macaulay, and in the accents of that overrated oligopoly, Oxbridge, their aspirations to the rights of Englishmen. England listened, but paid little heed. The Kaurava Party was a useful outlet for the frustrations of the English-educated, but since these were always expressed with the restraint born of English education, they posed no threat. The party had, after all, been founded by a liberal Scot, who had named it in a fuzzy misreading of Indian mythology and dedicated it to the perpetuation of his monarch's constitutional queenship over India, the radical idea being the adjective 'constitutional'. When Gangaji turned to politics the Kaurava Party had been in existence for thirty years and the British had not taken thirty steps toward Indian self-rule. With the advent of my Hastinapuris all this changed.

Dhritarashtra, for one, as you already know, Ganapathi, had acquired in England traces of the right accent along with streaks of the wrong ideas. He had returned fired with Fabianism, which taught that equality and justice were everybody's right, and which (with typical imprecision) omitted to exclude the heathen from the definition of 'everybody'. The Fabians had drawn up an all-embracing philosophy in order basically to make the point that it was the state's duty to provide gas and tap-water to the British working-man, and while the British working-man rapidly moved on to less elemental concerns, the philosophy travelled to distant peoples who had never heard of gas or tap-water. Dhritarashtra was one of its carriers. He heard speeches aimed at prodding Westminster to help the workers of Wigan Pier and drew from them the conclusion that it was also the duty of the government in India to serve the common Indian. Such a thought had not, of course, crossed the minds of those who had set up the government in India for the fun and profit of the indigenes of Ipswich, so that Dhritarashtra found himself drawing the corollary that the Indian government could only fulfil its duty if it were a government *of* India run by Indians for the welfare of Indians. This modest proposition, Ganapathi, took him far beyond the previous precepts of his party. It was a doctrine persuasively and passionately argued by the unseeing visionary. Within a short while he had captured the ideological heights of an institution low on ideas.

He did so, of course, because Gangaji's spectacularly unorthodox successes had shaken up the sterile verities of the party's past and opened it up for capture. In the old days the only — if sporadically — effective nationalist actions had been the bomb-throwings and the mob agitations from which the party elders had shrunk away. Now, in the actions I have described and innumerable others like them, Gangaji demonstrated that you did not have to be a hooligan to be effective. Non-violence, voluntary courting of arrest, even fasting — these were more acceptable to offspring of respectable families. Constitutionalists could hardly object to one who worked within the laws and willingly accepted the punishment for their violation. Gangaji's methods stoked the fires of true nationalism among those who had recoiled from violence and lawlessness. It was this warmth that welcomed Dhritarashtra when he began to preach to them. He found them ripe for conversion, and the Hastinapur connection bathed him in the light reflected from Gangaji's halo. If Dhritarashtra's socialist beliefs went beyond anything Gangaji himself had ever expressed, there was never any question of the Great Teacher's endorsement of his sightless protégé. The Kauravas were left in no doubt that Dhritarashtra was Gangaji's man.

At the beginning so, of course, was Pandu. In some ways he might have seemed a more natural heir to Gangaji, with his scriptural reading, his personal faddishness, his (albeit enforced) celibacy. Gangaji indulged Dhritarashtra and relied on Pandu. It was Pandu who took the party banners into the most remote villages, while Dhritarashtra toured the lecture-halls and the

meeting-rooms of urban India. This was, perhaps, inevitable, given both Dhritarashtra's strengths and his handicap. But it did mean that while Pandu trudged
in his dhoti through the mud and grime of the countryside, while Pandu led
the proletarian processions of stoic *satyagrahis* on defiant *dharnas*, while
Pandu took the blows on the head from the lathis – the long wooden arms –
of the law, Dhritarashtra endured little more than the hoarse barbs of bribed
hecklers, the strain of long speeches at mass meetings, the long nights
dictating pamphlets to adoring scribes. It was Gangaji who determined, who
ratified, who sanctified this division of labour; as a result Dhritarashtra was
before long the most famous Indian leader after Gangaji, while Pandu's
following was confined largely to the political activists who had toiled with
him in the villages. When, years later, Duryodhani spoke darkly of the
immense and unrivalled sacrifices her father and she had made for the nation, I
would think of poor Pandu, by then long turned to ash and almost forgotten,
poor, tough, scarred, calloused Pandu with the smell of sweat on his brow and
the dust of India on his sandals. And I would muse, Ganapathi, on the
injustices of Fate.

Of course Dhritarashtra too made sacrifices for the nation. His cause led as
surely to prison as Pandu's, and both spent years inside British jails. If
anything, Dhritarashtra's sentences as a convict of conscience amounted to
longer than Pandu's. But he turned his incarceration to profit, dictating books
and letters (and letters that became books) throughout his stay as a guest of
His Majesty, works that revealed again and again to the world his depth of
learning and breadth of vision. Prison confined others, but in Dhritarashtra's
case it only confirmed his reputation as India's leading nationalist after
Gangaji. The regularity with which each of his spells in prison resulted in a
book led one colonial cartoonist to depict him in the dock addressing a judge:
'Why did I break the law? Well, Your Honour, my publishers were getting
impatient . . .'

Was it inevitable, Ganapathi, that Pandu should become disaffected? Your
ponderous brow, your unblinking eyes, offer no answer. The inevitabilities of
history are for ideologues and fatalists, and I suppose I have belonged, at one
time or another, to each category. Yes, Ganapathi, it *was* inevitable. I watched
them both, my flawed, gifted sons; I watched them from afar as a humble
Kaurava Party worker in the plains; I watched them from nearer as a more
distinguished *ad hoc* member of the party's High Command; and I saw the
inevitability of their separation. Pandu became impatient of Dhritarashtra's
oratorical certitudes, his lofty convictions and vaulting ambition. Dhritarashtra,
in turn, had little time for Pandu's atavistic traditionalism, his political earthi-
ness, his pride in his wives' five boys. (Those who have no sons rarely

attach any importance to the priorities of those who do, but they resent them deeply.) If Gangaji saw any of this, he showed little sign. He carried on as oblivious as always to the dilemmas of others, doing nothing to heal the growing rift.

 *29*

That there was a rift became impossible to conceal. Pandu began to take positions at variance with Dhritarashtra's. He constantly urged the adoption of a harder line against the British than the party — its strategy guided by Gangaji's wisdom and Dhritarashtra's cunning — was willing to adopt. When the Prince of Wales, an empty-headed lad with a winsome smile, paid a royal visit to examine the most prized jewel in the crown he was briefly to inherit, Pandu urged that he be boycotted. But Dhritarashtra instead persuaded the party to permit him to present the Prince a petition (don't frown, Ganapathi, alliteration is my only vice — and after all, it is one thing you *can* do in Sanskrit). When the government in London then sent a commission of seven white men to determine whether the derisory 'reforms' of a few years earlier were helping Indians to progress to self-government (or whether, as Whitehall thought and wished to hear, the reforms had already 'gone too far' and needed reformulating), Pandu proposed a non-violent stir at the docks to prevent the unwelcome seven from alighting on to Indian soil. But this time Dhritarashtra wanted the party to content itself with — yes, Ganapathi, you've guessed it — a boycott; and once again, with Gangaji's toothless smile of benediction behind him, Dhritarashtra had his way. It became apparent to Pandu that Dhritarashtra's triumphs were basically of Gangaji's making, and that a large number, perhaps a majority, of the Kaurava Party were backing his half-brother not because of any intrinsic faith in his ideas but because they came with the blessing of the man Sir Richard had taken unpleasantly to describing as Public Enema Number One.

I myself caught a whiff of Pandu's bitterness at a Working Committee meeting of the party which I happened to attend. At one point I was talking to Dhritarashtra and the skeletal Gangaji when Pandu walked palely past. 'The Kaurava Trinity,' he muttered audibly for my benefit — 'the Father, the Son and the Holy Ghost'.

Of course he was exaggerating my own importance, for I sought no active role in the Kaurava leadership. The mantle of elder statesman had fallen on me when I was scarcely old enough to merit the adjective, and I was content with the detachment it permitted. But even my habitual sense of distance from the quotidian cares of the party could not prevent a stirring of disquiet, which was instantly confirmed by Dhritarashtra's next words. 'I should have thought,' he said lightly, but with his face set, 'that my dear brother would have done better to refer to the Hindu Trinity — the Creator, the Preserver and the Destroyer. But then he would have had to include himself at the end, wouldn't he?'

When rivals fling jokes at each other, Ganapathi, it means that there is no turning back. Between opponents who will not physically fight, a punch line is equivalent to a punch.

The disagreement came out into the open when the British convened what they called a Round Table Conference in London to discuss the future of India. It is not often that a major international event is named after a piece of furniture, but the round table in question was chosen quite deliberately (and after a great deal of diplomatic deliberation). It served two functions. One, unmentioned, was to hark back to the hosts' glorious chivalric past under the legendary King Arthur (who, if he existed at all, was a superstitious cuckold, which is hardly my idea of a national hero). The second, openly cited at background briefings for the press, was to place all the participants on an equal footing: to have had a conventional table with a 'head' might have implied that the British had their preferences among Indian leaders, and the British, of course, were noble and disinterested Solons who would never want anyone to think such a thing.

Well, Ganapathi, before you begin to suggest that that is all fine and democratic, let me tell you that the lack of preference is itself a preference. To put the true leaders of the people on the same level as princes and pretenders and pimps is not virtuous but vicious. In this case it meant reducing the Kaurava Party — the only nationwide nationalist movement, the only broad-based popular organization, the very party whose campaigns of mass awakening and civil disobedience had obliged the British at last, at least, to agree to talk with Indians — it meant reducing the Kauravas to a level of official equality with all the other self-appointed Indian spokesmen the British saw fit to recognize. And thus it was that Gangaji sat at his round table to parley with the British, surrounded by delegations of India's Untouchables and its touch-me-nots, representatives of Indians with their foreskins cut off and Indians with their hair uncut, spokesmen for left-handed Indians, green-eyed Indians and Indians who believed the sun revolved round the moon. Mind you, the Kaurava Party included members of every one of these minorities, and could claim with justice to be able to speak for all their interests, in the larger sense of the term; but the British were not interested in the larger sense at all. They wanted to introduce as many divisive elements as possible in order to be able to say to the world: 'You see these Indians can never agree amongst themselves, we really have no choice but to continue ruling them indefinitely *for their own good.*'

Now, all this was known before the conference even started, Ganapathi, that was the irony of it. What I am saying to you does not come with the benefit of hindsight (odd phrase, that: which of my readers will consider an old man's fading recollections a benefit?). No, Ganapathi, it is there in the public record, it is there in Pandu's impassioned entreaties to the Kaurava Working Committee. 'Don't go, don't let us be a party to this charade,' he pleaded. But the Working Committee, at Dhritarashtra's glib urging, agreed not only to attend but to send Gangaji as the party's sole representative to the conference. Pandu railed against 'this madness', as he called it. 'If we must go, let us go in strength, let us send a delegation that reflects the numbers and diversity of our following,' he argued. Once again he was disregarded; the Committee placed its faith in the man to whom many were already referring in open hagiology as Mahaguru, the Great Teacher.

So Pandu stayed in India and fretted, while the man he admired, but could not bring himself to surrender everything to, crossed his legs on a cold wooden chair and awaited his turn to speak after the Monarchists and the Liberals and the Society for the Preservation of the Imperial Connection, which had each sent more representatives to the Round Table than the Kauravas. But Pandu, though now bitter in his denunciation of his sightless sibling, was still a loyal party man. He remained so even when Ganga returned, having bared his chest on the newsreels and taken tea in his loincloth with the King-Emperor ('Your Majesty, you are wearing more than enough for the two of us,' the Mahaguru had said disarmingly) but won no concessions from the circular and circumlocutious conferees. Pandu resisted the temptation to say, 'I told you so' and concentrated instead on building up his support within the party councils. For once, my pale-faced hot-headed son was going to wait until the time was ripe before striking.

Do I give you the impression, Ganapathi, that between my pale and purblind progeny my sympathies lie only with Pandu? Do not be misled, my friend. India does not choose amongst her sons, and nor do I. They are both mine, their flaws and foibles, their vanities and inanities, their pretensions and pride, all mine. I do not disown either of them, any more than I could deny half my own nature.

And besides, Pandu could be wrong as well. As was amply demonstrated in the affair of the Great Mango March.

30

Some of our more Manichaean historians tend to depict the British villains as supremely accomplished – the omniscient, omnipresent, omnipotent manipulators of the destiny of India. Stuff and nonsense, of course. For every brilliant Briton who came to India, there were at least five who were incapable of original thought and fifteen who were only capable of original sin. They went from mistake to victory and mistake again with a combination of luck, courage and the Gatling gun, but mistakes they made, all the time. Don't forget that the British were the only people in history crass enough to make revolutionaries out of Americans. That took insensitivity and stupidity on quite a stupendous scale – qualities they could hardly keep out of their rule over our country.

The truth is that the average British colonial administrator was a pompous mediocrity whose nose was so often in the air that he tripped over his own feet. (It was just as well that so many of them had long noses, Ganapathi, for they could rarely see beyond them.) In the process, they made decisions that provoked visceral and lasting reactions. Don't forget, Ganapathi, that it is to one British colonial policy-maker or another that we owe the Boxer Rebellion, the Mau Mau insurrection, the Boer War, and the Boston Tea Party.

It all began, as these things tend to do – for the British have never learned from history – with a tax. Why the pink blackguards bothered to tax Indians I will never understand, for they had successfully stolen everything they needed for centuries, from the jewelled inlays of the Taj Mahal to the Kohinoor on their queen's crown, and one would have thought they could have done without the laborious extraction of the Indian working-man's pittance. But there has always been something perversely precise about British oppression: the legal edifice of the Raj was built on the premise that anything resulting from the filling of forms in quadruplicate could not possibly be an injustice. So Robert Clive bought his rotten borough in England on the proceeds of his rapacity in India, while publicly marvelling at his own self-restraint in not misappropriating even more than he did. And the English had the gall to call him 'Clive of India' as if he belonged to the country, when all he really did was to ensure that much of the country belonged to him. Clive's twentieth-century successors, who had taken the Hindustani word *loot* into their dictionaries instead of their habits, preferred to achieve the same results in more bureaucratic ways. They taxed property, and income, and harvests; they taxed our petrol, our patience and even our passing to the next world (through their gracelessly named 'death duties'). As the expenditure on foreign wars mounted they taxed our rice, our cloth and our salt. We had thought they simply couldn't go any further. Till the day they announced a tax on the one luxury still available to the Indian masses – the mango.

The mango is, of course, the king of fruits, though in recent years our export policies have made it more the fruit of kings – or of Middle Eastern sheikhs, to be precise. And the wonder of it is that – again before foreign markets became more important to our rulers than domestic bazaars – the mango was available to the common man in abundance. It was as if the good Lord, having given the Indian peasant droughts, and floods, and floods after droughts, and heat, and dust, and low wages, and British rule, said to him, all right, your cup of woe runneth over, drink instead from the juice of a ripe Chausa, and it will make up for all the misery I have inflicted upon you. The best mangoes in the world grew wild across the Indian countryside, dropping off the branches of trees so hardy they did not need looking after. And we took them for granted, consuming them raw, or pickled, or ripe, as our fancy seized us, content in the knowledge that there would always be more mangoes on those branches, waiting to be picked.

Then came the stunning announcement: the colonial regime had decided that the mango too had to earn its keep. Mangoes were a cash crop; accordingly, a tax was to be levied on the fruit, calculated on the basis of each tree's approximate annual yield. Trees in the vicinity of private property were to be attached to the nearest landlord's holdings for tax purposes; trees growing wild would be treated as common property and the tax levied on the village as a whole. District officials were instructed to conduct a mango-tree-registration campaign to ensure that the tax records were brought up to date. Poor village panchayats and panicky landlords chopped down their suddenly expensive foliage or fenced it. The days of the free munch were over.

At first the people reacted in stunned disbelief. Then, as the implications of the decision sank in, they gave vent – for they were simple people, used to calling a spade a white man's garden tool – to collective howls of outrage.

Gangaji heard the echoes and sensed a cause. He was at the ashram one day when a Kaurava Party member from Palghat, Mahadeva Menon, raised the matter over the Great Teacher's habitual lunch of nuts and fruit.

'Mahaguru,' he said in his high-pitched voice, lips rounding the flattest of English syllables – for English was the only language he had in common with Gangaji, as indeed it is my own sole means of dictating this memoir to you – 'there is something really terrible going on in our country these days.' (He actually said 'cundry', but you can spell that as you have been taught to, young man.) 'The peeble' – spell that 'people', Ganapathi, you really are getting to be quite difficult – 'in my nate-yew blace are zimbly so so miserable . . .' 'Native place', Ganapathi, 'simply'. I shall have to stop quoting people if you go on like this. Mahadeva Menon's English was as valid a language to him as its American or Strine variants are to their speakers, so there is no need to parody his accent in print. If every Australian novelist had to set down the speech of his characters to approximate the sounds they made rather than the words they spoke, do you think there would be a single readable Australian novel in the world? (As it is I am reliably informed there are two or even three.)

You are sorry? Good. You won't do it again? Very well, let us go on. Now, where was I? Ah, yes, Mahadeva Menon speaking to Gangaji about the terrible effects of the mango tax. A small man with a neat, trim black moustache, dressed in spotless white, with a folded white cloth flung over his left shoulder. A landlord from Palghat, converted to the egalitarian nationalism of Mahaguru Gangaji, describing the effects of the invidious mango tax on the well-being, on the depressed morale, of the masses of his district. 'You must do something about this, Mahaguruji,' he said.

Gangaji remained silent for a full minute, contemplating the suggestion and his bowl of dried fruit. At last he spoke. 'Yes, Mahadeva,' he said slowly. 'I think I must.'

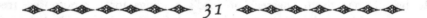 *31*

Pandu was aghast that Gangaji intended to make the mango tax an issue. 'There are so many other vital problems for the Kaurava Party to address,' he declared. 'If, at this time of increasing repression by the British, you devote your energies, your moral stature, to something as petty, as ridiculous, as mangoes, you will make yourself the laughing stock of the nation.' He placed his palms together in supplication. 'Please, Gangaji, please – do not trivialize our great cause like this.'

But the Mahaguru was not moved. 'Trust me, my son,' he responded, returning with due solemnity to the task Pandu had interrupted – the scrubbing of the ashram latrine.

Yes, Ganapathi, no endeavour was too trivial for our hero. And he prepared as assiduously for each, taking the same care to ensure his brushes and mops and soapy water and ammonia (he had a great faith in the cleansing properties of ammonia) were to hand as he did to ensure that the reasons for his national satyagrahas were widely known and well-understood.

Ganga's first step was to write to the Viceroy. The letter was a character-istic combination of impertinence and ingenuity, fact and foible:

Dear Friend,

As you are aware, I hold the British rule to be a curse. Your presence as its representative makes you the chief symbol of the injustice and oppression that the British people have visited upon the Indian nation. Yet I write to you as a friend, conscious of the immense potential for good that your post holds.

I have found it necessary on several occasions in the past to call into question some of the unjust laws that have been pressed upon the brows of my people. Indeed, I have been obliged on one or two occasions to disobey them and to lead others in disobeying them, in full consciousness and complete acceptance of the penalties for such disobedience. I consider non-violent civil disobedience to be one of the few morally just measures open to my fellow Indians and myself. Our cause is to defend ourselves and our own interests. I do not intend harm to a single Englishman in India, even if he be here as an uninvited guest.

I explain these things because I seek your help in undoing a great injustice which has recently been committed by the government you represent. I speak, of course, of the Mango Tax. This dreadful exaction has already caused untold suffering to the Indian masses amongst whose few humble pleasures is the fruit of the mango tree. The tax and its consequences have already caused a severe reaction amongst the people at large. I plead with you on bended knee to repeal this law.

I believe it will do your own cause far more good than harm to heed my plea. The estimates of your administrators speak of a potential revenue of some five million pounds sterling from this tax, which must surely be of little consequence to a government which earns more than 800 million pounds sterling from its other tariffs and taxes in this country. In addition, the repeal of this iniquitous tax will win you personally and your government much popularity, whereas its persist-ence can only add to the odium in which the British rule is held. The people at large are already saying that the oppressive foreigners will tax the sunshine next.

I therefore suggest that you rescind this decision as much in your own interest as in that of the people of India. Do not forget, dear friend, that your own salary is more than five thousand times that of the average Indian you tax, and that this colossal sum is paid for by the sweat of Indian brows. I would make so bold as to suggest that the action I urge upon you is nothing less than a moral obligation.

In concluding this plea, I must add that if you fail to heed it, I shall have no alternative but to launch a fresh campaign of civil disobedience against this unjust law. I would welcome this opportunity to educate the British people in the ethics of our cause. My ambition is no less than to convert the British people through non-violence, and thus make them see the wrong they have done to India. I do not seek to harm your people. I want to serve them even as I want to serve my own.

To this Ganga received, three weeks later, the following reply:

Sir,

I am directed by the Private Secretary of His Excellency the Viceroy to acknowledge your communication of the ninth instant.

I am instructed to inform you that His Excellency regrets the tone and contents of your letter, and particularly the threat to violate the laws of His Majesty's Government contained in its penultimate paragraph. His Excellency regards this as most unfortunate.

I am also directed to advise you that any breach of the regulations in force will be dealt with in accordance with the laws of the land.

The letter was signed by a Second Deputy Under-Secretary to the Private Secretary.

'Very well,' Ganga said, his lips pursing in that slight pout that legions of his female admirers continue to recall. 'Sarah-behn, please arrange to send the entire text of this correspondence to the press – the Indian papers and the foreign wire-services. And do not forget that very pleasant young man from *The New York Times* who came to see us last week.'

Sarah-behn did not forget. And it was she, sitting behind him on a raised platform erected outside the ashram, who recorded in her large clear hand the immortal words of the speech he made inaugurating the Great Mango March:

'My brothers and sisters,' Ganga said to the crowd assembled at his feet, 'I have called you here today to pray, as we usually do on this day each week. To pray for justice and Truth and the grace of God upon our benighted people. But today your prayers take on an additional meaning.

'In all probability this will be my last speech to you for a long time to come. As you know, I have resolved to embark upon a satyagraha to resist the unjust mango tax. Even if the British government allows me to march tomorrow morning, they will not allow me to return freely to this ashram and to you, my brothers and sisters. This may well be my last speech to you all, standing on the sacred soil of my beloved Hastinapur.'

(He was actually standing not on soil at all, whether sacred or profane, but on planks of wood erected to elevate him to the view of his audience. But the lumps were already forming in every throat in the audience, Ganapathi, and Ganga was poised to milk every tear-drop. I marvelled once more at how wrong Pandu could be. Trivialize the cause? Gangaji could dramatize and ennoble the most insignificant of causes when he chose to.)

'I shall personally break the law by violating the terms of the Mango Act. My companions will do the same. We will undoubtedly be arrested. Despite our arrests, I expect and trust that the stream of our volunteer civil resisters will flow unbroken.

'But whatever happens, let there not be the slightest breach of the peace, even if we are all arrested, even if we are all assaulted. We have resolved to utilize our resources in a purely non-violent struggle. Let no one raise his fist in anger. This is my hope and prayer, and I wish these words of mine to reach every corner of our country.

'From this moment, let the call go forth, from this ashram where I have lived for Truth, to all our people across the length and breadth of India, to launch civil disobedience of the mango laws. These laws can be violated in many ways. It is an offence to pluck mangoes from any tree which has not been marked as having been duly registered and taxed. The possession, consumption or sale of contraband mangoes (which means any mango from any such tree) is also, in the eyes of our British rulers, an offence. The purchasers of such mangoes are equally guilty. I call on you all, then, to choose any or all of these methods to break the mango monopoly of the British government.'

A cheer rose up at these words, Ganapathi, but Ganga was still drawing tears:

'Act, then, and act not for me but for yourselves and for India. I myself am of little importance, a humble servant of the people among whom I have been privileged to live. I am certain to be arrested, and I do not know when I shall return to you, my dear brothers and sisters. But do not assume that after I am gone there will be no one left to guide you. It is not I, but Dhritarashtra who is your guide. He is blind, but he sees far. He has the capacity to lead.'

And so Ganga soaked his listeners in their own emotions and anointed Dhritarashtra as his successor with their tears. It was at this point that Pandu, who had disdained the cause but come to the ashram out of loyalty to the Mahaguru, walked out, never to return to his teacher's side.

 *32*

The Great Mango March began the next morning. We all slept the night in the open air, in the grounds of the ashram, the reporters from the international press camping on the grass alongside sweepers and bazaar merchants and college students. Ganga awoke the next morning faintly surprised not to have been roused in his sleep by the clink of handcuffs. 'The government is puzzled and perplexed,' he triumphantly explained to the journalists, whom he had assured the previous day of his certain arrest. 'But have no fear – the police will come.'

We set out, then, Ganapathi, seventy-eight of us, volunteers culled from all over the country, on the Great Mango March. What a brilliant sense of the theatrical Ganga had. Mangoes could be found anywhere, but it was not enough for Ganga to march to the nearest tree and pluck its fruit: he knew that would not make good copy. He wanted to give the reporters with him something to report, and he wanted to inflate the issue to one of national importance by keeping it in the news for as long as possible. What better way to do that than by a 288-mile march from the ashram to the grove of a landlord with Kaurava Party sympathies who had refrained so far from registering his trees? Would not the impact of this *padayatra* exceed even that of his actual violation of the mango laws? And if the British arrested him *en route*, wouldn't that be even better?

It was brilliant, Ganapathi, what your generation would call a low-risk strategy. Don't ever forget, young man, that we were not led by a saint with his head in the clouds, but by a master tactician with his feet on the ground.

Look at the newsreels of that time, Ganapathi. The black-and-white film is grainy, even scratched, the people in it move with unnaturally rapid jerkiness, and the commentator sounds like an announcer at a school sports meet, but despite it all you can capture some of the magic of the march. There is Gangaji himself at the head of the procession, bald, more or less toothless, holding a stave taller than himself, his bony legs and shoulders barely covered by his habitual undress, looking far too old and frail for this kind of thing, yet marching with a firm and confident stride accentuated by the erratic speed of the celluloid. There is Sarah-behn by his side in her white, thin-bordered sari, looking prim and determined, and Mahadeva Menon, for all the world like a Kerala *karanavar* on an inspection-tour of his paddy-fields; and behind them the rest of us, in homespun *khadi* and cheap leather chappals, showing no sign of fear or fatigue. Indeed, there is nothing grim about our procession, none of the earnest tragedy that marks the efforts of doomed idealists. Instead,

Gangaji's grinning waves of benediction, the banners of welcome strung across the roads at every village through which we pass, the scenes of smiling women in gaily coloured saris emerging in the blazing heat to sprinkle water on our dusty paths, the cameos of little children shyly thrusting bunches of marigolds into our hands, the waves of fresh volunteers joining us at every stop to swell our tide of marchers into a flood, all this speaks of the joyousness of our spirit as we march on.

Twelve miles a day, Ganapathi, for twenty-four days, and yet there was no sign of weariness, neither in Ganga, nor in the women, nor in my own ageless legs. Nor was there any sign of the police, though Gangaji confidently asserted to the journalists at each halt for refreshment that he expected to be arrested any day. It was, of course, another clever ploy from the master tactician. The very prediction of imminent arrest kept the police away and simultaneously encouraged, indeed obliged, the journalists to stay on. But Gangaji knew perfectly well that he would not be arrested, indeed could not be arrested, for he had as yet broken no law.

At last we arrived at the mango grove, still unescorted by police, but with notebooks and cameras much in evidence. The landlord came forth to greet us; ladies of his household stepped forward with little brass pitchers to wash our feet. Gangaji walked on, towards the oldest and biggest tree in the grove. For a moment I feared that we would lose him in the crush of humanity, that the sheer numbers around him would swallow up the dramatic impact of what he was about to do.

But once again artifice came to the aid of Truth. The landlord's workers had erected a little platform for Gangaji, to be ascended by seven simple wooden steps. As silence settled expectantly around him, the Mahaguru, his little rimless spectacles firmly on his nose, his staff in his right hand, slowly, deliberately, mounted each step. At the top of the rough-hewn ladder, standing squarely on the little platform, he paused. Then, with a decisive gesture, he reached out a bony hand toward a ripe, luscious Langda mango dangling from the branch nearest him and wrenched it from its stalk. As the crowd erupted in a crescendo of cheering, he turned to them, his hand upraised, the golden-red symbol of his defiance blazing its message of triumph.

What poetry there was in that moment, Ganapathi! In that fruit, Ganga seemed to be holding the forces of nature in his hands, recalling the fertile strength of the Indian soil from which had sprung the Indian soul, reaffirming the fullness of the nation's past and the seed of the people's future. The cameras clicked, and whirred, and flashed, and Ganga stood alone, the sun glinting off his glasses, his hand raised for freedom.

From then on it was chaos, Ganapathi. The crowd cheered, and yelled, and swarmed around Gangaji as he stepped off the platform. The mango he had plucked, that first fruit of India's liberation, was instantly auctioned to enthusiastic acclaim, for the princely sum of sixteen hundred rupees. A hundred hands reached for the remaining fruit on that landlord's branches, plucking, tearing, pulling and inevitably, biting and sucking; before long the spotless white of the *satyagrahis' khadi* was stained with the rich yellow of their greed. Stones were flung to bring down less accessible fruit; some fell on stray volunteers, mingling bloodstains with the juice on their tunics. Thus it is, Ganapathi, that the sublime degenerates into the sub-slime; and there too, while I am sounding portentous, lies another metaphor for us, for our nationalist struggle, make of it what you will.

 *33*

But such metaphors come too easily to me, Ganapathi, for I was there then, and here I am now. Gangaji, fortunately, saw little of the immediate aftermath of his triumph, for he disappeared into the landlord's home to rest and refresh himself before the police came.

At last, as expected, they did; and the next day's newspapers were able to carry, alongside a front-page picture of Gangaji on the platform with his seditious mango held aloft, the news of his arrest and incarceration, along with the offending landlord and scores of volunteers. But Gangaji's action was the signal for a nationwide defiance of the Mango Act. Kaurava protestors across the country took to emulating their leader; wave after wave of *khadi*-clad *satyagrahis* plucked and planted the contraband fruit, openly bought and sold it, and non-violently prevented the government's mango inspectors from continuing with their work of enumeration and registration. The government's only response was to arrest the offenders, a course of action that cost them more in trouble, jail-space and unfavourable publicity than the mango revenues were probably worth. The protestors mocked the authorities by organizing elaborate ceremonies to consume the forbidden fruit. (Since the mangoes were plucked rather indiscriminately, this was not always a pleasure for the volunteers. 'Pretty awful stuff', Dhritarashtra confided to the policeman who arrested him.) As the mango agitation spread, the British found themselves having to make room for no fewer than 50,000 new political prisoners, jailed for offences even Western journalists found absurd. Ganga had not only made his point, he had held the imperialists up to ridicule. And colonialism, as the poet said, cannot bear very much hilarity.

Even Pandu, who had held himself conspicuously aloof from the agitation, was placed on the defensive: for once it seemed that he had been indisputably wrong in gauging the potential of one of Ganga's ideas. But then suddenly everything came unstuck.

Gangaji was still in prison when reports came in of what had happened in Chaurasta. In this small provincial town the mango agitation had, quite simply, got out of hand. The business of plucking and consuming forbidden fruit undoubtedly contains elements that appeal to the hooligan fringe that lurks at the edge of any mass movement. In Chaurasta the local Kaurava organizers had chosen their volunteers carelessly, or allowed too many outsiders to join them; whatever the reason, their civil disobedience became very uncivil indeed. Stones were being flung at fruit on the highest branches when the police arrived on the spot to make their routine arrests. The protestors, instead of submitting quietly to the guardians of the law, aimed their stones at the uniformed targets instead. The police – all Indians, mind you – turned their lathis on the *satyagrahis*; in the ensuing unequal battle a number of ribs and skulls were cracked and several bones and noses broken before the demonstrators were hauled off to prison. Word of the 'outrage' spread quickly, and by nightfall a howling mob had gathered outside the police *thana*, shouting, '*Khoon ka badla khoon*' – blood for blood, a slogan we were to hear later, in your own days, Ganapathi, from much the same sort of people and with equally tragic results.

It was late, and the *thana* was occupied by just two young policemen – Indians, Hindi-speakers. One of them, foolishly enough, stepped out to ask the crowd to disperse. Those were his last words; he was dragged into the mob and beaten and kicked to death. His terrified colleague inside was desperately trying to summon reinforcements when the screaming horde burst in and tore him literally to pieces. As they left, their bloodlust slaked, the mob set fire to the *thana*, with the dead or dying policemen still inside it.

The next day the Deputy Governor of Ganga's prison came into his cell with a newspaper: the headlines were bigger than any other so far devoted to the mango agitation. The official, a pugnacious Ulsterman, threw the paper on to a table in front of his prisoner. 'Is this the non-violent lesson you are trying to teach the British, Mr Datta?' he asked heavily.

Ganga read the article without a word, passing over a photograph of himself with the caption: '"Mahaguru" Ganga Datta: instigator?' At the end, he let the paper drop from his hand, and the prison official was surprised to see that the Great Teacher's eyes were brimming with sorrow.

'I shall suspend the agitation,' he announced dully.

'You'll what?' asked the incredulous Irishman.

'I shall suspend the mango agitation forthwith,' Gangaji said. 'If you will provide me with the facilities to make a public announcement, I shall do so immediately.' He saw the expression on his jailor's face and half-smiled. 'My people,' he explained sorrowfully, almost to himself, 'have not understood me.'

 *34*

Nor did they when the announcement came. Gangaji, in a British prison, calling off the most successful movement of mass civil disobedience the country had ever seen, all because of *one* incident? It was bewildering. To some, it was a betrayal.

'He has cracked under pressure,' Pandu concluded, addressing a meeting of those members of the High Command who were still outside prison. 'The British have got to him at last. Either that, or he has simply become a weak old man and lost the stomach to continue the fight.'

'Whichever it is,' someone interjected, 'he has let us down.'

'Now, wait a minute,' I said mildly (yes, Ganapathi, I had, with my usual slipperiness, evaded the clutches of the police myself). 'What's all this talk about letting *you* down? I didn't see any of you amongst the massed ranks of the mango marchers. You, for instance, Pandu – I thought you were against the whole business.'

'I *was*,' Pandu acknowledged without shame. 'But I don't mind admitting I misjudged the impact the agitation would have. The Mango March *did* fire the people's imagination; it stirred them up as few things before have ever done. In every corner of the country, in every little village, people who had never been political came out in support of the cause. Gangaji had struck a chord that I'm not even sure he expected to strike. Which Indian does not love mangoes? We had found an issue around which the whole country was rallying, and which was seriously embarrassing the British. And then what does he go and do? He personally, unilaterally, calls the whole thing off. Without even consulting any of us.'

'He didn't need to consult any of us to *start* the agitation,' I pointed out.

'That's what's wrong with our entire way of running this party,' Pandu declaimed bitterly. 'Is this a Kaurava movement, or a one-man show?'

There was, of course, no answer to the question, and no one ventured any, least of all me. But it had planted a doubt in the minds of the Kaurava High Command that would, Pandu knew, sprout richly for him one day.

'If you admit his judgement was right in starting the agitation,' I said in my best elder-statesman voice, 'admit that he may be right in calling it off too. Perhaps in time we will recognize that the principle of non-violence is more important than any single agitation.'

'Two lives,' Pandu said with uncharacteristic callousness. 'Two miserable policemen. Do you know how many Indian lives the British have taken in the last two centuries?'

'I believe I have an idea,' I replied quietly, 'and I also believe that is not the point. What Gangaji is showing the world through non-violence is a new weapon — one which can only be blunted if we go back to the old weapons. We cannot point to the injustice of British rule if our opposition to it takes equally unjust forms. That is why Gangaji has decided to call off the agitation. I should not have thought it would be necessary to explain this to leading members of the Kaurava Party.'

Dissent, Ganapathi, is like a Gurkha's *kukri*: once it emerges from its sheath it must draw blood before it can be put away again. I knew that blood would inevitably have to be drawn, and I felt the pain of the knife already, knowing that it was my blood that coursed through the veins of both potential victims: my blind son and my pale son, condemned to fight on history's battlefield.

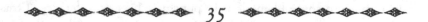 *35*

With the agitation suspended, the British, immensely relieved, dropped all charges and released the prisoners. In a gesture interpreted variously as one of appreciation, of consolation and of contempt, depending on who was analysing its implications, the Viceroy ('Dear Friend') invited Gangaji to tea.

To everyone's surprise but my own, Gangaji accepted the invitation. He entered the cavernous living-room of the viceregal palace swaddled in his habitual white, and found himself being greeted by our old friend Sir Richard, now Principal Private Secretary to His Majesty's representative in India.

'His Excellency will be with us shortly,' Sir Richard said, ushering him to a chair without the trace of a welcome on his lips.

Gangaji sat comfortably, his long spindly legs resisting the temptation to cross themselves on the Viceroy's brocade cushions. Sarah-behn, who accompanied him to most of his meetings, stood a few paces away behind a sofa. Sir Richard, regarding her with distaste, and standing himself, found it more convenient not to offer her a seat.

'While we are waiting, Mr Datta, may I offer you some tea?' he asked his patron's guest.

'Thank you,' Gangaji replied equably, 'but I have brought my own.' He moved his head in the direction of Sarah-behn, who held a stainless steel tiffin-carrier in her hand. 'Goat's milk,' he said by way of explanation. 'That is what I drink at this time.'

Sir Richard opened his mouth as if to speak, then – defeated by the occasion – shut it again. The ormolu clock on the wall ticked loudly in the silence.

'I hope I have not come too early,' Gangaji said at last.

'No, not at all,' Sir Richard found himself forced to reply. 'His Excellency has . . . er . . . been unavoidably detained.'

'Unavoidably detained,' Gangaji repeated. 'Unavoidably detained.' He savoured the words, seeming to taste each syllable as he uttered it. 'Another one of your fine British phrases, suitable for so many occasions, is it not? I wish I knew some of these myself. I always listen carefully to my English friends, like His Excellency or indeed you, Sir Richard' – Sir Richard coughed unaccountably – 'and I always intend to use these phrases myself, but somehow they never come out of my mouth at the right time.' He laughed, shaking his head, as Sir Richard reddened dangerously. 'I often say to Sarah-behn, we Indians will never learn this English language properly.'

Sir Richard did not know if his leg was being pulled, but he did know that he did not care too much for the trend of the conversation. He took a deep breath, as much to control himself as to punctuate his next utterance: 'I trust you are not greatly inconvenienced, Mr Datta. I am confident that His Excellency will be with us shortly.'

Gangaji laughed. 'Me? No, no, oh dear, not at all inconvenienced,' he chortled. 'I am sitting in this comfortable chair, in this comfortable room, large enough to accommodate a small train, with an eminent representative of His Majesty's government – you, Sir Richard – offering me tea. Why should I be inconvenienced?' He paused, waving a casual hand at his companion. 'Now she, Sarah-behn, she is not sitting in a comfortable chair. Perhaps if you asked *her* she might give you a different answer.'

It was, of course, Ganapathi, simply brilliant: it left the hapless Sir Richard no choice but to turn hastily and proffer a seat to the renegade Englishwoman. This, Sarah-behn, her expression unchanged, calmly took, smoothing down the folds of her sari and placing the tiffin-carrier with an audible clink at her feet.

'My goat's milk,' Gangaji said unnecessarily. 'She takes good care of it for me. It was all her idea, you know.'

'Indeed.' Sir Richard's tone was distant. He could not bring himself to feign interest in the dietary predilections of this oddly matched pair.

'Oh, yes.' Gangaji warmed to his theme. 'You see, I had this terrible dream one night.'

'A dream,' Sir Richard echoed dully.

'That's right. I dreamt a cow spoke to me.'

'A cow?'

'A large, sad-eyed white cow, with a long downturned mouth. "Don't let them do this to me, Mahaguru!" she was crying. And then I saw she was standing and swaying terribly, and there were all sorts of people crouching on the floor beneath her, boys and girls and children and adults and peasants and clerks, all tugging and pulling at her udders, milking her as she cried piteously to me.'

A choking sound emerged from Sir Richard.

'But it was not milk, Sir Richard, that was coming out. It was blood! And in my dream, I could do nothing. I woke shivering, with that cow's cries ringing in my ears. From that moment I resolved never to drink milk again. The cow is our mother, Sir Richard.' Gangaji suddenly and earnestly turned to him. 'Yours and mine. It is written in our scriptures. She provides nourishment and sustenance for us all. Is it right that we should cause her pain?'

Sir Richard remained speechless.

'Of course it is not. There and then I decided I could not cause her any more suffering. I was determined not to drink milk ever again.'

He stopped. Sir Richard slowly exhaled. 'I see,' he said, not knowing what he saw but relieved he would no longer have to hear.

'But then I fell ill,' Gangaji added abruptly. 'The doctors came. They said I needed minerals and protein in an easily accessible form.' He smiled. 'Another fine British phrase. I asked them what that meant, and they said I should drink milk. But I told them I could not drink milk. I had taken a vow in my heart never to drink milk again.'

Sir Richard looked toward the entrance of the room as if for deliverance. Gangaji went on.

'I asked the doctors what would happen if I did not drink the milk they wanted me to.

'"Why, then," they said, "you will die."

'"But we will all die one day," I replied. "What is wrong with that?"

'"It is just that you will die much sooner than if you did drink the milk," they said to me. "Next week, perhaps."'

Sir Richard looked wistfully gratified at the prospect.

'It was then that Sarah-behn came to my rescue,' the Mahaguru said. 'I was agonized at the thought of dying with so much work undone, so much left to do. Yet I was determined not to break my vow. I did not know how to resolve this terrible dilemma inside my heart, my soul. Then Sarah-behn said to me, "You must drink goat's milk." There I saw I had my answer. Just as nourishing, just as rich in minerals and proteins, yet free of the pain of the sacred mother-cow in my dreams.'

A footfall sounded faintly in the carpeted corridor, and a liveried *khidmatgar* entered, bearing a tea-tray. Gangaji accepted an empty cup, waved away the teapot, and allowed Sarah-behn to rise and pour him a cupful of goat's milk from one of the compartments of the tiffin-carrier.

A second bearer entered pushing a silver trolley, its filigreed top-rack all but obscured by lace doilies on which rested elegantly laden plates. 'Some cucumber sandwiches, surely?' Sir Richard asked in a weak voice. Rarely had his breeding and good manners been placed under such strain. 'I am sure your . . . er . . . doctors would wish you to have something to eat.'

An impish smile slowly spread across Gangaji's face. 'Don't worry about me, Sir Richard,' he said. 'I have brought my own food.' His hand disappeared into the voluminous folds swathing his torso and emerged holding a small, golden yellow, perfectly ripe mango. 'To remind us of a more famous Tea Party,' he announced. 'In – Boston, was it not?'

THE SEVENTH BOOK:

THE SON ALSO RISES

36

Just look at that, Ganapathi. I begin a section vowing to stay clear of Gangaji, and what does the man do? He takes over the section. As long as he is around it will be impossible for us to concentrate on other people, to dwell on Pandu's famous five or to pursue the darker destinies of Gandhari the Grim and the steatopygous Madri. In the olden days our epic narrators thought nothing of leaving a legendary hero stranded in mid-conquest while digressing into sub plots, with stories, fables and anecdotes within each. But these, Ganapathi, are more demanding times. Leave Ganga to his devices and start telling fables about Devayani and Kacha, and your audience will walk away in droves. The only interruptions they will stand for these days are catchy numbers sung by gyrating starlets, and Kacha isn't catchy enough, more's the pity.

So I suppose we may as well continue our tale, Ganapathi: give Gangaji a good run. But in order to do that we have to acknowledge that the Mahaguru was no longer the only runner.

Yes, Ganapathi, as the story of our impending nationalist victory gathers momentum, so too does a cause which Gangaji had barely begun to take seriously. A cause led by a young man whose golden skin glowed like the sun and on whose forehead shone the bright little half-moon that became his party's symbol. The cause of the Muslim Group.

The Muslims of India were no more cohesive and monolithic a group than any other in the country. Until politics intervened Indians simply accepted that people were all sorts of different things – Brahmins and Thakurs and Marwaris and Nairs and Lingayats and Pariahs and countless other varieties of Hindu, as well as Roman Catholics and Syrian Christians, Anglo-Indians and Indian Anglicans, Jains and Jews, Keshadhari Sikhs and Mazhabi Sikhs, tribal animists and neo-Buddhists, all of whom flourished on Indian soil along with hundreds and thousands of other castes and sub-castes. Indian Muslims themselves were not just Sunnis and Shias, but Moplahs and Bohras and Khojas, Ismailis and Qadianis and Ahmediyas and Kutchi Memons and Allah alone knew what else. These differences were simply a fact of Indian life, as incontestable and as innocuous as the different species of vegetation that sprout and flower across our land.

We tend to label people easily, and in a country the size of ours that is perhaps inevitable, for labels are the only way out of the confusion of sheer numbers. To categorize people is to help identify them, and what could be more natural in a country as diverse and over-peopled as India than the desire to 'place' each Indian? There is nothing demeaning about that, Ganapathi, whatever our modern secular Westernized Indian gentlemen may say. On the contrary, the application of such labels uplifts each individual, for he knows that there is no danger of him being lost in the national morass, that there are distinctive aspects to his personal identity which he shares only with a small group, and that this specialness is advertised by the label others apply to him.

So we Indians are open about our differences; we do not attempt to subsume ourselves in a homogeneous mass, we do not resort to the identity-disguising tricks of standardized names or uniform costumes or even of a common national language. We are all different; as the French, that most Indian of European peoples, like to put it, albeit in another context, *vive la différence!*

And, yes, when there are such differences, we do discriminate. Each group discriminates against the others. Your lot were free to be themselves so long as this did not encroach on my lot's right to do the same.

Mutual exclusion did not necessarily mean hostility. This was the prevailing social credo of the time, but there was a high degree of constructive interaction among India's various communities under these rules. It was, of course, Gangaji who taught us that the very rules were offensive. As with much else that he tried to teach the nation, we did not entirely learn to change our prejudices. But we became most adept at concealing them.

At any rate – and this is the point of my little sociological lecture, so you can wipe that the-old-man's-digressing-again look off your face, Ganapathi – we had never taken our social differences into the political arena. Maharajas and sultans had engaged their ministers and generals with scant regard for religion, creed or, for that matter, national origin. Aurangzeb, the most Islamic of the Mughals, relied on his Rajput military commanders to put down rival Muslim satraps; the Maratha Peshwas, the original Hindu chauvinists, employed Turkish captains of artillery. No, Ganapathi, religion had never had much to do with our national politics. It was the British civil serpent who made our people collectively bite the apple of discord.

Divide et impera, they called it in the language of their own Roman conquerors – divide and rule. Stress, elevate, sanctify and exploit the differences amongst your subjects, and you can reign over them for ever – or for as near to ever as makes no difference. Imagine the horror of the British in 1857 when their paid Indian soldiers revolted, Hindus and Muslims rallying jointly to the standard of the faded Mughal Emperor, deposed princes and disgruntled peasants making common cause against the alien oppressor. As soon as the national revolt – carefully disparaged by imperial historians as the 'Sepoy Mutiny' – was put down, British officials rediscovered their Latin lessons. *Divide et impera* was the subject of closely argued policy-minutes; everything had to be done to drive wedges between Indians in the interests of the whites and Whitehall. The British did not have far to look to place their wedges: they found the perfect opportunities in the religious distinctions which India, in its tolerance, had so long and so innocently preserved.

The strategy was amoral, the tactics immoral. The obvious cleavage to strike upon was between 'the Hindus' and 'the Muslims'. It mattered little that such terms themselves (concealing as they did so many complex divisions and identities) made little sense, nor that they covered groups which had never, in all of India's political history, functioned as monoliths. It mattered little, because Indians proved only too willing to echo Britain's political illiteracy and agree to be defined in terms imposed upon them by their conquerors.

So much for the strategy; but then look at the tactics. The British jettisoned or distorted many of their basic democratic precepts before applying them to India. Take elections, for instance. For a long time, there weren't any. Indians couldn't be trusted with the vote. Then, when the first set of 'reforms' introduced elections (to inconsequential bodies with absurdly limited powers, elected on the basis of a limited franchise, but still elections) a property qualification was required before you could vote. (The stipulation disenfranchised 90 per cent of Indians, and had been abolished decades earlier in the mother country.) When even the affluent voters showed a distressing tendency to vote for the moderate nationalism of the Kaurava Party, the Raj created 'separate electorates' for Muslims to vote for Muslim candidates. That was an example of the enlightened administration of the Raj. In their own benighted Britain they would never have thought of making the Jews of Golders Green queue separately to put a kosher *koihai* into the House of Commons – but such ideas were too good for the primitive, backward natives they were schooling in democracy. If you want to know why democracy is held in such scant respect by our present élite, Ganapathi, you need only look at the way it was dispensed to us by those who claimed to be its guardians.

So we had separate electorates, and inevitably the British encouraged separate political parties as well for each divisible minority interest. It did not take much to put up a few puppets to start a political association of, and for, Muslims. Every one of them was the recipient of a British title, a British subsidy, or (as in the case of their first figurehead, an overweight sybarite called the Gaga Shah) both. The Gaga's Muslim Group could easily have amounted to something. But the only problem was that he and his gigolous grandees were so embarrassingly grateful to their paymasters that they tripped over themselves to protest their undying loyalty to the British Raj, which didn't exactly help them win the popular esteem of the Muslim masses. The Gaga and his gang made speeches to each other, presented petitions to the British (to ask for the retention of separate electorates) and sailed off every 'hot weather' to spend their privy purses on the race-courses of Europe. Meanwhile, most serious Muslim politicians – and, for that matter, many Parsi and Christian notables – joined, supported and led the Kaurava Party.

So, too, did the man who was one day to lead the Muslim Group to its destiny. Karna emerged on the Kaurava political scene literally out of nowhere. Few things were known about this strange young man whose words glowed like his skin, who maintained a most un-Indian reticence about his origins, his family, his 'native place'. It was as if he had dawned on the present to shine in the future, while his past existed only in other people's imagination. But of his brilliance – and 'brilliant' was a word universally applied to his appearance, his intellect, his scholastic performance and his speech – there was no doubt.

He first came to national attention as a flourishing lawyer in Bombay, sharp, suave and self-assured, with a bungalow on Malabar Hill and an accent to match the cut of his Savile Row suits. Who he was, and what had made him, no one precisely knew. Mystery continued to swirl about him like mist at a Himalayan sunrise. He lived alone, seemingly without parents, friends, a background such as all Indians take for granted.

Inevitably the guessing-games were played, speculative stories floated, rumour-mills ground, till it became impossible to separate confirmed fact from culpable fantasy. For all one knew he was born into his present position, or rode into it on a white charger with nothing behind him but the sun silhouetted on the horizon.

Ah, the legends that built up around that young man, Ganapathi! Women gushed that he glowed like the sun from the heavens, and his imperviousness to them only made him more refulgent in their eyes. The matronly housewife in the adjoining bungalow swore that the sun emerged each morning from his window, and that on a grey afternoon he had only to appear on the verandah for the clouds to be dispelled. When he walked, crowds parted naturally, and people kept a reverential distance from him as if afraid to be singed by his warmth. The servants whispered that he used no soap or ointment to maintain that golden lustre, which shone untended by human hand. It was said he had all the skills of a classical warrior: some claimed he practised archery in the garden, and could shoot a single mango from a cluster without disturbing the others in the bunch; others spoke of his prowess at riding, recounting how one look from those blazing eyes could quell the most insubordinate of horses at the Mahalakshmi stables. If anyone, in the hushed discussions about him that animated every social gathering, so much as breathed curiosity about his unknown origins, someone was bound to retort that there was no point in trying to judge a mighty river by its source. In any case, Karna's was clearly no common pedigree, and his radiance was only the brighter for being encircled by the lambent touch of the unknown.

The young man himself did nothing to dispel the myths. The mystery of his past served him well, and as he rose dizzyingly to the pinnacle of Bombay's legal profession it was his future that attracted more attention.

Karna's poise and confidence were matched by his forensic skill. Few dared debate with him and those who did emerged shorn and shredded by his razor-edged tongue. His success in the courtroom brought him wealthier and more influential clients, invitations to speak at public meetings, and seats on major committees. Before long it began to be said that if there was an Indian of his generation born to shine and to lead, it was clearly the illustrious Mohammed Ali Karna.

Karna had joined the Kaurava Party upon his return from London to set up practice in Bombay as a barrister. He excelled upon its rostrums and soon represented it on various Raj committees and councils. But his view of the nationalist cause was, of course, quite different from Gangaji's.

Karna's concerns were those of the Inner Temple lawyer: Indians had a legal right to be consulted in their governance and he intended to obtain and assert those rights through legal means. It was as a skilled advocate of a constitutional brief that Karna approached his politics. Not for him the sweaty trudges through the *mofussil* districts, the mass rallies that Gangaji addressed in one or another vernacular; Karna, always elegant and well-groomed, was comfortable only in the language of his education and in the kind of surroundings in which he had acquired it.

These factors already pointed to a likely divergence from the path the party would take under Gangaji, but the actual incident that prompted Karna's exit ignited something more visceral in him.

Something that was destined to set our country ablaze.

 *37*

It was a major meeting of the party's Working Committee, where Kaurava policy and tactics were being discussed. The Gangaji group, already well on its way to dominance of the organization (these were the days, Ganapathi, when Dhritarashtra and Pandu were still comrades-in-arms), was being prevented from carrying the day only by the defiance of Karna, whose scathing sarcasm about the other side was proving, as always, effective. 'This party is not going to overthrow the British by leading rabble through the streets,' he was saying. 'The mightiest Empire in the world, with hundreds of thousands of soldiers under arms, is not going to be brought down by the great unwashed. There is no Bastille to break open, no feeble king to overrun, but a sophisticated, highly trained, deeply entrenched system of government which we must deal with on its own terms. Those terms, gentlemen' — and here Karna fixed his audience with that steely gaze above which the half-moon on his forehead seemed to throb with a light all its own — 'are the terms of the law, of familiarity with British constitutional jurisprudence, of parliamentary practice. We must develop and use these skills to wrest power from rulers who cannot deny it to us under their own rules.'

Karna looked around the table, confirming that every pair of eyes, even the tilt of Dhritarashtra's unseeing profile, was turned toward him. 'We cannot hope to rule ourselves by leading mobs of people who are ignorant of the desideratum of self-rule. Populism and demagoguery do not move parliaments, my friends. Breaking the law will not help us to make the law one day. I do not subscribe to the current fashion for the masses so opportunistically advanced by a family of disinherited princes. In no country in the world do the 'masses' rule: every nation is run by its leaders, whose learning and intelligence are the best guarantee of its success. I say to my distinguished friends: leave the masses to themselves. Let us not abdicate our responsibility to the party and the cause by placing at our head those unfit to lead us.'

Of course it was arrogant stuff, Ganapathi, but Karna's was the kind of arrogance that inspires respect rather than resentment. God knows how far he might have gone, and which direction the Kauravas might have taken, were it not for the knock on the door that interrupted him in full flow.

'Excuse me, Mr Karna, sir,' coughed an embarrassed *durwan*, 'but there is a man in a driver's uniform outside who says he must see you. I explained to him that you were busy and could not be interrupted, but he insisted it was very important. I . . . I . . . er . . . asked him who he was, sir, and he said . . . he said . . he was your father.'

Karna's burnished skin paled during this lengthy explanation, and then a voice sounded outside: 'Let me in, I say. My son will see me. I must . . .' And then the door was flung open, and a dishevelled figure appeared in a sweat-stained white uniform, peaked driver's cap in hand, anxiety distorting his face.

'Karna,' he cried in anguish. 'It is your mother . . .'

The young man was on his feet. 'I shall come at once, Abbajan,' he said, his face a yellow pallor.

'I see,' said Dhritarashtra mildly before Karna had even reached the door. 'A driver's son has been lecturing us on the unsuitability of the masses.'

'Such ingratitude,' murmured an obliging sycophant.

'Are we to let ourselves be swayed by the prejudices of someone who thinks he is too good for his parents?' asked Dhritarashtra. Karna shot him a look of pure hatred, which spent itself harmlessly on the dark glasses of its target. A hum of approval from around the table was cut short by the slamming of the door. Karna was gone, defeated – like so many of his compatriots – by his origins.

That is how things often work in our country, Ganapathi. If a man cannot be overcome on merit, you can always expose him by uprooting his family tree. Family trees are versatile plants, Ganapathi; in our country incompetence and mediocrity also flourish under the shade of their leafy branches.

So Karna strode out, and I followed him, muttering that I would be back. I still don't know what animated my impulse. Kunti had told me she would come by the building where we were meeting in order to wait for her husband, and I was seized with the urge to escape the stifling air of our petty quarrels. It would, I thought, do me good to spend a few minutes in more congenial company.

It was just as well. I reached Pandu's wife on the landing just in time to catch her as she swooned into my arms.

I eased her on to a sofa and wondered, with all the incompetence of the lifetime bachelor, whether it would be appropriate to splash water on to that still exquisitely made-up face. I had not come to a decision when Kunti stirred, and opened eyes whose redness owed nothing to any cosmetic.

'It's him!' she gasped.

'What's who?' I asked, taken aback.

'The young man . . . who just walked out.'

'Mohammed Ali Karna?'

'Is that who it was? I've heard them speak of him, but never seen him before.' She began to sit up now, the colour slowly pulsing back to her cheek. 'What do you know about him, VVji?'

I wished I knew more than I did. After all, information was my speciality; with my sources, I knew everything about everybody. But Karna had proved an exception. 'Nobody knows very much about him, Kunti. He's a successful Bombay lawyer, London-trained, a little arrogant. And today we have just learned he is the son of a driver.'

There was a little intake of breath. 'A driver?'

'You know, a chauffeur. Karna left with him. His mother is apparently very ill.'

Kunti straightened herself on the sofa and pushed a strand of elegantly greying hair absently back from her eyes. 'His mother,' she said faintly, 'is feeling much better now, thank you.'

It was my turn to swallow air. Her words woke me like the first shafts of sunlight through half-open eyes. Of course: the mystery of Karna's origin was resolved at last.

The error of Kunti's adolescence, the result of the plausible temptations of a passing foreigner, the offspring of a travelling man of the world, who had travelled out of his mother's world in a small reed basket, had not perished. He had survived after all; he had been found; and he had grown to become Mohammed Ali Karna.

'Kunti,' I breathed.

'Oh, VVji, he's alive,' she said, her eyes glistening. 'I'm so happy.'

I tend to become the stern sage at the wrong moments. 'You must never acknowledge him, Kunti,' I cautioned her.

'Do you think I don't realize that?' The retort was sharp, but I shall never forget the pathos in her voice. 'Oh, VVji, won't you find out more about him for me? Who this driver is? What exactly happened?'

'Of course,' I reassured her. With that basic clue, I knew that I, Ved Vyas, savant of other people's secrets, would have no difficulty.

Indeed: a few discreet inquiries confirmed that Kunti's instinctive faith in her first, lost son's survival had been entirely justified. The basket had floated gently down the river and become enmeshed in some undergrowth on the right bank. As Fate would have it — for such things, as you well know, Ganapathi, are willed from above — a childless couple was picnicking on the riverside. The husband was a humble modern successor to the noble profession of charioteering, in other words a chauffeur, and he had profited from his employer's absence to drive his wife to the river for a rare outing. Of such coincidences, Ganapathi, is history made.

The couple found the child and raised their hands heavenwards in praise of Allah, for they were Muslims. And thus it was that the child they adopted, the natural son of Kunti, acquired the basic qualification for membership of the party he would lead so decisively one day: the Muslim Group.

The other elements of his curriculum vitae then fell implausibly into place. Implausibly, for few who saw the Inner Temple barrister would have easily guessed the prosaic facts I discovered or inferred: a slum boyhood; scholarships to secondary school and college; a wealthy patron, his father's employer — the opulent Indra Deva — to finance a stay in London. Karna was not born to affluence, as everyone thought; and yet, in a curious way, Ganapathi, he was.

But the more I probed, the more the story of Mohammed Ali Karna dissolved again into myth and speculation. Even when the incident of the chauffeur's arrival at the Kaurava Party meeting became widely known, and the gossips and the rumour-mongers circulated fanciful and malicious versions of it to all who would listen, the golden youth remained untarnished. Instead, though the identity of those he called his parents could not be concealed, there were odd stories, awed stories, circulating about his extraordinary qualities, almost as if to make up for the apparent ordinariness of his ancestry.

These stories stressed not just his brilliance, but the determination and self-control which would one day win him a country. A typical tale, quite probably apocryphal, Ganapathi, told of how he came by his unusual name.

His father, devout Muslim though he was, had been reluctant, the story went, to risk the slightest harm to his golden foundling, and had left the boy uncircumcised. One day the young Mohammed Ali, bathing in the river with his father, asked him why he was different in that crucial respect.

'Because you are not really my son,' the grey-haired chauffeur replied; 'God allowed me to find you, but that did not give me the right to change the way He had made you.'

'But I *am* your son,' the boy declared. 'I do not care what I was before you found me; my past abandoned me. I *will* be like you.'

Whereupon he seized a knife and circumcised himself.

Hearing of the boy's deed the chauffeur's master, Indra Deva, expressed his admiration of the lad. 'You shall be known, in the glorious tradition of our national epic, as Karna,' he announced. 'Karna, the Hacker-Off.'

And thus it was that Mohammed Ali, adopted son of a rich man's driver, became Mohammed Ali Karna, destined to be Star of the Inner Temple and Defender of the Mosque.

You don't seem particularly convinced, Ganapathi. Well, neither was I. It is only a story. But you learn something about a man from the kind of stories people make up about him.

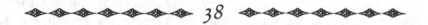 *38*

Of course one must be wary of history by anecdote.

It would be too facile to suggest that the incident at the meeting alone led to Karna's resignation from the Kaurava Party. There undoubtedly were a hundred complex reasons that drove Karna out of the party, and that might have led him to leave it at another stage of its development. It was clear, for one thing, that his position was undermined by the demonstrable effectiveness of Gangaji's methods; he could at best have slowed the capture of the party by the Hastinapuris, but he could not have prevented it. There was, for another, his own ego, which could not have abided the subordinate or at least co-equal role that Dhritarashtra and Pandu, let alone Gangaji himself, would have imposed upon him. Karna was one of those who would rather be king of an island than courtier, or even minister, in a great empire.

And then there was the altogether more complicated matter of religion. Don't get me wrong – Mohammed Ali, for all that he had earned his 'Karna', bore no resemblance to the robed-and-bearded ayatollahs of current Islamic iconography. He disdained the mullahs and disregarded their prohibitions. Where Dhritarashtra learned to brew his own tea in England, Karna acquired a taste for Scotch and cocktail sausages. Far from praying five times a day, he prided himself on his scientific, and therefore agnostic, cast of mind. His outlook was that of an Englishman of his age and profession: 'modern' (to use an adjective that has outlived more changes of connotation than any other in the language), formalist, rational, secular. It was not Islam that separated him from Gangaji, but Hinduism.

I see from the look of astonishment on your face that I shall have to explain myself. It is really very simple, Ganapathi. Karna was not much of a Muslim but he found Gangaji too much of a Hindu. The Mahaguru's traditional attire, his spiritualism, his spouting of the ancient texts, his ashram, his constant harking back to an idealized pre-British past that Karna did not believe in (and was impatient with) – all this made the young man mistrustful of the Great Teacher. The very title in which Gangaji had acquiesced made Karna uncomfortable: in his world there were no Mahagurus, only Great Learners. And Gangaji's mass politics were, to Karna, based on an appeal to the wrong instincts; they embodied an atavism that in his view would never take the country forward. A Kaurava Party of prayer-meetings and unselective eclecticism was not a party he would have cared to lead, let alone to remain a member of.

In other words, Karna found the Kauravas under Gangaji insufficiently secular, and this made him, paradoxically, more consciously Muslim. Gangaji's efforts to transcend his Hindu image by stressing the liberalism of his interpretation of it only made matters worse. When the Mahaguru, in one of his more celebrated pronouncements, declared his faith in all religions with the words, 'I am a Hindu, a Muslim, a Christian, a Zoroastrian, a Jew,' Karna responded darkly: 'Only a Hindu could say that.'

This doesn't mean, Ganapathi, that Karna slammed the door on the Kauravas and went off straight away to join the Gaga's discredited Group.

When, in his absence, the Kauravas passed the policy resolution that committed the party firmly to Gangaji's line, Karna, humiliated and bitter, felt he could no longer return to the cause. Yet he still believed, like almost everyone else, that the Kauravas were the nationalists' only hope. If they were going to persist in error, Karna decided, then he had no party left. He did not simply return to his law practice; he packed his bags and set sail for England.

Karna was never a man for half-measures. Once he had decided to make a break it was always a clean break, and a complete one. It was a characteristic that would have a profound and lasting impact upon the nation.

 *39*

For it was obvious to anyone who had followed his career that Karna could not be kept out of Indian politics for ever. He was in London when the Mahaguru and his motley crew of Round Tablers conferred so fruitlessly, and he found himself unable to hold back in public the contempt he felt for the state of the nationalist organizations. 'As an Indian,' he said to an inquiring reporter, 'I am ashamed and disgusted to see my fate and that of my country being discussed and resolved by such a collection of has-beens, never-wases and never-will-bees.'

'If you feel so strongly,' asked the journalist, 'why do you not return to Indian politics yourself?'

Karna's unblinking gaze directed the questioner to his notebook. 'I am waiting,' he said, 'for the right invitation.'

The right invitation. There was the tragedy of *divide et impera*. If the British had not sought to split up our people along sectarian lines, the invitation Karna was so openly soliciting might have come from, say, a Conservative Nationalist Party, one differing from the Kauravas on issues of political principle rather than religion. Instead the call came from the Gaga Shah, head of the Muslim Group: a gilt-edged card requesting the pleasure of Karna's company for tea at the Savoy.

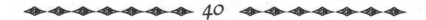 *40*

'So glad you could come, old chap,' the Gaga said, half-rising, with great effort, from his capacious chair. Karna took his hand unsmilingly. 'Sit down, won't you, there's a good fellow. Tea?'

Steaming cups were poured, not by a Savoy waiter, but by a menial in a cummerbund who bowed as he handed the refreshment to his master. Karna declined with a curt shake of the head the offer of a silver tray laden with pastries. The Gaga looked astonished. 'Really?' he asked, as he stuffed a glazed pink object into his mouth and, almost in the same gesture, helped himself to a cream puff. 'Don't know what you're missing, old chap.'

Karna remained pointedly silent.

'Must eat, you know,' the Gaga went on bonhomously. 'All in the cause of duty for me, of course. My followers weigh me against gold and diamonds every birthday, and it wouldn't do to let them down by placing a sylph-like figure on the scales. Ruins the spectacle, don't you know. And doesn't make for much of a birthday present, either.' He guffawed into his tea. Karna seemed incapable even of a polite smile. The Gaga decided to try again. 'One of my wives, can't remember which one – put pearls around their neck and they're all alike, ha-ha – used to go on and on at me about my eating. Don't take this, put that down, not another helping, you know the sort of thing. Till I told her that each bite of *foie gras* meant another sapphire for her collection. Quite literally. And then I couldn't stop her shovelling the stuff on to my plate.' He chuckled at the memory, then noticed Karna sitting, stiff and unmoved, his cup untouched on the table by his side.

The attempt at banter past, the Gaga took an elaborate sip of tea, one pudgy and bejewelled little finger held delicately in the air. 'S'pose you're wondering why I asked you here,' he said at last.

'The question had occurred to me,' Karna said drily.

The cup rattled in the Gaga's hand. This was not a tone of voice he was accustomed to hearing. 'Quite,' he exhaled sharply. 'Quite.' He reached for a chocolate éclair and munched it reflectively. 'Fact is, we'd like you back in India.'

'We?' Karna sat still, one eyebrow raised in interrogation.

'The Muslim Group,' the Gaga explained. 'Our party needs men like you.'

'Oh?' Karna seemed to want him to go on. How much easier it was, the Gaga thought, to deal with men of the turf. They were content with a pat and a nod, and the occasional packet of cash. This cold, aloof lawyer with the arrogant eyes was another sort of customer altogether. And yet – he was just the sort of jockey needed to spur an overweight, complacent thoroughbred into purposeful motion. The Gaga sighed.

'You are aware of the current political position in India,' he began.

'I have been following events, yes,' Karna confirmed.

The Gaga sensed an opportunity to let the other do the talking. 'Good,' he breathed his relief. 'And how do you assess the situation?'

'I believe it is quite deplorable,' the lawyer replied. 'Ganga Datta and his Kaurava Party are the only actors of any consequence on the stage, and they stand for all that is retrogressive and populist in Indian politics. If they are to triumph we shall witness neither democracy nor progress but mobocracy and anarchy in India.'

'Hindu mobocracy,' the Gaga added.

'Perhaps. Though rioters have no religion, as we have seen during this wretched mango business. It galls me to see the leadership of India fall into hands stained by mango juice.'

'Well put,' the Gaga said, thinking enviously of the mangoes wasted on the agitators. They were his favourite fruit, and he had made an annual practice of sending a basket of choicest Alphonso to every Englishman of distinction he sought to cultivate. The unusual gift, accompanied by a crested card bearing the calligraphed compliments of the Gaga Shah, had opened the doors of many a stately home for him in the past. This year, thanks to Gangaji's bad taste, they had had a disastrous effect. Few new invitations had been prompted by what some saw as a symbol of sedition, and in two cases his baskets had been sent back to him, their contents intact. Next year, the Gaga sighed, he would have to think of something more appropriate to give.

'I'm afraid I don't believe any of the other parties have covered themselves with glory either,' Karna added. 'The Muslim Group . . .'

'. . . is moribund,' the Gaga completed the sentence for him. 'Quite. But then what can you expect from a gathering of nawabs and zamindars? We have wealth, we have status, we have positions of influence. But I will be candid with you, my dear Karna, we lack energy.' He helped himself to a madeleine. 'That is why I have asked you here today, old chap. The Muslim Group needs you.'

Karna looked at him in silence for a long moment. 'What exactly are you proposing?' he asked at last.

The Gaga looked nonplussed. 'Why, that you should come back, of course. And join the Group, dear fellow. Give us the benefit of your perception. Your advice.'

'Advice.' Karna looked hard at his host, and the Gaga noticed how the half-moon glowed at him, like a third eye.

'Yes. And . . . and . . . counsel.'

Karna rose to his feet. 'In that case, we have nothing to discuss, Your Highness,' he said curtly. 'Your proposal is of no interest to me. Good day.'

The Gaga, struggling free of the enveloping embrace of the cushions into which he had sunk, nearly choked. 'But . . . here . . . where are you going? I don't understand.'

'I shall make myself perfectly clear. I have no desire to offer advice, as you put it, or counsel, to an ineffective covey of irrelevant old men. If you'll pardon my language, sir. And now I shall take my leave. I have other pressing matters to attend to.'

The Gaga, to Karna's surprise, chuckled, restraining the young man with a pudgy hand. 'Come, come,' he said, pushing the lawyer with surprising strength back towards the chair. 'Pardon your language!' he gave vent to a throaty chortle. 'I shall do nothing of the kind. That is precisely the kind of language we need to hear more of in the Muslim Group. Sit down, dear chap, and tell me what *you* think you could do for us. Apart from giving us advice, that is.' He laughed heartily and clapped his hands for more pastries. Karna, mollified, his half-moon fading to blend with the golden skin around it, allowed himself to be steered to a seat.

'Good,' said the Gaga, subsiding once again into the upholstery. 'Now, tell me.'

'I have given the matter some thought,' the lawyer said. 'At first I hesitated even to come here; I have never had a very high opinion of the political achievements of your Group, despite my personal regard for many of its members.' The Gaga acknowledged the courtesy, and the criticism it modified, with a gracious nod. 'In the ordinary course I would have been reluctant to identify myself solely with one community. But I do not like the direction that the Kaurava movement is taking, and I am forced to acknowledge that of the available political alternatives, the Muslim Group, which at least enjoys a certain prestige in the eyes of the Raj, has the best potential.'

He paused here to look meaningfully at the Gaga, who nodded, a lemon tart between his cheeks making other communication difficult.

'I say potential, Your Highness, and I use the word advisedly,' Karna continued. 'Because I do not believe the Group as it is at present constituted has any prospect worth the name, except to serve as a forum for the landed Muslim interest and to speak for the secular concerns of the community from time to time – without, that is, wielding any real political power. The only positions the Group has gained are those to which the British have chosen to appoint its members. We must be grateful for that, but we cannot afford to be content with it.'

'Quite so,' the Gaga concurred, hastily swallowing a morsel. 'Quite so.'

'We are reasonably secure under the British, but we must think of the future,' Karna went on. 'A future under Ganga Datta's Kauravas does not bear thinking about. Neither you nor I would have any place in the kind of India they are likely to construct.'

'I quite agree,' the Gaga intoned. 'Go on.'

'That is why we must prepare our battlements now,' the young man concluded. 'And that is why you do not need *advice*. You need leadership.'

'Leadership which you can provide?' the Gaga asked.

'Leadership,' Karna said firmly, 'that *only* I can provide.'

The Gaga was silent for a long moment, weighing the implications of the words as if they were diamonds he was being called upon to give away. 'Very well,' he said at last. 'Name your terms. I believe we can meet them.'

Karna pulled a piece of paper out of the inside pocket of his double-breasted jacket. 'I thought this might be required,' he said impassively. 'Here they are.'

The Gaga took the sheet from him and read it carefully, and this is where my narrative falters, Ganapathi, for the young man in the cummerbund, standing discreetly attentive behind a thick curtain, could not make out the writing from where he stood. Yes, Ganapathi, he was one of my men. I have told you repeatedly, haven't I, that I have my sources. They were everywhere, even on the Gaga Shah's personal staff. I am glad to see that how-could-he-possibly-have-known look, which you have been wearing ostentatiously throughout this scene, disappear from your face. A little more faith, Ganapathi, a little more respect, a small suspension of disbelief, and you will find our story sailing smoothly on, without all these breaks for justification and explanation which your furrowed brow periodically imposes upon me.

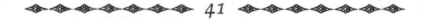 *41*

As it happens, we do not need the contents of that piece of paper to be able to guess what Karna's terms were. For within months of his return to India everything had become clear. He was introduced into the Muslim Group and made its President with almost indecent haste. The Committee of Elders, which had hitherto guided the activities — such as they were — of the party, was reconstituted into an advisory panel named by President Karna and serving at his pleasure. The party's Constitution was redrafted to confirm the President's supreme position and to proclaim a new objective: the advancement (not just the defence) of the rights and interests of India's Muslims. Using the immense resources of its patrons, the Group established offices, and launched membership campaigns, in every district of the country. Karna was creating his constituency.

I said earlier that in the country's political race for independence the Mahaguru was not the only one doing the running. Karna's Group declared itself for the first time in favour of freedom from the British. It was no longer pleading and pledging its loyalty to the colonial masters in exchange for favours: it was now a nationalist movement in its own right, like the Kaurava Party. The only difference was that the Group considered nationalism to be divisible. 'Independence without Hindu domination' was Karna's new slogan. If that seemed less than consistent with his previous non-sectarianism, he couched it in constitutionalist terms, speaking glibly of the need for a new form of federalism, the protection of minority rights, the importance of each community being able to advance unobstructed by the others. Some, at least, refused to take him at his word. 'What he really means is the importance of Mohammed Ali Karna wielding power over at least one part of the country, unobstructed by anyone else,' Dhritarashtra said mordantly to the Kaurava Working Committee. 'You can hardly accuse him of inconsistency in that. He's never believed in anything else.'

Picture the situation then, Ganapathi. The Kaurava Party, riven by the dissent of the Panduites, its most successful popular movement of civil disobedience suspended in the wake of the Chaurasta deaths, its eccentric but charismatic leader continuing to thumb his nose at the Raj. And in the opposite corner, the Muslim Group, richly endowed, favourably looked upon by the rulers, decisively led. The clash was as inevitable as its outcome was uncertain.

THE EIGHTH BOOK:

MIDNIGHT'S PARENTS

42

L et us leave them there for a minute, Ganapathi, and take a quick look at the others. The wives and children of politicians may not lead such momentous lives, but that is no reason for us to ignore them. Pandu's extended family, for instance, flourished in his absence. Though Madri did tend once in a while to look long and wistfully at herself in the mirror, she and Kunti ran a remarkable household for their five sons.

And what sons they were, Ganapathi! Yudhishtir showed every sign of rapidly vindicating his father's astral prophecies by excelling at his studies, making a habit of standing first in his class at every examination he took. And if he was overly fond of starched shirts and encyclopaedias, neither was likely to do him much harm in the courtroom career for which everyone believed he was destined. Bhim developed stature and musculature with each successive meal, and from the first became the strong-armed protector of his brothers. He was too heavy to swagger, but his lumbering tread was held in dread – no, no, Ganapathi, I am not returning to verse, keep your pen on the same line there – by every would-be juvenile bully. Arjun, of course, was perfection with pimples. Fleet of foot and keen of mind, supple and sensitive, lean and strong, a sportsman and a scholar, Arjun united all the opposite virtues of human nature: he was prince and commoner, brain and brawn, yin and yang. As for the twins, Nakul and Sahadev, they were the right foils for their exceptionally endowed brothers, for each was pleasant, simple, decent and honest, exemplifying all the merits of the amiable mediocrity they shared with millions of their less illustrious countrymen.

And so grew the five brothers, known variously as the Famous Five, the Hastinapur Horde or quite simply as the Pandavas. While all by herself, in Dhritarashtra's wing of their palatial home, Priya Duryodhani, away from her cousinly brood, cozenly brooded.

She was a slight, frail girl, Ganapathi, with a long thin tapering face like the kernel of a mango and dark eyebrows that nearly joined together over her high-ridged nose, giving her the look of a desiccated schoolteacher at an age when she was barely old enough to enrol at school. She might have even been labelled plain had not Nature, with her marvellous flair for genetic compensation, given blind Dhritarashtra's disappointing daughter the most striking pair of eyes in Hastinapur. Dark and lustrous, they shone from that pinched face like blazing gems on a fading backcloth, flashing, questioning, accusing, demanding in a manner that transcended mere words.

Not that words were of much use to Priya Duryodhani. She had little feeling for them, and her high-pitched squeaky voice would have made a poor vehicle for any figure of speech. But those eyes more than made up for all her other deficiencies, Ganapathi. They gave her a strength, a dynamism, that everything else belied. Gandhari the Grim, let down by the fates in both the number and the gender of her offspring, had been blessed with savage irony in the one aspect of her daughter she would never be able to appreciate.

Unappreciative and unappreciated, Gandhari wasted away in the home she had hoped to make with her perennially absent husband. She had given up her most precious possession for him, but he was not there to share the darkness with her.

Yet Gandhari refused to accept that her sacrifice had been pointless, and clung to her blindfold with the intensity that only Indian women accord their marital symbols. What sustained her it was impossible to imagine, but it certainly was not her husband. Dhritarashtra addressed all his letters from prison to Priya Duryodhani, well before she was old enough to understand any of them, rather than to the long-suffering wife who had offended by delivering her. As her health deteriorated, Gandhari's world remained circumscribed by her silken blindfold, and she became withdrawn and increasingly grim.

There are those who make much of Dhritarashtra's devotion to his daughter and use it to explain her subsequent actions. I prefer to give far more importance, Ganapathi, to the years at her mother's darkened bedside, to her exposure at so impressionable an age to the sad betrayal of Gandhari's sacrifice, to her profound realization of her own aloneness. After what she saw in her childhood Priya Duryodhani would never be able to trust another human being, no, not even — especially not — her own father.

Some aspects of her unique character manifested themselves early. Such as the time she decided to get rid of Bhim.

43

Bhim, you will recall, Ganapathi, was one of those disgustingly strong children who are excessively healthy and hearty, and whose good spirits burst out of them to the general inconvenience of others. Growing up with Bhim meant having dust flung in one's eyes, finding one's clothes in the river after a swim, being picked up and dropped into slushy puddles, all to the tune of his uproarious laughter – and it also meant having no choice other than to grin and bear it. The experience must have been something along the lines of being a team-mate of Ian Botham on a cricket tour. Boys who climbed trees to pluck fruit were liable to find themselves shaken off the branch, along with the fruit, by Bhim rattling the trunk as if it were a sapling. I can see why Duryodhani, who at the best of times saw little to laugh at in life, found this all a bit tiresome. But her proposed remedy was, even then, a little on the drastic side.

Imagine the situation for yourself, Ganapathi. A dark, introverted, frail Priya Duryodhani shakes free the last dead spider from her dress, wipes off the last mud-stain, or puts the last drenched letter from her father out to dry – and decides to act. Not in haste, mind you – that would not be characteristic of her. She waits till her twelfth birthday is to be celebrated and then invites her cousins to a children's picnic at Pharmanakoti, on the banks of the river. It is she who has chosen the spot.

What lies behind the pinched face and lustrous eyes of little Duryodhani? She is not normally one for parties, even less for picnics. But neither her parents nor her guests – both relieved at this apparent sign of advancing normality – question her intent. 'Thweet Priya Duryodhani,' says her aunt Madri, 'it ith *tho* thweet of her to think of thith.' Little does Madri know that she might just as well have lisped the word 'think' too.

Yes, Ganapathi, thinking and sinking are both terms that apply to our heroine's intentions. For she has found a bottle in her mother's overflowing medicine-chest whose label reads 'Poison – keep out of the reach of children.' Wrapping it carefully in fine lace, Priya Duryodhani takes this with her to the picnic-spot. And she takes care – for she always follows instructions, especially written ones – to keep it out of the reach of the other children.

Think of it, Ganapathi. An idyllic scene from a Basohli painting. The sun shines brightly from a powder-blue sky, while on the thick, moisture-rich grass boisterous princelings play rowdily together. Duryodhani, whose luke-warm interest in the proceedings has led to her gradual exclusion, eases herself, unmissed, out of the group. She walks to where the servants have been busy laying out the contents of the three picnic hampers they have brought. 'Very good,' she says after a cursory inspection. 'You may go now. Return in two hours to clean this up. We should have finished by then.' It is an interesting choice of words, Ganapathi. There is much that Duryodhani intends to finish.

The boys are still far away as the servants retreat. At one place, as is by now customary, they have served twice as much food as for the others; this is, of course, for Bhim. Priya Duryodhani sits there, taking care to ensure that she has a view of her guests frolicking in the distance. Then, from her own shoulder-bag, from under her books and magazines and the inevitable letter from her father, she takes out a little bottle wrapped in lace. Opening it with care, she liberally douses the serving before her with its contents. Then, carefully closing the bottle, she wraps the lace meticulously around it once more, restores the bundle to her bag, takes out a book and, primly crossing her thin legs, begins to read.

Aha, Ganapathi, I see you thinking, something is not right here. Surely our illustrious Leader-to-be did not commit juvenile homicide? Perhaps there is something wrong about the label on the bottle; or perhaps she has not poured enough of it to do any serious harm; or perhaps, Heaven forfend, she has simply poisoned the wrong serving? I am afraid, Ganapathi, you must think again. The bottle that the diligent Duryodhani has pilfered does indeed contain poison, and there is very little of it left now that it has been put back in her bag. And she has indeed picked the right mound of pilau to soak. And what is more, the undiscriminating Bhim, who would consume anything provided there was enough of it, tucks voraciously into his plateful and before long has eaten it all.

Think of it, Ganapathi! The tranquil scene of your Basohli begins to disintegrate into a Tzara. The bright sun swims before Bhim's eyes, like an orange disintegrating in a storm. He complains of feeling tired and nauseous. 'You've eaten too much,' Duryodhani says without sympathy. Through the gathering mists he hears her suggesting a rest by the river bank. While his unsuspecting brothers turn to French cricket, Bhim loses consciousness on the water's edge.

Out of view of her rumbustious cousins, Duryodhani tiptoes to her sleeping victim. She looks around her: not a leaf stirs. She drops a pebble on his chest, to find out whether he might lightly wake. When this provokes no change in the rhythm of his heavy breathing, she tries a larger, sharper stone. Still there is no reaction. Now acting with unpractised efficiency, she bends to thrust an umbrella under Bhim's bulk. Using it as a lever, and with surprising strength for one of her frame, she topples him with a splash into the river.

Imagine it, Ganapathi, as a silent film of the 1920s. There stands Priya Duryodhani, a thin cotton dress on her bony frame, contemplating for one jerky moment of uncertainty the riverine ripples eddying from her action. Then it is all swift movement. She looks around with a rapidity only the celluloid of the era can record, to ensure that no one has seen her. Satisfied – imagine the close-up, Ganapathi, at that firmly set mouth, those grim thin lips, that determined face with its blazing eyes – Duryodhani slips quickly away.

You can invent the caption to that shot, young Ganapathi. Bhim has sunk like a boulder; with the poison also working its way inside him, it is a reasonably safe bet that he will not resurface alive. 'A job well done!' the titles would say on the screen. Fade and dissolve, to Duryodhani returning to join the others, her expression giving nothing away. Years later an American Secretary of State would sigh with regret at the loss that Priya Duryodhani's political success had meant to the world of poker.

But no, Ganapathi, do not fear the worst. A reasonably safe bet, it certainly was; but she was quickly to learn that with the Pandavas there are no reasonably safe bets.

Pan our film back to the shot of the riverside. As Bhim rolls into the water – slowly here, it is over in an instant – he is bitten by a venomous snake. Thus does Fate protect her favourites, Ganapathi, for the scheming Priya Duryodhani had poured the contents of a poisonous snake-bite antidote into her victim's lunch. The sharp fangs wake Bhim from his drugged stupor just as the serpent's venom encounters its antidote in his bloodstream – and neutralizes it. Bhim, instantly awake and cured, takes a deep breath as he goes under, comes back to the surface and swims back to the shore in a few strong strokes. Applause, Ganapathi, from the cinema floor, from the youths in the 25-paise seats. Cat calls and cheers as Bhim hauls his bulk out of the water and wrings his singlet dry.

Cut! Turn to Priya Duryodhani, twelve years old, and cheated of her best birthday present. As the screen fills with her sallow face Duryodhani does not betray the slightest hint of astonishment when Bhim rejoins her group, soaking and as large – quite literally – as life. 'Been taking a swim, brother?' she asks casually, her heart pounding for fear that he had seen her.

Bhim laughs, his customary reaction to most questions. 'Must have dozed off and rolled into the river in my sleep,' he says, tossing water off his forelocks. 'Unless one of you . . .' but he dismisses the unspoken thought with another laugh, and any fears of discovery that Duryodhani may have are soon drowned in the squeals of the others as Bhim proceeds to chase them towards the river for a fraternal dunking.

There I must end our little film sequence. But you see what I mean, Ganapathi. Priya Duryodhani acted only according to the dictates of her own conscienceless mind. Even at the age of twelve, overkill was already her problem.

Perhaps things might have been different had Dhritarashtra taken her in hand, rather than his pen. But he did not, and there is no point in speculating about what might have happened if he had. History, after all, is full of ifs and buts. I prefer, Ganapathi, to seek other conjunctions with destiny.

 *44*

With their father away on political errands or in prison, the Pandavas also lacked a stable paternal presence in the home. Kunti was determined not to let them suffer in this regard, and began looking for a regular tutor to take them in hand. But the wilful boys proved more than a handful for the various forlorn Bachelors of Arts Kunti engaged, and after several such failures she realized they would only respect a tutor they chose themselves. Yet none of the prospective candidates who answered her advertisements met with the boys' approval, and Kunti despaired of ever finding them a suitable guru.

One day the Pandavas were playing their favourite sport – cricket, of course, Ganapathi: that most Indian of organized pastimes, with its bewilderingly complex rules that are reduced in practice to utter simplicity, its underlying assumption of social order, its range and subtlety that so suit our national temperament – when a mighty swipe by Bhim sent the ball high over the others' heads, soaring out of the ground and landing with a loud splash in a disused well. Five sheepish ex-princelings were soon gathered round the brick structure, helplessly watching the red cork-and-leather object float twenty feet below them. It was a sheer drop; the fungus- and slime-covered wall offered no purchase, no crevice or projection, for a descent down its slippery side. There was not even a bucket attached to the threadbare rope that dangled uselessly from the wooden cross-beam above the well. The boys leaned despairingly over the edge, seeing their prospects of an innings ebbing with the water around their irretrievable ball.

'What have you lost, sons of Hastinapur?' asked a gravelly voice. They turned, startled, to discover a saffron-robed sadhu, his full beard still more black than grey, the staff and bowl of his calling in each hand, surveying them with an amused smile.

'Our ball,' replied Yudhishtir, the most direct. 'But how do you know who we are?'

'I know a great deal, my boys,' came the answer. 'A ball, eh?' He looked with casual curiosity into the well. 'Is that all? You call yourselves Kshatriyas, and you can't even recover a ball from a well?'

'Actually, we don't call ourselves Kshatriyas, because our family doesn't believe in the caste system,' Yudhishtir replied, revealing yet again the obsessive earnestness, the desire to lay all his cards on the table face up, that was to become his best-known characteristic.

'And if you think we're so stupid, can you do any better?' asked Bhim a little more aggressively.

'Why, certainly, if you wish,' the sadhu said, unoffended by the challenge. 'But my services don't come for nothing. If I can get your ball out for you, will you give me dinner tonight?'

'Just dinner?' Yudhishtir asked in surprise. 'I'm sure we can offer you something that will last longer than that.'

'Dinner will do for now,' the saffroned savant smiled. 'A sadhu's lot is a hungry one.'

He reached up for the old rope hanging above them, which in better days would have carried a bucket into the depths.

'If that's your plan, forget it,' said Arjun, who had so far remained silent. 'The rope is old and frayed. We've already worked out that it won't support the weight of one of us, let alone an adult like you.'

The sadhu gave him a darting, sidelong look, as if briefly acknowledging the perspicacity of the speaker. But he did not reply, and the smile was still on his face as he looped one end of the rope and balanced the decaying hemp in his hand. Then, with the briefest of glances at the position of the ball, he tossed the rope in a casual curve into the water, tightening the loop as it landed. When he hauled the rope up, the ball, its redness dulled by the soaking, was safely imprisoned in the knot he had made.

As the boys stared at him in astonished gratitude, he slipped the ball free and tossed it to Yudhishtir. 'Next time,' he said, sounding at last like a sage, 'be more careful.'

'That's fantastic!' the twins exclaimed in one breath. 'Can you teach us how to do that, sir?'

'Don't be silly, Nakul and Sahadev,' began an embarrassed Yudhishtir, turning to the sadhu. 'Thank you, sir . . .'

'Why not?' the sage cheerfully addressed the little twins. 'And many other things besides, if you're only willing to learn.'

'Can you teach him to bat properly?' Nakul pointed at his twin. 'He was out for zero again.'

'Zero?' the sadhu laughed. 'Well, that is nothing to be ashamed of. The English game of cricket would never have taken shape without the Indian zero.'

'What do you mean?' This was Arjun, intrigued but wary.

'It's quite simple,' the sadhu replied. 'While some of our historical-scientific claims (to have discovered the secret of nuclear fission in the fourth century AD, for instance) are justly challenged by Western scholars, no one questions the fact that our ancestors were the first to conceive of the zero. Before that mathematicians, from the Arabs to the Chinese, left a blank space in their calculations; it took Indians to realize that even *nothing* can be something.

Zero, *shunya, bindu*, whatever you call it, embodies the unchanging reality of nothingness.'

'But zero's still zero,' Nakul said.

The sadhu roared with laughter. 'Not quite,' he said. 'The Indian zero is no empty shell. It reflects the perpetual intangibility of the eternal, it embodies the calm centre of the whirling tornado of life, it stands for the point where our verifiable values are transcended by the enigma of the void. Yes, young man, it is empty of numerical value. But it is full of non-empirical possibilities. It is nothing and everything; it is the locus of the universe.' He chuckled at the puzzlement on the twins' faces, even as he took in the sharper look of insight that had appeared in Arjun's and Yudhishtir's eyes. 'Now do you see, my friends, why your zero is really something very special, very Indian?'

'But can you teach him to bat?' asked Nakul, as his elder brothers burst out laughing.

'Perhaps,' side-stepped the sage. 'But first, what about that dinner?'

45

So they took him home, Ganapathi, and sat around him in an adoring semicircle as he deftly did justice to an appetite as prodigious as his skills. In between courses, he told Kunti and the Pandavas his story.

'My name is Jayaprakash Drona,' he said. 'I was born a Brahmin, and believed from my youth in the great tradition of Brahmin learning, unrelated to any profession or material gain. When I felt ready I took leave of my family and, adopting the robes of a mendicant, set forth into the world. All my knowledge and skills I acquired from a rishi at the foot of the Himalayas, and as for my food, I was given whatever I wanted by those to whom I extended my empty bowl, since I believed, in the tradition of our great sages, that my material needs were irrelevant, for a Brahmin's upkeep is the responsibility of society. Having learned all that my rishi had to teach me, and upon his advice, I returned to the plains, there to impart some of my learning to those who sought it, asking in exchange nothing more than the occasional bowl of rice and dal.

'In the course of my wanderings I came across an Englishman, who was then visiting the remote district in which I happened to be travelling. He was a civil servant sent out to administer justice in a complicated matter involving land. (How ironic, is it not, my sister, that the British, those great usurpers of land in this country, presume to tell us Indians what to do with the little they have left us?) Anyway, this Englishman clearly found his stay onerous and had little to do in his spare time in that place, until he chanced upon me. He spoke our language, after a fashion, and we talked. He professed interest in our ancient practices and customs, our traditional knowledge and skills. I answered his questions, and he seemed greatly interested in what I had to tell him. During the time that he remained in that district I saw him for at least an hour every day. When he left he said that he owed all that he knew of India to me, and that he would never forget it. He gave me his personal card and said that if ever I needed assistance I should not hesitate to call on him.

'It was not long after that I found a good woman to bear me a son. I called him Ashwathaman, and his birth obliged me, if not to settle down, at least to acquire a dwelling where I could leave him as I set forth each day. The responsibilities of parenthood are not meant for us who have taken saffron; and yet I must confess that my son became the be-all of my life, much as I imagine these fine young boys are to you, sister.

'At first I never doubted that I could provide all that Ashwathaman might need. I could offer him learning, and for food he shared what I was given each day; as for clothing, its lack never bothered me, for what does a Brahmin need but his sacred thread? Or so I thought; but sages, alas, sister, do not know everything.

'The needs of the son are sometimes the making of the father. I did not want, and so assumed I had brought my son up not to want. But one day Ashwathaman asked me – sister, you will understand this – he asked me for a glass of milk. He had seen rich children drinking this thick white liquid, and he too wanted to have some.

'Well, sister, I had none to give him. Who in my position would have? You know the price of milk, you know the purposes for which it is used, for tea and sweets and cheese, all luxuries beyond the means of a humble man of learning. But I could not bring myself to tell my son this.

'I promised him I would get him some, and set out the next morning with but that one purpose in mind. But you know, sister, how people are these days. They will gladly give a sadhu some of the rice and dal they cook in abundance each day, but milk is too valuable a commodity to be wasted on such as me. In the old days a holy man could have knocked on the first sizeable door and be given a cow if such was his need, but I could not get so much as a glassful. Household after household turned me away. "Milk, indeed!" some said. "What do *you* need milk for?" Or "*Hai ya*, what will these sadhus expect next? Rice-bowls made of gold or what? Really, there's a limit, I tell you." When at last, weary and disheartened, I came home, I found Ashwathaman with a glass in his hand, his eyes shining with excitement.

"Father, father, I have tasted milk at last!" he exclaimed. "I asked my friends, and they gave me some." I took the glass from him, sister, and put my lips to it. What Ashwathaman had been given to drink was cheap rice-flour mixed with water.

'I could not bear to look at the child, gazing at me with an expression of such simple joy in his wide eyes. The pain and hurt that suffused my heart stifled my breathing. That my learning and wisdom had brought my son to this! It is all very well to renounce the material pleasures of the world, but one has no right to renounce them for another. I resolved never again to beg for a living. I would find myself a patron, I vowed, and bring my son up to know the good things of life, not just the important ones.

'I thought instantly of the Englishman who had given me his card. He was now an official of even greater importance in the province. Taking my son with me, I went to his residence. At first the guards would not even let me past the gate, but when I produced the card, a little bent and soiled and curling at the edges, but still unmistakably his card, I was allowed in. Mr Ronald Heaslop, for that was his name, himself met me on the steps of his porch. He was wearing a silk dressing-gown and had a glass in his hand, and he was weaving slightly as he walked, but his speech was clear and his grip on the glass was firm.

'"Yes," he said as I approached, "what can I do for you?"

'I did not like the brusqueness of his tone, but I put it down to the manner of superiority that all Englishmen seem to have instilled in them at an early age, and which they mistake for a sign of good breeding. The haughty stare, the taciturn manner, are simply, I thought, their equivalent of the politeness and respect for elders we teach our children to show. "You remember me, Mr Heaslop," I began, and saw from his unchanged expression that he did not. "You gave me this card."

'He took it, almost snatched it, from me. "What of it? I give my card to hundreds of people. You could have picked it up from the ground."

'My bile was rising, sister, but having come so far I felt I could not simply turn away. "You gave it to me," I said, "on your departure from Devi Hill *taluk* six, seven summers ago, in return for all the knowledge and instruction I imparted to you, on the subject of the holy *shastras* and our tradi –"

'"Knowledge? Instruction?" he interrupted me derisively. "You have no *knowledge* you can *instruct* me in, black man. I remember now – yes, I gave you the card. A lot of superstitious twaddle you told me, and I found it amusing, a diverting way to pass the time. But I was much younger then. I'm afraid I no longer find your kind of prating very interesting. Is that all you came here about? Because I'm afraid I really don't have time for this."

'I was smarting at these words, sister, but I was determined not to slink away like some wounded dog. "I came," I said with as much dignity as I could muster, "because I was in need, and I thought I could call upon our past friendship –"

'"*Friendship?*" he interrupted me again. "Don't be stupid. We are not here to be your friends, black man; we are here to rule you. There is no friendship possible in this world between the likes of you and such as me; not now, not here, not yet, not ever. You say you are in want; it is no concern of mine, but here – Ghaus Mohammed! Bring me my purse!"

'I should have turned on my heel and left at that very instant, but exhaustion and astonishment kept me rooted to the spot. The Englishman's servant arrived with the purse; Heaslop put his hand in and stretched out a fistful of change towards me. Not in the name of any supposed friendship, of course, nor even in acknowledgement of our past contact, but because this gesture defined the proper relations between a British national and a native beggar. I could not bear to move; little Ashwathaman, his eyes wide in fear and discovery, clung to my leg as I stood transfixed. Heaslop waited for a brief moment, saw me immobile; then with a casual, almost careless flick, he flung the coins in my face.

'Thunder rolled within my breast, sister, lightning flashed through my mind, a storm drenched my eyes. The skies opened, and through the rain that poured down upon us I saw Heaslop returning a little unsteadily to his house. And little Ashwathaman scrabbling in the mud for the fallen coins.

'A rage filled me such as I cannot begin to describe. "No!" I bellowed. "No!" I seized Ashwathaman by the scruff of the neck and began shaking him in fury. "Not one of those coins, boy, not a single one!" I screamed. His little hands unclenched, and one by one the coins, some big, some small, began to fall out of his grasp. The last one to fall was a rupee coin – yes, sister, more than enough to buy him a glass of milk. But I was determined my son would not drink of an Englishman's charity.

'Still holding him by the neck, I propelled my son out of the compound. Ashwathaman, snivelling, kept trying to look behind us. I turned briefly to see the servant Ghaus Mohammed bend to pick up the fallen coins.

'We walked on, sister, and from that moment a new determination was born in my heart. Of what purpose is our cultural and philosophical heritage, our learning and our history, if it condemns us to being offal at the feet of a Heaslop? I vowed to work for the defeat and expulsion of Heaslop and the government he represents, not only by supporting the Kaurava Party in its just struggle against the oppressor, but by educating and training those who will one day rise to lead our people when we replace the alien system they have thrust upon us.'

'Will you educate and train us, Dronaji, sir?' asked Yudhishtir.

'It will please me,' Kunti added, 'if you would accept.'

'Certainly,' said Drona equably. 'Indeed, I should have been quite embarrassed had you not asked. For it is this very task that has brought me here. Gangaji engaged me as your tutor last week.'

 *46*

One day, Ganapathi, when I was visiting the home of one of our younger party leaders – never mind his name – I found myself the object of the curiosity and admiration of his little son, aged, oh I don't know, maybe seven. He was sitting at my feet, chin cupped in his hands, and at one stage when his parents were both out of the room, he said to me, 'Dadaji, won't you tell me a story?'

No one had asked me to do that before, Ganapathi – one of the hazards of the peripatetic procreation I had practised was the loss of any claims to grandfatherhood – and I was touched by the request. 'Certainly,' I said, and embarked upon a story. It was a tale from our ancient annals, the *Panchatantra* or the *Hitopadesha*, I am no longer sure which, and I was telling it rather well, spinning the yarn along with a fluency worthy of a real grandfather, when the boy cut in to ask: 'But Dadaji, what happened in the end?'

What happened in the end? The question drew me short. The end was not a concept that applied particularly to that story – which, as it happens, involved one of the characters embarking upon another story in which one of the characters tells another story and . . . you know the genre, Ganapathi. But even more important, 'the end' was an idea that I suddenly realized meant nothing to me. I did not begin the story in order to end it; the essence of the tale lay in the telling. 'What happened next?' I could answer, but 'what happened in the end?' I could not even understand.

For what, Ganapathi, *was* the end? I know where our modern Indians have acquired the term. It is a contemporary conceit that life and art must be defined by conclusions, consummations devoutly to be wished and strived for. But 'the end' isn't true even in the tawdry fictions that reified the phrase. You want one of those Hollywood films that conclude with the hero and heroine in a passionate clinch, you watch the titles on the screen announce 'The End', and you know perfectly well even before you have left the hall that it is not the end at all: there are going to be more clinches, and a wedding, and more clinches, and tiffs and arguments and quarrels and perhaps saucers flying against the wall; there will be the banalities of breakfast and laundry and house-cleaning, the thoughts of which have never crossed the starry-eyed heroine's mind; there will be babies to bear and burp and birch, with flus and flatulence and phlebitis to follow; there are the thousand mundanities and trivialities that are sought to be concealed by the great lie, 'they lived happily ever after'. No, Ganapathi, the story does not *end* when the screenwriter pretends it does.

It does not even end with the great symbol of finality, death. For when the protagonist dies the story continues: his widow suffers bitterly or celebrates madly or throws herself on his pyre or knits herself into extinction; his son turns to drugs or becomes a man or seeks revenge or carries on as before; the world goes on. And – who knows? – perhaps our hero goes on too, in some other world, finer than the one Hollywood could create for him.

There is, in short, Ganapathi, no *end* to the story of life. There are merely pauses. The end is the arbitrary invention of the teller, but there can be no finality about his choice. Today's end is, after all, only tomorrow's beginning.

I was struggling inarticulately with these thoughts when the boy's mother returned to drag him off to bed. Saved by the bed! 'I shall tell you tomorrow,' I promised the impatient child. But of course I never did, and I fear the boy thought me a very poor story-teller indeed.

Or perhaps he grew to understand. Perhaps, Ganapathi, he came to manhood with the instinctive Indian sense that nothing begins and nothing ends. That we are all living in an eternal present in which what was and what will be is contained in what is. Or, to put it in a more contemporary idiom, that life is a series of sequels to history. All our books and stories and television shows should end not with the words 'The End' but with the more accurate 'To Be Continued'. To be continued, but not necessarily here . . .

Ah, Ganapathi, I see I disappoint you once more. The old man going off the point again, I see you think; how tiresome he can be when he gets philosophical. Do you know what 'philosophical' means, Ganapathi? It comes from the Greek words *phileein*, to love, and *sophia*, wisdom. A philosopher is a lover of wisdom, Ganapathi. Not of knowledge, which for all its great uses ultimately suffers from the crippling defect of ephemerality. All knowledge is transient, linked to the world around it and subject to change as the world changes. Whereas wisdom, true wisdom, is eternal, immutable. To be philosophical one must love wisdom for its own sake, accept its permanent validity and yet its perpetual irrelevance. It is the fate of the wise to understand the process of history and yet never to shape it.

I do not pretend to such wisdom, Ganapathi. I am no philosopher. I am a chronicler and a participant in the events I describe, but I cannot accord equal weight to my two functions. In life one must for ever choose between being one who tells stories and one about whom stories are told. My choice you know, and it was made for me.

> My choice you know, and it was made for me.
> Does the river ask why it flows to the sea?
> I share with you a fragment of experience –
> Embellished no doubt, a figment of existence;
> But it is true.
>
> It moves me, I do not control it.
> When the pantheon marches, can the police patrol it?
> It is a shard of ancient pottery –
> Awarded to a spade as if by lottery;
> But it is true.
>
> The song I sing is neither verse nor prose.
> Can the gardener ask why he is pricked by the rose?
> What I tell you is a slender filament,
> A rubbing from a colossal monument;
> But it is true.
>
> I claim no beginning, nor any end.
> Does a tree in the wind know why it must bend?
> The picture I show you has colour and cast
> A snip from a canvas impossibly vast;
> But it is true.
>
> I am not potter, nor sculptor, nor painter, my son.
> Do the victor or loser know why the race must be won?
> I am not even kiln, not hand, no, not brush;
> My tale is recalled, words plucked from the crush –
> But it is true.

It is my truth, Ganapathi, just as the crusade to drive out the British reflected Gangaji's truth, and the fight to be rid of both the British and the Hindu was Karna's truth. Which philosopher would dare to establish a hierarchy among such verities?

Question, Ganapathi. Is it permissible to modify truth with a possessive pronoun? Questions Two and Three. At what point in the recollection of truth does wisdom cease to transcend knowledge? How much may one select, interpret and arrange the facts of the living past before truth is jeopardized by inaccuracy?

I see once again the furrow of incomprehension on your brow, Ganapathi, wrinkled there by the frown of impatience. The old man is being wilfully obscure, your forehead grumbles.

Do not seek to answer these questions, my friend. I shall not pose them again.

Instead, Ganapathi, we shall return to the story.

 47

But to which story shall we return?

Shall I tell of Karna's dramatic rise to national importance through his dominance of the Muslim Group? Of the mass meetings he began to address, in impeccable English, with robed and bearded mullahs by his side, speaking to Muslim peasants to whom he seemed as foreign as the Viceroy, and who yet – another Indian inconsistency – hailed him as their supreme leader? Shall I speak instead of Gangaji, unwithered by increasing age, but often resting one arm on his sturdy Scottish sister as he walked to his prayer-meetings, Gangaji whose message turned increasingly to love and peace and brotherhood, even as foreign journalists and photographers clustered round him in droves to make him a global legend? Or of Dhritarashtra, the man to whom the Mahaguru left the political leadership of the Kaurava Party while he devoted his own time to the moral and spiritual values that informed his cause? Dhritarashtra, who derived his ultimate authority from a man whose basic beliefs he did not share, but whose benediction had made him the unquestioned heir-apparent to the Kaurava crown? Or should I turn instead to Pandu, my disenchanted son, and tell you of the rebellion of the man whose victory, unlikely though it always seemed, might have changed the course of our history?

He was no smooth politician, my pale son; he had no head for the philosophical niceties of his trade, the intellectual arguments over right and left and right and wrong. Pandu was in the Kaurava movement to overthrow the British, and he was not convinced that Gangaji's methods – endorsed, as he saw it, opportunistically by Dhritarashtra – were working, or working quickly enough. As we have seen, the anointment of his blind half-brother as Crown Prince rankled deeply; but it was the abandonment of the mango agitation just when it seemed to be achieving results that led Pandu to break ranks. He announced his candidacy for the presidency of the Kaurava Party at its next annual session.

'What do we do now?' Dhritarashtra, leaning heavily on his cane, his voice laden with anxiety, asked the Mahaguru. 'I had thought my re-election was assured.' He sucked in his sallow cheeks in an expression of dismayed petulance. 'Unopposed,' he added.

'So had I, my son,' Gangaji replied, untroubled. 'This is most unfortunate. But do not worry about it.'

'Do not worry?' Dhritarashtra almost choked on the words. 'Do you know the kind of support he can muster on his rabble-rousing platform? I could even – lose.' He spoke the unmentionable word with a shudder: it expressed an unthinkable thought.

'A possibility that has occurred to me,' the Mahaguru responded equably.

'We can't allow it to happen,' Dhritarashtra said. 'You must speak to him.'

'I have already done so.' The Mahaguru's response was casual.

'And?' Dhritarashtra could not keep the eagerness out of his voice.

'He will not be moved.' The Mahaguru held himself very still when he spoke these words. 'He assured me of his complete respect and devotion – that is always a very bad sign, V.V., is it not? – but told me very gently and firmly that his candidacy was irrevocable.'

'On what grounds?'

This time it was I who answered. 'Time for a change. Need for renewal in the party. New ideas about the direction of the movement. His slogan is "A Time for Action". People are listening to him.'

Dhritarashtra let out a long and bitter sigh. 'The bastard,' he breathed.

'So are you, don't forget,' Gangaji retorted, allowing himself an idiosyncratic chuckle. 'Eh, V.V.? And the legitimacy of his aspirations is not in doubt. But do not worry, my son. I have no intention of risking your humiliation at the election.'

I imagined Dhritarashtra's eyes lighting up behind those dark glasses. 'So you will speak to some leaders – make it clear you support me for the post?'

'I have no intention of risking my own humiliation either,' Gangaji replied briskly. 'No, that is not what I had in mind.'

'Then what, Gangaji?' the note of despair was back in his tone.

'You will step down,' the Mahaguru said. 'Gracefully.'

Dhritarashtra looked as if he had been struck by his own cane.

'You will behave as if you never had any intention of seeking re-election,' the Mahaguru went on. 'You will explain that you do not believe it is healthy for the party that one man hold the presidency for too long. A single one-year term, for instance, would be preferable. Perhaps two. Of course, you have had three, but that was wrong and you do not want to see the mistake repeated. You welcome other candidacies.'

'You just want me to give in,' Dhritarashtra breathed.

Gangaji ignored the remark. 'There will, of course, be another candidate. Not you. Not, in fact, anyone particularly well-known in the country. Perhaps an Untouchable – I mean a Child of God. He will be a more appropriate symbol for the party than another former princeling. And I shall let it be known that that is my view.'

A glimmer of understanding lightened my sightless son's features. 'So you're not going to let Pandu get away with this.'

'I think this would be the most judicious way of meeting this challenge to the authority of the party leadership,' Gangaji said. 'I do not know whether my discreet support for the other candidate will prevent an undesirable result. But should it fail, it will not be my closest follower and – what is the word they use? – *protégé* who will have been defeated.'

'And should it succeed?' I asked.

'Why, we shall have just the sort of president we need,' Gangaji said. 'A symbol. What, after all, is the presidency? It is a title that confers a degree of presumed authority on the holder. The British King, too, has such a title. But he is not the most powerful man in England.'

'Of course,' said Dhritarashtra. The colour was returning to his cheek.

'Whoever wins the presidency, the party must prepare itself for the future,' the Mahaguru went on. 'There are changes in the offing, constitutional changes, for which the party must be ready. My last talk with the Viceroy has paved the way for the establishment of a new political system. Partial democracy, it is true. But our friends in the civil service have helped advocate our cause. Vidur has done his work well. Indians will hold elected office in the provinces, even if with limited powers. All our efforts have come to some good. The British know they cannot continue to arrest us, to lathi-charge us. They have to give us a share in their system. The passage of the Government of India Act by the British Parliament now seems assured.'

We knew all this already, but Gangaji undoubtedly had a good reason for reminding us of what we knew. 'Our sights must now be set on the governments to be formed in the provinces. They are a stepping stone to a central government one day, a dominion government for all of India, a government of Indians. The Indians who will make up that national government of the future are the ones the British will want to talk to. It will not matter what title they hold – certainly not that of a rotational party presidency. The British, my dear Dhritarashtra, will be less interested in who is president today than in who might be prime minister tomorrow.'

'Of course, Gangaji,' my blind son replied humbly.

Of course. For the Mahaguru was right, as always. Dhritarashtra could afford to step aside from the presidential fray, and aim higher.

48

Pandu did not merely *stand* for the presidency in the traditional idiom – he ran for it. He waged an energetic and aggressive campaign amongst the delegates to the All-India Kaurava Committee. Those who had trudged with him through the villages, those who had stood in his orderly phalanxes of protestors to bear the bamboo blows of the British, those who had marched and sweated and suffered outside the range of the cine-cameras, at last found in him one of their own kind to vote for. The visible leadership of the party had always come from the highly educated, highly articulate stratum of lawyers and men of property, who had had themselves elected by the rest. Even Gangaji, who had broadened the party's support and given it a mass base, had done little to change the pattern at the top, where a handful reigned, derided as 'party bosses' by the British and hailed as 'people's leaders' by the Kauravas. (Observe, Ganapathi, how the cynic's élite is the revolutionary's vanguard. Your tyrant is my inspiring leader; one man's slave is another's disciplined adherent to the cause. So it is that democracy produces oligarchs, and mass is always ruled by class.) In the first election featuring candidates from the ranks, Gangaji's handpicked Godchild was too obviously a stalking-horse to be convincing. The Mahaguru dropped some hints, but did not allow himself to venture too far out on a limb. As the campaign progressed the way of my pale son, Gangaji's 'days of silence' increased. So Pandu, the former princeling, became the first President of the plebeians.

For a brief moment we all inhaled the whiff of revolution. Pandu made a stirring speech of acceptance, promising action in place of inaction. He was careful not to say the slightest word against the Mahaguru; indeed, he expressed his unbounded reverence for the party's mentor and spiritual guide. But the very phrasing of his praise implied that his respect for Gangaji did not extend to his political methods. And his constant exhortations to break new ground were couched in terms that the Mahaguru's (and Dhritarashtra's) admirers could never accept, even if they brought sections of the crowd to their feet, clapping and whistling.

It was exhilarating, Ganapathi, but it could not last. However right Gangaji had been in the strategic sense when he implied that the presidency did not matter, he could not wish away the prominence that the position gave Pandu. The excitement of his supporters at Pandu's election posed a threat that could not be allowed to grow. From the expressions on the faces of the others it was clear to me that Pandu's presidency would destroy either the party or him.

The Mahaguru was never one to tolerate divisiveness. And he said as much, in one of his characteristically long and complex letters, to the new President of the Kaurava Party, who saw the text in the newspapers a day before the letter reached him.

'I couldn't agree more,' Pandu said when he read it. 'Which is why I would appreciate it, Gangaji, if you would urge the recalcitrant elements of the party to rally around their elected President, instead of making such divisive noises.' He wrote that down in more diplomatic terms, posted it to the Mahaguru's ashram and released it to the press a day later.

Gangaji didn't particularly care for this reply. 'The roots of division must be traced deep in the soil,' he declared in an editorial in his weekly newspaper. 'It will not do merely to cut off its branches.'

'Divisiveness and disloyalty do not flourish in the bright heat of the sun,' Pandu said sententiously to a peasant rally the following week. 'They grow in the shade afforded them by the leafy boughs of an old banyan tree.'

The first moves had been made in an elaborate game of chess. But if chess is so much more civilized than boxing – one sport to which Indians have never taken – its attraction for us lies in the careful unfolding of calibrated stratagems, the open warnings to be on guard, the ever-present possibility of an honourable draw: the very things pugilism does not permit. The contest between Gangaji and Pandu, however, admitted of no defensive moves, no side-steps toward stalemate; from the moment it began, a knockout punch was the only objective. It was a match in which, for either side, no draw was possible.

'There is an old Indian proverb,' Gangaji told a blond photographer from *Life* magazine who was taking notes as well as snapshots of the great man. 'It says, "United we stand, divided we fall."'

'But that's an old American proverb,' the blonde blinked.

'Perhaps, but the Indian version is older,' the Mahaguru replied. 'And it goes together with another Indian proverb: always respect your elders.'

When this was published, Pandu was being interviewed by *Time*. 'A young modernist poet of Lucknow expressed the attitudes and aspirations of his generation in a recent couplet, which I shall translate for you,' he informed the journalist. 'It goes roughly like this:

"I do not reject you; rather,
I measure the years I have grown;
I worship your grey hairs, Father,
But – I must comb my own."'

Fallen pawns littered the edges of the board.

'The Indian literary tradition places little value on satirical verse,' Sarah-behn spoke for Gangaji on one of his days of silence. 'So too, the Indian political tradition is one of utmost seriousness and respect for established institutions – provided these institutions are popularly supported and seen as reflective of the people's will.'

Check.

'The best reflection of the people's will,' declared Pandu in a speech to his supporters, 'is the figure at the bottom of the voting tally in a democratic election.'

A daring manoeuvre, Ganapathi. But one which left a flank exposed.

'History teaches us,' the Mahaguru told a prayer meeting, 'that it is always dangerous to mistake the enthusiasm of a select few for the support of the broad mass.'

That was when the castle fell. The letters began arriving at Pandu's home and at Kaurava Party headquarters – letters from party workers and leaders across the country, bearing addresses even Pandu could not recognize. The letters deplored the party's drift from the path of truth and moderation always espoused by Gangaji. Many of them found their way to the newspapers, colonialist and nationalist alike.

'I've been President barely three months,' mused a bewildered Pandu. 'What drift are these people going on about?'

Two letters in the same vein appeared in Gangaji's own paper, without accompanying editorial comment.

'Those who welcome the new directions of the movement,' Pandu declared defiantly to a Kaurava crowd meeting on a famous beachfront, who were more used to slogans than swimming, 'should let their voice be heard amidst the orchestrated clamour of the die-hards. Do you all not give me your loyal support?'

'N-o-o-o-o,' rose the crescendo from the sands.

Shaken, Pandu wrote to his former mentor. 'There appears to be a systematic campaign within the party to undermine me and question my leadership of the party. Such elements seem to derive solace from your silence on the matter, which could even be construed as tantamount to tolerance of anti-party activities. I shall be grateful if you would kindly lend your voice in support of my attempts to move the Kaurava party forward. A statement from you dissociating yourself from some of the excesses of those who claim to be your followers would be greatly welcome.' He sealed the letter and marked it 'confidential'. This time there was no copy for the press.

But now it was the Mahaguru who published the correspondence. 'It is not for me to advise faithful servants of the Kaurava cause against acting according to the dictates of their consciences,' Gangaji stated piously in his printed reply. 'Leaders should never lose sight of the concerns of their followers.'

Pandu's ranks were decimated. He attempted one last gambit at a meeting of the Kaurava Working Committee.

'In view of the variety of attacks on my position and principles within and outside the party of late,' he announced, 'I should like, as party President, to seek a vote of confidence from this committee.' He looked directly at me for a response, staking everything.

I could sense the unease of the others around the table. I felt like Caesar pushing a knife into Brutus. 'Don't do it, my son,' I said, my voice hoarse. 'Do not ask this of us.'

The look of pain that crossed his pale face still haunts me. Not to receive a vote of confidence was as bad as receiving a vote of no-confidence.

The game was over: Pandu had toppled his own crowned head. He resigned.

 49

Gangaji did not make much of his victory. There were no self-congratulatory declarations, no statements to the press. His objective attained, the Mahaguru saw to it that the Untouchable defeated by Pandu was appointed Acting President by the Committee. The following year, this worthy was elected to the post in his own right – unopposed. Today, you have to turn to history books to find his name.

You seem disturbed, my dear Ganapathi. Anxiety creases your brow and narrows your eyes. Never mind, I know what is troubling you. The idea of saintly Gangaji, paragon of Truth, ruthlessly squeezing an insubordinate ward out of power sits ill with you. How could the Mahaguru, you ask yourself, the Great Teacher, a man of vaulting vision and pristine principle, conduct himself like a Tammany Hall politician? You are disappointed.

You should not be, my son. No great man ever achieved greatness by sincerity of purpose alone. If Gangaji believed in Truth, it was *his* Truth he believed in; and by extension the actions he undertook were founded on the same belief. Pandu, for whatever reason, represented a challenge to his unremitting quest for this Truth. 'Trust me, my son,' Ganga had said to him at the start of the Mango March, but Pandu had not followed; and once the agitation was called off, trust had died between the two princes of Hastinapur. The Mahaguru had chosen Dhritarashtra as his heir, and who was to gainsay his choice? Pandu could have accepted it and continued to serve the cause, following the Mahaguru and his own blind brother. He chose the path of dissent instead: the way (as the Mahaguru saw it) of untruth.

The righteous reaction was to eliminate the dissenter. Not by having him hit on the head in the dark by hired thugs, nor by cheating at the elections; Gangaji would never countenance such means to attain his ends. But dharma enjoins firmness in defence of righteousness, Ganapathi. (There is nothing particularly new, or even cynical, about that. Our own traditions prescribe such action – not just in the Machiavellian handbook for royal survivors, the *Arthashastra*, but in our epic political treatise the *Shantiparvan* of my namesake Vyasa.) The moral pressure (and mind you, the Mahaguru never thought of it as anything else) – the moral pressure he placed on Pandu to bring about my pale son's capitulation was merely the political equivalent of the flattened tyres of Raja Salva early in our story. No violence done, no blood spilled – but oh, Ganapathi, what hurt and humiliation, what sadness and suffering can be caused in the defence of Truth!

I cannot bear to think much longer of my pale pained son, Ganapathi. I do not wish to prolong his stumbling saga through the various stages of this narrative. Let us pay the price of chronological inexactitude to follow the rest of his story now, so that I may relinquish this heavy burden of historical memory, strained by the additional weights of paternity and helplessness. Come, Ganapathi: we shall leave the others frozen in their places in time as we unravel Pandu's destiny in the only form that suits its bathos.

50

To tell the tale of Pandu
Will not detain us long;
His slogan was a 'can do!'
And on his lips a song.

Oh, pour some draughts of red wine
Into history's bloody jars;
Learn there's just a thin line
'Twixt tragedy and farce.

When Pandu, hale and hearty
Was declared too sick to lead
He upped and quit the party
To protest the dirty deed.

'Goodbye to all my dear friends –
I say this with a lump –
Your means justify another's ends;
I was pushed, I did not jump.

'Your cause and mine are noble:
To make our people free.
But one fact is simply global:
One can't do this easily.

'To speak, and write, and walk and fast
Will never break our shackles;
But those who still live in the past
Well, they just raise my hackles.

'We've been good too long, we never fail
To play by Britain's rules;
When we break the law, we go to jail
And bow our heads like fools.

'The time has come, I say tonight
To cast aside our veil;
To stand like men, to arm, to fight –
To think of blood, not bail.

'Tonight non-violent Pandu dies!
No more shall I be weak;
From now I toil and exercise
To be strong as Indian teak.

'Away with Tolstoy, Ruskin, Buddha:
Their ideas just make little men littler.
No more "truth-force", only *yuddha* –
It's time to learn from that chap Hitler.'

So saying, our angry hero
Became the country's first Fascist;
Admiring Roma's latest Nero
He practised how to clench his fist.

'Our Aryan brothers, full of go-go
Have revitalized the German nation.
As India's SS, I announce the O O –
Short for Onward Organization.

'Onward, my friends! our cause must march,
In discipline we must never slacken.
Our military shorts we must always starch,
For Britain's foes will need our backing.'

Then Poland fell, and the Nazi Panzer
Overrode Chamberlain's 'Peace with honour'.
'Let's join Hitler's extravaganza –
Britain will soon have our jackboots on her!'

So saying, Pandu bought a ticket
(First-class, appearances must be kept)
To Berlin; 'The rest of you can stick it –
Pandu acts while the Kauravas slept!'

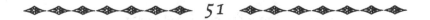 *51*

But when our hero began his trip
(He'd got as far as the aerodrome)
The Brits, who'd briefly lost their grip
Declared war on Berlin, and on Rome.

Standing at the excess-baggage counter
(He'd packed too much for the winter season)
Pandu's plans began to flounder
When he was arrested – for intending treason.

Handcuffed, the O O's home-grown Führer
Was carted off to the central jail;
For him there'd be no judge or juror –
The Raj didn't want him out on bail.

And there a lesser man might languish,
Rotting away behind prison bars;
His mind and spirit prey to anguish
As he mourns his lot, and curses his stars.

But our Pandu was made of sterner stuff!
He was never one to stand and gape.
Now that the Brits were playing rough
He resolved to make his own escape.

Each day he plotted his great jailbreak:
– Shall I saw? or dig? or provoke battle?
Can I get a knife in a chocolate cake?
Or pretend to faint, and flee the hospital?

His plans might well have been doomed to failure
Had the fates not played into his hands;
For a man assigned to be his jailor
Turned out to be one of the O O's fans.

'Honoured to meet you, Panduji, sir,'
He whispered when they were first alone.
'As I shake your hand, I must aver
I think of you as our Saint Joan.

'We men in khaki have had to fret and fume
At the namby-pambiness of the Kaurava Party.
Bharatmata would surely be led to its doom
Were it not for the O O and its *Chakravarti*.'

(The OO, Ganapathi – here I must explain –
Took its terminology from the Indian *dharti*:
Its men-scouts were *sainiks*, its H Q Ujjain,
And its Supreme Leader a Chakravarti.)

'I'm glad to hear that,' Pandu replied,
'We need men of spirit in jobs like yours.
But while I'm locked up, strong men have died
For the nation's illnesses need the OO's cures.'

He fixed his captor with an unblinking stare.
'It's time for you to serve the cause.

I can't stay here when they need me there –
You must help me get out, to fight our wars.'

The jailor shuffled from foot to foot,
Looking determined and chagrined in turn.
'From the top of my cap to the toe of my boot,
I've always merited the wages I earn.

'Now you want me to be untrue to my salt.
That's a difficult decision to make.
You know how I'll be condemned for my fault
And the spiral my career will take.

'I admire you, Chakravarti – this is no homily –
I wish I could help you to flee;
But I must think of my job, my wife and family
And I must do my painful duty.'

'Yes, you must do your duty,' said Pandu quickly,
'But where does your duty lie?
When the nation, oppressed, was never so sickly
Can a true man just stand and sigh?'

He could see his words had won him a pause
In the train of the jailor's thought;
The uniformed patriot guarding the laws
Was torn 'tween the must and the ought.

'And then, of course, there's something, son,
Which you might well have overlooked;
When freedom comes, and the O O's won
The rewards won't be overbooked.

'At that time, then, where'd you rather stand?
Among the heroes of Bharatiya Swaraj?
Or will you be counted with the shameful band
Who betrayed the foes of the Raj?'

'Forgive me, Chakravarti,' the jailor wept,
'For having hesitated at all.
I don't have the keys, but I know where they're kept,
And I can get you over the wall.'

Though the alarm bells were rung, and every port watched,
By eagle-eyed British police,
Pandu evaded them all – *this* flight wasn't botched
For they couldn't spot the wolf through the fleece.

Yes, it was Pandu's disguise that got him past
The checkpost – as Begum Jahan,
The fat, *burqa-ed* wife (ah, I see you're aghast)
Of a fiercely possessive Pathan.

You may disapprove of our hero's disguise
– How could a leader dress like a fool? –
But there's no denying it evaded the eyes
Of policemen right up to Kabul.

From neutral Afghanistan, dressed well again
In battledress from the bazaar
Chakravarti booked himself on to a plane
To Berlin (cabling Adolf to send him a car).

There was a slight hitch, I've got to admit
For our brilliant *swadeshi* Caesar,
Busy ensuring his fatigues would fit,
Had forgotten he needed a visa.

Oh, the terrible ways of bureaucracy!
The airline wouldn't take him on board –
The avatar of Indian autocracy
Explained, shouted, ranted, implored;

But 'Sorry, sir, that's a strict regulation,'
Said the manager (not sorry at all),
'Try the embassy of the German nation –
And would you mind not blocking the hall?'

Defeated, at last, with one more plane missed,
Pandu went off to apply,
'Mr Consul-General – I must insist
I can't wait for Berlin's reply.

'Do you know who I am? Herr Hitler's best friend
In the Indian sub-continent;
From Kanyakumari to London's West End
I'm known for my Fascistic bent.'

(All this, Ganapathi, if truth be told
Was cunning deceit by my son;
He was really no Nazi, my decent cuckold,
But a patriot in search of a gun.

Oh, he'd flirted, it's true, with Fascist ideas,
But those didn't count in the end;

As he'd said to his wives, 'It's simply, my dears,
That my enemy's enemy's my friend.')

'*Sehr gut, mein Herr*,' the Consul said,
'In that case I'll give you your visa.
Good luck — and when you see the nation's head
Don't forget to salute the old geezer.'

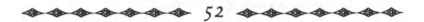 *52*

He remembered; first day, Pandu snapped a salute,
Palm out, in the Nazi style,
It caught the Führer right in the snoot,
And made him see stars for a while.

'Heil — ouch! Oh, hell,' Chakravarti said,
As the Führer winced in pain,
'I'm sorry — I wish I were dead —'
'You will be, if this happens again.'

An inauspicious start! — but that's how it was
For our fighter in exile throughout;
His valiant efforts to work for the cause
Were hamstrung within and without.

'Radio broadcasts — that's what you can do,'
Said the Germans, when he asked for tanks;
So instead of invading, our disappointed Pandu
Made speeches to the other ranks.

Every Sunday and Thursday, on *Deutsche Welle*,
Chakravarti broadcast to the East;
But his stirring exhortations to march on Delhi
Came through like the yelps of a beast.

'What's this?' men would say, twiddling knobs on their sets,
As an awful squawk assaulted their ears,
And whine followed squeal like the screech of ten jets,
All braking while changing their gears.

'Can't make out a word!' — 'Is it a new song?'
'An announcement from Washington DC?'

'No, I think it's a girl, and she's speaking Bong! –
Let's get back to good old BBC.'

So Pandu's prating received a low rating –
His oration could hardly be heard;
And the long months of waiting led him to start hating
His exile – so futile, absurd.

Then came the break! Hitler's Nippy allies –
The Japanese in their Far Eastern sphere –
Hacking through jungles, raining death from the skies
Defeated Blimps quaking with fear.

So much, my friends, for the imperial myth –
Of ruling invincibly;
The claim that Britannia's kin and kith
Were supreme militarily.

(In fact, Ganapathi, if truth be told
The bloody 'white man's burden'
Was what our coolies – cudgelled, cajoled –
Bore on their heads and cursed in.)

But when the Japs, those sturdy chaps
Gave the pinkskins their come-uppance,
Hope dawned in Indian hearts and laps
That we too could win Independence.

For the supremacist claims of colonial toasts
Stood revealed as shabby deceits:
Vainglorious boasts from undefended posts
Mocking disgraceful retreats.

'Hooray!' said Chakravarti, 'Let's fight! Let's go!
Let's salute the rising sun!
With the help of Japan and the noble OO
Our battle will be won.'

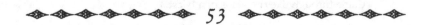 53

In due course ('after uneventful trip')
He arrived at the scene of his war
The ex-British playground, now out of their grip –
The island of Singapore.

'Welcome, Chaklavalti,' a young Chinese said,
'I'm your intehpleteh tonight;'
A Japanese general then bowed deep his head:
'Hurro, have you had a good fright?'

'Yes, thank you, sir!' Pandu replied
(As the Chinese had translated the greeting)
'I'm extremely glad to be on your side –
Together we'll give them a beating.'

'Together?' harrumphed his little host.
'I'm not sure I quite understand.
The Brits here have arready given up the ghost –
And we noticed no Indians at hand.

'In fact,' he went on, warming to his theme,
'The onry Indians we saw
Were fighting on their side – that's not a dream:
Our prison camps have Indians garore.'

'Of course,' Pandu hastened, 'but what could we do?
Our boys were enslaved in their ranks.
Now they're certainly chastened, like bears in a zoo
And dissension flows in their flanks.

'Just let me at them, just give me some time,
And I'll deliver an army to you;
The best Indian soldiers, fighters sublime
Lined up for Tojo to view.

'I'll fire them with freedom and nationalist pride
Urge them to enlist in our cause;
Tell them it's more easy with Japan on our side
To kick the oppressor outdoors.'

'Orright,' said the Jap, ('All light,' said the chap),
'We'll give you the access you want;
An I D card, cap, a jeep and a map,
And permission to embark on this jaunt.'

So Pandu set out, in full battledress,
His topee at a jaunty angle;
From exercise ground to officers' mess
The spurs on his booties would jangle.

'*Namaskar! Sieg Heil!* Now harken to me –
All you wretched P-O double-yous:
I offer the chance to save your *janmabhoomi*
And pay Bharatmata her dues.

'What kind of life is this? Just sitting around
And waiting for your next dish of gruel –
When you could instead be out of this ground
And fighting the nationalist duel.

'Or would you much rather sit and break rocks for the Japs
Doing prisoners' work till you die?
Dig trenches, latrines, look for landmines and traps,
Build a bridge on the nice River Kwai?'

'But our oaths? Our careers? We must be true to our salt,'
Ventured one or two men in doubt.
'If the Brits couldn't save you, it's hardly your fault,'
Said my son: 'What's an oath in a rout?'

Ah, he struck a chord there, my pale son Pandu!
He knew what would appeal to the men;
If you've any doubt of what a golden tongue can do,
Consider his triumph again.

They flocked to him in the proverbial droves,
Proclaiming their desire to enlist;
Attracted, perhaps, by the fishes and loaves
But also by Pandu's raised fist.

His message to them was loud, it was clear,
To soldiers in prison immersed:
'If you fight for the freedom of your nation so dear
You'll get your own freedom first.'

Platoons, companies, divisions were raised
Of the O O's Swatantra Sena;
In their political harangues Hirohito was praised
But Chakravarti was the overall gainer.

How he strutted, my son, how proud he became!
You'd think he'd just won a battle.
When in fact (as the Brits would snidely claim)
His men just hung around like cattle.

Oh, they trained, and they drilled, and they marched in parade,
Their uniforms were ironed every day,

But the ex-POWs of Pandu's brigade
On the war-front, made little headway.

The Japanese were pleased as the numbers increased
– It made very good propaganda –
But when it came to the crunch, politeness ceased,
And they spoke with ruthless candour:

'Trust traitors? Oh, we know what you'll say,
"They're not traitors, but patriots and heroes" –
'But if the oath they had sworn can be broken today,
Can't they just as easiry break tomorrow's?

'We don't blame them at all, for swallowing their pride –
Our prison camps aren't much fun;
They make good PR, but we must set them aside
When there's serious soldiering to be done.'

'So I'll wait,' swore Pandu, 'what the hell!
My forces will just bide their time;
And though the Japs are now doing well
Soon they'll need us, as reason needs rhyme.'

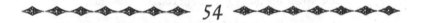 *54*

But while waiting, my son was determined
Not to suffer the grim solitude
That in Berlin (with door locked, and food tinned)
He had borne with such fortitude.

So he smuggled a message to Madri
Through a Japanese network of spies:
'Your husband needs you very badry –
Could you come? Discretion'd be wise.'

Excited and anxious, our princess
Wipes a tear of farewell from her eye;
'Take care of my thonth' (Kunti winces)
'I mutht join my *patideva* – goodbye.'

After a journey both risky and torrid
Full of dangers (too many to relate)
Madri arrived – 'Oh dahling, 'twath horrid!' –
In Singapore, to seal Pandu's fate.

'Overwhelmed' would be an understatement
To describe my son's attitude;
He beamed and glowed *sans* abatement
In marital beatitude.

'Now all's well,' he proclaimed to his helpmeet,
'I can bear any weight, any wait;
My companion is here to help beat
All ennui, all frustration, all hate.'

But to ease Japanese suspicions
About his commitment to the cause,
And to reaffirm his ambitions,
Pandu enrolled her in the wars.

'Captain Madri! How you'll impress the Japs
In your battledress of khaki!
A little tight around the chest, perhaps –
But you'll shine in the General's marquee!'

And indeed she looked a sight to behold
In the fatigues of the Swatantra Sena;
The cut of her shirt was not itself bold
But when she moved, no cloth could restrain her.

For years, the thought of sexual functions
Pandu had instantly banished;
As he rigorously heeded the doctor's injunctions
All fleshly temptation had vanished.

But the iron restraint of *satyagrahi* life
Had grown flaccid in his forced exile
And the new proximity of his bosomy wife
Woke passions dormant the while.

For weeks Pandu continued to resist
As Madri stirred life in his loins;
But despite meditation, he could not desist
From contemplating a union of groins.

'Oh fatal flaw! I can't commit such a sin –
What is happening to my concentration?
The British offensive is about to begin –
And I think of the wrong kind of penetration!'

For yes, Ganapathi, the fortunes of war
Had turned; now the Japs bore the brunt:

Instead of 'Attack India', 'Defend Singapore'
Became Japan's battle-cry at the front.

At last Pandu's men were given the chance
To fight – but the going got rough,
And his war-weary *sainiks*, unable to advance,
Found Pandu's slogans no longer enough.

Oh, when it came to fighting the Brits
Or traversing the jungle terrain
Some *sainiks* were valiant, at least in bits
With many heroes who battled in vain.

But few soldiers can shoot at their brothers-in-arms
And Pandu's were also thus hindered;
Under fire, forgetting his eloquent charms
They fled, or simply surrendered.

Disgraced, with defeat looming real and large,
The Japs ordered Pandu to withdraw;
In a rickety plane (he was offered that or a barge)
He left the island of Singapore.

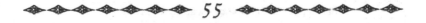 55

As the aircraft rose with a shudder
Into the darkened tropical sky
And the pilot pushed the rudder
On a course for safe Shanghai –

Pandu looked down into the failure
Of the plans he'd left behind;
'I couldn't have been sillier,'
Pandu sighed. His face was lined;

There were crow's-feet at the corners
Of his tired and bloodshot eyes,
And his pale face was like a mourner's
(Sagging with grief, you realize).

'I had such hopes, my dearest one
Of rising to the fore;
With the swastika, and the rising sun
I thought we'd win the war.

'I'd hoped then to have proved my point
To the Brits and Kauravas too;
To Gangaji, who might then anoint
Me his heir and Number Two.

'But had he not, it wouldn't have mattered
What the non-violent ones thought;
For the people, once the Brits were battered
Would have crowned me, like as not.

'Instead, Madri, my hopes lie shattered
In the dust under British boots;
The man who fought as the Kauravas nattered
Now flees — and who cares two hoots?

'As I look at you, my heart fills with sorrow
At the fate that awaits you too:
There is no hope of a bright tomorrow
For the wife of brave Pandu.

'If the Brits win, as now seems probable,
There'll be nowhere for us to hide:
Their cops are smart, their judges not bribable,
I'll be arrested and summarily tried.

'There's not much hope of escaping the rope
For inciting the men to mutiny;
I wish I believed you'd be able to cope
With the shame — and the ignominy.'

'Don't talk like that!' A teardrop shone
On Madri's glistening cheek;
'Oh, thweetheart, I love you, the thought of you gone
Maketh me feel empty and weak.

'My darlingeth Pandu, let me thay to you
— I thwear thith upon Vithnu and Thiv —
If anything happenth to my deareth Pandu
I thimply don't want to live.

'My husband, you gave me thuch wonderful joy
By calling *me* to your thide in your need;
Do you think I'm some thameleth Helen of Troy
To trot off on another man'th thteed?

'No! Pandu my lord, by your thide I'll thtay
Through thick and thin, better and worthe;

We'll fathe the Raj, fight on night and day –
And I'll help you, for whatever that'th worth.'

'Oh Madri!' and here our Pandu was moved
By the sincerity of her love,
If anything, her declarations proved
She was a gift from the heavens above.

'Oh, Madri!' He took her in his arms
And kissed her long and wetly,
Till, attritioned by her charms,
His will collapsed completely.

'No – Pandu – don't!' his loved one cried,
As his hands explored her buttons;
'Remember the doctor – when you nearly died –
Let'th kith, but not be gluttonth!'

'Twas of no avail, he was possessed
By a need he could not define;
After years of restraint, now obsessed
To unite with his concubine.

'I want you!' his hiss was urgent
As he peeled off layers of clothes;
In the cold seat, his passion emergent
Repulsed his wife's feeble 'No's.

Poor Madri! Denial was not in her nature,
'No' was not a word she liked to speak;
Indeed (at the risk of caricature)
Her flesh was willing, and her spirit weak.

And Pandu was in no mood to be denied;
His hands moved with a probing persistence.
He caressed her: 'I want you!' he cried,
'You're the only joy left in my existence!'

In love and heat, Madri conceded defeat,
And yielded to her husband's great ardour.
Soon, despite her fears and the tilt of the seat,
She was gasping, 'Oh, yeth! Harder! Harder!'

'Oh, yes!' he breathed back in pneumatic bliss.
'Onward! That's my immortal credo!'
But then his lips, after a pulsating kiss,
Turned blue, and exhaled a croaking 'O . . . O . . .'

Tracers exploded outside in the sky
Shooting incandescent streamers of light
Across the window where our lovers lie
Entwined 'tween the silence and night.

'Thank you,' Madri sighed in orgasmic relief,
'You were wonderful — wath it good for you, too?'
Then, looking at him, almost beyond belief:
'P. . . Pandu! What hath happened to you?

'Why are you tho limp? Why lie you tho thtill?
My huthband, my lord, king of the O O?
Pleathe rithe — pleathe thmile — oh tell me you will —
Oh my God! You're not . . .! Oh . . .! Oh no . . .!'

She screamed; and it was as if her heart-wrenching cry
Had carried her spirit to where his had flown:
Soaring up and across the illuminated sky
To its celestial home, where no one is alone.

For in that terrible cry of desolation
Was embodied a plea no god could deny;
Her intense refusal to accept her isolation
Carried its message to the forces on high.

Two powerful beams of terrestrial light
Criss-crossed on the wings of Pandu's Zero;
Revealing to Madri a last vivid sight
On her breast, the beatific head of her hero.

Then she knew; and she smiled, in the stillness that followed.
The shell that was coming made scarcely a ripple.
She lifted his head, kissed him, slightly swallowed;
Then lowered him gently, his mouth to her nipple.

When the shell hit she could have sworn she felt
A life-seeking tug at her soft swollen breast;
A split-second, perhaps, and then came a pelt
Of death-dealing shrapnel that tore open her chest.

For another split second the plane hung on there
Spotlit in the beams of the gunners below;
Then it burst into a flaming ball in the air
Burning crimson, consuming my son — and widow.

As Pandu plummeted to the fiery fate
That all Hindus know as we leave this world,

Madri, his devoted (though second) mate
Kept the proud banner of Sati unfurled:

She attained eternity – an all-too-rare case –
In the glorious blaze of a purifying fire,
Finding, in the flames of the plane, her place
On her husband's aluminium funeral pyre.

That must have made Pandu happy, Ganapathi. With all his deep delving into the scriptures, his theological sanctions for procreative cuckoldry, he must have savoured the satisfaction of going like that – burning with his dutiful wife in fulfilment of the classic ideals of marital love. It must have gladdened his atrophied heart.

When the news reached us here, it affected all of us deeply, even Dhritarashtra, whose place at the head of his generation it made more secure. My blind son issued a touching little statement about his 'immeasurable sadness' and the 'incalculable loss to the grieving nation'. He pledged to 'keep the flame of my brother Pandu's deep-seated patriotism aglow'. Ah, Dhritarashtra, for ever those visual metaphors.

And what of Gangaji? The Mahaguru was moved enough to sit in silence and spin for hours, talking to nobody, immersed in reflection. He presented the cloth that emerged from that session to Pandu's surviving widow, Kunti. But it was practically unusable – the woof was all warped, or was it that the weft was not right? – which showed that for once Gangaji's mind had not been on what he was doing. Pandu's loss diminished us all.

THE TENTH BOOK:

DARKNESS AT DAWN

56

But there was no time to grieve. We all had more vital business at hand. Neither the nation nor the party had been standing still during Pandu's years of exile. Now it was the moment to reap the bitter harvest that had been sown since our digression began. In other words, Ganapathi, this is flashback time.

We had left the others frozen in their places when we embarked upon Pandu's story – frozen in the aftermath of his resignation from the Kaurava presidency. Let us examine this curious tableau again. There is the Mahaguru, studiously bent over his spinning wheel, assiduous journalists at his feet; Dhritarashtra, white stick held slightly aloft, fist clenching its knob with index finger pointing towards Delhi or destiny or both; Karna, the half-moon throbbing on his forehead, declaiming in a three-piece suit to a group of Muslim notables in stuffed armchairs; the five Pandava youths, agilely imbibing their lessons from their bearded preceptor; and Duryodhani, sitting on the ground at the foot of the darkened bedside of her mother Gandhari the Grim, determinedly arranging her *khadi*-clad dolls in the shadows as the woman in the blindfold sinks inexorably into another world.

'What are you doing, Priya Duryodhani?'

'I am playing with my dolls, Mother.'

'What – what are you playing with them, my child?'

'I am playing family, Mother. This doll is all tied up. It is going to jail. This doll is not feeling well. It is lying down. This other doll is left to fight the nasty British all by herself. She is strong and brave and she knows she is all alone, she will always be alone, but she will win in the end . . .'

No, Ganapathi, let us leave them there and unfreeze another section of the tableau. The five Pandavas and Drona.

But wait! There are *six* boys surrounding the saffron-clad sage. Yes, the five sons of Pandu have been joined by Ashwathaman, Drona's son. They are together as knowledge is poured into them like milk and honey: the science of history and the mysteries of science; physics and the traditional martial arts;

geography and geometry; ethics and arithmetic; the *vedas*; classical music and folk dance; rhetoric and oratory. And then, Drona's own 'special skills'.

These are special indeed, these skills. Drona has given the lads a glimpse of his abilities by his deft removal of their ball from the well. But there is so much more: unerring accuracy with ropes, strings, catapults, bows; the ability to find targets with stones, arrows, and (in due course) bullets; the preparation of cocktails to which Molotov would not have been ashamed to lend his name; the uncanny knack of blocking roads, starting avalanches, demolishing bridges, just by knowing where to place a small amount of explosive. Not all of this is in the course-description that Gangaji has approved for his ward's children; but, 'There are many kinds of nationalism,' says Jayaprakash Drona, 'and I believe you must be well-versed in all of them.'

Some, perhaps, better versed than others? As the special skills sessions increase in range and complexity, the time and individual attention Drona is able to devote to each student becomes crucial to their speed and skill. Ashwathaman, who sleeps in his father's room, gets extra lessons: ciphers and codes, powerful yogic *asanas*, breathing exercises. Arjun, catching on, knocks one night on his teacher's door. 'Dronaji, may I too sleep at your feet, that I may learn better from you at all times?' The sage, pleased at his student's devotion, accedes to the request. Arjun soon becomes as proficient as Ashwathaman.

And what proficiency! Ganapathi, you will not believe it when I tell you of the range and subtlety of Drona's training, from dialectics to diuretics. Of his methods, by which what was taught was only as important as how it was taught. Of his convictions, whose singular angularities would be retained in different ways by each of his charges.

Take, for instance, the time he summoned his wards and pointed out a picture on the wall, one he had torn from a magazine, an ordinary picture of a rather porcine English politician.

'Imagine you are all members of an élite group of hardened revolutionaries,' he told them. 'Your target is that man.' He jabbed his finger towards the florid face looking smugly down upon them from the wall. 'You each have your favourite weapon at hand – gun, grenade, rock, bow and arrow, it doesn't matter. Your mission is to get him. Is that clear?'

They chorused their comprehension.

'Step forward, Yudhishtir,' Drona declared. 'Take up your weapon. Look at your target. What do you see?'

'I see my target,' Yudhishtir replied.

'Is that all you see?'

'I see an imperialist political figure,' Yudhishtir replied, trying to guess what was required of him. 'Born thirtieth of November 1874. Prominent family. President of the Board of Trade at thirty-four, Home Secretary at thirty-six, First Lord of the Admiralty, Colonial Secretary, Chancellor of the Exchequer . . .'

'Go back to your place, Yudhishtir,' Drona interjected, expressionless. 'Nakul, you. What do you see?'

'An overweight, over-the-hill and overrated politician, a teller of bad after-dinner jokes, a gasbag . . .'

'Bhim?'

'A fat man who seems to enjoy a good cigar. But I'll kill him if you tell me to.'

'Sahadev?'

'A representative of the worst of British colonialism, a die-hard enemy of our people, an oppressor who conceals his racialist tyranny beneath a cloud of rhetoric about upholding freedom — the freedom of those with his colour of skin.'

'Ashwathaman? Do you see all this too?'

'Certainly, my father. And more.'

'And Arjun? What about you, Arjun?'

Arjun stepped forward, his eyes narrowing upon the picture. 'I see my target,' he said.

'What else?'

'Nothing else. My mission is to hit this target. I see nothing else.'

'His background? His biography? His position?'

'I need know none of that. I see my target. I see his head. Nothing else matters.'

Drona sighed audibly. 'Take aim, then, Arjun. Shoot.'

Arjun aimed his imaginary weapon, his clear eyes never wavering from his target, and a gust of wind burst into the room, ripping the picture off the wall, sending it flying in a scudding spiral into Drona's hands.

'I shall make you,' Drona breathed, 'the finest Indian of them all.'

But there is one sour note. After one set of school examinations Arjun comes back with thunderclouds on his brow. He has come first; but for all his private tuition he is only joint first. And the child who has tied with him is from a lowly government school.

'His name is Ekalavya,' Arjun announces.

'Ekalavya? But that is the son of one of the maidservants in the palace!' Bhim, who knows all the maidservants, exclaims.

The twins rush off to investigate, and return with a dark, dust-smeared little boy in a frayed shirt. He bends to touch Drona's feet.

'Stood first, eh? And who taught you what you know?'

'Why, you – sir.'

'Me? You are not one of my students, boy.'

'Sir . . . I stood, sir, outside the door, while you were teaching the others. And I listened, sir.'

'An eavesdropper, eh, boy? And a free-loader. You know what a free-loader is, boy?'

'Yes, sir. It's . . . it's American, sir. Someone who doesn't pay for what he gets. I'm . . . very sorry, sir.'

'That's right, boy. And that's what you are. A free-loader. You have been learning from my lessons, and you haven't paid my fee.'

'Your . . . your fee, sir? I'll gladly pay what I can.'

'What you can, boy? And how much is that, I pray?'

'Sir, not very much, sir. My mother is a maidservant here.'

'A maidservant's son presumes to call himself my pupil? Very well, I shall name my fee. Do you promise to pay it?'

'If I can, sir, of course,' says the boy, still looking down at Drona's rough calloused feet and horny nails.

'No conditions, boy. It is a fee you can pay. Will you promise to pay it?'

The boy's voice is soft and trembly under the intimidating line of questioning. 'Of course, sir,' he whispers. Yudhishtir looks troubled, but says nothing.

'Good. My fee, Ekalavya, is the thumb of your right hand.'

There is a collective gasp from the twins and Bhim. Yudhishtir starts forward, then stops, restrained by the hand of a frowning Ashwathaman. Only Arjun looks supremely untroubled, even at peace.

'The . . . the . . . th . . . thumb of my *hand*, sir?' asks the bewildered boy. 'I . . . I don't understand.'

'Don't understand?' Drona bellows. 'You come first in class, boy, and you don't understand? You promised me my fee, if you can pay it. And I want the thumb of your right hand.'

'B . . . but without my th . . . thumb, sir, I won't be able to write again!' The boy looks despairingly around the room, and finally at Drona, who stands impassively, his arms folded across his chest. 'Oh, pl . . . please, sir, not that! Ask me for anything else!' The tears smart at his eyes, but he fights them back. 'Pl . . . please sir, what have I done to deserve this punishment?'

'You know perfectly well what you have done. You have intruded where you do not belong. And this is no punishment – it is my fee.'

The boy throws himself at Drona's feet. 'Please, revered teacher, please forgive me,' he blurts out. 'If I do not do well and make a success of my studies, who will look after my poor mother when she becomes too old to work? Please do not demand this of me.'

Drona looks down at the boy sprawled before him. 'That is no concern of mine,' he says brutally. 'Will you pay my fee?'

The boy looks disbelievingly up at him, then slowly raises himself from the floor. He stands, and for the first time he is looking the sage in the eye.

'I cannot pay it,' he says.

'Cannot pay it? You call yourself my pupil, and dare to refuse me my fee?'

The boy does not shift his gaze. 'Yes,' he affirms.

Drona advances upon him, bringing his face so close to the boy's that the hairs of his beard graze Ekalavya's nose. 'If you do not pay your guru the fee he seeks, you are unworthy of what he has taught you,' he snarls, his spittle flecking the boy's forehead.

Ekalavya stands his ground, but swallows, his dark face burning darker in his dismay. 'I . . I'm sorry, sir, but I cannot destroy my life and my mother's to pay your fee,' he says faintly but firmly.

'Get out!' Drona barks. 'Get out, worthless brat! And if I catch you anywhere near my classes again, I shall exact my fee myself!'

The boy steps back, looks wildly around him, and trips hastily out of the room. Drona's uproarious laughter follows him mockingly down the stairs.

Later, when the class resumes, Yudhishtir raises his hand. 'If the boy had readily agreed to the fee you asked of him, guruji, would you have taken it?'

Drona laughs shortly, waving the question away. 'Study,' he says, 'study your epics, young man.'

Next time, Arjun stands first in the examinations — alone.

I see you are troubled, Ganapathi. I have been inflicting too many moral dilemmas on you of late, haven't I? But there is no point turning your nose into a question-mark, Ganapathi; I am not going to resolve all your problems for you. Was Drona playing an elaborate game that none of the others was sophisticated enough to understand, or was he just doing to poor Ekalavya what Heaslop had done to him? Had the poor boy been less of a literalist and gladly stuck out his thumb as a gesture of devotion and subservience, would Drona have hacked it off with a knife or laughingly invited the lad to join his class? I do not know, Ganapathi, and the ashes of the only man who does have long since flowed down the Ganges into the sea.

 *57*

But enough of such speculation; we have left too many of our dramatis personae inconveniently frozen in various parts of our tableau. There is Karna,

for instance, declaiming to his party elders; let us approach him and hear what
he is saying.

'Gentlemen, the facts are plain. We entered these elections – the first under
the new Government of India Act – as the self-proclaimed spokesmen of
India's Muslims. We contested in reserved constituencies, putting up Muslim
candidates for seats only Muslims could vote for. And yet, at the end of the
day, when the votes were counted, we discovered that Kaurava Muslims –
followers of the underclad Mahaguru – have won more Muslim seats than we
have. It is galling, but it is reality, and we must accept it.

'The question obviously arises, what next? There are those amongst us
who feel that all we can do is to sulk in our tents. I am not able to prescribe
such a bitter pill myself. We contested the elections in search of power, and
power is what we must continue to seek if we are to justify our existence as a
party. There are many routes to power; in my view we must first attempt the
most obvious one. We must ask to join the Kauravas in a coalition government
– at least in the one province where we have done well enough to stake a
claim to doing so.'

The Muslim grandees around him nod, some vigorously, some with
evident scepticism. Let the lights dim on their bobbing hennaed heads,
Ganapathi, and let us turn the spot, and our attention, to our Kaurava friends
who, too, have emerged from our tableau and are conversing animatedly.

'But why should we?' The voice is Dhritarashtra's. 'We have an absolute
majority in the Northern Province ourselves – we don't need a coalition with
anybody, let alone Karna's puffed-up little group of bigoted nobodies.'

'Tactically,' says a quiet voice, 'and forgive me for speaking, gentlemen,
since I do not, indeed, cannot belong to your party' – it is, of course, Vidur
the civil servant – 'it would be a wise step. The British would be taken aback
by a coalition of the two strongest opposing political forces in the country.'
And then he spoils his argument with bureaucratic propriety by adding: 'But
you, of course, have a political choice to make.'

'Precisely,' says the mellifluous Mohammed Rafi, a Northern Province
Kaurava – and a Muslim whose aristocratic pedigree is as impeccable as his
exquisitely tailored sherwani. 'We have a political choice to make, and with all
respect to Vidur-bhai, he cannot be expected to see things the same way. If
we enter into a coalition with the Muslim Group, what are Kaurava Muslims
like myself going to say to our supporters when they ask us to explain our
supping with the Shaitaan we have just been denouncing? We have declared
that the Kaurava Party is the only true national party, that we represent all
groups and interests, including naturally those of Muslims. Having been
elected on the strength of those beliefs, how can you ask us to cede

ministerial portfolios that Kaurava Muslims might have expected, to the very people who allege we do not represent Muslims? If the Kaurava Party dispenses with *our* claims so lightly for mere tactical considerations, it will only confirm the Muslim Group argument that we are stooges of the Hindus, with no real power of our own in the party. No, I agree with Dhritarashtra. Let us put principles before tactics, my friends.'

This is probably news to Dhritarashtra, whose argument has not been noticeably long on principle, but he assents vigorously. The discussion continues, and it is clear that Mohammed Rafi has made a telling point. 'We must not,' an elder statesman concedes, 'win the partnership of Karna's Group and lose the faith of our own Muslim comrades.'

'Hear, hear,' murmur some; 'Well said, V. V.,' echo others.

At last Gangaji ends the debate. 'There will be no coalition,' he announces in a voice wearied by conciliation.

The spotlight shifts, for the curtain-ringer.

'The bastards!' Karna's voice itself seems to wear gloves, but there is no mistaking the knuckledusters underneath. 'Well, gentlemen, that is that, then. I said to you there are other routes to the acquisition of power: we shall now proceed to carve out a few of them. As far as the Kauravas are concerned, gentlemen, it is war.'

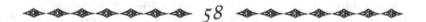 *58*

War – Pandu's war – the successor to the 'war to end all wars' – erupted in Europe, and as German bombs exploded over Poland, the blast buffeted us in India.

'Well, what's the form, then, Sir Richard?' asked the Viceroy at his daily meeting with his cherubic Principal Private Secretary. 'Don the glad rags and deliver a proclamation from the steps of the viceregal palace, or does the rule-book prescribe something different?'

'We don't have many precedents for a declaration of war, Your Excellency,' his aide admitted. 'I could have one of our chaps look it up, but I imagine you can pretty much make up the drill as you go along.'

'What did we do the last time?' the Viceroy asked, idly toying with a thirteenth-century miniature Siva lingam that served as a paperweight.

'The last time? Do you mean the fifth Afghan war, or the seventeenth campaign against the Waziris? I think we went in rather less for protocol than for powder in those engagements. In the British Indian tradition, when you wanted to declare war you tended to do it with a cannon. Unless, of course, you weren't planning a war at all but a sort of extended picnic, like Sir Francis Younghusband, who went out one morning with five horses and a Christmas hamper and came back having annexed Tibet. It was rather embarrassing at the time, because nobody really *wanted* Tibet, but Sir Francis shrugged and explained that when he rode into Lhasa the local warlords got up and surrendered and he had no choice but to accept their tribute. He'd really intended just to see the tourist spots and to get a few good pictures of the Potala Palace, but one of his rifles went off accidentally and when he then saw all the notables on their knees cowering he couldn't really disappoint them by *not* conquering them. I think his punishment for taking Tibet was to have to work out what to do with the place. But to return to your question, I'm afraid there was no formal declaration of war there either, Your Excellency.'

'Sir Richard,' the Viceroy smiled amiably, his hand straying from the lingam to a jewel-encrusted dagger from Maharaja Ranjit Singh's collection that was now used to slit open confidential envelopes, rather than throats, 'I don't mean any of those wars, of course. The last one in Europe we were mixed up in. The Great War.'

'Ah.' The Principal Private Secretary reflected briefly. 'I think we heard about that one in India a few weeks after it had started in the old continent. And by then there wasn't much point in a formal declaration. Of course, the Great War never touched this part of the world very greatly. Except for all the Indian soldiers we sent off to fight in France and Mesopotamia.'

'This one may, Sir Richard. Touch this part of the world, I mean. The Japanese are in alliance with the Germans and may attack our possessions in the Far East. India is still a long way from their forces, but distances in today's world mean a good deal less than they did twenty-five years ago. No, this time, when war is declared in India, it could really mean something for this country and her people. India may have to fight to preserve her freedom.'

'I'm not sure all our Kaurava friends will see it quite like that.' Sir Richard smiled humourlessly. 'Mr Datta and his *khadi*-clad companions seem to think that's what they're doing already – with us on the wrong side of the argument.'

'Quite.' The Viceroy nodded. 'But I think they'd draw a distinction between the two kinds of fight. The Mahaguru and his friends are "fighting" – if that's the word for their non-violent agitations – for, in the celebrated phrase, the rights of Englishmen. It's democracy they want. I hardly think they'll consider the Nazis a model of *swaraj*, except for the fringe in the Onward Organization, and we can lock that bunch up soon enough. Don't forget that Ganga Datta was on our side the last time round, quite actively in fact – the Ambulance Association in Hastinapur, was it not?'

'I haven't forgotten, Your Excellency.' Sir Richard, who tended to think of Hastinapur as a personal heirloom, harrumphed. 'But a lot of water, and some blood, has flowed under the bridge since those days. I've made something of a special study of Mr Ganga Datta over the years, and I'm not convinced for a minute by his pontifical pacifism. Today the sainted Mahaguru is just as opposed to British interests as his fellow vegetarian in Berlin.'

The Viceroy put down the dagger and gave his seniormost advisor a sharp look. 'I do believe your prejudices are showing, Sir Richard,' he said mildly. 'India's non-violent saint-statesman lending moral support to Germany's jackbooted stormtroopers? No, I think Ganga Datta and most of the Kauravas, certainly Dhritarashtra and his socialist followers, will be happy enough to go along with a declaration of war on Nazi Germany. They've been quite critical of the Nazis in their public pronouncements on international affairs. The point is, how do we go about it? It's easy enough to declare war, but do we, ah, consult them first, and in what manner? There were no elected Indian ministries to think about at the time of the last war. Now there are.'

'I don't see how it's any of their business,' Sir Richard, defeated, scowled.

'Come, come, Sir Richard. We propose to declare war on behalf of India and we don't think it's the business of the Indian leaders we have?'

'Precisely, sir.' Sir Richard's eyes glowed redly above his pink cheeks. 'You, the Viceroy of India, will be declaring war on behalf of His Majesty the King-Emperor, whose representative you are in this country, upon those who are his enemies. *India* only comes into the picture at all because it is one of the King-Emperor's possessions. It has no independent quarrel with Herr Hitler and his friends. I know you don't agree with my view that Ganga Datta and his ilk would support Attila the Hun if it would help drive the Raj out of Delhi, but leaving the political reliability of the Indians aside, the point is that the only reason for India to be at war with Germany is that she is ruled by Britain. *Britain* is at war with Germany. *British India* must follow suit. The Indians governing their provinces – under the supervision, in any case, of British Governors appointed by the Crown – have nothing to do with it at all. Defence isn't even their business; it's ours.' He raised an eyebrow at his sovereign's representative. '*Quod erat demonstrandum*, Your Excellency.'

'*Nec scire fas est omnia*,' the Viceroy riposted. 'None the less why not consult them anyway? It should buck up that po-faced lot the Kauravas have in office.'

'All the more reason not to, sir.' The Principal Private Secretary was emphatic. 'They're insufferable enough as it is. Why should we give them the additional satisfaction of being consulted, when it is our nation that is under attack, our homes under threat, our armies and aircraft under fire? Personally, sir, I'd think it humiliating to have to seek the consent of the loincloth brigade before we placed His Majesty's subjects here on a war-footing. In my view, it's neither politically appropriate nor constitutionally necessary.'

'Perhaps you've got a point there,' the Viceroy conceded, rubbing a reflective chin.

'With respect, indeed, sir. And think what propaganda the Kauravas would make of it. The all-powerful Viceroy has to ask them before he can declare war on another European state! It would be disastrous for our credibility with the man-in-the-street, Your Excellency.'

'Hmm. I think you may be right there, Sir Richard. It's just that I don't think they'll take it very well. And the last thing I need here at the beginning of a war is a new set of political convulsions on my hands.'

'Don't worry about a thing, sir. As Virgil put it, *"Experto credite".'*

'I hope you're right, Sir Richard. As Horace reminds us, *"Nescit vox missa reverti".'*

Horace was, of course, right — words once published cannot be taken back. When the declaration of war was made without the slightest semblance of consultation with the elected Kaurava ministries in the states, the Mahaguru's followers resigned their offices *en bloc.* An appointed official had no moral authority, they announced, to declare war on behalf of a nation whose elected representatives had not been consulted. The Kaurava Party, Dhritarashtra added, might conceivably have endorsed a request to join the Viceroy in a declaration of war, not so much out of a desire to come to Britain's aid in her hour of peril, but simply because of the nationalist movement's dislike of international Fascism. But the callous disregard by the colonial authorities of the legitimacy of the democratic process — a process, Dhritarashtra pointed out, by which Britain pretended to set such great store and in whose defence it was supposedly fighting — had made such an endorsement impossible. The Kaurava Party could not possibly remain in office in these circumstances, and it would urge all Indians not to cooperate with the war effort.

Vidur tried to advise his compatriots and relatives against such precipitate action. 'Make your point by all means, but for God's sake don't resign,' he pleaded with his sightless half-brother.

'You do not understand politics, Vidur,' Dhritarashtra told him.

'Perhaps not, but I understand administration,' my youngest son responded. 'And one of the first rules of administration is, do not give up your seat until you know how much standing-room there is.'

But they did not listen to him, Ganapathi. A sheaf of identical resignation letters were wired to Delhi. As always, there was one governmental institution that never failed to do well out of a political crisis: the Post Office.

There were thunderclouds on the Viceroy's brow the next morning, but Sir Richard persisted in seeing the silver lining.

'Jolly good thing, this, if you'll pardon me, Your Excellency,' he beamed, his jowls quivering with satisfaction. 'With one stroke, or rather the absence of one, we have cut the dhoti-wallahs down to size and got rid of a number of dangerous troublemakers from vital positions of power. Imagine Kaurava seditionists and anti-colonials in control of the Ministries of Supply, Food and Agriculture, Power and Electricity in the major provinces at a time of war and national peril – it could have proved disastrous.'

'Indeed?' The black clouds seemed to lighten a little on the viceregal forehead.

'Instead,' the Principal Private Secretary affirmed, 'we can run these departments ourselves with tried and tested officials, or even' – and he glowed at the ingenuity of the thought – 'even place other parties in office from amongst the minorities in the legislatures. They will be beholden to us, and since the Kauravas have forfeited their responsibility we can hardly be blamed for turning to other elected Indians to do their job for them, can we? This will, in turn, weaken the Kauravas' base of support, because they will no longer have any patronage to dole out, no more jobs for the boys, no more opportunities to operate the levers of power. And we will, therefore, have a weaker nationalist party to contend with in the years to come, after the war. Oh yes, Your Excellency, I see a lot of good coming out of your excellent decision not to consult the Kauravas.'

The Viceroy let the implications of his advisor's last sentence pass. He was not yet convinced he wanted the paternity of his unilateral announcement ascribed to him. 'I hope Whitehall sees it that way, Sir Richard,' he replied, absently fingering the lingam and then drawing his hand away as if scalded by its procreative symbolism. 'And I trust you will draft a suitable note on the matter to ensure that they do.'

59

He did; and Whitehall did; and as events unfolded it appeared that Virgil was right too, and it was advisable to trust the man of experience. For the Kauravas sat at home while the provincial legislatures carried on without them, gaining neither the advantages of being in office within the country nor those of leading a glorious crusade in exile as Pandu was doing. In due course, other parties and alliances staked their claims to form ministries in some of the provinces, and when it suited them, the British admitted these claims. The Muslim Group of Mohammed Ali Karna, which had failed to win a majority in any of the provinces, formed minority governments in three where the Kaurava ministries had resigned. They set about systematically increasing their following through every means at their disposal. One story quoted Karna as saying: 'We shall win the hearts and minds of the people, however much it costs us.'

Thwarted, frustrated, excluded, the Kaurava Party chafed in its self-imposed irrelevance. Then, in a desperate and not entirely well-thought-out bid to regain the political limelight, the party met under Gangaji's chairmanship and proclaimed a new campaign of civil disobedience. The message to the British was simple and direct: 'Quit India.'

Oh, Ganapathi, how those two magic words captured the imagination of the country! The new slogan was soon over all the walls; it was chalked, scrawled, painted on notice-boards, on railway sidings, on cinema posters. Little newspaperboys added it *sotto voce* to their sales cries: '*Times of India*. Quit India. *Times of India*. Quit India.' The magic refrain was taken up by chanting crowds of students, office-goers, political workers, hoarsely orchestrated by the Kaurava Party and its vociferous cheerleaders: 'Quit – India. Quit! India. Quit? India!' The words beat a staccato tattoo on British ears; they were the heartbeat of a national awakening, the drum roll of a people on the march.

It lasted twenty-four hours. Oh, there may have been sporadic resistance in some places for a little longer, but the organized movement to get the British to Quit India was snuffed out within a day of its proclamation. The Raj had been watching the Kauravas closely, very closely. It arrested the principal leaders within hours of the Quit India call, in one notorious case arresting a dilatory Working Committee member as he was coming out of the meeting-hall. (I had gone to the bathroom when the others dispersed, Ganapathi, if you must know.) By the next afternoon the lower-level organizers – the men who actually got the crowds out on to the pavements, who told them where to march and led them in their sloganeering – were behind bars. It was all over before it began.

At least the non-violent campaign was. Jayaprakash Drona, tutor to the Pandavas, abandoned his charges to wage a one-man battle against the Raj. He blew up two bridges and derailed one goods train before the long arm of the law caught him squarely on the tip of the jaw. He was interned in a maximum-security prison and the only significant result of his bravado was that the education of my five grandsons suffered.

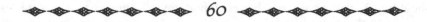

60

So, Ganapathi, as Pandu strove and struggled in Berlin and Singapore, Gangaji and his Kaurava followers languished in prison while two very different individuals moved closer to realizing their ultimate ambitions of thwarting the Mahaguru.

Mohammed Ali Karna, with three provincial governments dancing to his tune and unchallenged as the most prominent Indian out of captivity, glowed with the lustre of quasi-divinity in which his followers had cloaked him. His name could no longer be taken in vain by lesser mortals: he was now referred to almost exclusively by the honorific 'Khalifa-e-Mashriq', or Caliph of the East, a choice of cognomen which ignored – indeed, blandly denied – his secular Anglicization. And as the Muslim Group consolidated its hold on, and its taste for, power, a vocal section of its adherents began openly calling for the creation of a new political entity where they could rule unchallenged, a state carved out of India's Muslim-majority areas. This Islamic Utopia would be called Karnistan – the Hacked-off Land: simultaneously a tribute to its eponymous founder and an advertisement for its proponents' physical political intent. The party's younger hotheads had already devised a flag for their state. It would carry, on a field of Mohammedan green, a representation of the half-moon that throbbed on their caliph's burnished forehead.

Yet there were already signs, if only we had known how to recognize them: signs that Karna, at his peak, had peaked. His long face began to look increasingly pallid at the post-sundown cocktails and receptions which celebrated and reinforced his prominence. As the darkness gathered Karna would withdraw even more into himself, until all that remained was the vividness of his birthmark against the pallor of his skin. Sometimes he would withdraw altogether, slipping out of the reception rooms where his awed followers gathered in respectfully distant clusters. It was thus that I found him once, shivering in an unlit garden while the hubbub of conversation continued on the terrace behind.

'It *is* late, isn't it?' I ventured conversationally.

'It is dark, Vyas,' Karna replied.

'You don't like the dark?'

My question seemed to ignite a dying ember in him. 'I hate the dark,' he replied with sudden vehemence. 'I hate the blackness of night. Even as a child, it was the sun I yearned for. The sun, enveloping me in its glow, setting me ablaze with its light. When the sun is up there I am warm, I am safe. But as dusk drops and the light fades, I feel the shadows creeping up behind my shoulder. A chill enters my bones; I find myself shivering. The nameless demons of the dark keep sleep from my eyes, Vyas. I can only rest with the light on.' He seemed to pull himself together with a physical effort. 'But let the morning come, let the flames of the sun touch my skin and scorch the dreadful memory of night from my brain, and I am myself again.' He shook his head, as if realizing just in time whom it was that he was confiding in. The dapper lips twisted in deliberate irony. 'Good night, Vyas,' he said self-mockingly, inclining his head as he walked away, away from the starless night sky and into the well-lit acclaim that awaited him indoors.

If the Khalifa-e-Mashriq constituted a growing threat to what Gangaji stood for politically, a slight, embittered figure was beginning, unknown to all of us, to cast an equally dangerous shadow on the Mahaguru's person. Amba, the slim, doe-eyed princess whose nuptial bliss the Regent of Hastinapur had once so thoughtlessly blighted, was almost ready to exact her revenge.

She was no longer the lissom beauty of Salva's fancy. Long years of neglect and frustration, of vainly seeking familial, royal and finally criminal help to redress her plight, had altered the soft lines of her face and body to reflect the hardness of her hate-filled heart. Yes, Ganapathi, the very twist of her mouth mirrored the warping of her soul. Only her eyes shone with the spirit of corrosive determination that had extinguished every other spark of her being.

For decades she had been obsessed with one thought only: how to get her own back on Gangaji. When all those she approached, from hesitant rajas to reluctant hit-men, proved unwilling or unable to take on her mortal enemy, Amba turned from human help to divine doxology. She meditated, prayed, arranged for a succession of priestly rituals of increasing obscurity and malevolence. She took up Tantrism, participating in rites where blood and semen spurted into yellowing skulls as acolytes screamed their frenzied invocations of the powers of Shakti. She practised austerities, sitting motion-less for days in mortifying postures, her mind concentrating solely on her overwhelming clamour for retribution. At last — and she knew not in what state of consciousness this occurred, whether she was awake or dreaming or on that translucent plane where all experience is intensely, unverifiably personal — a dark figure appeared before her, erect above her half-closed eyes, bearing a trident and a look of infinite wisdom.

'What you want shall come to pass,' said an ethereal voice that echoed round the spaces of her mind. 'But know this: under the boon conferred by his father, Ganga Datta will only leave this world when he no longer wishes to remain in it. When such a moment comes, he can be destroyed — but only by a man made unlike all other men.'

And then the voice was gone, leaving only the vibrations of its message in her mind, so that when Amba opened her eyes and saw the haze swirling around her it was as if she had been touched by the intangible, as if she had been possessed by the ineffable, as if she had been filled up by an absence.

She remained as she was for many hours after that, savouring the texture of the experience through all her senses, giving herself up to the meaning of that moment. Finally, she knew, and she rose to her feet with a terrible purpose etched into her will.

Amba would have her revenge at last. But it would not be as Amba, the betrayed beauty of Bhumipur, that she would exact it.

In a small disreputable clinic in the back-streets of Bombay, behind the quarter where the transvestites flaunt their gender at perspiring clients, beyond the dark betel-stained stairways ascended by pairs of swaying herm-aphrodites, Amba stood naked before a sharp-toothed figure in a grimy white coat.

She spoke to the surgeon in a voice hoarse with strain.

'Take from me these milkless breasts, doctor, seal this unseeded womb. Make me a man, doctor. A man made unlike all other men.'

61

The war was over. The destruction, the fire-bombing, the rocket blitzes, the lingering deaths on the battlefields, all ended with a bullet in a Berlin bunker and a thousand suns exploding over Japan. But in India, Ganapathi, the violence was just about to begin.

It was clear that this was one victory which would cost Britain as much as defeat. The old Empire had been brought to its knees by the effort of self-preservation, like a householder crippled in his successful resistance to a burglar. At the moment of victory, as he was sharing his triumph with his allies, the Prime Minister who symbolized John Bull's indomitable will was unseated by an electorate that wanted eggs rather than empire and valued indoor gas over imperial glory. When Labour came to power it was evident even to the purblind members of the Society for the Preservation of the Imperial Connection (SPIC) and its marginally more progressive rival the Society for the Promotion of an Anglophile Nationalism (SPAN) that the days of the Raj were numbered. Wearied by war, Britain no longer had the stomach for colonial conflict. His Majesty's grasp on the reins of his Indian Empire was now noticeably feeble.

Freed from their disastrous incarceration, the leaders of the Kaurava Party blinked at the sunlight of a new reality. They discovered a nation whose nationalism had been left directionless too long, and a rival organization unrecognizably stronger than it had ever been, newly wise in the ways of power, tested by office and already flexing muscles developed while the Kauravas' were atrophying in jail. Suddenly, the Independence stakes were a two-horse race, with the two horses aiming for different finishing-posts.

Elections were called: the democratic way out of the dilemma. The Kauravas did well, but not as well as before. It was not possible to make up for six years away from the field in six weeks of energetic campaigning. The Mahaguru's men still won a majority of the provinces, but the Muslim Group emphatically carried most of the Muslim seats. In all but one of the provinces where their co-religionists were in a majority, they triumphantly assumed the reins of office – and demanded separation.

At the twilight hour, the Raj realized what it had done. *Divide et impera* had worked too well. A device to maintain the integrity of British India had made it impossible for that integrity to be maintained without the British.

In a gesture so counter-productive it might almost have been an act of expiation, the Raj clumsily gave the warring factions a last chance of unity. It decided to prosecute Pandu's traitors, the soldiers who had discarded their Britannic epaulettes for the swastikas of the OO's Swatantra Sena. Pandu himself was gone, though there were still die-hards who insisted he had not died in the plane crash and was lurking underground on some tropical island waiting to re-emerge at the right time. In either case, the Supreme Leader was not available to be tried, and the Raj had to find scapegoats amongst his lieutenants. In a desire to appear even-handed amongst the main communities, the British chose to place three Panduites on trial in Delhi's historic Red Fort: a Hindu, a Muslim and a Sikh.

The result was a national outcry that spanned the communal divide. Whatever the defects and the derelictions of Pandu's unfortunate followers, they had not been disloyal to their motherland. Each of the three defendants became a symbol of his community's proud commitment to independence from alien rule. Neither the Muslim Group nor the Kaurava Party had any choice but to rise to the trio's defence. For the first time in their long careers Mohammed Ali Karna and Dhritarashtra accepted the same brief. The OO trials were the last issue on which the two parties took the same stand. Pandu brought them together in death as he could not have done in life.

But the moment passed. The defence of three patriots was no longer enough to guarantee a common definition of patriotism. The rival lawyers for the same cause hardly spoke to each other. Karna began to lose interest when he discovered that his Muslim guinea-pig was no fan of Karnistan (indeed, Ganapathi, he was to stay on in India and die a minister). The ferment across the country made the result of the trial almost irrelevant. The men were convicted, but their sentences were never carried out, because by the time the trial was over it was apparent that the ultimate treason to the British Raj was being contemplated in its own capital. London, under Labour, was determined to liquidate its Indian Empire.

By this stage, Ganapathi, the vultures had scented the dying emanations and were already beating their wings for pieces of the corpse. Karna made it clear he had no desire to content himself with a few provincial satrapies. He wanted a country: he wanted Karnistan. When it briefly seemed that the sentimental British were unwilling to contemplate the break-up of the dominion they had so assiduously built, he exhorted his followers to 'Direct Action'. Several thousand cadavers, burning vehicles, gutted homes, looted shops and rivulets of blood later, everyone except the Mahaguru began thinking about the unthinkable: the division of the motherland.

Gangaji refused to be reconciled to the new reality. He walked in vain from riot-spot to riot-spot, trying to put out the conflagration through expressions of reason and grief. But the old magic was gone. Where he was effective it was in very specific areas for very limited periods of time; against the scale and magnitude of the carnage that was sweeping across the country, he was broadly ineffectual. It was almost as if the Mahaguru and his message had only touched a corner of the national consciousness, a corner reserved for the higher attributes of conscience and historical memory, but one unrelated to the dictates of reality or the needs and constraints of the present.

History was catching up with itself, and it was running out of breath.

 62

As the communal strife — the American news-magazines and the British tabloids were already calling it a 'civil war' — swept across the country, the British government decided to bring matters to a head. In fact, to a different head: they changed the Viceroy, appointing a new representative with a mandate to negotiate an orderly transfer of power.

Viscount Drewpad was the right man to give away a kingdom. Tall, dapper, always elegantly dressed, he wore his lack of learning lightly, cultivating a casual patter that impressed anyone he spent less than five minutes with — which was almost everybody. It helped, of course, that in

their ruling classes the British valued height more than depth. It helped
even more that he was related in at least three ways to the royal family,
whose patronymic (like his) had been changed from the German during the
unpleasantness of 1914.

'In-jyah! How exciting!' exclaimed his wife Georgina when he straightened
his collar before one of three bedroom mirrors and gave her the news. 'Aren't
you rather young to be ruling a continent?'

'I won't be ruling it, dear, just giving it away,' her husband replied,
patting cologne on to his cheek. 'And, besides, I think they've chosen me
because I'm young. We're the glamour brigade, you see, marching forth to the
skirl of bagpipes. They can't send an old dodderer who'd make it look as if
we were only leaving India because we haven't the strength to carry on.'

'Why *are* we leaving India, then?'

'Because we haven't the strength to carry on.' Lord Drewpad picked up a
small pair of silver scissors and delicately trimmed the black moustache which,
along with his tweezered eyebrows, framed an aquiline nose like the two bars
of the capital letter 'I'. 'But there are ways and means of pulling out. We're
going to do it in style.'

'Oh, good,' said Georgina. 'India,' she said dreamily. 'You took me there on
our honeymoon.'

Lord Drewpad adjusted a cuff and turned to give her an affectionate look.
'And I wasn't the only one to, ah, *take* you there either,' he pointed out. 'Now,
that sort of thing won't do, Georgina. You'll have to remember we'll be far
more visible this time.'

'Bertie, you've got a wicked mind!' Georgina trilled girlishly. Over the
years she had bounced on some of the best mattresses in England, with her
husband's amused consent. Now . . . 'The beds i' the East are soft,' she quoted
mischievously.

'If you must think of Shakespeare, choose *The Taming of the Shrew*,' her
husband retorted, combing a recalcitrant curl back into place. 'Look, Georgina,
we have appearances to maintain. I mean, when we're in India we won't be
just anybody. We'll be there in a symbolic capacity.'

'Oh, really?' Georgina gurgled. 'And what will we be symbolizing?'

'Surrender,' replied Lord Drewpad, putting down the comb and squinting
critically at the mirror.

'Oh, I don't mind symbolizing that at all,' said his wife, lying back
languorously on her bed.

'Now, Georgina, none of that,' her husband warned her waggishly. 'Remember, withdrawal is the larger theme of our presence.' He lifted his chin so
that the light fell more clearly on it. The shaved skin was still smooth,

complementing the first-person-first emblem of the prominent I on the middle of his face. He nodded to himself in approval.

'Tell me about it, dear,' his wife went on. 'What does it all mean?'

'In a nutshell, headlines in the papers, footage in the newsreels, tea with the holy Mahaguru in Delhi, a cavalry escort in turbans and braid, and an army of servants,' Lord Drewpad replied, practising a toothy grin into the mirror. Dissatisfied the first time, he bared his teeth again, more successfully. 'Jolly good, what?'

'And the work?' Lady Drewpad asked. 'Will there be a lot?'

'Good God, they're not sending me out there to *work*, Georgina,' the Viceroy-designate grimaced. 'There are plenty of civil servants to do that. They're sending me there to give the Raj a great big grand farewell-party. With colour, and music, and lights and costume, and enough pomp and circumstance for the natives to remember us by for a long, long time.'

'Is that what the *Labour* government wants you to do, Bertie?' Georgina could not keep the astonishment from her voice.

'Well, not exactly,' Lord Drewpad admitted, critically examining his finger-nails. 'I have an idea they'd probably prefer me to set an example in self-restraint for the ration-ridden populace at home. But once I'm in India, there's not much they can do about it. You see, the Viceroy doesn't live off the British taxpayer. Indian revenues are considerable, and I intend us to enjoy them considerably.'

Lady Drewpad sighed in anticipatory wistfulness. 'It all sounds delightful,' she murmured.

'Hmm,' her husband agreed, busying himself with an emery-board. 'And the thing is, we'll be making everybody happy at the same time. The government here, because they want the problem off their hands. The British in India, because after a long time they'll have a Viceroy — and Vicereine — who will dazzle the natives with an unstinting display of imperial glory. And the Indians, because they know they'll be getting their country back at the end of it all.'

'Are you sure the Indians won't mind? All the pomp and ceremony, I mean.'

'Mind? Don't be silly.' Lord Drewpad put his fingers out, nodded approbation, and put away the nail-file. 'Do you know,' he said in the tone of erudition he habitually used to convey his nuggets of half-knowledge, 'that the very word "ceremony" comes from India, from the Sanskrit *karman*, a religious action or rite? What we shall be performing in India is nothing more, and nothing less, than the last rites of our Indian Empire.' He swivelled on a slippered heel, flashing a dazzling smile: three mirrors smiled back at him. 'Let this be my epitaph: "Alone amongst his peers, he did not hesitate to stand on ceremony".'

'Sounds marvellous.' Georgina purred contentedly. 'But for now, are you finished, dear? Will you put out the light?'

Her husband took one last self-satisfied look at his reflection. 'Yes, I think I've done my exercises for the day,' he said, allowing himself a yawn. 'Time for bed. Good night, dear.'

He switched off the lamp with a fragrant hand, plunging the room into darkness, while five thousand miles away in the country he was to rule, the flames of communal frenzy burned brightly across the land.

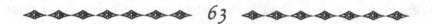

63

The Drewpad viceroyalty was conducted just as Georgina had been promised – in the light of chandeliers and flashbulbs, beneath the glitter of diamond tiaras and shimmering gold braid, and to the tune of the bagpipes of the Royal Scots Fusiliers. The last representatives of His Majesty the King-Emperor were not lacking in company: 913 servants in cummerbunds and scarlet livery attended to their individual needs, from perfumed bathwater to choice chicken breasts for their dogs; 500 horsemen guarded their corporeal persons; 368 gardeners trimmed and watered their manicured lawns (assisted by 50 youths whose sole job was to run about scaring away the crows). On the first day in his new palace Drewpad, in silk sash and gold aiguillettes, his beribboned breast awash with medals and orders he had not had to fire a shot in order to obtain, ambulated in stately fashion down miles of red-carpeted corridor, his satin-gowned consort on his arm, to be sworn in as Viceroy in a ceremony only marginally less elaborate than a coronation. Within hours he embarked with Indian leaders on the negotiations whose breathtaking pace was to characterize his incandescently brief tenure.

'Five *minutes*?' protested a bewildered Dhritarashtra, his stick tripping over the threshold, as he was ushered out of his first meeting with the new Viceroy. 'Is that all he's prepared to listen?'

'That's about as far as his attention-span seems to stretch,' confirmed Mohammed Rafi, Gangaji's latest choice as President of the Kaurava Party. 'Something tells me we're not going to have an easy time with this man – or indeed much time at all.'

'I have no intention of giving them room to argue,' the new Viceroy explained to his Vicereine in the relative privacy of her capacious dressing-room, while she divested herself gradually of several lakhs of rupees' worth of antique jewellery. (He had himself earlier been meticulously undressed, from epaulette to silver boot-buckle, by a winsome aide-de-camp. In the course of a meteoric cavalry career Drewpad had become, in the American phrase, somewhat A C/D C, a proclivity reflected in his choice of A D Cs – and in his indulgence of his wife's extra-curricular romps.) 'That's one mistake my predecessors made – to talk endlessly with these Indian politicians in the hope of arriving at some sort of conclusion. Absolutely hopeless business, of course.'

'But if you don't talk to them, how will you ever solve the problem?' asked Lady Drewpad, tilting her head to remove a heavy earring.

'Oh, I'll talk to them all right,' her husband responded airily. 'But I won't listen to them. All I want to hear from you lot, I'll tell them, is a yes or a no. We've had enough of reconciling different plans for the transfer of power with both groups haggling over each clause.'

'But what if you can't get the different sides to agree?'

'Not important.' Lord Drewpad shrugged. 'We'll try and charm the blighters into being reasonable, but if they persist in their bloody-mindedness we'll tell them where to get off. Darling, put that on again, will you?' He inclined his head towards the diamond tiara which had crowned her golden curls. 'I want to look at you like that for a moment.'

She smiled, flattered, and turned to face him. On a sudden impulse, she slipped her blue silk *peignoir* off her shoulders. There she stood, Ganapathi, as Britannia had first come to us: naked, with outstretched hands, about to place our crown on her head.

Drewpad took her elegant fingers in his own. 'How I wish I could present you to all India like this,' he said. 'My jewel, in a crown.'

She laughed, and tossed her *coiffeured* head. 'It might stop them talking, for a while.'

'And then their next words might just be, "Yes". Several times.' Drewpad bent to kiss her hands. 'You're an essential part of my plans, darling. We've got to charm these humourless fellows into being more accommodating. You're my secret weapon.'

64

In another high-ceilinged but considerably darker room in distant Hastinapur, with a small kerosene lantern flickering yellowly in a distant corner, Gandhari the Grim lay dying.

'Has he come?' The voice was strained and feeble, and Priya Duryodhani, hunched near her mother at the head of the bed, had to lean closer to hear it.

'Not yet, Mother.' She looked towards the curtained doorway without hope, knowing she would have heard the tap of her father's stick long before he appeared at the entrance to their room. 'Word has been sent. He will be coming soon.'

The faded face seemed to sink deeper into the pillow. I was reminded then of that other night, so many years ago, when Dhritarashtra's daughter had fought her way into the world.

'Don't strain yourself, Gandhari,' I said gently. 'He must have been detained. You know how things are these days.'

'These days?' The pale dry lips, highlighted by the bandage that still concealed her eyes, parted slightly in a bitter smile.

I said nothing. It had been no different in earlier days. The light from the lantern flitted briefly across the shadows.

'Water.' There was a sudden urgency in the voice. Duryodhani reached for the brass pitcher on a bedside table and poured the lukewarm liquid into a tumbler. Gandhari tried to raise herself, then gave up the effort. Her daughter's hand quickly interposed itself, half-raising Gandhari's head, while the other tilted the tumbler towards her mother's parched mouth. A little water dribbled down Gandhari's chin.

'Good boy.' Gandhari was holding her daughter's free hand in a tight grip. 'My son. You are all − all I had.' The words were coming out in gasps now. 'Alone. Always alone. In . . . the . . . darkness.'

We were both still, Duryodhani motionless in her mother's grasp and I, destiny's observer, unable to move from my place in the shadows at the foot of the bed. And in the stillness I realized that nature too was quiet. There was an unnatural silence outside. The crickets had stopped their incessant chirping, the mynahs were no longer twittering in the trees, the hundred and one sounds that always came in from the garden at this time of day had mysteriously died. It was as if all creation was holding its breath.

'Darkness!' Gandhari screamed in one convulsive gasp. Her hand left Duryodhani's and seemed to reach for the bandage across her eyes; but before it could touch that slender satin shroud it fell back lifelessly across her breast.

'Mother!' Duryodhani sobbed, burying her face in the folds of Gandhari's garment. It was the only time I would ever see her weep. 'Mother, don't leave me, don't leave me alone!' The tumbler fell from her hand, clattering against the marble floor. A trail of water flowed slowly from it in a winding rivulet towards the doorway.

A cane tapped its way down the corridor and came to a stop. The curtain was pushed aside.

'Don't cry so, my child,' said a gentle voice. 'See, your tears have wet my feet.'

'Papa!' Duryodhani turned her tear-stained face to her father, and her cry was heart-rending. 'She was waiting for you!'

'I'm .. sorry.' Dhritarashtra took a hesitant step forward. 'Won't you come to me, my child?'

For a moment the stillness continued; then a solitary koyal cooed in a tree outside, and Duryodhani was on her feet, running towards her father, who dropped his cane and caught her in an all-enveloping embrace . . .

I stepped soundlessly forward to where Gandhari lay, neglected in death as in life. Tenderly, in a gesture that I could not explain, I crossed her palms across her chest. Then, ignored by her husband and daughter lost in mutual consolation, I eased that terrible bandage off her face.

Her eyes were open.

Gandhari was gone, but her dark, devastated pupils spoke of greater suffering and solitude than most of us can endure in a lifetime of light. But she was right, Ganapathi. There are some realities it is better not to see.

I placed my hand on her forehead and very gently closed her eyes. Then, for the last time, I slipped her bandage back into place.

'Goodbye, Gandhari,' I said.

THE ELEVENTH BOOK:

RENUNCIATION –
OR, THE BED OF ARROWS

65

'Gentlemen,' announced Viscount Drewpad, 'I have summoned you here today to tell you that His Majesty's Government – in other words, I – have had enough.'

He looked around the table at the representatives of the three parties the British had chosen to deal with: the Kauravas (Dhritarashtra, the ebullient Mohammed Rafi and myself), the Sikhs (Sardar Khushkismat Singh, whose stock of jokes about his community was rivalled only by other people's anecdotes about him) and the Muslim Group (Karna, a robed mullah in a hennaed beard and a surrogate for the Gaga Shah, who was himself already out of the country arranging his post-Independence future abroad). We all looked back at the Viceroy, but none of us spoke: with this superficial and supercilious man even Karna was at a loss for words.

'Whitehall has formulated, and successive Cabinet missions have presented, a number of plans to you all relating to a possible transfer of power from British rule to Indian self-government,' he went on. 'Each and every one of them has foundered on the intractable opposition of one or other of you.' To avoid giving gratuitous offence with those words he fixed his gaze directly on the Sardar, who had, in fact, cheerfully given his assent to each and every variant of the Independence formulae thus far proposed. But he might as well have looked at Karna, because *we* had tried to bend as far as we could to accommodate him, and each time he had balked. Various schemes had been drawn up, grouping the Muslim provinces separately, proposing 'lists' of states in a weak confederation, devising elaborate guarantees of minority rights and communal representation. Each had foundered on the rocks of Karna's intransigence. At one point Gangaji – who no longer came himself to these negotiations, saying he preferred to give us moral guidance from outside – suggested that as the price of keeping India united we should simply offer Mohammed Ali Karna the premiership of all India. So central was Karna's personal ambition to his political stand that it might even have worked, but this time it was Dhritarashtra who refused to countenance the suggestion. Drewpad was really speaking for all of us as he went on: 'We cannot, with the best will in the world, go on indefinitely like this.'

Karna glowered at him. 'We have not come here, Viceroy, to be lectured at like errant schoolchildren,' he snapped.

'I have not finished.' Drewpad fixed him with an amiable gaze. 'I wish to tell you today that I, for my part, have decided to wash my hands of your squabbling. You all agree on one thing: that in the end you want the British out. Very well, we shall proceed on that basis. Whether you agree on anything else or not, the British *will* pull out – on August the fifteenth, 1947.'

To say that the seven of us around the table gasped in astonishment might seem a cliché, but like most clichés this too was true. 'But that's barely eight months away!' Karna, as usual, was the quickest to recover. 'What made you choose such a date?'

'It's my wedding anniversary,' Drewpad responded innocently.

'This is preposterous!' Rafi was shouting. 'You can't do this!'

Lord Drewpad picked up his papers and drew his chair back. 'Oh, yes? As our American cousins say, Mr Rafi, can't I just!'

And before we knew it he was striding out of the room.

The deadline was impossible. 'Leave us,' Gangaji had written to Drewpad's predecessor when he was jailed for his Quit India call. 'Leave us to God or to anarchy.' It had sounded good at the time; but now, when the British seemed to be about to do precisely that, we felt sick to the pits of our stomachs.

We met, the Kaurava Working Committee, at the Mahaguru's feet the next day. It was one of his days of silence, which meant that he would listen sagely to what we were saying, then scrawl a few words on the back of an envelope that Sarah-behn would read aloud to the rest of us. 'One hell of a way to chair a meeting,' Rafi breathed in an aside to me as we sat cross-legged on the floor. 'Especially the most important meeting of our lives.' But of course, Gangaji wasn't chairing it at all; Rafi was the President of the party. Yet everyone knew whose view mattered the most in our conclaves.

'The first thing to be sure of is, does he mean what he says?' someone asked.

'From what I have seen of Drewpad,' responded Dhritarashtra wearily, and without irony – you know how he was for ever speaking in visual images – 'he strikes me as the kind of person who always means what he says.'

'In that case we have our backs against the wall.' This was Rafi. 'All that Karna and his cohorts have to do is to stick obstinately to their demand for a separate state. With the British scheduled to leave for certain by a specific date, they know that sooner or later we'll have to give in.'

It was a difficult thing for Rafi to say, because as a Kaurava Muslim he was amongst the party's strongest opponents of the demand for Karnistan. If a separate Muslim state came into being it would, after all, leave him and his co-religionists in the Kaurava camp isolated, on both sides of the communal divide.

A hubbub of comment followed, largely tending to agree with the President. Gangaji raised his hand. We were all silent as he traced words on to a scrap of paper in his spiky pencilled hand.

'You must never give in,' Sarah-behn read, 'to the demand to dismember the country.'

'Gangaji, we understand how you feel,' Dhritarashtra said. 'We have fought by your side for our freedom, all these years. We have imbibed your principles and convictions. You have led us to the brink of victory.' He paused, and his voice became softer. 'But now, the time has come for us to apply our principles in the face of the acid test of reality. Rafi is right: Karna and his friends will simply dig in their heels. Separation or chaos, they will say; and on Direct Action Day last year they showed us they can create chaos. How much worse will it be without the British forces here? Might it not be better to agree in advance to a – the words stick in my throat, Gangaji – civilized Partition, than to resist and risk destroying everything?'

The Mahaguru had already started writing before Dhritarashtra had finished. 'If you agree to break the country, you will break my heart,' he wrote.

'It will break many hearts, Gangaji,' his chosen heir said sadly. 'Mine, and all of ours, included. But we may have no choice.'

'Then I must leave you now,' Sarah-behn read in a quavering voice. 'I cannot be party to such a decision. God bless you, my sons.'

The Mahaguru waited until the last word was read, then nodded, his Adam's apple bobbing visibly like a painful lump in his throat. He slowly got up and, with one hand on Sarah-behn's shoulder, hobbled out of the room. Nobody spoke; and nobody tried to stop him.

His departure, as we had all known it would, made the rest of the meeting much easier. Misgivings were voiced on all sides, but we had struggled too long for freedom to want to tarnish it when it was within our grasp. It was better to give Karna what he wanted and build the India of our dreams in peace and freedom without him.

That evening, the Working Committee of the Kaurava Party resolved unanimously to accept in principle the partition of the country. It was the first time we had ever gone against the expressed wishes of Gangaji. His era was over.

 *66*

Some people said later that we had acted too hastily; that in our greed for office we sacrificed the integrity of the country; that had we been willing to wait and to compromise, Partition would never have occurred; that Karna was the most surprised man in India when our resolution was passed because he was only asking for the mile of separation in order to have the yard of autonomy and we should have called his bluff. To all these theorists, Ganapathi, I say: That's absolute cow-dung. Or its male equivalent. We gave in to Partition because Karna's inhuman obduracy and Drewpad's indecent haste left us no choice.

Of course, there was a great deal we didn't know, although the whole horde of hindsight historians act as if we did. We had no idea that the sun was burning out behind Mohammed Ali Karna's increasingly pallid skin, and that within nine months of the vivisection of our land the half-moon on his forehead would throb feebly into eclipse. We could not have imagined, either, that Partition, which we accepted as a lesser evil, would lead to a carnage so bloody that anything, even the chaos of an unresolved Independence settlement, might have been preferable to what actually happened.

Nor could we have even begun to guess what the practical process of partitioning the country would involve. The appointment, for instance, of a political geographer who had never in his life set foot on any of the territories he was to award either to India or to the new state of Karnistan.

'It's really quite easy,' the stout, bespectacled academic announced, standing with a pointer before a small-scale map. 'One takes a given cartographical area – there – one checks the census figures for religious distribution and then one applies the basic principles of geography, choosing natural features as far as possible for the eventual boundary, studying elevation and relief – see these colours here? – not forgetting, of course, heh-heh, the position of these thin lines, which are roads or rivers, and then . . . then one draws one's boundary line v-e-ry carefully, like this.' Lips pursed in concentration, he proceeded to trace, in a shaky hand, a sharp slim line on the map. 'That, ladies and gentlemen,' he declared, 'will be the new frontier between India and Karnistan in this area.' He put down the pointer and half-bowed, as if expecting applause.

'Congratulations, Mr Nichols!' A veteran administrator named Basham rose to his feet. 'I have lived and worked in that very district for the last ten years, and I must take my hat off to you. You have just succeeded in putting your international border through the middle of the market, giving the rice-fields to Karnistan and the warehouses to India, the largest pig-farm in the zilla to the Islamic state and the Madrassah of the Holy Prophet to the country the Muslims are leaving. Oh, and if I understand that squiggle there correctly,' he added, taking the pointer from the open-mouthed expert, 'the schoolmaster will require a passport to go to the loo between classes. Well done, Mr Nichols. I hope the rest of your work proves as – easy.'

'Of course,' stammered a beet-faced Nichols, 'given the cir . . . circumstances in wh . . . which we're working, and the short dead . . . deadlines, m . . . m . . . mistakes are possible.'

'Of course,' commiserated the old India hand.

'Field visits are out of the question. Simply not feasible, in the circumstances. We have no choice but to work from maps.'

'Quite so,' sympathized Basham. 'Field visits out of the question, of course I understand. Just think, Mr Nichols, if only Robert Clive had felt the same way about field visits at the time of Plassey, you wouldn't even have this problem, would you now?'

Yet somehow, Ganapathi, it all went on. Fat little Nichols drew his lines on his maps, and each stroke of his pencil generated other lines, less orderly and less erasable lines, lines of displaced human beings leading their families and animals away from the only homes they had ever known because they were suddenly to become foreigners there, lines of buses and bullock-carts and lorries and trains all laden with desperate humanity and their pathetic possessions, lines too of angry vicious predators with guns and knives flashing as they descended on the other lines, lines now of shooting hitting wounding raping killing looting attackers ripping apart the lines of stumbling fleeing bleeding crying screaming dying refugees . . . In those days, Ganapathi, lines meant lives.

67

There were other lines too. Lines of glittering socialites queuing up to be received at one of the numerous soirées and balls organized at the Viceroy's house ('almost as if he wants to spend the rest of the government-hospitality budget while he still has one,' a cynic commented). Lines of journalists and cameramen queuing outside his study for quotographs as he emerged after his breezy summits with a succession of dignitaries ('almost as if he only meets them for the sake of the pictures afterwards'). Lines of stiff soldiers in starched uniforms, ceremonial swords at the ready, to welcome him to airfield after airfield on his whirlwind tours of the country ('almost as if he wants to see it all before they take away his plane'). Lines of nawabs, maharajas and allied potentates anxious to wheedle some assurance out of him that they wouldn't have to merge their principalities into either the new democracy or the emerging Karnocracy ('now there he did the right thing by us: he told the princelings they wouldn't get a pop-gun out of Britain if they sought to resist').

At last Vidur came into his own. He was by now sufficiently senior in the States Department, the organ of government that dealt with the princely states, and Drewpad needed an Indian in his higher councils on the eve of a transition from British to Indian rule. Within a short while – and remember a short while was as much as Drewpad gave anybody – he was amongst the Viceroy's closest advisors. It was he who did the meticulous paperwork that allowed Drewpad to deliver his startling pronouncements on everything from princely privilege to constitutional prerogative. And if occasionally he slipped away to brief Dhritarashtra or myself in advance of an impending development of some importance to the future of the country, he was only doing his larger duty – to the nation, rather than just to the government. As a result of which India did not do too badly out of the partitioning of the army or the division of governmental assets. Vidur, as always, did his work well.

Ah, Ganapathi, those were proud paternal days for me, unacknowledged father though I was. One son was poised to inherit the first free government of India, another had been martyred in the attempt and was revered in almost every Indian home, and the third stood side by side with the British Viceroy as the last arrangements were made for the withdrawal of colonialism. There were few fathers, Ganapathi, who could say, as I could, that history had sprung from their loins.

But I would rather procreate history than propagate it. There are moments in my own story I would rather forget, and that terrible year of 1947 was full of them. For the last time I took to the dusty roads in my sandals to see and learn what was happening, and I saw too much, Ganapathi, I heard too much. The killing, the violence, the carnage, the sheer mindlessness of the destruction, burned out something within me. I could not understand, Ganapathi, even I could not understand, what makes a man strike with a cleaver at the head of someone he has never seen, a son and husband and father whose sole crime is that he worships a different God. You tell me, Ganapathi. What makes a man set fire to the homes and the animals and sometimes the babies of people by whose side he has lived for generations? What makes a man tear open the modesty of a girl he has never noticed, spread her legs apart with a knife to her throat, and thrust his hatred and contempt and fear and desire into her in a spewing bloody mess of possession? What madness leads men to seek to deprive others of their lives for the cut of their beards or the cuts on their foreskins? Where is it written that only he who bears an Arabic name may live in peace on this part of the soil of India, or that raising one's hand to God five times a day disqualifies one from tilling another part of the same soil?

Yet such were the assumptions and actions of ordinary men in those days, Ganapathi (I will not add the obligatory 'and women' because for the most part they did not perpetrate the madness, they were caught up in it, they were the victims of it). And those of us who saw it as madness, who saw it destroy everything we had lived and struggled for, were powerless to stop it. We tried, each in our own way, where we could, but found it too strong for us. Like Gangaji, we walked rather than wept, preached and prayed rather than giving up in despair. But each time we opened our eyes it was to a new anguish, a new despair, which ground its heel into the already unbearable torment of our nation's suffering.

If only – if only we had said no to Drewpad, and not obliged people to flee! It is flight that makes men vulnerable, it is flight that makes them violent; it is the loss of that precious contact with one's world and one's earth, that pulling up of roots and friendships and memories, that creates the dangerous instability of identity which makes men prey to others, and to their own worst fears and hatreds. Those of us whose spirits are moored in a sense of place, whose minds can still climb up the leafy branches of family trees with roots plunged deep into the soil, who from those branches can wave to other friends, neighbours, cousins, rivals similarly perched on theirs, who can recognize the countryside around and name the seeds from which the surrounding fruit had grown – *we* do not murder other people's children, burn their homes or slaughter their cattle. But those who have been deprived of such security are prompted by their anxiety and bitterness into the roles of either perpetrators or victims – yes, both, because it is often the man who has lost everything who is also the most convenient target, for he is faceless, homeless, placeless, and his lack of identity invites and seems to mitigate attack. After all, no one mourns a nobody.

But we cannot blame only Drewpad. He had a job to do, and that job was to exit, pursued by a bear; if the bear was of his own creation rather than the cause of his departure, it was a bear none the less, and we, as its hereditary keepers, remained responsible for its appetites. Gangaji recognized this, and took upon himself the tragedy of the nation. He saw the violence across the land as a total repudiation of what he had taught. All his later life he had seemed ageless; suddenly he looked old.

It was at this stage that he turned to that unfortunate nocturnal experiment which was to cause so much needless controversy amongst his later biographers. In his despair, in his dejection over the state of the country, and in his resultant ageing, he seemed to have lost that incredible physical self-sufficiency that had let him stride up the steps of Buckingham Palace in the English winter in his dhoti. He now trembled as he stood up, needing to lean on both his stick and Sarah-behn; and at night he was given to terrible fits of shivering. Perhaps that was what sparked it off – an old man feeling the cold at night – but Gangaji attributed no such simple motive to the decision that he, with characteristic lack of embarrassment, announced to his entourage one morning.

'Many of you,' he said, with that combination of simplicity and shrewdness that was uniquely his, 'will notice a change in my sleeping arrangements from tonight. Sarah-behn will sleep in my room from now on – and in my bed.' He paused, seemingly oblivious to the consternation his words had engendered. 'Some of you may wonder what I am doing. What has happened, you may ask, to that terrible vow of old Bhishma, and the principles of celibacy he has enjoined on all of us? Do not fear, my children. Sarah-behn is like a younger sister to me. But I have asked her to join me in an experiment that will be the ultimate test of my training and self-restraint. She will lie with me, unclad, and cradle me in her arms, and I shall not be aroused. In that non-arousal I hope to satisfy myself that I have remained pure and disciplined. And not merely that. It is my prayer that this test will help me to rediscover the moral and physical strength that alone will enable me to defeat the evil designs of that man Karna.'

The Mahaguru, at his venerable age – an age when most normal men should have been dandling great-grandchildren on their arthritic knees – thinking, and speaking, of testing his capacity for arousal! It was, to many, downright indecent, and the thought of their saintly sage wrapped up in the commodious pink flesh of the formidable Sarah-behn was more than most of his followers could bear. Various whispered explanations were discussed, from the obvious one of senility – that this was simply eccentricity compounded by age – to the more esoteric one of Shunammitism, that Gangaji was decadently seeking his rejuvenation through the ministrations of a younger woman. There was no consensus on the matter, but there was rapid agreement on one thing: the story had to be kept from the press. A tight blanket of loyal self-censorship descended on all of us, covering our own discomfort and our leader's nakedness.

But inevitably, word leaked out about Gangaji's latest experiments in self-perfection. And while it never circulated verifiably enough to appear in print, it attracted a fair amount of both vicious gossip and sincere curiosity. I think it was in the latter category that the eminent American psychoanalyst, who had questioned the Mahaguru periodically since Budge Budge, came up to him and asked in all earnestness:

'Could it be that your inability to become the Father of a united India drives you to seek maternal solace in British arms?'

 68

Dhritarashtra was the one man who was equal to the situation. His affliction, of course, spared him the worst scenes of horror and devastation. Not for him the walks through burning villages; not for him the sight of a corpse-laden train, steaming into the station with every man, woman and child in it butchered in the very vehicle of their escape by the people from whom they were fleeing. Instead, Dhritarashtra busied himself in the committees and meetings that planned the end of the empire and the birth of the nations that would replace it. He frequented the conference-rooms and situation-rooms from where what could be controlled of the country was controlled. And he developed a relationship with Lady Drewpad that curiously – and usefully – made him all the more welcome in the Viceroy's antechamber.

They made a strange pair, those two – the blond patrician and the blind politician, engaged in animated conversation in the rose garden as the world turned itself upside-down around them. Sometimes they would walk, and I saw the deepening lines on Dhritarashtra's face soften as her words soothed his spirit, heard her infectious laughter dissolve the perennial frown on his prominent forehead, sensed her gently take his hand to lead him over the unfamiliar steps into her life.

Georgina Drewpad, amatory adventuress of libellous renown, might not have had the most impeccable credentials of all our vicereines – women who themselves, thanks to their marriages, had slipped into the history of our country on their backs – but she changed India, and India changed her. She eased the tragic tension that might otherwise have destroyed our first Prime Minister, and restored to him the faith and the will he needed to take on the burden that would soon be his. And despite the almost insuperable handicap of being married to a man shallower than the River Punpun in drought, vainer than a priapic peacock in heat and less sensitive than a Kaziranga rhinoceros in the summer, Georgina revealed a remarkable capacity for constructive caring. When she was not with Dhritarashtra – and sometimes even when she was – she was busy coordinating charity collections for the victims of the violence, visiting the injured in hospitals and touring the slums in her official jeep to bring succour to women whose God-given maladies (from cholera to *kala-azar*) had been neglected in the face of the overwhelming man-made calamity around them.

But some things, about both people and places, do not change. No woman who had given and taken the currency of love as had Georgina Drewpad could have remained indefinitely untouched by the blind temptations of foreign exchange. No country whose colonists' imagination had created an Adela Quested and a Daphne Manners could have denied its seed to the most yielding of its vicereines.

And so it happened; on the soft capacious bed of the Vicereine's private suite, within four posts of fragrant sandalwood, cushioned by the finest down ever stuffed by colonized fingers, my blind son of India took possession of all that Britannia had to offer him. And as the passion and the coolness of their coupling, the touch and the withdrawal of their contact, the tenderness and the rage of their caresses, mounted into a dizzying, tearing burst of final release, the fireworks burst white, saffron and green in Dhritarashtra's mind. Midnight exploded into dawn. He was free.

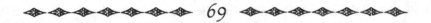 69

So it was over, and we had won. India had conquered Great Britain; Gangaji's *khadi*-clad coolies, his homespun hordes, had triumphed over the brass-and-braid brigades of the greatest empire the world had ever known. You cannot imagine, Ganapathi, and I mean that literally, you cannot imagine the excitement, the exhilaration, the exultation of that midnight moment when the nationalist tricolour rode up the flagpole and Dhritarashtra, his voice breaking with emotion, announced to the nation in the most enduring of his visual metaphors:

'At the hour of darkness, as the world slumbers, India awakes to the dawn of freedom.'

When the clock struck twelve that night it struck for the hopes in all our hearts. The cheers that resounded from the massed ranks of the legislators in the Constituent Assembly found their echo in the crowds on every city street, in every village *panchayat*, atop every lorry, aboard every train. They were cheers, Ganapathi, of the kind that greets the end of a Ram-Lila performance at a *maidan*, when the demon has been slain and the giant effigy of Ravana, the alien king who has crossed the sea to usurp and ravish India's innocence, is ceremonially set alight. That is when you shout in an affirmation of triumph, truth and teleology; you cheer the fact that you knew what would happen, and you cheer the fact that its happening has confirmed your faith in the world.

But one man was not cheering that night. Gangaji sat on the cold floor of a darkened room, sunk into his white wrap, his lower lip extended in a gloomy pout, his long arms listless by his side. Almost alone among his colleagues, the Mahaguru saw no cause for celebration. Instead of the cheers of rejoicing, Ganapathi, he heard the cries of the women ripped open in the internecine frenzy; instead of the slogans of triumph, he heard the shouts of crazed assaulters flailing their weapons at helpless victims; instead of the dawn of Dhritarashtra's promise, he saw only the long dark night of horror that was breaking his nation in two. The bright lights of the gaily coloured bulbs strung across all the celebratory *shumianas* of Delhi could not illuminate that darkness, Ganapathi, nor could they shine in his eyes as brightly as the blazing thatched homes of the poor peasants. He had preached brotherhood, and love, and comradeship in struggle, the strength of non-violence and the power of soul-force. Yet it was as if he had never lived at all, never preached a word.

He saw the shadow fall across him before he saw the haggard man framed in the doorway. He looked up at the tall awkward figure without curiosity.

'Yes?' Sarah-behn asked.

'Do you remember me, Bhishma?' the visitor asked in a ragged choking voice. Something stirred in Gangaji's eyes.

'Who are you?' Sarah-behn asked.

The visitor coughed redly into a stained handkerchief. He looked in wonder at his own blood, his indeterminate features twisting in pain. 'I now call myself Shikhandin. Shikhandin the Godless. Bhishma will understand.' The lips parted in a crooked smile. 'He knew me as Amba, princess and bride. Did you not, Bhishma?'

Gangaji looked at him in widening comprehension, but said nothing.

'I have been through much to get here, Bhishma.' The voice was unsteady, and one hand was holding in the side of his stomach as if to keep the guts from falling out. 'The butcher who unmade my womanhood hasn't left me much time. But some things are easier for a man. Just travelling here, walking through the streets of this flaming city, entering this compound – Amba could not have done it.'

Sarah-behn was staring in horrified fascination at the gaunt figure with the indeterminate voice. But she, like the few others in the room, did not – could not – move. And Gangaji sat calmly looking at the unnatural apparition, an ineffable peace lightening his face.

'What a wreck you are, Bhishma!' the voice went on. 'What a life you've led. Spouting on and on about our great traditions and basic values, but I don't see the old wife you ought to be honouring in your dotage. Advising everyone about their sex life, marrying people off, letting them call you the Father of the Nation, but where is the son you need to light your funeral pyre, the son of your own loins? I've been looking everywhere, Bhishma, but he's nowhere to be found!' The visitor spat redly on the floor. 'You make me sick, Bhishma. Your life has been a waste, unproductive, barren. You are nothing but an impotent old walrus sucking other reptiles' eggs, an infertile old fool seeking solace like a calf from the udders of foreign cows, a man who is less than a woman. The tragedy of this country springs from you – as nothing else could after that stupid oath of which you are so pathetically proud. Bhishma, the pyre has already been lit for you in the flames that are burning your country. You have lived long enough!'

The twisted figure bent sideways in pain, then straightened itself with a visible effort of will. 'They say, Bhishma, that you will go only when you no longer wish to live,' Amba/Shikhandin coughed. 'Look at the mess you've made.' A hand swept out to the world beyond. 'You don't still want to live, do you?'

Gangaji looked steadily at his nemesis and slowly, wearily, emotionlessly shook his head.

'I thought so.' The hand swept back. It was holding a gun.

Sarah-behn screamed.

Three bullets spat out in quick succession. The screaming did not stop; it was joined by other screams, which dissolved into wails and sobs. For a second it seemed that the occupants of the room were all frozen in shock, and that all that moved were the waves of grief from the screaming women. Then everyone sprang into motion. Sarah-behn ran to Gangaji. Two or three of his male followers seized Shikhandin, who did not resist. The assassin leaned on his captors like a bride reluctant to leave her father's home, but there was defiance in his weakness, and his arms were pinioned behind his back. Shikhandin looked with bitter satisfaction at the Mahaguru, lying crumpled on the floor, life oozing from his wounds.

'Gangaji.' It was Sarah-behn, frantic with grief and fighting to conceal it, beside herself and beside him. 'Don't worry. The doctors are coming. Everything will be all right.'

The Mahaguru smiled with effort, as though at the absurdity of the proposition.

Or at least I imagine he did: that is the way in which I have heard the story. For I was not there, Ganapathi. I, who had spent so many of Gangaji's waking hours with him, who had trudged by his side through the indigo fields of Motihari and the mango groves before Chaurasta, I could not reclaim that place as he lay mortally wounded amidst his followers.

I have had nightmares about that moment since, and in my nightmares the Mahaguru fell, pierced not by bullets but by arrows, sharp shafts that cut deeply into his body and his being. 'Let Ganga Datta die in a manner befitting his life,' I heard an ethereal voice saying, perhaps his own, and then a hundred hands were raised to lift the Mahaguru from the floor where he had fallen and carry him gently to his deathbed. And when they placed him on it I realized in my nightmare that it was a bed of a hundred arrows, all planted firmly in the stony ground, their sharp triangular heads embedded in Gangaji's back, his lifeblood pouring from each in a crimson flow that merged and mingled with the darker trickle from his assassin's weapon, till it was impossible to tell which he was dying from, the injury inflicted by the killer or the unremitting incisions of the bed of arrows on which he was lying – the bed which was all that a torn and jagged nation could offer its foremost saint to rest on.

In the helpless horror of my nightmare I watched his life ebb away, unable to move an arm, lift a finger, raise a voice to change anything that was happening. Yet Gangaji was in no torment. He bore his fatal impalement calmly, as another campaigner for justice and peace had accepted the catharsis of crucifixion. And when he called for that final sip of water which is the dying Hindu's last prerogative on earth, a lustrous youth stepped forward to shoot another arrow into the ground by the Mahaguru's head. The arrow sprang from his bow as if released from an unbearable tension, flew through the air and imbedded itself quivering in the earth.

From that spot, Ganapathi, gushed the best and the worst of all the water of India, its crystals clear with the sparkle of love and truth and hope, its flow muddied by the waste and the offal that are also flung into the holiest of our rivers. This water spurted up near Gangaji, bathing and soothing and inflaming his wounds, and dropping in thirst-quenching rivulets on to his parted lips.

As Gangaji drank, my nightmare faded into received memory, and the Mahaguru was back in the arms of his sobbing Scottish sister on that cold unforgiving floor, with Shikhandin's bullets bleeding the life out of him.

'Thirsty,' he uttered in a fading voice.

A boy brought him a tumbler. 'I am Arjun, Pandu's son,' he said softly. 'I was just arriving when I heard the shots. Look, I have brought some water for you. Pure Ganga-*jal*, from Hastinapur. Please drink it.'

The Mahaguru, Ganga Datta, bent forward gratefully for a sip, placing a weak hand of benediction on the youth's head. Then he turned his cow-eyes of infinite sadness to his constant companion.

'I . . . have . . . failed,' he whispered.

And then he was gone, and the light, as Dhritarashtra was to say, went out of our lives.

 *70*

No obituaries, Ganapathi. You won't get those from me. Anyone who wants eulogies can look them up in the local library — 'generations to come will scarce believe that such a one as this ever in flesh and blood walked the earth' (Einstein), 'the noblest Roman of them all' (Sir Richard), 'a great loss to the Hindu community' (Mohammed Ali Karna). What I feel about Gangaji can't be put into words, and in a sense everything I have been telling you, and everything we are living today, is the Mahaguru's funeral oration.

No questions, either. I will not ask whether Amba/Shikhandin was truly responsible for the Mahaguru's death, or whether it was not India collectively that ended Gangaji's life by tearing itself apart. Nor will I ask you, Ganapathi, to reflect on whether Ganga Datta might in fact have been the victim of an overwhelming death-wish, a desire to end a life that he saw starkly as having served no purpose, a desire buried deep in the urge that had led him, all those years earlier, to create and nurture his own executioner.

No questions, Ganapathi, because I have no answers. And yours, or anyone else's, would be as irrelevant as an old man's nightmares.

But there is one story I ought to mention, just so that you have it, even though I don't believe it myself for a moment.

It is said, around the smoky fires where villagers in what used to be Hastinapur warm their hands on a winter night, that as Gangaji lay dead, wrapped as in life in his white sheet, a tall figure with a half-moon glowing on his forehead stepped in and sat by his bed.

Yes, Ganapathi, Karna.

And Karna spoke — for that is how they sing it in the desert huts of western Rajasthan in the wailing chants of the Langas and the Manghaniyars, how they hear it in the arrack shops below the palm-fronds that fringe Kerala's highways, as men gather to drink and talk politics — he spoke in a low insistent voice, seeking the Mahaguru's forgiveness and his blessings. Yes, blessings, for did not the Mahaguru realize that he, Karna, was only doing what he had to in fulfilment of his own karma? Could a man be blamed for performing too well the script of destiny?

Then — and this is where I really part company with the popular version —

as the unacknowledged son of Kunti rose to leave, the story goes, a hand slipped out from under the shroud and grazed his shoulder.

Gangaji disagreed with no man more profoundly, yet he would not deny Mohammed Ali Karna his blessing when he asked for it.

That, at least, is the story as it is told; make of it what you will.

THE TWELFTH BOOK:

THE MAN WHO COULD NOT BE KING

71

Is this all I can recall of the glorious period of our attainment of Independence, I see your elephantine frown ask me. Can death, destruction, and despair be my only recollections of the first flush of national freedom? No, Ganapathi, I too was not oblivious of the excitement of the age, the exhilaration of change. I can and do recall other things about 1947, petty moments, perhaps, which reflected and affirmed that things were no longer the same. I remember Englishmen who edited newspapers in the big cities suddenly discovering virtues in the nationalists they had reviled till noon the previous day. Signs being taken down in exclusive establishments, signs which read 'Indians and dogs not admitted beyond this point'. Children being born at inconvenient times of the night who would go on to label a generation and rejuvenate a literature. Pink-skinned civil servants with worthless lifetime contracts frantically arranging their own premature retirements and passages home while learning to be attentive and obsequious to Indians who had suddenly been placed above them.

Like Jayaprakash Drona, Minister of State for Administrative Reform, who sat in his saffron robe, black beard flowing messily over his desktop, as perspiring I C S officials pressed him to put his newly valuable signature on to pieces of paper they had drafted with meticulous attention to the interests of their kind.

'Routine paper, sir. Annual leave chart. The leave's already been taken, sir.'

'All right.' Drona signed suspiciously.

'Now this file, sir, approves *ex gratia* compensation payments to all those whose career expectations have been, ah, affected by, er . . . recent events in the country.'

'No.'

'But you must, sir! It's been carefully worked out. On a sliding scale, taking into account seniority, length of service . . .'

'No.'

The official swallowed, then placed the offending docket in a tray labelled 'Pending'.

'This is an altogether simpler matter, sir. An individual case. Civil servant who lost everything, all his possessions, papers, antiques, in a nasty disturbance during the Partition riots. Most unfortunate case, sir, in fact I've just seen him this morning at the ministry, pretty distraught as you can imagine. If you'd just sign here, sir, we'd make him a special one-time grant in partial restitution, authorize an advance on his next six months' salary to get him back on his feet again, and allow him exceptionally to convert into cash the freight costs he would have claimed from the government if all his furniture hadn't gone up in flames.' Drona opened the file and picked up a pen. 'Thank you, sir,' his Secretary went on. 'I think you'd really be doing a fine thing for poor Heaslop. He's spent all his career in India and . . . sir?'

For Drona, who had put pen to paper, had lifted it again and was looking at him with what the poet, some British poet, had called a wild surmise.

'Did you say his name was Heaslop?'

'Yes, sir, I . . .'

'*Ronald* Heaslop?' The Secretary nodded. 'And you say he is here, now, in the ministry?' The Secretary nodded again, unhappily. 'Send him in,' Drona directed. 'I want to talk to him.'

Ronald Heaslop was duly ushered in, sporting white ducks a shade too large for him, borrowed from a friend while the only suit that had survived the arsonists was receiving the none-too-tender attentions of a dhobi. The suit accentuated the extent to which he seemed to have shrunk, physically and in spirit.

Drona leaned back, his fingertips steepled in a gesture of greeting or reflection, it was not clear which. 'Mr Heaslop,' he asked, 'do you remember me?'

The Englishman looked at him blankly for a moment, then with an effort summoned up a recollection. 'Why, of course! Devi Hill – you talked to me about Indian spiritualism.'

'Amazing what adversity will do for the memory cells, isn't it, Mr Heaslop?' Drona asked in his most *swadeshi* voice. He now made a special effort to Indianize his diction with the colonials: they had to realize he had both an axe and an accent to grind. 'While you are being so amazingly accurate, you would not be able to recall a more recent encounter, no?'

Heaslop looked at him again, hesitated, then slowly began to flush red, like a toilet after the Holi celebrations.

'Shall I give you clue, Mr Heaslop? A visiting card? A request for help "Ghaus Mohammed, purse *lao*"? Or were there several such incidents in your distinguished career in this country that you are knowing so well?'

Heaslop began to speak, but the words would not get past his throat. 'I . . . I'm . . .' he croaked.

'And now it is your turn to be coming to me in need,' Drona remarked, with the subtlety of a juggernaut. 'Now what shall we do, Mr Heaslop? What would *you* do in my place? Shall I, too, summon my Ghaus Mohammed?'

Heaslop remained redly speechless.

Drona pushed a button on his desk. A peon poked his head round the door. 'Secretary-sahib *ko bula do*,' he commanded. Sir Beverley Twitty, KCMG, emerged with a promptness accelerated by apprehension.

'Ah, Sir Bewerley,' Drona said expansively. 'You were putting a certain file before me just now, isn't it? File of Shri Heaslop? You have it?'

The Secretary handed it over with a set face.

'Now, let me see.' Drona examined the paper before him with exaggerated care. 'What is it you are proposing, Sir Brewerley? "Special one-time grant in partial restitution for losses suffered to private property in performance of service-related functions." My my, what long sentence, Sir Bewerlily. I must be learning how to write like this soon. Otherwise how I will manage when you and your fellow British are no longer remaining here? What were these losses, Shri Heaslop, that you, er . . . suffered in performance of service-related functions?'

'They set fire to my house,' Heaslop replied bitterly. 'I lost everything I had – or almost everything. Fact is, I was rather lucky to escape with my life at all. I woke up smelling smoke and leapt out of the window. Seconds later the place was gone.'

'Most unfortunate,' Drona clucked. 'So you were asleep in your home at the time this happened?'

'Yes.'

'I see. So that was your service-related function – sleep?'

Heaslop looked nonplussed. Sir Beverley, still unsettled by Drona's way-wardness with his name, sprang to his junior's defence. 'Well, sir, everyone has to sleep.'

Drona ignored him. 'There was a riot going on in the city?'

'Yes,' replied Heaslop eagerly. 'Nasty business, it was. Hindus killing Muslims, Muslims butchering Hindus – oh, the Muslims were much worse,' he added hastily, in deference to Drona's saffron robes. 'And probably both sides turning on the British.'

'A major riot, would you say?'

'Oh, definitely. Decidedly major.'

'And you were asleep? A major riot between two sections of His Majesty's subjects in your district, and you, Mr Heaslop, were sleeping? You surprise me, Shri Heaslop. I would have seen you instead in your official jeep, restoring law and order and sanity to the population. *That* would have been your . . . "service-related function", would it not?'

'But –' Heaslop spluttered. Drona interrupted him ruthlessly.

'In the circumstances, I am hardly thinking this one-time payment recommended by Sir Brewerly is justified,' he commented. 'What is it – 20,000 rupees, is it, Sir Bewarley – 20,000 rupees for being asleep at the wrong time in the wrong place. No, no, Sir Bowerley, goodness gracious, this will not do at all.' He moved his fingers to the next line on the file. 'Six months' salary advance? Six months? But my dear Mr Heaslop, will you be working six months still with this dreadful native government? I am rather thinking not. I am rather thinking that your name will be figuring on the list of those recommended for early termination of service and reversion to the Home cadre.' Sir Beverley seemed about to speak. Drona added meaningfully, 'And there may be other names too.' The Secretary relapsed into silence.

'Now let us see,' Drona went on, 'what else? Exceptional conversion of freight into cash? But I am surprised, Sir Liverbelly. A civil servant recommending exceptions? Never am I hearing before of such a thing. Exceptions in a time of national calamity? I think not.' He put the file down and wrote across it in bold, decisive letters. 'I very much regret to be rejecting your recommendation, Sir Lewerbey,' he said with a pleasant smile. 'But Mr Heaslop, though I as a minister of the government of India cannot help you, as an individual I am simply overcome with sympathy for your predicament. Sir Weberley, you must start a collection for poor unfortunate Mr Heaslop. Here is my own contribution.'

His hand disappeared into the saffron folds of his garment and produced a fistful of small coins.

Drona got up, leaned over the table and very slowly and deliberately poured them, in a tinkling cascade, into Heaslop's lap.

No, in fact it didn't happen that way, Ganapathi. Sometimes I wish it had, that Indians had proved capable of paying the Raj back, if you'll pardon the metaphor, in its own coin. But I've let an old man's vengefulness get the better of me, and I have been untrue to Drona. Revenge was the one quality conspicuously absent in the way he, and other members of the independent Indian government, treated their former masters.

Forgive me, Ganapathi. What happened was far more prosaic than my fantasy.

'Mr Heaslop,' Drona asked, 'do you remember me?'

'Why, of course!' the Englishman responded, after a pause. 'Devi Hill – you talked to me about Indian spiritualism. I had no idea that you –'

'No,' Drona interrupted him mildly. 'I don't imagine you did. I believe, though, that you might recall a later encounter.' He looked directly at

Heaslop, who shifted uncomfortably in his chair, but said nothing. 'Well? Do you?'

'I . . . I . . .' Heaslop stammered, his mouth opening soundlessly as it used to during his old exchanges with Sir Richard. Drona's unflinching gaze seemed to pin him to his seat, nailing his squirming conscience to the truth. 'Y . . . yes,' he said at last, miserably. 'I . . . I say, I'm afraid I behaved most aw . . . awfully. I'm sorry.'

Drona's face lightened, as if that had been what he was waiting to hear. 'I am not,' he responded equably. 'That meeting taught me a great deal, Mr Heaslop. In fact, you could almost say that that is why I am here today.' He smiled, and there was no rancour in his voice. 'So you see, I am really quite grateful to you.' He turned the pages of the file before him and looked up from them to the speechless Englishman. 'I am most distressed to read of your misfortunes, Mr Heaslop. Of course I shall approve the recommendations submitted by Sir Beverley. With one addition.' He paused, seeking the right paragraph in the dossier before him. 'The Secretary-sahib has suggested that – where is it now? – "Consideration be given", that's right, consideration be given to your transfer to New Delhi, in the circumstances, pending any decision you might wish to make about your future career.' Drona looked up from the file inquiringly.

'Yes,' Heaslop nodded, since confirmation seemed to be called for. 'It would help me, and I don't really want to go back to the district, after all . . . all that's happened.' He stopped unhappily, aware of the awkwardness of his situation, made no more bearable by the solicitousness of the saffron-robed figure across the desk.

'I see,' Drona said. 'In that case, I will give consideration immediately.' He wrote on the file as he spoke. 'You shall be transferred to New Delhi with immediate effect, Mr Heaslop.' His eyes briefly met those of the Englishman, who was reddening with embarrassment and gratitude. 'To my department, in fact. As long as you wish to remain in the service of this government, you are welcome here. I believe we shall work very well together.'

Heaslop rose, stretched out his hand, and found the minister's palms folded in a polite but correct *namaste*. Clumsily, he retracted his own and mirrored the gesture. There seemed to be nothing else to say.

 72

And through this delightful era, what, you may well ask, of the Viscountess Drewpad? Till Drewpad's final exit she continued to come to my blind son's arms. There were many opportunities for the relationship to . . . er, fructify, as her husband prepared for the ceremonial handover of his symbolic position, now no longer that of Viceroy but Governor-General, to his Indian successor, the scarred and decrepit but undoubtedly symbolic Ved Vyas. (Who held it, I might add, Ganapathi, for that brief interregnum between Drewpad's departure and the proclamation of the Indian Republic, when the country was a dominion under an appointed Indian Governor-General. But I had not cut many inaugural ribbons or cracked many coconuts against the hulls of ships when I had to make way, in turn, for an elected President. They say every dog has its day, Ganapathi, but for this terrier twilight came before tea-time.)

But I am getting away from Georgina Drewpad. She came, as I was telling you, to Dhritarashtra, and she came back even after her official position had elapsed. Some exits, Ganapathi, are simply to permit a different sort of entrance. Lady Drewpad had waved a composed official farewell by her husband's side from the steps of a B O A C Constellation as her husband departed into the relative obscurity of uniformed nepotism. But she came back soon enough, Ganapathi, and often enough, the nation's unofficial First Tourist, slipping quietly into the country on unpublicized visits to Priya Duryodhani's widower father.

Nature and history would not be denied. Soon after one of those journeys she returned much earlier than expected. This time she stayed incognito, clad in billowing caftans and noticeably preferring the curtained indoors, for longer than she had ever done before. At last, on 26 January 1950, as the Constitution of the new Republic of India was solemnly promulgated by its founding fathers, Georgina Drewpad, her face awash with tears, delivered herself of a squalling, premature baby.

The infant girl, bearing the indeterminate pink-and-brown colouring of her mixed parentage, a tiny frail creature with strong lungs, used frequently and well, was immediately handed over to the faithful low-caste servant who had served Dhritarashtra and his companion throughout this difficult period. She was to be adopted; neither of her natural parents could openly acknowledge the intimacy that had produced her.

The baby was called Draupadi, a subtle Indianization of her mother's family name, and she took the uncouth patronymic of her adoptive father, Mokrasi. Draupadi Mokrasi. Remember the name well, Ganapathi. You will see a lot more of this young lady as she grows up in independent India.

 *73*

History, Ganapathi — indeed the world, the universe, all human life, and so, too, every institution under which we live — is in a constant state of evolution. The world and everything in it is being created and re-created even as I speak, each hour, each day, each week, going through the unending process of birth and rebirth which has made us all. India has been born and reborn scores of times, and it will be reborn again. India is for ever; and India is forever being made.

The India of which Dhritarashtra assumed the leadership on 15 August 1947 had just been through a cathartic process of regeneration, another stage in this endless cycle. But you must not think, Ganapathi, that the trauma of Partition represented a disruption of this constant process, a side-step away from a flowing dance of creation and evolution. On the contrary, it was a part of it, for the world is not made by a tranquillizing wave of smoothly predictable occurrences but by sudden events, unexpected happenings, dramas, crises, accidents, emergencies. This is as true of you or me as of Hastinapur, of India, of the world, of the cosmos. We are all in a state of continual disturbance, all stumbling and tripping and running and floating along from crisis to crisis. And in the process, we are all making something of ourselves, building a life, a character, a tradition that emerges from and sustains us in each succeeding crisis. This is our dharma.

Throughout this unpredictable and often painful process of self-renewal, despite the abrupt stops and starts of the cosmic cycle, the forces of destiny remain unshaken in their purpose. They are never thwarted by the jolting and jarring of history's chariots. The vehicles of human politics seem to run off course, but the site of the accident turns out to have been the intended destination. The hopes and plans of millions seem to have been betrayed, but the calamity turns out to have been ordained all along. That is how a nation's regeneration proceeds, Ganapathi, with several bangs to every whimper.

This constant rebirth is never a simple matter of the future slipping bodily from the open womb of history. Instead there is rape, and violence, and a struggle to emerge or to remain, until circumstances bloodily push tomorrow through the parted, heaving legs of today.

So it was in our story: Gangaji died, his assassin Shikhandin was hanged, Karnistan was hacked off the stooped shoulders of India, Dhritarashtra attained the prime ministry of a land racked with chaos and carnage, and out of this all, Draupadi Mokrasi was born, cried and, not without struggle, grew up — into an admirable, beautiful, complicated, desirable (I could do this for another twenty-two letters of the alphabet, Ganapathi, but I won't) creature whose life gives meaning to the rest of our story.

The India of those early years of Independence was a state of continual ferment. It was constantly being rethought, reformed, reshaped. Everything was open to discussion: the country's borders, its internal organization, its official languages, the permissible limits of its politics, its orientation to the outside world.

One of the first issues confronting the new government was the future of the 'princely states' – the hundreds of fiefdoms and kingdoms that had nominally remained outside British rule, as had Hastinapur before Gangaji incurred the Raj's wrath. Even before the British left they had made it clear to the nawabs and maharajas of these principalities that they were obliged to accede either to India or to Karnistan. Most made their choice according to the dictates of geography and common sense, but one or two of the bigger states dragged their constitutional feet in the hope that they might be able to hold out for their own independence. One of these was the large, scenically beautiful and chronically underdeveloped northern state of Manimir.

Manimir, with its verdant valley and its snowy mountain peaks, had been linked politically to the rest of India since the sixth century A D. Its Maharaja, in fact, traced his descent from the Rajput warrior-kings of western India, though this was elaborated in the officially inspired myth to imply a higher ancestry, both geographically and spiritually (the Maharaja numbered the sun and the god Shiva amongst his progenitors, and Shiva, at least, made his celestial home on the top of Mount Kailash in the Himalayan ranges to the north of Manimir). Whatever his genealogy, though, Maharaja Vyabhichar Singh was a soft-jowled hedonist, with pudgy hands and a taste for Caucasian carnality that had already dragged him at least once through the British courts. (There the Indian Office had succeeded in having him referred to throughout as 'Mr Z', an expedient which, far from concealing his identity, only presented his numerous detractors with another epithet of abuse.)

While princes to the south of him, with varying degrees of good grace, merged their possessions into the Indian Union and accepted ambassadorships and seats in Parliament as revised symbols of contemporary status, Vyabhichar Singh obstinately refused to cede either throne or title. He declared himself to be independent, a condition no other nation recognized, and sent 'ambassadors' to India and to Karnistan, who were ostentatiously ignored by all except the printers of visiting cards.

All this might have been mildly amusing, were it not for two inconvenient facts about Manimir. One, it was sandwiched between the border of what remained of India and what had emerged from Mr Nichols' tender mercies as the new state of Karnistan. Two, its population was overwhelmingly Muslim, while the religion of the Maharaja, inasmuch as sybaritism did not qualify as one, was Hinduism.

'We can't let that concupiscent coot get away with this much longer,' Mohammed Rafi, his aristocratic lip curling, said with feeling in the Prime Minister's study. 'The longer that fool Vyabhichar Singh takes to make up his mind, the more time Karna and his minions have to stir up communal feeling for the state's accession to Karnistan. And,' he added, 'we can't afford to lose Manimir.'

The 'we' was, let's be frank, as much a personal pronoun as a patriotic one: the greater the number of his co-religionists on Karna's side of the population ledger, the lower the credibility and influence in India of party President Rafi and his fellow Kaurava Muslims. Already it was clear that they were doing none too well from the haemorrhaging exchange of populations that was taking place in the wake of Partition, particularly on the western border. But even politicians have principles, and Rafi's concerns about Manimir were more than mere electoral mathematics. The future of India as a secular nation depended on its ability to integrate a Muslim-majority state successfully, to nail Karna's lie that India's Muslims needed a country of their own in order to breathe free and flourish.

'With respect,' said a quiet voice. 'I believe the Maharaja thinks he *has* made up his mind.' Vidur's tone was the epitome of the senior civil service: his voice contained an omniscient reserve, as if concerned that the knowledge it carried might be frightened away by too dramatic an octave. 'He wishes to remain Independent in perpetuity. Of course, he is not being very realistic.'

'He is being a damned fool,' Dhritarashtra said. 'What's worse, of course, is that for years we have supported the Manimir National Congress of Sheikh Azharuddin against Mr Z's undemocratic rule, and now the Sheikh is likely to find his support being cut from under his feet by the Muslim fanatics clamouring for merger with Islamic Karnistan. What can we do, Vidur?'

'Not a great deal, I'm afraid, Prime Minister.' The Principal Secretary for Integration, as he now was, was always scrupulously correct in official meetings with his half-brother. 'As you know, in the course of my missions to most of the wavering princes in 1947 I pointed out rather forcefully, with Lord Drewpad's acquiescence, the unviability of the independence option to those who were contemplating it. In most cases the palace guard was the only armed force in these princely states, and they could easily have been overwhelmed by a small detachment from the nearest police-station in British India, so the princes did not require much persuasion. In Manimir, regrettably, though the palace guard is even more effete and less effective than most, the

Maharaja did not possess enough, ah, good sense to make the decision he should have.'

'Why don't we just march in?' asked Rafi, with nawabi impatience.

'It's a little delicate, Mr Rafi,' Vidur replied, in the tone of a doctor circumspectly advising a wealthy patient of one more indulgence he would have to give up. 'It is one thing to, er, as you put it, march in to a little fiefdom surrounded completely by Indian territory. Quite another to contemplate military action in a state the size of Manimir, which has an even larger frontier with Karnistan than it does with us.'

'So what *can* we do?' Rafi asked, impatiently echoing his Prime Minister.

'I'm afraid we must wait a little longer,' Vidur said, his face assuming the mournful manner that bureaucrats adopt when saying things they know politicians don't want to hear. 'You know, sir, await developments. A number of things could happen that might end the stalemate.'

'Such as?'

'One possibility is an internal uprising, led for instance by Sheikh Azharuddin, which might overthrow the Maharaja and proclaim adherence to India. Our intelligence reports to date do not, however, suggest that the Sheikh is capable of mounting and leading such a rebellion, at least in the near future. We could seek to finance, supply and even organize an uprising, but that, of course, calls for a . . .' he paused before uttering the next word, to make it clear it rarely passed his lips, 'political decision which is yet to be made.'

'Well, let's make it, then,' said Rafi.

'Suppose we do,' Dhritarashtra said mildly, 'these things would still take time to, ah, become operational. We are speaking now about the immediate future. You were indicating, Vidur, that an Azharuddin-led rebellion is a possibility, but not, right now, a probability. What if our intelligence fellows are wrong?'

Vidur raised an eyebrow as if the very thought was blasphemous.

'Well sir, if they are, and if Sheikh Azharuddin is capable of leading a popular rebellion against the Maharaja, and if he succeeds — all of which, as you will appreciate, sir, is purely hypothetical — it is still far from certain that the Sheikh, despite the affinity between his party and yours, will necessarily accede to the Indian Union. It is said that he needs India — he needs Manimir to join the Indian Union — in order to obtain power, but if he gets power without Indian help he may decide he does not need us.' Vidur coughed discreetly.

'And the other possibilities you want us to wait for?' asked Dhritarashtra.

'Intervention by Karnistan,' Vidur replied. 'If Karna decides *he* won't wait any longer and tries to take over in Manimir by force, we can step in on behalf of the legally constituted authorities, assuming of course the legally constituted authorities ask us to.'

'You mean Mr bloody Z has to invite us in before we can do anything about a Karnistan invasion?' This was, of course, Rafi again.

'I'm afraid so. Otherwise we would be invaders ourselves, without the head start the first invaders would have. It would not be an easy position to sustain, militarily or' — Vidur grimaced like a headmaster obliged to utter an indelicacy — 'politically'.

'I wonder how my friend Sheikh Azhar would react in that sort of situation,' Dhritarashtra mused.

'It is not very clear, Prime Minister,' Vidur replied. 'It is said that though he has been sympathetic in the past to Kaurava aims, he is increasingly frustrated by what he is beginning to see, most unfortunately, as Indian complacency about a Hindu maharaja. If Karna were to seek to exploit this by invading with the declared intention of putting the Sheikh in power in Manimir as the true representative of the people of the state, we might lose Manimir for ever.'

'Never. They can't stand each other,' Rafi pointed out.

'There's an even more important reason why that won't happen,' the Prime Minister said. 'Karna is the only leader of any consequence in Karnistan. Azhar's popularity in Manimir is equally undeniable. If I know the Khalifa-e-Mashriq, he will never risk placing someone in power in one part of his domain who could be a popular threat to himself. No, Vidur: if Karna decides to act, it will be without Azhar. He will want Manimir, but he will want it, like everything else, on his own terms.'

'And that, Prime Minister, may offer us our best chance,' Vidur said. Having expressed a political opinion, he blushed self-consciously, like a chartered accountant who had accidentally indicated a preference for shapely rather than binomial figures.

There was a knock on the door. I haven't done this to you too often, have I, Ganapathi? Stretching the limits of coincidence unacceptably far? I mean, it's not always in this narrative that a character has said, 'It would be really convenient if the sky were to fall on us right now' — and the sky has fallen on the next page. Fair enough? So do you think you can excuse me now if a sweat-stained despatch-rider bursts into the room and announces that Manimir has been invaded by Karnistani troops?

No? Very well. Take away the despatch-rider then. A secretary walks in. Not one of your ICS types with a capital S, but a secretary, a chap who takes dictation and passes messages. 'Prime Minister, Sahib,' he says urgently. 'Excuse me for interrupting you, but I thought you'd like to know immediately.

A message from the Defence Ministry has just been flashed in. The minister is on his way over to see you. Manimir has been invaded from Karnistan.'

Notice, Ganapathi, *from*, not *by*, Karnistan. Not by regular troops either – the spit-and-polish-wallahs hived off from the Indian Army – but by 'irregulars'.

'What do you mean, "irregulars"?' Dhritarashtra asked the Defence Minister when he arrived. 'If you ask me, the whole thing seems quite irregular to me.'

The Defence Minister – none other than our jovial Sikh friend Sardar Khushkismat Singh – laughed dutifully. There was not much he failed to laugh at. 'It seems they are not soldiers at all, but Pathan tribesmen,' he explained. 'Though we don't doubt for one minute that they have been armed and supplied by Karna's government. Their declared objectives are certainly identical – the "liberation" of their Islamic brothers from tyrannical Hindu rule, and the merger of Manimir with Karnistan.'

'Well, what do we do *now*?' asked Rafi, transforming the gathering into an impromptu council of war.

'How long will it take for our troops to reach the Manimir border in invasion strength?' Dhritarashtra asked.

'I've already spoken to the Chief of Staff,' replied the Defence Minister. 'Assembling the men, arranging logistics, vehicles, supplies, the troop-movement itself – about twelve hours.'

'That's it, then.' The Prime Minister turned to the Principal Secretary for Integration. 'That's how much time you have to fly to Manimir, see the Maharaja and get him to accede to the Indian Union. The moment he does so, Karna's irregulars are no longer invading a defenceless princely state but the sovereign territory of India. And he will have a war on his hands.'

'I shall leave immediately,' Vidur said in his low bass. 'But . . . ah . . . Prime Minister, if I do *not* succeed in obtaining accession, what do you propose to do?'

'The orders that go out now will not be rescinded,' Dhritarashtra announced firmly. 'Our troops will march in anyway. If you do your job quickly enough, the invasion will be legal. If not . . .'

He did not need to complete the sentence. 'I'll do my best, sir,' Vidur said, gathering his papers with a swift and practised hand, and left.

 *74*

When his plane landed in Devpur, the capital of Manimir, it was snowing. The off-white flakes unevenly covered the habitual grime of the city like silver foil stuck on a discoloured *barfi*. Vidur, who preferred his cities clean and his *barfi*s without silver foil, suppressed a shudder. His radio message had apparently got through: a corpulent uniformed official was at the airport to greet him, looking very like a doorman employed at the better class of hotel.

'Mr Principal Secretary?' The official snapped a round-armed salute that nearly popped the brass-buttons on his ill-fitting coat. It was clear he had put on some weight since it was tailored – perhaps for the previous winter, Vidur thought. Uniformed officialdom in Manimir was rarely required to exert itself. 'Bewakuf Jan, Colonel of the Guards. Welcome to Manimir, sir. Your bags?'

Vidur gestured apologetically at the black briefcase in his hand. 'This is all I've come with,' he said, in the tone of a physician who has brought all he needs for the delivery. 'I'm afraid we haven't very much time.'

'Haven't ... very much ... time?' the colonel seemed genuinely taken aback. 'But aren't you planning to see the Maharaja tomorrow?'

'I am planning,' Vidur said firmly, 'to see the Maharaja tonight.'

'Tonight! But that's quite impossible. The Maharaja has been entertaining an important private guest and ... and ... they have already retired for the night. He has left strict instructions that he not be disturbed.'

'Then I'm afraid he is very likely to be disturbed by the rattle of Pathan rifle-butts on his window-pane tomorrow morning,' Vidur replied. 'As for me, I shall not need to trouble you further, colonel. I shall return to Delhi as soon as my plane has been refuelled.'

'Come, sir, come; I am sure that won't be necessary,' said the colonel. Despite the freezing temperature in the unheated airport, Vidur saw he was perspiring. 'His Highness will be most disappointed. Please follow me. The car is waiting.' He turned to lead the way.

Vidur did not move. 'I am here to see the Maharaja,' he said. 'And I am expected to report back to my Prime Minister in Delhi before dawn.'

'Before dawn,' the colonel echoed dully.

'Exactly.' Vidur went on without pity. 'In the circumstances, I see little point in accepting your invitation to drive to the palace. Good day, colonel.'

Colonel Bewakuf Jan swallowed, and looked skywards for inspiration. 'In the circumstances,' he said miserably, 'I suppose the Maharaja will have to be disturbed.'

'I suppose he will,' Vidur concurred. 'And in the circumstances, I'm sure he'll understand,' he added confidently. The colonel nodded, as if he were considerably less sure.

The palace limousine – an enormous vehicle with a seating capacity half-way between a London taxi and a Delhi bus – purred them to the pink-and-guilt Devpur Palace, a similarly immense rococo edifice overflowing in gaudy ornamental detail. Ochre exterior lighting cast a yellowish glare on asymmetrical rockwork, randomly-cast shells, flowing scrolls and marble curves abruptly begun and ended, as if the architect had been paid on a per-feature basis. Crenellated battlements completed the structure – appropriate, Vidur thought, for an embattled Maharaja.

Vidur and the colonel walked up red-carpeted stairs and down endless red-carpeted corridors until they entered what Vidur guessed – from the somnolent guards who slouched to attention as Colonel Bewakuf Jan appeared –were Vyabhichar Singh's private quarters. Two immense oak portals guarded by fiercely moustachioed (and surreptitiously yawning) *subedars* in red opened to admit them into shorter passageways laid with carpeting of a deeper pile in more opulent hues. At last they were alone before an elaborately carved door from which emanated a faint whiff of sandalwood.

'The Maharaja's bedroom,' the colonel whispered.

'Why are you whispering?' Vidur asked.

'So as not to wake up the Maharaja,' the colonel whispered back.

'We are here,' Vidur pointed out, 'to wake up the Maharaja.'

A gale of giggly laughter from inside suggested the deed did not need to be done. *'Arrête.'* A girlish Gallic scream floated through the keyhole. *'Mais non!'* came the high-pitched response of indeterminate provenance. *'Continue!'*

The colonel blanched. 'His Highness is . . . er . . . entertaining an overseas guest,' he whispered. 'I really think we should come back later, Mr Principal Secretary.'

'And risk him going to sleep? Look, I'm sorry to interrupt his little party, but at least we know he's awake. And apparently in a good mood. I really have no time to waste, colonel. Shall I knock on the door or will you?'

The colonel suffered again the agony of irresolution, then lifted the brass knocker and dropped it gently on the door. A peal of laughter sounded from the room.

'That is either the most sophisticated door-bell I have ever seen, or they haven't heard you,' Vidur said after a moment. 'Allow me?' And before the horrified colonel could prevent him Vidur had seized the brass knocker and swung it against the door with a crash.

There was a startled silence from the other side. Then a peremptory voice raged in a squeaky bellow: 'Who the hell is that?'

The colonel's corpulent features crumpled. 'It's . . . me, sir,' he articulated through paralysed vocal chords.

'Who? Speak up, son of a donkey.'

'Me, sir. Colonel Bewakuf Jan. With the Pr –'

'Bewakuf?' The voice cracked in incredulity at its highest pitch. 'Colonel Bewakuf? I thought I told you I was not to be disturbed, Major Bewakuf.'

Tears seemed to spring to the colonel's porcine eyes. 'Yes, sir, but . . .'

'There are no buts, offspring of a rancid pig!' screamed the royal voice on the other side of the door. 'How dare you disobey a direct order, Captain Bewakuf?'

'I'm sorry, sir, but . . .'

'You're *sorry*? You're sorry, licker of a eunuch's behind? You try and break down my door when I am trying to sleep, Lieutenant Bewakuf, and you say you are *sorry*?'

'Sir, it was not I, but *he* said . . .'

'*He*? He said? You mean there is someone else with you, turd from a tenotomized transvestite? Are you having a party outside my bedroom door, Havildar Bewakuf, in the middle of the night? I shall have each of my guards horsewhipped tomorrow, Lance-Naik Bewakuf, and as for you, Bewakuf, I shall spend all night thinking up a suitable punishment. Now get out, do you hear? Get out, and if your shadow so much as falls on my door again, eater of a dog's offal, I shall personally come out and wring your neck! Is that clear, Sepoy Bewakuf?'

'Yes, sir.' The ex-colonel was visibly in tears.

'Just a minute, Your Highness.' Vidur addressed a busty carving on the sandalwood door just above the brass knocker he had so improvidentially wielded. 'I apologize for this intrusion, but it was not the colonel's fault. I insisted he bring me here.'

The effrontery of the unfamiliar voice seemed to take away the Maharaja's breath. At any rate his response was a somewhat more subdued scream. 'And who, may I ask, are you?'

'Vidur Hastinapuri, Principal Secretary for Integration of the Government of India, and special emissary of His Excellency, Prime Minister Dhritarashtra,' Vidur announced at his most official. 'I must leave Devpur shortly, sir, and I have flown here from Delhi expressly to see you. I had understood such a visit would be welcome and I have very little time.' He paused, then added firmly, 'I must see you immediately, Your Highness.'

'Oh you must, must you?' Vidur might have preferred another choice of words, but the voice was decidedly less strident. 'Do you realize what time it is?'

'I had understood this was an emergency,' Vidur replied drily.

There was a moment's silence, then a slapping sound, like that of a palm against flesh. 'Very well,' the Maharaja said, amid the splutter of giggles being stifled, 'if you insist, I shall receive you now. Just a minute.' A rustle of sheets – or was it something else? – was briefly heard, and the murmur of low voices. 'You may come in.'

The door was not locked. Vidur opened it and stepped in. The colonel seemed undecided as to whether he should enter or not, and stood on one foot on the threshold.

'Wait outside, Bewakuf!' the Maharaja barked. The colonel hopped backwards like an offended, if overweight, ostrich. The door swung shut behind him.

 75

Vidur had expected to find Mr Z in his dressing-gown, entertaining a female friend (or friends — he had not been sure of the number of distaff voices). He was startled to see the Maharaja propped up in bed, covered by an enormous silk *razai* that reached up to the lowest of his several chins. Its nearer length rose as a large mound, almost as if the Maharaja had chosen to throw so many blankets on to his lower extremities that half his anatomy reposed under a small hill.

'I'm sorry, Your Highness,' Vidur apologized. 'I didn't realize you were in bed. The colonel and I heard voices and I . . . er . . . I thought you were still awake.'

'I am awake.' The Maharaja giggled. 'My guests have . . . er . . . retired.' This time the giggle seemed to emanate not from the Maharaja's throat, but from lower down. 'Please take a seat.'

Vidur turned to the nearest chair, a Louis-Quinze piece that might have been designed by the palace architect. A garment had been flung over its side. Vidur meticulously picked it up. It was a smooth satin lady's slip. He gazed stupidly at it, nonplussed.

'Put it anywhere,' the Maharaja waved a pudgy hand.

Vidur looked around in increasing embarrassment, and found a heap of similar apparel on an identical chair. He walked to it and dropped the garment on to the pile as if it was burning his fingers. It slipped to the floor, bringing a lace brassière down with it. Vidur flushed.

'Never mind,' the Maharaja said, gesturing him back to his chair. 'What can I do for you?' One of his hands suddenly disappeared under the *razai*.

Vidur sat down delicately. 'With respect, Your Highness, I think it is more a question of what we can do for you,' he said.

He was taken aback by another giggle; this time, he could have sworn, from the region of the Maharaja's belly.

'What exactly do you mean?' the Maharaja asked, an expression of intense concentration on his face.

'We have information that a large band of Pathan irregulars has streamed across your borders,' Vidur replied. 'They are encountering practically no resistance and are already making considerable inroads into Manimiri territory.'

'I know all that,' the Maharaja said impatiently. His other hand had now disappeared under the embroidered quilt. He seemed to be straining at something, with considerable effort. Vidur was reminded of his own bouts of constipation.

'I realize Your Highness is aware of the problem,' he said. 'What Your Highness may not know, however, is that these tribesmen have raised the slogan of liberating Manimir from your ... ah ... oppressive rule. And that they are almost certainly armed, supplied and directed by the government of Mohammed Ali Karna, which intends to annex Manimir.'

The Maharaja gasped, and a gurgling noise sounded from beneath the mound of the *razai*. Vidur was gratified by the reaction, but could not escape the feeling that it was not his statement that had caused it.

'But — that's terrible!' The Maharaja breathed heavily, squirming under his silken covering. He seemed to be sliding under the quilt as he spoke. 'Why haven't ...' his neck had almost disappeared from Vidur's line of vision, 'why haven't my own people been telling me how serious this is?' He sat up suddenly again with a jerk, a bare pale chest popping startlingly into view.

'Perhaps because they can't get in to see you,' Vidur couldn't resist replying. He was tired of the odd behaviour of this peculiar little man, and conducting such a discussion in a bedroom removed certain constraints, as far as he was concerned. 'The point is, Your Highness, that by this time tomorrow, and probably sooner, this palace will be in Karnistani hands.' He paused for dramatic effect. 'Unless you act now.'

A short high-pitched giggle emerged in reply. Vidur had been looking directly into the Maharaja's hooded eyes and could have sworn he hadn't seen the lips move — but the sound was unmistakably oral.

'I hardly think this is a laughing matter, Your Highness,' he said sternly.

'No — of course not,' the Maharaja breathed, the words emerging in gasps. 'I'm sorry.' His hand, under the *razai*, slapped flesh. 'Bugs,' he explained, superfluously.

'I understand,' Vidur replied, far from certain he understood at all. 'I assume you need help.'

The Maharaja twisted again under the covers, his eyes rolling. 'No ... thank you. I ... simply must get this bed changed tomorrow,' he said, breathing heavily.

'I meant military help.' Vidur was finding the conversation increasingly difficult to control. 'That is why I am here, Your Highness.'

'I am most grateful.' An expression of rapture was beginning to suffuse the royal face. Vidur was amazed at how the Maharaja could alternate so easily between discomfort and bliss in response to a fairly consistent line of argument from himself. Decidedly a most peculiar character.

'Can . . . you . . . send . . . us . . . Indian . . . troops?' the Maharaja panted.

'Certainly, Your Highness.' Vidur began to feel alarmed by the Maharaja's tone. 'Are you quite sure you're well, Your Highness?'

'Yes,' Vyabhichar Singh nodded vigorously, 'yes – yes.'

The mound moved.

'As I was saying,' Vidur began, and then stopped, because he no longer recalled what he was saying and because the hillock on the lower half of the Maharaja's bed was now moving up and down to a remarkably steady rhythm and . . .

'Exercises,' the Maharaja breathed. 'Every day. Don't pay 'tention. Ah, yes. Yes.' His eyes closed and his fleshy round head turned from side to side. 'Troops. Yes. Please. As many. Ah! As you can. Yes! Yes! Troops.' The *razai* was positively heaving now, and little beads of perspiration were appearing on the Maharaja's forehead.

'We'll need a formal request from you, of course, Your Highness,' Vidur said, shrinking into his chair.

'Yes. No – problem. Formal request. Ah. Bring a paper. I'll sign. Yes. Ah. Ah. Yes. Yes! Aaah!'

Vidur found himself speaking rapidly, as if to shut out of his mind the horrible supposition that had entered it and which he found too unthinkable to be allowed to linger there. 'We believe the most appropriate course would be for you to sign an Instrument of Accession and then appeal formally for Delhi to intervene,' he said, looking at the marble floor, the wool carpet, the velvet bedroom slippers, anything to avoid that quivering quilt. 'That would, of course, legitimize the entry of Indian troops on to Manimiri soil and permit India to act officially without the slightest constraint against the bandits who have encroached upon our – I mean your – sovereignty. I shall . . .' He stopped short, his eyes having travelled from the carpet to the foot of the armchair – and to the flimsy female undergarments he had knocked on to the floor.

'No!' The Maharaja cried, half-sitting up and then subsiding again on to his pillow. 'Ah. Yes. No. No accession. Never! Yes. Ah. Why? Yes. Can't you send? Ah. Indian troops? Ah. Yes! Friendly basis? Why accession? No! Yes! Yes!'

'I beg your pardon, Your Highness?' Vidur asked in some confusion.

'Yes! Dammit, no! No! No, don't stop – *n'arrêtes pas* – yes! Yes!' The words were emerging in little grunts. 'Send me. Troops. Aah. Save my state. Aah. Then go away. Aah. No accession. Aaah. Understand?'

'I don't think *you* understand, Your Highness,' Vidur stood up. 'If what you are suggesting is that India should send you her armed forces as a gesture of friendship, defeat the invaders and then restore your kingdom to you, I am afraid you are . . . you are living, sir, in' — he found himself looking at the mobile mound again, and his tongue switched on to automatic pilot — 'a fool's paradise.' As soon as the words were out he regretted them; one simply did not speak to a Maharaja like that, not even to a colossal fool like Mr Z. 'I . . . I'm sorry, Your Highness, I . . .'

But the Maharaja did not seem to have heard him; his 'ahs' had become too frequent and too loud now to permit conversation. The royal eyes were completely hooded, the hands were moving under the *razai*, and the discernible portion of the Maharaja's trunk was arched in unabashed ecstasy.

'Your Highness!' Vidur expostulated.

'Yes . . . yes . . . YES!' screamed the Maharaja. The heaving mass of silk and embroidery gave one last convulsive jerk, and Vidur found himself staring as a bare white foot popped briefly into view and slipped back under the *razai*. It was a soft, delicate foot, with painted nails pointing downwards; but the Maharaja was still lying on his back . . .

Vidur closed his incredulous eyes, and tottered heavily on to his chair. 'Aaaaaahh!' he heard the Maharaja say, expelling air like a deflating brown balloon. When he opened his eyes again Vyabhichar Singh was sitting up against the pillows, his hands pudgily outside, holding the edge of the *razai* up to his uncollared collar-bone. 'That feels much better,' the Maharaja said cheerfully. 'Nothing like a spot of exercise last thing at night. Does wonders for the constitution.'

Vidur nodded silently, his vocabulary defeated by the occasion.

'Now you were saying, Mr Secretary . . .'

'I was saying,' said Vidur at last with uncharacteristic bluntness, 'that the only basis on which India will send you troops, Your Highness, is if Manimir accedes to the Indian Union.'

'You can't be serious,' the Maharaja said, bliss fading rapidly from his face.

'I'm afraid I am.'

'You mean you'll let me down, expect me to cope with these marauding Muslim hordes all by myself, let Manimir fall into Karna's hands, unless I sign my throne away?'

Vidur thought about the truckloads of troops even now rolling towards India's border with Manimir, and decided that honesty was not, the

Mahaguru's teachings notwithstanding, the best policy. 'Yes,' he lied for the only time in his life. 'The Prime Minister has no intention of sending Indian troops to fight for your throne, Your Highness. But we will fight – for Indian soil.'

'It's not much of a choice, is it?' the Maharaja asked bitterly. 'If I don't get your help, I lose my throne; if I get your help, I still lose it. What difference will it make whether I sign or not? I'm finished as Maharaja either way.'

The mound stirred at these words.

'It will make a world of difference, Your Highness,' Vidur said. 'If you sign the Instrument of Accession, I will fly you in my plane tonight to your winter palace in Marmu, a few hundred miles further from the marauding hordes you refer to; Indian troops will move in, beat back the invaders and preserve your palace and your property; and the Cabinet in Delhi will undoubtedly express its gratitude to you in a . . . a tangible way.'

'Ambassador to Outer Mongolia?' Vyabhichar Singh's lip curled.

'On the other hand,' Vidur went on, 'if you prefer *not* to sign, the Pathans will push aside the opposition of your royal guard as if they were swatting flies, take over this palace and all within it, and conceivably string you up, Your Highness, from the nearest flagpole.' A little shriek was stifled under the *razai*. Vidur found himself relishing every word. 'Probably not before they have worked their gentle touch on you and any – companions and friends of yours they may find,' he went on cruelly. 'You know the reputation of our dear ex-countrymen from the North-West Frontier. They stay bottled up in those dry, drab hills for months on end, and then they have an opportunity to let off a little steam when someone finances a jolly little expedition like this. The kind of steam, Your Highness, that scalds rather deeply. I wouldn't say it is such a poor choice after all.'

The Maharaja swallowed. 'I'll need time to think about this,' he said.

'Time, I'm afraid, is one thing I haven't got, Your Highness. Even as I speak to you, my plane is warming up to fly me back to Delhi – and, if you wish, to drop you at Marmu. I am carrying in my briefcase a typed draft of the Instrument of Accession. All you have to do is put your signature to it – I shall even provide the pen – and Indian troops will begin to advance into Manimir. Otherwise, it is best I take my leave now. I have no desire to be stuck in Devpur when the Pathans get here.'

'I –' The Maharaja had barely begun to speak when the mound rose abruptly and the *razai* was flung back off the foot of the bed, burying him under its heavy embroidered folds. A steatopygous blonde wearing nothing but a look of panic turned to the well-swathed Maharaja. *'Mais c'est affreux,'* she exclaimed as the Maharaja struggled to free himself from his silken encumbrances. *'Qu'est-ce que tu attends? Que ces Pathans me violent ou quoi? Signe!'*

She bent forward, presenting Vidur a perfectly proportioned behind, and proceeded to pummel her helpless helpmeet. Mr Z flailed his hands in a vain bid to escape from the all-embracing quilt and the relentless assault. *'Signe!'* she screamed. 'Sign!' Vidur closed his eyes and tried to recall long-forgotten French lessons, but the words kept getting mixed up in his mind with his only previous recollection of a bare Caucasian behind, glimpsed during a *Folies* show at a daring private club in the country's great eastern metropolis. *'Oh, Calcutta!'* he breathed. (Now you know, Ganapathi, how old that malapropism is.)

Four hours later he walked into Dhritarashtra's study – my blind son had been up all night waiting for him, but then night and day mattered little to our Prime Minister – and flapped a piece of paper under his half-brother's sensitive nose.

'Here it is,' he declared in what were to become (thanks to a pair of indiscreet biographers) the most historic words ever spoken by an Indian civil servant. 'We've got Manimir. Mr Z has signed the Instrument of Accession. And now that I've done my job, I hope the bloody army can do theirs.'

76

As you can see, Ganapathi, Vidur spoke a very different language in private from that which he employed in official meetings ('that which' – got it? Good). But he had usually, throughout his long career, been right. What he had said to the Maharaja about the Pathans, for instance – though you would have been forgiven for thinking it was just a ploy to scare Mr Z into signing – turned out to be, in the army phrase, 'spot on'. The Pathans believed fully in enjoying their all-expenses-paid opportunity to 'let off steam', and so threw away the great tactical advantage of their initial stealthy advance into Manimir. They digressed into little forays of loot, rape and pillage that diverted them from the main objectives their Karnistani paymasters had charted. As a result, an invasion that could quite conceivably have taken the Manimiri capital before the Indian troops even got under way, became stalled first at the shelves of successive shops (rapidly stripped by the raiders) and finally at a wayside convent full of German nuns and white wine (ditto). While the Pathans indulged themselves in every kind of Liebfraumilch, the First Sikh Regiment and nine metric tonnes of Indian Army *matériel* were airdropped on Devpur. When the Maharaja's accession to India was announced, a furious Karna committed regular troops to the fray to make up for the unprofessionalism of the irregulars. The first Indo-Karnistan War had begun.

Apart from the distractability of Karna's chosen instruments, there was one other important element in India's favour. Sheikh Azharuddin, the Manimir National Congress leader, announced his welcome to the Indian troops early in the campaign, at a massive public rally in Devpur after the Maharaja's flight from his palace with Vidur and his panicky companion. 'When our friends from Karnistan are attacking and violating our sisters and our homes in the name of Islamic brotherhood,' he declaimed passionately, 'I say, to hell with Karnistan! The Indians have deposed the tyrant who has oppressed us for so long. They offer us the prospect of people's rule – *our* rule – democracy. I pray for their success.'

With Azharuddin on their side, Ganapathi, the Indians had won half the battle – that crucial half which is fought in the hearts and minds of the people. There were no fifth columnists to worry about, no fear of having to defend their backs from the treachery of a resentful population. The Indian Army rolled back the invasion with panache. They were poised to push the unfirm irregulars and the uniformed regulars completely out of Manimir when they were drawn up short – several hundred miles short – by an inopportune cease-fire cast over their heads like an ill-directed fishing net. My blind and visionary son had decided to appeal to the UN.

Many of us who never forgave him for that decision found all sorts of indefensible impulses behind it. It was common talk, for instance, that Georgina Drewpad had chosen this period to visit her old dominion, and ventured a viceregal opinion to which Dhritarashtra had been unduly susceptible. Others thought that it was my son's education that was to blame, that his mind had been formed by the very sort of people who had founded the United Nations to meddle in other people's affairs. Still others suggested that had the Prime Minister been able to see, even just a tiny little crack, he would not have made such an obviously stupid decision. I think all these critics were overlooking one thing: that Dhritarashtra had not, after all, been the Mahaguru's handpicked heir for nothing. The boy had a conscience, and his conscience would not allow him to let soldiers take and lose lives for land he was certain India would regain at the conference table, in an international court of law or in a democratic referendum. Of course he was wrong, but he was wrong, Ganapathi, for the right reasons.

So Manimir remained condemned to the label of 'disputed territory', part of it in Karnistani hands, the bulk in ours. The state whose attachment to India was the most eloquent possible repudiation of the religious Partition paid a high price for Dhritarashtra's idealism. To this day it is scarred by tank-tracks, amputated by cease-fire lines, exploited by rhetoricians and fanatics on both sides of the frontier who prostitute its name for their own meretricious purposes.

Yet, Ganapathi, what a story it was. A story of India: of the decadence and debauchery of princes, of the imperatives and illusions of power; of the strengths of secular politics and the weaknesses of internationalist principle. An Indian story, with so many possible preambles and no conclusion.

It was also over Manimir that Dhritarashtra first revealed the technique of political self-perpetuation that he was to develop into such a fine art in the years to come. When the first criticisms were openly raised within the Kaurava Party, Dhritarashtra silenced them promptly by offering to resign. He knew perfectly well that with Gangaji gone and Pandu dead, Karna across the new frontiers and Rafi sidelined by the fact that much of his community had suddenly become foreigners, there was no obvious alternative leader the party could find. The critics responded by muting their objections; and Dhritarashtra learned how easy it was to get his own way.

The consequences of idealism and the imposability of individual will were prime ministerial lessons also learned, and profoundly absorbed, by the dark-eyed young daughter whom the widower Prime Minister had appointed as his official hostess. Yes, Ganapathi, Priya Duryodhani listened, and watched, and imbibed tone and technique from her paternal model. With Manimir, she learned her first exercise from her father's political primer. It was an education from which the country was never to recover.

77

And what of the offspring of India's blind leader and Britain's all-seeing Vicereine, the infant Draupadi Mokrasi?

The frail girl quickly overcame the handicaps of her premature birth, her health improving as Dhritarashtra quietly devoted a discreet eye – forgive me the expression, Ganapathi, but it was one of Dhritarashtra's – and an equally discreet cheque-book to her welfare. It was soon clear she would grow into an extraordinarily beautiful woman, but in childhood her other traits of character were apparent in a way they would not be in later years, when her beauty too often blinded men to everything else.

One of her teachers at the time, a Professor Jennings, was asked to describe the young Draupadi. He cleared his throat in that unnecessary British way and spoke in a voice as dry as the tomes he had authored, looking through horn-rimmed glasses at a point just above the questioner's tilted head.

'To her exquisite looks,' he said in a self-consciously passionless tone, as if he were describing an English breakfast, 'she added an open manner, an ability to learn from and adapt to the conditions in which she found herself, and a willingness to play with all the children in the neighbourhood, irrespective of caste, creed or culture.

'If Miss D. Mokrasi had a fault,' he went on, knowing he was expected to be aware of one, 'it was that she spoke a little too readily, in a voice that for a young girl was somewhat too loud, and in terms that ought to have been more self-restrained. She did not always eat enough, and though she studied hard she often tended to learn by rote; but that completed the list of her disabilities. While she was not always the equal to every situation with which she was confronted, she was blessed with great faith in herself. She might not always perform brilliantly, she knew; but she could always muddle through.'

A true daughter of India, little Miss Mokrasi. With her, we felt that we, too, could always muddle through.

THE THIRTEENTH BOOK:
PASSAGES THROUGH INDIA

78

As Draupadi Mokrasi grew up, my five grandsons the Pandavas stepped out into the world. They shared a rare heritage and an unusual education, and inevitably proved unable to shake off another inheritance: they all decided to follow their father and their teacher into politics.

Drona did not last long in government. His style was a little too idiosyncratic and his attitude to administration a little too personal for him to have been able to make a success of it. Not long after ensuring the rapid repatriation of the Englishmen in the civil service, he resigned, stating that he preferred to devote himself to 'constructive work' in the countryside rather than in a paper-laden office. His five students and his son immediately offered to join him. 'Look,' said their mentor candidly, 'I'm not sure I want to inflict my plans on you. For Ashwathaman, of course, it's a different matter — he's my son. But the rest of you, princes of Hastinapur, wandering with me seeking social change in the villages — I don't think it's going to work. For one thing, you've never wandered around before. Ashwathaman and I have.'

'We thought you said that we were all equal in your eyes as your students,' Nakul said. He used the first person plural as a matter of habit, because he more often than not spoke for Sahadev as well.

'Of course,' replied Drona. 'But education is one thing, experience another. Ashwathaman and I have had the experience. You haven't. You'd be miserable.'

'I think you should leave it to us to judge that, Dronaji,' Yudhishtir said quietly. 'We wish to go with you. Will you deny us that privilege?'

'All right, all right,' said Drona crossly, though he was, as you can probably imagine, Ganapathi, quite pleased by his protégés' devotion. 'Come along, then. But don't tell me later I didn't warn you.'

The five went together to take leave of Kunti. She was seated in the living-room, half-smoked Turkish cigarettes overflowing from a near-by ashtray whose silver matched the tint of the hair at her temples. Her Banaras sari, Bombay nails, Bangalore sandals and Bareilly bangles all advertised her fabled elegance — an elegance betrayed only by the strain at the corners of her red eyes and by the quick darting puffs she took through her ivory cigarette-holder.

'Don't tell me,' she said as Yudhishtir stepped forward from the little group to address her. 'Let me guess. You all remembered it's my birthday and you have a surprise present for me.'

'But your birthday's next month, Mother,' Nakul said.

'How clever of you to remember, Sahadev,' Kunti trilled cuttingly. 'So it can't be that, then. I know! You're all taking me to the cinema.'

Yudhishtir shifted uneasily from foot to foot. 'No, Mother,' he said.

'No? Then it must be something nicer. I've got it! For the first time in so many years you have decided you want to spend your afternoon with me. Talking. Or playing a board game, perhaps. Have I guessed right? Scrabble? Monopoly?' She laughed hollowly. 'Monopoly! That would make a change from solitaire.'

Yudhishtir shuffled again, looking unhappily at the others. 'No, Mother,' he repeated weakly.

'No, Mother? But how can that be? You couldn't possibly be standing here to tell me, could you, that you have decided to leave me alone in this house and go off with that smelly wretch Drona and that scruffy son of his to do "constructive work", whatever that means, in the dirty villages?' She looked levelly at Yudhishtir, but her hand pulled the cigarette-holder in and out of her mouth with the jerky speed of a wound-up marionette. 'No, that's simply not possible.'

'You knew all along, Mother,' Yudhishtir said.

Kunti ignored him. 'I'll tell you why it's not possible,' she went on. 'It's not possible that my five grown and nearly grown sons could be so thoughtless, so selfish, so ungrateful, as to repay all my years of devotion to them by walking out on me like that. Just like their thoughtless, selfish, ungrateful father. Leaving me,' she added bitterly, 'alone.'

'Mother,' Yudhishtir said gently, 'you know we have never disobeyed you, in anything. If you forbid us to go we shall stay.'

'Forbid you?' Kunti turned her face away so that they would not see the tears come smarting to her eyes. 'And then have you hulks moping around the house looking at me as if I have sentenced you all to death? No, Yudhishtir, don't try and make it easy for yourself. I shall not forbid you. Go, if you want to. All of you. Go.'

They looked hesitantly at each other. 'Mother, you will be all right, won't you?' Bhim asked.

'Oh, I'll be all right,' Kunti replied, the sun reflecting off the moistness of her pupils. 'As all right as I have ever been.' She ran the back of a hand across her eyes. 'There – that does it: I've smudged my eyeliner. It's not even as if the five of you are worth it. What sort of company have you been for me, anyway? It'd be just the same whether you were here or not.'

'Mother, I promise you,' Yudhishtir said earnestly, 'that we shall come back to you whenever you need us. And that we will never, ever disregard a single instruction you give. We swear never to disobey anything you say, however big or small the issue.'

The promise took on a new dimension: it was the corollary and the condition of their autonomy. Solemnly, in an instinctual ritual of affirmation that seemed to belong to another world, they each echoed the promise. It thus acquired a reality of its own, which would come back to haunt them years later.

Kunti, touched, looked up at her eldest son.

'Will you give us your blessing, Mother?' Yudhishtir asked. 'Before we go?'

'Yes,' she said at last, wrenching the word from her heart. 'God bless you, my sons, in whatever you do.' She found she could not stop the tears from coming. 'Now go. I hate you seeing me like this. For my sake, all of you, go!'

They went, slowly filing out of her presence, and when the room was empty at last she raised her tear-soaked face to the window and spoke bitterly to herself, and to the rays of the sun that streamed in to mock her misery with their brightness.

'Why me, Lord, every time? Why must I be abandoned by every man to whom I give myself? Even by the sons I bore with such pain?'

There was, of course, no answer. But the celestial breeze that swept into the room and dried the tears upon her cheek also left the echo of an answer in her mind. '*It is*,' the echo whispered, '*it is your karma, Kunti.*'

But then it could as easily have been her imagination.

 *79*

'Ah, Kanika, is it you? You walk so softly I cannot always tell.'

'Yes, Prime Minister. In fact I have left my sandals outside the door. After all the months of being cribb'd, cabin'd and confin'd in the shoes England obliges me to wear, I find even sandals too much of an imposition when I am home.'

The visitor's padding footsteps neared him and Dhritarashtra recognized the familiar aromatic combination of Mennen after-shave ('if they are willing to name a cologne after me, I may as well use it') mingled with onion-and-red-chilli *samandi*, the favourite breakfast chutney of his High Commissioner in London. 'Prime Minister, it is good to see you,' V. Kanika Menon breathed powerfully as the two men embraced.

'As your American friends say, likewise.' Menon laughed: he had no American friends. The usual consequence of contact between him and 'those of the American persuasion,' as he liked to describe them, was apoplexy – on the part of the Americans. Kanika invariably remained his cool, acerbic self throughout these encounters, while everyone else present felt they had just been through a wringer and had come out still wet. Dhritarashtra was probably his only friend in the world.

'How are things across the black water?' the Prime Minister asked as his guest made himself comfortable.

'Tolerable, though Albion remains as perfidious as ever,' Kanika replied. 'But let me not waste your time on petty routine. I have been debriefed – I believe that is the current expression, though I am always tempted, when I hear it, to make sure I still have my undershorts on – by the mandarins of the External Affairs Ministry.' He shook his head expressively, a gesture wasted on his friend: how easily one forgets Dhritarashtra's blindness, he thought. 'I have often wondered, Prime Minister, where you pick up some of these characters. All terribly solemn fellows in elaborate three-piece suits and better accents than I am accustomed to hearing when I am summoned to Whitehall. But ask them for a decision and it's as if you had suggested a dirty weekend. Send them a cable and they will contrive brilliantly to lose it amongst themselves. I cannot recall a single transaction with them that has not taken weeks rather than days. Are you sure, Prime Minister, that some of them haven't misread the name of their enterprise as the Ministry of *Eternal* Affairs?'

Dhritarashtra laughed. 'You are incorrigible, Kanika. No wonder your Russian friends think so poorly of our boys in South Block. The ideas you must put into their head!'

'Me?' Kanika Menon put all his injured innocence into his voice, regretfully shelving the expressive gestures for which he was famous on the international rhetorical circuit. 'I have no Russian friends, Prime Minister, you know that. Several acquaintances, perhaps. And they don't need *me* to tell them about our ministry. You know what the Russian ambassador said to me the other evening?' Menon assumed a booming voice and the accent of a Volga boatman. 'Come here, Menon, and I will tell you what they are saying in the Kremlin about your Indian diplomacy,' he quoted. 'They say it is like the love-making of an Indian elephant: it is conducted at a very high level, accompanied by much bellowing, and the results are not known for three years.'

'Oh, Kanika,' laughed the Prime Minister helplessly, 'I don't know what I do without you in Delhi most of the year. But I am glad you have taken this little holiday. You are just what the doctor ordered.'

'Problems?' Kanika asked, instantly sympathetic.

'Well, of a fashion,' Dhritarashtra replied. 'No, not really. Well, let me put it this way: some of our people in the Kaurava Party think there is a problem.'

'You are speaking, Prime Minister, in riddles. You will have to make allowances for your uninformed cousin from the country.'

'I don't think you know Jayaprakash Drona,' Dhritarashtra said. It was more of a statement than a question: Kanika had spent the years of the struggle for freedom running the Indian Home Rule League in London, where Dhritarashtra had met him. His personal knowledge of Indian politicians was largely based on whether they had travelled his way during his long self-exile. Drona had not.

'You mean the saintly anarchist? Only by reputation.'

'Well, that's something,' the Prime Minister said. 'A *good* reputation?'

'More or less,' Kanika responded cautiously. 'Nationalist, idealist, willing to lay himself on the line, or so the American military attaché said to me at the time of the Quit India business.'

'Really? I wouldn't have thought the Americans took much notice of the Quit India movement.'

'Oh, they did. The moment it was announced. I think they saw Gangaji's choice of a slogan as a definite tilt towards America. "Quit" is very American, you know. Though the Yankees are more used to hearing it applied to them in the Latin world. I was a little surprised myself: the British stopped using "quit" in that sense about the time of Spenser.'

Dhritarashtra laughed. 'And did you confirm the American's analysis for him?'

'Of course not. I told him we were still three hundred years behind in our use of the English language.'

'Disappointing,' Dhritarashtra said lightly. 'I wonder when we'll ever make a diplomat out of you? Anyway, so you know about Drona. If you have been following developments at home as you are supposed to, I suppose you also know he quit the Council of Ministers some time ago and went off into the villages, accompanied by Pandu's five sons and his own.'

'I seem dimly to recall something along those lines,' Kanika replied, as fastidious about not splitting his infinitives as he was about infinitely splitting hairs. 'As you can probably guess, it failed to make much of an impact in the imperialist press, and I read the Indian papers, when they get to me five weeks late, only for the domestic cricket scores. But why on earth did Drona do this?'

'To work for the political transformation of rural India,' Dhritarashtra sighed. 'And no, you wouldn't have seen much about it in the Indian newspapers even if you had looked beyond the sports page, because their reporters never venture out into the countryside. The Indian press purveys news of, by and for the urban élite. Drona doesn't belong to any of those categories.'

'Oh, the jute-bag press will notice him all right, the moment his rustic crusade impinges on their owners' interests,' Kanika replied sardonically. 'My personal recipe for getting the attention of the Indian press is to attack the jute industry. Gangaji did it, and he was front-page material for the rest of his life. Mind you, he did a few other things too, but you can't overlook the fact that the largest shareholders in at least half a dozen of the country's leading newspapers are jute barons. But I digress. You were telling me about Drona, who, I presume, has so far left jute alone.'

'Oh, yes. But he has made some inroads in other areas, with his young followers. Raising the villagers' consciousness of their democratic rights. Ensuring that tenants on large farms get their due, and clamouring for land reform. Exposing corruption and maladministration in the police and the village councils.'

'And this worries you?'

'It delights me!' Dhritarashtra was emphatic. 'Kanika, these are the sorts of things that I have spoken and written about all my life, the kinds of things that the Kaurava movement was, as far as I am concerned, all about. You know my views — we were Socialists in London together. How could you ask such a question?'

'Because you seem troubled. And because you implied there may be a problem about Drona.'

'Of course. I'm sorry, Kanika. It's just that — that this whole business is so terribly unworthy, if you know what I mean. Some people have been advising me that Drona and his young followers are becoming too popular. They feel I ought to be doing something to — make life a little difficult for them. Cut them down to size.' Dhritarashtra exhaled his anguish. 'I just can't bring myself to, Kanika. I need your advice.'

Kanika was silent for a moment, as if weighing two answers in the balance. 'In questions of political judgement, Prime Minister, I am something of a traditionalist,' he said at last. 'I go back to the lessons of the *Arthashastra*, from which Machiavelli plagiarized so effectively, and the *Shantiparvan* of Vyasa. I hope you won't mind what I am going to tell you, but for what it's worth, it comes sanctified by the centuries:

It's never that easy to be a king
And rule a populace;
For popularity's a fickle thing
Which might easily gobble us.

A king must always make it clear
That in his realm he's boss;
Nobody else, though near and dear,
May inflict on him a loss.

A king must always show his might
Even 'gainst kith and kin; .
It doesn't matter if he's right
But he must be seen to win.

There's not much point in being strong
If no one sees your strength;
A tiger shows power all along
His striped and muscular length.

Any weakness must be concealed
As a tortoise hides his head;
A king must never be revealed
Quaking under his bed.

Stealth and discretion are the means
To employ in making plans;
A clever king, though, never leans
In trust on another man's.

Pretend! Conceal! Find out! Mistrust!
These are the vital things;
Maintain a cheerful outer crust
But permit no rival kings.

Keep your intentions to yourself –
Don't reveal them on your face;
Purchase silence with your pelf
And pack a knife (in case).

Give orders only when you're sure
Of their effective execution;
Make certain you are seen as pure
– Innocent of persecution.

Eradicate the slightest threat!
Don't forget the thinnest thorn
Embedded in your flesh, might yet
Fester; and this I warn:

A small spark can start a forest fire –
No enemy's too minor –
Before the danger gets too dire
Don't make the fine points finer.

There never is a genuine need
To issue an ultimatum;
Before a rival does the deed –
Simply eliminate him.

Do it sharp, and do it quick!
But never let him catch on.
(To be safe, keep a big stout stick
And always sleep with the latch on.)

Dissimulate! When angry, smile;
Speak soft; then strike to kill;
Then weep – oh, never show your bile –
And mourn your victim still.

Amass all the wealth you can;
Cash, jewels, humans too;
Resources are needed for every plan,
And any means will do.

Remember it's said a crooked stick
Serves just as well as a straight one
When it's fruit from a tree you wish to pick
(An early plum, or a late one).

So employ your own crooked men
To gather information;
From the market and the gambling den
Let them take the pulse of the nation.

Regarding enemies, I only wish
You'd learn from the fisherman's book;
He traps and slits and strips his fish,
And burns what he doesn't cook.

That's the only way to treat all those
Who pose a threat to you;
They may genuflect, and touch your toes –
But don't let them get to you.

Think of the future; it's time to start
To anticipate the threat;
If you don't grow callouses on your heart
You might just bleed to death.'

Dhritarashtra sighed. 'Thank you, Kanika. I know you're speaking with my best interests at heart, but that's simply not me. I can't do it.'

'You asked for my advice,' Kanika Menon shrugged. 'I gave you the only advice I could.'

'I know,' Dhritarashtra said. 'Now let's try and forget I ever asked you, shall we?'

'Certainly,' his visitor said, the sharp, hawk-like face a mask. 'It'll go no further.'

But it already had. Just beyond the half-open door leading to the Prime Minister's private study, Dhritarashtra's dark-eyed daughter put down the book she had been pretending to read and smiled a quiet smile of satisfaction. She was glad her idealistic father had some less idealistic friends. Dhritarashtra might forget Kanika's advice, but Priya Duryodhani would remember every word of the acerbic High Commissioner's brutal counsel.

And she would not hesitate to act on it.

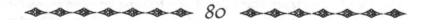 *80*

The government jeep seemed to hesitate before turning into the small village lane. When it gradually eased its way past the corner and entered the dust-track, its gear-grinding reluctance proved amply justified. There was scarcely enough space between the walls of the mud houses on either side for it to progress smoothly, and the road-surface available would not lightly have been classified by the Automobile Association as motorable. But once the turn was past, it was almost easier to continue than to retreat. The jeep bumped and jolted its way down, scattering shrieking children and squawking chickens in all directions like seeds flung by a tipsy farmer.

At last it drew to a noisy halt before an open space where a throng of villagers had gathered in front of a red-and-white banner proclaiming 'Land Reform Rally' in Hindi and English. A bearded speaker was declaiming to the crowd without the benefit of either text or microphone. The wayward breeze carried some of his phrases erratically towards sections of the crowd, which punctuated his eloquence with the occasional ragged cheer. The arrival of the jeep lost him the fringes of his audience: from where they stood the intruding vehicle had a clear advantage in audibility.

A rumpled figure emerged from the jeep and stood outside it, squinting at the scene with his hand to his brow like a sailor looking for land. A generous layer of dust had settled on his face and hair and streaked his unfortunate choice of garment, a cream-coloured cotton suit. In his hand he held a battered black briefcase.

'Uncle Vidur!' a youthful voice rang out above the speculative murmurs of the crowd. 'Uncle Vidur!' its twin echoed.

A tall, distinguished-looking young man in a cotton shirt and trousers detached himself from the knot of people near the platform and made his way after the two younger boys to the jeep. 'Uncle Vidur,' Yudhishtir said. 'What a pleasure to see you! What brings you here?'

'You,' Vidur said shortly. He was clearly in no mood for pleasantries. 'Where are the others? I have to talk to you all urgently.'

'Dronaji's on the platform and Bhim is pretty much holding it up for him – one of the supports gave way: we think it was sawed through by one of the landlords' people last night. Oh, and Arjun is up there somewhere keeping an eye on the crowd; we've had a couple of ugly incidents recently. But if you'll wait just a few minutes, Uncle Vidur, the rally's almost coming to an end.'

Vidur looked dubiously at the crowd. 'Oh, all right,' he said at last. 'But try and signal to him to finish fairly quickly. I haven't a great deal of time.'

Up on the platform Jayaprakash Drona was building up to an impassioned climax. 'We hear a great deal of socialist talk from New Delhi,' he declared. 'The government tells us it is reserving the "commanding heights of the economy" for the people – for the public sector. And what are these "commanding heights"? Iron and steel, to build big ships in which none of us will ever sail. Power, to light the homes of the rich who have electricity. Banking and finance, for those who have money to put into them.' (Answering echoes from the throng.) 'But what about the land, the earth, the soil which each of you and four fifths of your countrymen till to feed yourselves, your families, and the ration-card-wallahs in the cities? No one in Delhi is talking about land!' (Angry shouts.) 'While the bureaucrats and ministers stand on their "commanding heights", the common peasant of India is trodden into the demanding depths – of starvation and ruin! *They* do not care about ruthless exploitation by the landlords in the villages, because they are too busy in the cities. Busy worshipping at what our Prime Minister, Dhritarashtra, a man for whom I have great respect,' (ironic cheers from a section of the crowd), 'no, seriously, a man whom I greatly respect, called the "new temples" of modern India – the gleaming new factories his government has erected. Why "new temples"? Because Dhritarashtra hopes that our people will abandon their old temples, their real temples, to pray at the altar of his new machinery.' (Shouts of outrage.) 'I know this is difficult for you to believe, but that is what our Prime Minister wants. Well, he is not going to get it for a while, because his ministers dutifully echo his views, and then they make the new temples just like the old ones: they go to inaugurate a steel factory or a chemical laboratory, and they break a coconut and perform a puja outside.' (Appreciative laughter.) 'So I say to you all, it is time we forgot about the new temples and spent a bit of time thinking about the people who go to the old ones.' (Hear, hear.) 'You!' (Roar of applause.) 'This government has got to be pressed into implementing the land reforms the Kaurava Party has promised since before Independence. The honest peasant must be rewarded for the sweat of his brow! Land to the tiller! Down with landlord exploitation! Long live the humble Indian farmer!' (And echo answered, 'Zindabad!')

The speaker descended from his platform, and the crowd dispersed slowly, like ants abandoning a crumb. Drona walked with rapid strides to the visitor.

'Well, how did you like that?' the sage of the sansculottes asked, wiping the sweat from his brow as he greeted Vidur.

'Not bad,' the civil servant responded, 'except that I thought you were a little hard on poor Dhritarashtra there. After all, he believes in precisely the same things – land reform, tillers' rights, and so on. But he can't just wade in and change everything overnight. He's got a party, and a country, to run.'

'Well, he'd better realize soon that these people are his country,' Drona retorted. 'But it's clear you haven't come all this way to discuss politics. Or' – he looked shrewdly at the bureaucrat – 'have you?'

'Good Lord, no,' Vidur replied hastily. 'Look, isn't there some place we can talk?' He looked around him at the small circle of villagers who had gathered around them and were staring at Vidur with unashamed curiosity.

Drona grinned. 'You shouldn't dress like that, Vidur, if you want privacy in an Indian village,' he remarked mischievously. 'Come – there is a place we can all go to, if you'll promise to take off your shoes. The Shiva Mandir is normally closed at this hour, but the priest has given me a key to the back gate of the temple. We can sit under the shade of a large banyan by the side of a somewhat fungal tank, and talk to your heart's content in the courtyard of the Lord.' He regarded the jeep with interest. 'Is this your vahana? "Government of India, Central Bureau of Intelligence",' he read from the licence plate. 'Is that what you're doing these days?'

'The CBI is one of the departments that report to me, yes,' replied Vidur, whose success over Manimir had elevated him to the rank of Secretary of the Home Ministry. 'And that's why I want to talk to you. Can we get a move on?'

The six of them — Ashwathaman was away organizing the next day's rally at a near-by village — sat around their unexpected visitor, shoeless, at the temple tank, as he explained the reason for his unexpected visit.

'I'm afraid things are no longer safe for you,' he said, addressing himself directly to Yudhishtir. 'Someone — someone powerful, and I think it could be Priya Duryodhani — has given instructions that the five of you should be attacked, possibly killed.' He saw astonished questions rising to their lips, and raised a hand. 'Don't ask me how I know, or why I can't do anything about it. In time, perhaps, I can get Dhritarashtra or even Duryodhani herself to put an end to this madness and take back these insane instructions if she has anything to do with them, but right now they've already gone out and I was terrified they'd be acted upon before I could warn you. You're particularly vulnerable in this highly visible campaign of Drona's — it would be very easy to organize a riot or a violent disturbance in which you could be harmed.'

'Let's see who will try to harm us,' said Bhim with typical bravado. 'I will take on anyone and his father.'

'Don't be silly, Bhim,' Vidur said unkindly. 'You can't take on a bullet in the back or an expertly thrown knife from a crowd. I wouldn't have come all this way, at some personal inconvenience, if I hadn't believed the situation was more than even the five of you could cope with.'

'Of course, Uncle Vidur,' said Yudhishtir. 'Please go on.'

'I want the five of you to come with me immediately, in the jeep. It will be a bit of a squeeze, but the journey won't be long. I have a boat waiting on the banks of the Ganga a little way from here, just beyond the next village. A man will be waiting on the other side who will escort you to the town of Varanavata. It's a bit off the beaten track, but large enough for you to get lost in the crowd. Lie low for a while there, until this thing blows over. I can get messages to you through the local postmaster, but since it is an open wire they may be somewhat elliptical.'

'We will decipher them, Uncle Vidur,' Yudhishtir said quietly. 'What about Dronaji?'

'Yes,' said the saffron-clad firebrand, 'what about me?'

'You're quite safe, for the moment,' Vidur replied. 'Oddly enough, the threat seems directed only at the five of them, which suggests it may be personal rather than political — or at least more personal than political.'

'I still can't believe Duryodhani would be involved in anything like this,' Yudhishtir said.

'We can,' said Nakul candidly.

'I'll never understand that girl,' said Vidur with a tired shake of the head. 'If it weren't for a very strong instinct to the contrary, I'd have had it out with her directly. But something tells me it would be better if she did not know I am aware of what is going on – I can be more useful to you all in this way. I hope I'm right.'

'I'm sure you are, Uncle Vidur,' Yudhishtir said dutifully.

'Oh – and there's one more thing. Someone will be waiting for you at Varanavata – someone from whom I don't think you ought to be separated at this time.'

'Mother?' Arjun asked.

Vidur nodded. 'Be good to her, boys. She's been through a lot.'

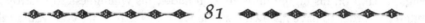

81

The news of the death of Karnistan's eponymous founder reached Dhritarashtra during his morning massage, when he had his major cables read to him.

'How did it happen?' he asked his half-brother, who had interrupted the uninspired elocution of a particularly truculent dispatch from London to give him the news. The Prime Minister lay on his front, wearing shorts and his ever-present dark glasses, as a burly *pahelwan* dissolved the knots of tension on his neck with the subtle pressure of his expert thumbs.

'Well, he hadn't been too well for some time now,' Vidur replied. 'You remember, that golden skin of his had begun to take on a decidedly yellowish tinge by the time Partition occurred. And there were moments when one almost felt one could look through that translucent half-moon on his forehead to the twisted mess inside.' Vidur stopped, embarrassed by his own imagination. 'But anyway, the actual climax was rather bathetic. Seems his official vehicle got stuck in the mud somewhere on an inspection tour. Karna barked at the driver, which only made the poor fool more nervous, so nervous he revved the engine too strongly and got the wheel embedded even more deeply in the mud. The Khalifa-e-Mashriq was apparently beside himself with rage. Leapt out of the car screaming imprecations at the hapless driver. Said he'd pull the wheel out of the mud himself with his bare hands.'

'Good God,' Dhritarashtra murmured, feeling other bare hands – stronger than Karna's – relax his shoulder-blades with long, deep strokes. 'And did he try?'

'Apparently. When the driver tried to help him Karna sent him back to his seat. It seems there were people around, but no one dared approach the Khalifa in this mood.'

'And then?'

'He apparently actually tugged at the wheel, which didn't budge, of course. And then he did something rather peculiar – I mean even more peculiar.'

'Oh?'

'He shook his fist at the sun.'

'Strange.'

'And almost immediately, so the story goes, keeled over and died,' Vidur completed the tale. 'With his hands still locked hopelessly on the wheel of his car.'

Dhritarashtra was silent for a moment as the muscular masseur kneaded life into the unexercised flesh of his thighs. 'I can't say I ever liked the man very much,' he said at last. 'With his overweening ambition, the glaring pseudo-religious chip on his highly un-Islamic shoulder, his willingness to destroy a country in order to have his own way, he wasn't exactly what you would call likeable. And yet . . . I wonder sometimes: if we had given him his due in the Kaurava Party, might he not today be remembered as one of the finest Indians of us all?'

He winced as the masseur's palms slapped his slackening waist more vigorously than usual. But Dhritarashtra did not take that as a political comment. He knew the masseur held the country's highest security clearance, shared only with a dozen members of the Cabinet and a handful of the top civil service. The *pahelwan* had been engaged with the most impeccable of credentials – a recommendation from me.

We historians, you see, Ganapathi, had to have our sources.

Far away, in a nondescript hotel room in charmless Varanavata, Kunti Devi Yadav, relict of the much lamented Pandu, heard the news on a tinny radio and wept. She wept for the son she had never known, and for the fate that had deprived her of that knowledge. She wept, too, for lost innocence and acquired guilt: the innocence she had surrendered in the arms of Hyperion Helios, and the dreadful guilt that only a mother who has survived a child can know. A mother who, in this case, was obliged to mourn her son alone, and in silence.

Kunti wept. She walked unsteadily to the barred window of her hotel room. And then, in a completely incongruous gesture, she pushed her braceleted arm out of the window, and shook her fist at the sun.

THE FOURTEENTH BOOK:

THE RIGGED VEDA

82

'Delighted to receive you, noble sirs.' The hotelier's brace of gold teeth gleamed in a beaming smile. 'My good name is Purochan Lal. I am very much honoured to welcome you to my humble hostelry. Will you be staying long?'

'A few days,' Yudhishtir replied non-committally. 'We have not decided yet.' He cast a look around the premises, unimpressed.

'Naturally, naturally.' Purochan Lal was scrapingly obsequious. 'It is only fit and proper that you should take your time to pronounce on the merits of our fair city. Er, town.'

'Can you show us to the room of our mother? She is expecting us.'

'Your mother? Most certainly.' Purochan Lal walked behind a rudimentary counter to a well-thumbed register. 'And what is her good name, please?'

'Kunti Devi. She must have arrived — oh, about a day ago. From Hastinapur.'

'Srimati Kunti Devi! But of course!' Purochan Lal seemed almost excited. 'You are saying she is your mother? You are her son?'

'Yudhishtir,' the eldest confirmed. 'And these are my brothers Bhim, Arjun, Nakul and Sahadev.'

'We are pleased to meet you,' said Nakul gravely. Arjun nodded. Bhim beamed.

'But what an unexpected honour!' The hotelier rubbed his hands in a combination of reverence and glee. 'The five sons of the meritorious Pandu! Our late great Chakravarti, scourge of the British!' He leaned over the counter in conspiratorial confession. 'I was myself a member of the Onward Organissation,' he announced in a sibilant whisper. 'Your wiss is my command.'

Yudhishtir looked embarrassed at the unexpected reception. 'Our only wiss, I mean wish, is to be taken up to our rooms,' he said. 'We are very tired, and we want to see our mother soon, if it's no trouble.'

'Trouble? No trouble at all. It is my pleasure to be of service to Chakravartissons. My only sorrow is that my rooms are so unworthy of such distinguished visitors. Hai, hai.' He shook his head in mournful self-reproach.

Then, suddenly, his regretful face lit up. 'But wait! I have an idea. My new house is almost ready. It is not far from here, and my family do not plan to occupy it till after Diwali. Why not you live there instead?'

'Really, we wouldn't dream of giving you such trouble,' Yudhishtir said. 'I'm sure we'll be perfectly comfortable here.'

'What talk is this? I am already telling you, it is no trouble at all,' Purochan Lal replied. 'I insist. It will be honour for me and my family to have you sleep under our roof. I must go and fetch the keys. But no, first I must take you to your mother. Then you all wash and be comfortable, and within one or two hours, I shall ready the new house for you.' He smiled and bowed and rubbed his hands again, as the three older Pandavas looked at each other and shrugged. 'You will accept? You will stay in my house? I am truly honoured. Please follow me.'

Early the next morning, the Home Secretary in Delhi grimly studied the smudged carbon delivered to him by his staff in the cable interception service. 'CONTACT ESTABLISHED STOP FIVE FULLY TRUSTING STOP MOVING TO PRE-TREATED HOUSE TOMORROW STOP PREPARATIONS MADE AS DISCUSSED STOP PLEASE ADVISE WHEN TO START STOP KINDLY CONTINUE REMIT FUNDS WITHOUT STOP STOP PUROCHAN LAL.' The cable had been sent from Varanavata the previous evening. It was addressed to Priya Duryodhani.

Vidur had to buy time.

He pulled a writing-pad toward him and rapidly drafted three cables in his quick, sloping hand. Thank God his most reliable man in Varanavata was the postmaster.

'FOR PUROCHAN LALL STOP MESSAGE RECEIVED STOP DO NOT DO ANYTHING TILL EYE TELL YOU TO START STOP CONTINUE YOUR PREPARATIONS AND DO NOT STOP STOP PLEASE DRAFT CABLES MORE CAREFULLY AND DO NOT END SENTENCES WITH STOP STOP STOP YOU SEE HOW CONFUSING THIS IS STOP FUNDS ARE MY RESPONSIBILITY AND THEY WILL NOT STOP STOP ESPECIALLY IF YOU STOP STOP STOP STOP.'

He signed that one Priya Duryodhani.

The next cable was to the postmaster. 'DO NOT DELIVER TO PUROCHAN LAL ANY CABLE OTHER THAN THOSE BEGINNING WITH WORDS QUOTE FOR PUROCHAN LALL UNQUOTE.' He signed his full name and title, and made sure he assigned the instruction an official reference number.

His last cable was the most difficult one to compose.

'FOR YUDHISHTIR CARE GPO VARANAVATA STOP YOUR LATEST

ASTROLOGICAL FORECAST STOP BE WARY TROJAN HOUSE STOP
GUARD AGAINST HEADLESS PARSON STOP DONT LET ON COLON
NO IMMEDIATE REARRANGED GARDEN STOP AM SENDING RABBIT
TO HELP BURROW STOP TRAVEL BROADENS THE HORIZONS STOP
LET STARS LIGHT YOUR PATH STOP UNCLE VIDUR.'

He re-examined the text with a critical eye. 'Trojan house' was a fairly obvious allusion. Had Yudhishtir done enough crosswords to deduce that 'headless parson' was 'arson' and 'garden' could be 'rearranged' as 'danger'? He hoped so. If the superfluous punctuation and the Confucianisms of the rest of the message proved more opaque, he could not help it: there was no way he could risk being more explicit. But the meaning could be guessed at, and it was only intended to place the Pandavas on guard until his man got to Varanavata.

It was time to send for the Rabbit.

 *83*

'What's this about a rearranged garden?' Bhim asked.

'Danger,' Arjun said shortly.

'I don't see what's dangerous about this garden,' Bhim looked around him contemptuously at the few scraggly bushes around the perimeter of the lawn. 'In fact it's not much of a garden at all, if you ask me.'

'Am sending rabbit to help burrow,' Yudhishtir mused.

'Burrow – that's a hole in the ground,' Arjun said reflectively. 'Rabbits make them. I think Uncle Vidur is suggesting either that someone will help us find a safe hiding place, or . . .'

'. . . will help us dig our way to one,' Yudhishtir agreed.

'Did I hear you say dig?' Bhim asked. 'In this garden? Forget it. You'd be lucky to get a cactus to grow here.'

'Travel broadens the horizons?' Yudhishtir asked.

'I suppose that means prepare to escape. And "let stars light your path" must refer to escaping at night.'

'Look, what are you two on about?' Bhim, who had caught only the occasional word of their exchange, asked belligerently. 'Sitting here talking about gardens, and digging, and looking at the stars in the night, as if we've got nothing more important to do! When are you going to tell Ma and me about the cable that came from Uncle Vidur?'

'Just as soon as we've worked out what it means, Bhim-*bhai*,' Arjun said mischievously. 'Here – why don't you look it over and have a try?'

Bhim took the pink form with its lines of erratically stuck strips of white paper and frowned at its contents. He raised his finger as if to scratch his head and then, realizing how the gesture might stereotype him, put it down again.

'Well?' asked Yudhishtir.

'It's in code, of course,' replied Bhim.

'Ten out of ten so far,' said Yudhishtir. 'But what does it all mean?'

'Roughly . . . We should watch out for a Trojan horse — "house" here's just a misprint, everyone knows what a Trojan horse is. I don't suppose he means a large wooden creature full of soldiers, but someone slipped into our company — I know! The servant maid!'

'The maidservant! How clever of you, Bhim!' Arjun marvelled. 'You mean toothless, sixty-year-old Parvati is really a sinister secret agent in disguise? I'd never have worked that out by myself.'

But Bhim was too engrossed in the rest of the text to catch his younger brother's mocking tone. ' "Guard against headless parson." That's more difficult. There must be a parish-priest type about who's dangerous.'

'And headless?'

The question threw Bhim for a moment, but he recovered quickly. 'Certainly, you know, when he loses his head. A sort of violent, schizophrenic type. Goes crazy on full-moon nights and runs about with an axe. That sort of thing.'

'Right, Bhim. So we'll be on our guard against Parvati and a lunatic priest. What else?'

'It says, "Don't let on colon". What part of the body is the colon, Yudhishtir?'

'It's the large intestine,' replied his polymath elder brother, 'from the caecum to the rectum.'

'It's also the monetary unit of El Salvador and Costa Rica,' Arjun added helpfully.

Bhim shot him a suspicious look. 'Are you trying to be funny, Arjun? Because this cable's got nothing to do with El . . . El Alamein and Costa Brava, or wherever. All this means is we've got to make sure the crazy parson never gets near our large intestines.'

'Keep away from our caecums, we'll say when he approaches.'

' "No immediate," Uncle Vidur says. An immediate no.'

'That's all very well, saying no and all, but Bhim, if this parson's that crazy do you think he'll listen?'

'Perhaps you have a point there,' Bhim admitted. 'Wait — maybe that's where the rearranged garden comes in. If we rearrange the garden, perhaps this priest will not go for our colons.' Bhim looked around him again. 'But I'll say this again: there's not much garden to rearrange.'

This might have gone on for ever, Ganapathi, were it not for a fortuitous interruption – the arrival outside of their mother. Kunti Devi, dressed in a simple cotton sari, walked to her sons with a frown on her face.

'Tell me, boys,' she asked with the directness for which she was known, 'do you feel there is something strange about the house?'

Yudhishtir and Arjun exchanged glances. 'In what way, Mother?' the elder asked.

'The smell,' their mother replied. 'I can't explain it, but there's something odd about the smell from the walls and floors of this house.'

'I thought so too,' Yudhishtir admitted, 'but knowing it was a new house, not yet occupied, I thought it might just be fresh paint.'

'There's no paint on the floors,' Kunti said, 'but they smell the same.'

Yudhishtir looked again at the cable in his hand, and at Arjun. 'I'll go and see, Mother,' Arjun said quietly.

'Don't just see, sniff!' Bhim bellowed after him.

'What are you boys discussing? Is that a telegram?'

'It's a telegram from Uncle Vidur,' Bhim announced. 'It's in code. I was just explaining it to them.'

'Really? From Uncle Vidur?' Kunti seemed disturbed. 'What does he say?'

'Just to be careful about certain things,' Yudhishtir said cautiously. 'There's nothing to worry about, Mother.'

'No,' said Bhim reassuringly. 'I can handle any number of schizophrenic priests and Trojan maidservants for you, Ma.'

Kunti's startled reaction might have merited a few clarifications, but at that moment Arjun stepped out of the house wearing a grave look.

'I think I know what it is,' he said as he approached them.

'The smell? What?'

'Lac,' Arjun replied.

'What do you mean, lakh?' Bhim asked. 'That's not a smell, it's an amount.'

'I didn't say lakh, Bhim, but *lac*. The word's from the same root, but this one's a resin, produced by coccid insects on the twigs of trees. It's transparent, so you can apply it anywhere and it won't hide the wood or whatever surface there is beneath, though it will give it the reddish look we all noticed. Of course, its smell takes some time to disappear, as Ma has just found out.'

'So that's all,' Kunti smiled, relieved. 'Well, I'd better go and see about some tea for all of us.'

'Wait, Ma.' Arjun paused. 'Keep the stove well away from the wall and the floor, and don't stub your cigarettes out anywhere but in an ashtray. You see, there is one property of lac I haven't mentioned yet. It's highly inflammable. We're living inside a petrol-can.'

 84

'Your report?' Vidur asked, leaning back in his chair.

'I went as instructed,' (said the Rabbit)
'Quite promptly – as is always my habit.
The five whom you said
Might even be dead
Had a chance – and I told them to grab it.

'Your cables had worked very well.
Purochan was confused as hell.
With your "start" and your "stop"
You had him on the hop –
So into our little net he fell.

'Obeying your telegrams, he'd waited.
His trap was all ready and baited.
Your nephews had no reason
To suspect him of treason;
Their extinction seemed virtually fated.

'It just was a question of time
Before Purochan committed the crime.
A touch of the torch
To the lac-covered porch
Was all it would take to fry 'em.

'Of course, he had started to wonder
If Duryodhani had made a blunder,
As day after day
He was asked to delay
The deed that would cast them asunder.

'Thank you, sir, for your delaying tactics:
Without them, we'd have been in a real fix.
But you gave us the time
To outsmart the slime
With our spades, hoes, shovels and picks.

'As soon as I'd established contact
And confirmed that your nephews were intact,
We started to dig
A tunnel so big
It made a geological impact.

'We all set to work with a will.
That Bhim! He'd eat his fill,
Then with enormous power
Dig out in an hour
Enough mud to form a small hill.

'In a short while our work was complete –
A remarkable engineering feat:
A spacious tunnel
Ventilated by funnel
And insulated from the inevitable heat.

'And all this was done surreptitiously.
(Purochan mustn't find out adventitiously.)
The opening (quite large)
Was concealed by camouflage:
Some shrubbery – placed most judiciously.

'At last we were ready to flee
The death-trap of Duryodhani.
Invitations were sent
For a festive event –
Dinner, offered by Kunti Devi.

'Purochan, unsuspecting, arrived,
With those of his henchmen who'd strived
So long and so hard
And so cleverly, toward
The elimination of the Pandava Five.

'They ate, drank and made merry
Uplifted by Kunti's spiked sherry;
By eleven o'clock
Quite downed by the hock
They dozed on the floor, quite unwary.

'At a signal from me, your five,
Like worker-bees fleeing the hive,
Slipped into the hole,
Each like a large mole,
And scurried to safety – alive.

'I went on to Stage Two of the Plan.
(The Rabbit's a reliable man.)
I touched a flame to the door
To the curtains, the floor –
And as the fire blazed, I ran.

'So Purochan had the end he had cherished:
The fulfilment of the plot he had nourished.
His house burned as he'd planned
(With the lac, you understand)
But it was Purochan himself who perished.

'In the meantime, under cover of night
The Pandavas made good their flight.
Guided by the stars
And the lights of passing cars
They sought refuge at another site.'

'Thank you,' said Vidur. 'I can take the story up from there.

'The papers all spoke of disaster:
The death of the heirs of the Master.
Foul play was feared,
For Purochan had disappeared,
And his walls had been of lac, not plaster.

'"Heinous crime!" screamed the press.
"National disgrace! What a mess!"
Said the PM on the morrow,
"I'm overcome with sorrow";
And Duryodhani – well, you can guess.

'I sent word to the boys: "Lie low.
Wait for this whole thing to blow.
Adopt a disguise,
Avoid prying eyes,
But as for coming back – no, no."

'So now they have started to wander.
Elegant Kunti has to cook and to launder.
From place to dim place

Across the great face
Of India, they walk, talk and ponder.

'It is, of course, an education.
They will learn about their great nation.
Though of no fixed address
And ignored by the press,
They'll be Indian (unlike others of their station).

'I've told them it will take some time
Before they can restart their climb
To public acclaim
And national fame;
For now they must remain in the grime.

'My nephews will travel in obscurity.
Do good work in strict anonymity.
But even if they chafe,
At least they are safe —
And not increasing too much their popularity.

'Several birds I kill with one stone:
Duryodhani doesn't break any bone;
Drona's wings are clipped,
(For he's just not equipped
Without my nephews, to succeed alone;)

'Dhritarashtra, my brother, is pleased
That the threat in his party has ceased;
My stratagem stifles
His potential rivals;
And with everyone, my own stock has increased.'

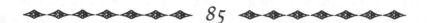 *85*

'So they will wander about, perfectly safe, and I shall be even safer? Brilliant, Vidur, simply brilliant.' The Prime Minister's relief shone brightly between his upturned lips. 'You see, Kanika, how Vidur has attained all that you were advocating, without any of the terrible means you proposed? I'm so glad, Vidur, that no violence was necessary.'

'There is, of course, Prime Minister, the slight matter of Purochan Lal and his associates,' said Kanika Menon, who rarely hesitated to voice an inconvenient truth. (Or, indeed, a convenient falsehood.)

'Ah ... yes.' Dhritarashtra was briefly dampened. 'I suppose that was unavoidable, was it, Vidur?'

'I'm afraid so, Prime Minister.' Vidur's tone was neutral, professorial. 'The police had to find bodies, and they had *not* to find Purochan. This was the only way to attain both objectives. And to protect your sister-in-law and nephews, of course.'

'Of course.' Dhritarashtra suddenly seemed less enthusiastic. 'But enough of all this. Divert me, Kanika. What have you been learning during this visit to our newly independent land? You must have a great deal to tell me.'

'Where can I begin, Prime Minister? Each day I am here I discover what a priceless collection of collaborators you have surrounded yourself with. Have you heard the latest about your Defence Minister?'

'No,' Dhritarashtra confessed. 'Unless it is the one about him asking for an appointment with the head of the Afghanistan Navy.'

'Ah, the old land-locked leg-pull. But really, P M, it's not as funny as all that – after all, even you've received the U S Secretary of Culture.' Kanika advertised his prejudices like a supermarket its sales, in large red letters. 'No, the story I had in mind originated during Sardar Khushkismat Singh's last visit to London. You know how much he likes a good joke, even – or especially – if he can't understand it. At a dinner in his honour, Churchill, whose standards are definitely slackening in his anecdotage, announced to the men over the port and cigars: "Gentlemen, I have a terrible confession to make." There was, as you can well imagine, a stunned silence. "For seven years in my dissolute youth, I slept with a woman who was not my wife." All eyes were upon him at these words, all ears strained with incredulity, none more so than Sardar Khushkismat Singh's. Churchill timed it to perfection. "She was, of course," he added carefully, "my mother." The guests laughed in relief as much as appreciation, and our good Sardar, albeit a little mystified by the British sense of humour, made a mental note of what had apparently been a highly successful joke. Last week, he gave a little dinner for me with some of the resident diplomats and military attachés, and after dinner, as the *saunf* was brought out, he decided to try out the witticism. "Gentlemen," he announced, "I must confess that in my dissolved youth, I slept with a woman who was not my wife." The consternation of his guests rivalled that of those at Churchill's party. The good Sardar practically tripped over himself in his haste to reassure them. "Not to worry, not to worry," he waved his hand. "It was Winston Churchill's mother."'

Dhritarashtra was laughing helplessly. 'Oh, Kanika, I don't know how I manage without you in Delhi,' he said. 'But then I don't know how I'd manage without you abroad. Eh, Vidur? Who'd stand up for us in the United Nations and defend us passionately over Manimir?' His face darkened. 'You know, I never thought, Kanika, that the Karnistanis would so completely turn the diplomatic tables on us as they have over Manimir. Had I known, I'd never have gone to the United Nations in the first place.'

'No, Prime Minister, but *they* might have,' Kanika Menon said. 'And outsiders who know nothing of our struggle for freedom, our history, our people, would have continued to sit in judgement on us. Karnistan was created for the Muslims, most Manimiris are Muslims, ergo Manimir should be in Karnistan. That is the extent of their political geography. I, of course, stand up and tell them that India does not consider that religion should determine statehood, and that the bulk of Manimir's Muslims were behind us when our troops marched in to protect them against the Karnistani invaders. But then they ask why, if that is the case, the most prominent of these Manimiri supporters of Indian intervention, your own friend Sheikh Azharud-din, is in jail.'

'I had to put him there, Kanika,' Dhritarashtra muttered unhappily. 'He was getting out of control. Vidur will tell you.'

'You don't have to tell me,' Kanika said. 'I know all the answers. In some cases I made them up myself. Remember I hold the record for the longest speech ever made at the United Nations, and it was on Manimir. There were a lot of answers in that speech, and a lot of counter-questions too. Would any of them in India's place have tolerated a Sheikh Azharuddin on their most sensitive border, flirting with the idea of his state's independence? That's what I asked them.'

'I know,' Dhritarashtra said. 'Kanika, you have done an excellent job abroad, defending and projecting India's position before and since Independence. Now I think it is time you came home. I will find you a safe seat at the next election. I want you in politics, and I want you in my Cabinet. I have even decided which ministry to give you.'

'The Foreign Ministry?' Kanika asked hopefully. 'Will you let me sink my teeth into the bloodless hounds of South Block?'

'No,' Dhritarashtra said. 'You know, Kanika, that is the one ministry I have always wanted to hold myself. Foreign affairs is the only subject where it doesn't matter that I can't see: everything else requires an empiricism of which I'm incapable. You understand?'

'Of course.' Kanika's hawk-like features concealed his disappointment. 'But then, whose place do you intend me to take?'

Dhritarashtra smiled wickedly. 'Sardar Khushkismat Singh's,' he said.

 *86*

Travelling southwards, guided by the stars and by their own instincts, the Pandavas sought security in constant movement. At each place, they performed some good deed, much like the itinerant cowboys of the more idealistic Western films, who rode into terrorized towns, guns blazing, demolished the good, the bad and the ugly, and rode off into the sunset, leaving the populace less miserable if more mystified.

The Five found themselves performing a different if not entirely dissimilar order of service in their peregrinations. They would enter a village in which the local priest, defying the new Constitution, was refusing to allow the Untouchables, Gangaji's Children of God, to enter the temple; or another where a landlord had evicted a pathetic family of tenants because they had been less than fully cooperative with his exactions; or a third in which a corrupt village official, a policeman or a *patwari*, was exploiting the poor and the illiterate for his personal profit. In each case, Yudhishtir would intervene in the name of righteousness; should his appeal fail, Arjun would attempt the method of reason; and if even this did not work, Bhim would settle the issue decisively with his highly personal techniques of persuasion, with Nakul and Sahadev standing by to pick up the pieces afterwards (and Arjun, marvellous Arjun, returning to the scene to reconcile his brothers' victims to the new dispensation). In each case the villagers were awed and grateful and anxious to offer a permanent home to the five strangers, but the Pandavas always picked up their few belongings and moved on before the villagers' demands became irresistible. On buses, bullock-carts, passing lorries but mainly on foot, our five heroes and their mother disappeared unobtrusively into the horizon, leaving behind, in each locality, a lesson and a legend.

Yes, Ganapathi, in villages across the alluvial trans-Gangetic heartland of India, in the dusty squares where the poor congregate to forget their misfortunes, in the twilit housefronts where old women tell the stories that their daughters and nieces will cherish and repeat and pass on like precious oral heirlooms, the legends grew of the five wanderers who came and did their good deeds and went. The stories always developed in the telling, being modified and embellished by each teller, so that eventually the details differed so greatly from one village's version to the next's that they might have been tales of totally different people. In one the five princes of Hastinapur became mendicants and holy men; in others their education and confidence proclaimed them quite clearly as exiles from a distant city; in some it was said that their impossible combination of attributes could only have been divinely inspired, and so they had come from Heaven to ensure that the dictates of dharma were followed in dusty Adharmapur. The ever less elegant figure of Kunti in their midst became variously that of a mother, a sister, a cook and a goddess — Shakti — in person, with her five arms in human form bringing justice to an evil world. And the legends grew, Ganapathi, even though it was not long after the Pandavas' passage that the reforms they had wrought quietly lapsed, and their erstwhile victims, convinced the wanderers would not return, returned to their old ways with a vengeance.

No, let me not be so categorical. Of every five good deeds they performed, four did not long outlast their departure, but in about one case out of five the Pandavas left behind a true convert, an unalterable new reality or a genuine change of heart. So it was in the country as a whole, Ganapathi. As the giant that was independent India lumbered into wakefulness and slowly purposeful motion, Parliament passed laws that a few implemented and many ignored, reforms were enacted that changed the lives of the minority and were subverted by the majority, idealistic policies were framed that uplifted some and were perverted to line the pockets of others, and everywhere it was five steps forward, four steps back. But the one step that was not retraced still made a difference. That was the only way that change would come to a changeless land.

In Delhi blind Dhritarashtra ruled with Priya Duryodhani by his side, and he pledged the nation not so much to the gas and hot water of his Fabian preceptors but to the smoke and steam of the modern industrial revolution their ancestors had denied his country. So factories sprang up amidst the mud and thatch of our people's homes; gigantic chimneys raised themselves alongside the charcoal braziers of our outdoor kitchens; immense dams arose above the wells to which our women walked to draw their clay urns full of water. India was well on the way to becoming the seventh largest industrial power in the world, whatever that may mean, while 80 per cent of her people continued to lack electricity and clean drinking water.

It was the same for the people themselves. Institutions of higher learning, colleges of technology, schools of management mushroomed in the dark humid forests of our ignorance. The British had neglected village education in their efforts to produce a limited literate class of petty clerks to turn the lower wheels of their bureaucracy, so we too neglected the villages in our efforts to widen that literate class for their new places at the top. Within a short while we would have the world's second largest pool of scientifically trained manpower, side by side with its largest lake of educated unemployed. Our medical schools produced the most gifted doctors in the hospitals of London, while whole districts ached without aspirin. Our institutes of technology were generously subsidized by our tax revenues to churn out brilliant graduates for the research laboratories of American corporations, while our emaciated women carried pans of stones on their head to the building-sites of new institutes. When, belatedly, our universities became 'rurally conscious' and offered specializations in plant pathology and modern agricultural methods, their graduates were to bid a rapid farewell to the wastelands of Avadh and Annamalai and earn immense salaries for making Arab deserts bloom.

But, as usual, Ganapathi — you are not strict enough with me — I digress; my mind wanders across this vast expanse of our nation like the five heroes whose tale I am trying to relate. Yet we cannot tell it all; we must soar above the mountains and the valleys, the hillocks and the depressions of India's geography and take the larger view of our cavalcade of characters as their wheels scratch the surface of our immense land. And occasionally we must swoop down to watch them at closer quarters, as they perform the acts and utter the words that give our geography its history.

87

Thus we spot our five in a village torn by the conflict between two landlords, Pinaka and Saranga. Pinaka, wealthy and powerful, always seen with an eagle on his shoulder, has immense holdings, farmed by battalions of tenants who are paid well for their services but have no title to the land. Saranga, an immense bear of a man, controls as big an area, but has signed over to his share-croppers the land they till, though he still exacts a tribute from them for this act of emancipation. Both landlords employ gangs of toughs armed to the teeth to protect those on their side of the divide and make menacing noises at their rivals. The Pandavas are the first people in the village who have no stake in the conflict; they arrive, they take up lodgings, they stay neutral. Both Pinaka and Saranga are suspicious, then solicitous; each assumes, the first because he is generous, the second because he is just, that the Pandavas will join *his* side. When they do not — for they see merit in aspects of both arguments, and are fully convinced by neither — they invite the opprobrium of both.

'How could you refuse to condemn Saranga when his hired hoodlums beat up poor Hangari Das, molested his wife and abducted his children merely because he wanted to keep his own harvests for himself?' Pinaka asked bitterly.

'What good would it do to condemn him?' Arjun replied. 'Would it have restored his teeth, his wife's pride or his children?'

'How can you refuse to join me when Pinaka fails to give his tenants their land, earns so much profit and heartlessly replaces a tenant when he finds another who can produce more revenue by his work?' Saranga was equally bitter.

'What good would it do to join you?' Yudhishtir replied. 'Would it change Pinaka's ways, give his tenants full title, and grant security to those among them who are ill or idle?'

They both went away, denouncing the Pandavas as hopeless and untrustworthy. At last, seeing that there was little they could do in this divided village, the Pandavas quietly left, abandoning both sides to their endless quarrel.

So too, Ganapathi, rising from our perch near the village of Pinaka and Saranga, we may flap our wings above the concrete and asphalt of the nation's capital. There, poised in the warm middle of a global cold war between the former colonizers and their allies on one side, and well-armed barbarians on the other, Dhritarashtra and Kanika evolved and elaborated the concept of 'non-alignment'. In their articulate exegeses this emerged as a lofty refusal to take sides in an immoral and destructive competition that could enflame the world. Yes, Dhritarashtra and Kanika developed into a fine art the skill of speaking for the higher conscience of mankind. To the brash and moralistic money-makers with whom the former colonial powers were allied, India's refusal to join the forces of God, light, and the almighty dollar was downright immoral, and Kanika Menon was portrayed on the covers of their international news-magazines – an honour even Gangaji had been denied – with his sharp face and hooded eyes drawn to resemble a poisonous cobra. To the bluff and amoral slavers and statists on the other side, India's rhetoric was insincere, either a Brahminical ploy to conceal the brown Britishness of their language and education, or a canny camouflage for the capitalist course being pursued beneath India's veneer of democratic socialism.

They were both right and they were both wrong, for Dhritarashtra was guilty only of the insincerity of the blind and Kanika of the inaccuracy of the ivory-tower. Both – Dhritarashtra for idealistic reasons, Kanika for ideological ones – believed in the non-alignment they preached, but neither could control the convictions or even the conduct of those who were to implement their policies.

Nor could either control indefinitely his own desire to flex the nation's muscles, which many outside thought to be atrophied by disuse and pacifism. Just as the loudest proponent of celibacy is most vulnerable to the temptation of easy sin – for restraint must always be sustained by lack of opportunity – so too non-violent India was being stirred into a frenzy by the provocations of a weak and wanton neighbour. This was the last remaining colonial enclave on the Indian coast, the picturesque Portuguese possession of Comea, a land of long beaches and cheap liquor, a haven for loose women and tight-lipped spies from which its foreign masters obdurately refused to withdraw.

After years of gentle persuasion by Dhritarashtra and his smoothest diplomats had failed, the hawk-faced Defence Minister persuaded his Premier that it was time to embark on a new course. The armed forces of the Indian Republic would take over the defiant but ill-defended colony.

Under the two bachelor statesmen, India's soldiers would at last enjoy their first foreign affair — and return home with a fair and fertile bride.

 *88*

It was at this time that the Pandavas, fatigued by a long day's marching on their passage through India, decided to settle down for the night in a wood.

It had been a tiring journey, and long before they reached the wood Kunti and the twins had felt too exhausted to carry on. Bhim lifted them up in his immense arms, but even his arborescent biceps began to feel the strain, and when they reached the first clearing in the forest Bhim simply put his burdens down and tore the PRIVATE PROPERTY – NO TRESPASSING sign off its post, flinging it with a crash into the bushes.

'What the hell was that?' asked Hidimba, a large man with a small goatee who owned the wood and the sprawling bungalow at the centre of it. He patted his enormous belly, yawned the sleep out of his colossal body and turned to his sister, who was serving him. 'Will you go and see what that is?' he asked. 'If it is an animal or a gust of wind, I shall go to bed. If it is a human trespasser, I shall have some sport.' He pushed his chair back and rose, a mountainous creature who towered over his sylph-like sibling as if he had absorbed her share of growth chromosomes in their common womb.

The girl stepped tentatively out, her fear of the darkness outweighed by her terror of her brother. A few paces into the forest brought her within sight of the clearing. She stood at its edge, saw the woman and the four youths asleep on the grass, and Bhim, sitting with his back to a tree, keeping guard. She took in the size of his chest and the strength of his arms, the straightness of his back and the solidity of his shoulders, the sinews on his neck and the subtlety in his eyes, and she fell instantly in love.

If you had seen the monstrousness of her brother Hidimba, my dear Ganapathi, you would not look so surprised.

She stepped into the clearing with her finger to her lips.
Bhim looked up at the vision of her firm and shapely hips.
'Who are you?' asked the girl, with a gentle winning smile;
'Don't you know this land is private for at least up to a mile?
My brother puts a sign up warning trespassers away;
If he finds them here he beats them like a farmer thrashes hay.
But if you'll follow me now, I shall lead you to a spot
Where Hidimba cannot see us, and the world can be forgot.'

She swayed her hips suggestively just as she spoke that phrase.
Her eyes both misted dreamily like a cool pond in a haze.
Her fingers played seductively with the beads around her throat;
She looked at Bhim as longingly as an MP at a vote.
'Don't say a word,' she whispered, as he seemed about to speak;
'Don't risk my brother coming to discover what I seek.
He's a nasty, cruel monster, and he keeps me like a slave,
To cook and clean and stitch for him, heat water for his shave.

'He doesn't let me go out, and no one can come in;
The very thought of another is an inexcusable sin.
And if he catches someone with no business to be here,
He beats him very badly, makes him really pay dear.
I was sent to see what had made the noises in the dark;
If I tell him he will come out and eat you like a shark.
But if, my dear, you come with me, as a flame welcomes a moth,
I'll hide you all and save you from my brother's terrible wrath.'

She was so sweet, so lovely, from small feet to ripened breast,
That her passionate entreaties might put any man to test.
But Bhim, though not unable to enjoy a bit of fluff,
Was – even in these matters – made of much sterner stuff.
'You are a fool, you silly girl, despite your many charms,
To think that at a time like this I'd take you in my arms,
Forgetting my first duty to my family sleeping here,
Whom I am closely guarding as the stag protects the deer.

'And let me tell you, woman, that you can tell your brother,
I can handle his assaults as I can handle any other.
There is no man I have yet seen who ever lived or died –'
'But you've not seen him!' the girl exclaimed; and sighed;
'. . . who frightens me,' Bhim went on, 'upon this blessed globe!'
'. . . And you've not seen me,' she said, slipping off her robe.
For a very long moment then our hero was struck dumb
As he stared at this creation whose ruby lips called, 'Come.'

Her eyes like silver fishes flashed him signals of desire,
Her breasts like heavy conch-shells set his manliness on fire;
Her curved round brown midriff with its oval opening
Was taut like a tabla ready for a man's drumming;
Her swaying hips and tapered thighs offset her downy jewel
Which mesmerized his malehood as if challenged to a duel.
Bhim found he could no longer speak; his throat was parched and dry,
And he might well have given in – but for a curdling cry:

'Whore! Slut! Lustful woman!' erupted a banshee shriek,
But it was no ghost nor female who provoked his sister's 'Eek!'
The gigantic man who entered, each nostril breathing fire
Left no doubt of his physical strength, and considerable ire.
Advancing with a heavy tread he raised a ham-like paw
And in an instant would have struck his sister to the floor;
But the naked girl in terror flung herself away from him
And took shelter behind the sturdy back of the startled Bhim.

'Hold on a sec,' our hero said, 'what kind of man are you?
You get your kicks from bashing girls?' (He spat:) 'Tch-Tchoo!
If that's the case, my outsize friend, with you I'll pick a bone
I shall teach you, in the future, to leave the weaker sex alone.'
'Aagh!' screamed the tyrant in inarticulate outrage,
'I'll take that girl and whip her and lock her in a cage.
And as for you, fat stranger, it will be stranger still
If I don't tear you limb from limb and leave you very ill.'

'Why don't you start?' Bhim sprang up: 'or shall we toss a coin?'
With one swift move he thrust a knee into Hidimba's groin.
The giant screamed, and hopped about, and Bhim stepped on his toe:
And then, as Hidimba swung, nimbly evaded the blow.
As the fight began the others stirred; their sleep was now disturbed,
And what they saw, when they took it in, left them most perturbed.
(Imagine waking from your dreams to see Bhim, his trousers torn,
Grappling with a monster, while a nude girl cheers him on.)

'Who are you, girl?' Kunti asked, anxious to establish a nexus,
As Bhim drove a sledge-hammer fist into Hidimba's solar plexus.
'The monster's sister,' she replied, scrambling for her dress,
Which in the fight had been reduced to something of a mess.
'My brother owns this land,' she said, 'in fact, this very wood;
And when he sees intruders he gets angrier than he should.'
'I see,' said Kunti, as the giant emitted a roar of pain,
'My son gets angry too – oh! There he goes again!'

'I know!' the girl, all bright-eyed, said; 'isn't he terrific?
Of all the men I've ever seen, he really is the pick!'
'Ah,' said Kunti, understanding, 'and how many have you seen?'
'Two,' confessed the girl, 'and the other one's so mean.'
Her mean brother was certainly having the worst of the fight;
Each jarring blow opened his eyes as if he was seeing the light.
'Does that explain,' Kunti asked, waving an embarrassed hand,
'Your . . . er . . . state of dress?' (A picture would be banned.)

'Oh – yes.' The girl modestly cast down her almond eyes:
'I deeply love your son; and though I'm not his size,
I know that given half a chance I could make him very happy.
I cook, I clean, I sew and stitch, and I'm really quite snappy.
And then I think' (she blushed at this) 'speaking as a woman,
I believe my body pleases him'. 'Well, yes, it's only human.'
Hidimba's grunts and awful groans were now too hard to bear;
'Oh, stop it, Bhim,' Yudhishtir called; 'stop, and leave him there.'

'All right,' said Bhim, with a final punch to his rival's groggy head;
Hidimba fell, lay still. Said Kunti: 'Bhim, it's time to wed.'
'What?' The strong jaw dropped; Bhim stopped like a broken carriage;
'I can't believe it! As I fought, you were arranging my marriage?'
'It seemed somehow appropriate,' Kunti replied, unflapped,
'If you fight for a girl you can hardly tell her later you were trapped.
And besides, this fit young lass will be a great help to me –
You boys never think of the awful strain of your itinerary.'

'It's all too sudden – I've got to think.' Bhim leaned against a tree;
'An hour ago, I was sitting here . . . it's all too much for me.'
'I'm not too much, am I, my dear?' asked the girl with a gentle smile;
Her face was bright, her eyes alight, innocent of any guile.
Bhim looked at the girl, and then he thought of the woman he had seen:
The hips, the lips, the breasts, the rest, the face of a beauty queen –
A beauty she had offered him with a love transcending shame.
'All right,' he said. 'I'll marry you. Er . . . what is your name?'

89

Comea had fallen. Nationalists danced in the streets at the expulsion of the last colonial power from Indian soil, the only one that had not had the intelligence or the grace to withdraw amicably in time. Kanika was a national hero for having – as Defence Minister – planned and led the decisive action.

It was being said that, for all his talk of peace and morality, Dhritarashtra had learned a lesson from his namby-pambiness over Manimir; there were some things for which cannons were far more effective than conferences.

To the north, however, there were frowns on the anti-colonialist faces of the mandarins of the world's most populous tyranny, the People's Republic of Chakra, as they contemplated the hubris of their southern neighbours.

'They are glowing too big for their boots,' said the Chairman, and a dozen inscrutable faces nodded as vigorously as the tight collars of their regulation tunics would allow.

The two countries had, for nearly two thousand years, been separated by the vast expanse of Tibia, a large nation of few people which had served as a willing conduit for a number of Indian religious innovations from Buddhism to Tantrism. Despite periodic ritual genuflections to the north (whenever the Chakars had a central regime strong enough to warrant Tibian circumspection), Tibia had maintained its independence till its casual conquest – in circumstances almost indistinguishable, in fact, from that of its homonym Tibet – by Sir Francis Oldwife. The British, eventually convinced it was the one place on earth to which it was not worth assigning a civil service, withdrew from Tibia not long after. But in order to feel they had got something for their pains, they took the trouble to conclude a peace treaty with their recent subjects, a document which among other things defined the border between Tibia and British India. Since it was drawn by a crusty Scot named MacDonald, the now-defined frontier came to be known as the Big Mac Line.

When Chakra's glamorous Generalissimo gave way before the raucous regiments of the cherubic Chairman, Dhritarashtra had been amongst the first to applaud, for sound anti-imperialist, pro-socialist reasons. India's was even the first government to accord the Communist regime the honour of formal diplomatic recognition. During the early phase of international ostracism endured by the People's Republic, India was seen frequently by Chakra's side, advocating its admission to various international forums, speaking regularly in favour of 'peaceful co-existence' with Snuping, as the capital of Chakra was then still called. As Dhritarashtra and Kanika bobbed and beamed alongside their yolk-hued counterparts for the benefit of the world's flashbulbs, a new slogan was, with official encouragement, given wide currency in India: 'Hindi-Chakar *bhai-bhai.*' That meant that, faith and physiognomy notwithstanding, Indians and Chakars were brothers; and since *'chakar'*, carefully pronounced, also meant 'sugar' in Hindi, the slogan implied that sweetness infused the relationship. Little did its originators realize how easily it would soon be twisted into a pointed 'Hindi-Chakar bye-bye'.

The problem arose on two levels. On the more elemental level the Chakars, despite their new egalitarian ideology, did not particularly care for what, to the inheritors of the Middle Kingdom, seemed the patronizing support of their ethnically inferior neighbours. And then, on the geo-political level, there was the Big Mac Line. Since the Chakars had marched into Tibia and taken it over with even less trouble than Sir Francis had, the Scot's handiwork now represented the border between Chakra and India.

It was, from Snuping's point of view, a most inconvenient line. For one thing, it was tainted by having been imposed by a colonial power in negotiations with a state that had ceased to exist: logic, therefore, called for it to be renegotiated with the People's Republic. For another, MacDonald had made it inconsiderately difficult to cross from Tibia into the Chakran province of Drowniang (an activity which he may not have considered strictly necessary, given that the two did not at that time belong to the same rulers). A few border adjustments seemed, to Snuping, to be essential.

The Chakars could well have tried, Ganapathi, through amicable negotiations based on good neighbourliness and mutual realism, to come to an understanding with India. After all, not many of us – and I, don't forget, was a Cabinet minister in Dhritarashtra's government in those days – had any particular affection for a line drawn by a Scot, and drawn, let us face it, on the basis of mapping techniques which were so primitive as to justify revision on cartographical grounds alone. But such a procedure would have addressed only the second level of Snuping's problem. They preferred a method which would simultaneously tackle the first – which would, in the words MacDonald might have used, give us a bloody nose, cut us down to size and put us in our place. Ironically, it was Kanika's far-too-easy conquest of Comea which showed them the way.

My heart still weeps at the thought of the condition of our army in those days, Ganapathi. They were cock-a-hoop, in their military lingo, after having captured an ill-defended enclave by the simple expedient of marching into it in numbers large enough to discourage any resistance. The only shot in the Comea campaign was fired by a young soldier who accidentally marched into a house of pleasure and discharged his rifle in startled excitement, bringing down a chandelier of imitation crystal on the heads of several of the territory's Portuguese notables. He received a medal for their arrest and penicillin injections for the other consequences of his intrusion.

The major consequence of the conquest of Comea was complacency. Kanika felt vindicated in his stewardship of the Defence Ministry, and took his triumph as a licence to devote even more time to the prolix speeches and scabrous character-assassination that were his favoured pastimes. It is said that there was a report on his desk pointing out that the *jawans* in our mountain regiments had no all-weather rations and were obliged to wear canvas tennis-shoes in the Himalayan snow, but that he had placed it in an overflowing 'Pending' tray. Dhritarashtra, meanwhile, was so content with the company of his popular and successful Defence Minister that he had no desire to listen to the warnings that the few of us who cared to, dared to give him. Indeed, nor did the people at large share our misgivings. The year after Comea, Dhritarashtra went to the polls for the third time since Independence in the quinquennial exercise that affirmed our status as the world's largest democracy, and triumphed handsomely. Kanika was returned to Parliament with a record plurality.

Imagine it, then, Ganapathi: our soldiers with their ill-clad and unprotected backs turned, warming gloveless hands before domestic stoves in the icy mountain passes, as Defence Minister Kanika Menon pirouettes on the world stage in the Kathakali mask of a confirmed conqueror, Dhritarashtra makes visionary speeches about non-aligned unity and the brotherhood of Indians and Chakars, and the massed millions of the Chakra People's Liberation Army slant their jaundiced eyes to the sights of weapons whose gleaming barrels are pointed towards New Delhi.

90

At this very time the Pandavas, after years of promoting rural uplift, had arrived in the market town of Ekachakra, their number swollen by the birth of Bhim's son Ghatotkach. 'A few months of domesticity will do us all some good,' the new father had proclaimed, to his mother's undoubted relief, and they had taken up residence as the paying guests of a friendly Brahmin. It was in the first full flush of their indolence that word reached them of the challenge thrown down by the famed wrestling champion Bakasura, who had pitched his tent in the city.

'We saw the posters all over the town,' Nakul said excitedly, 'and everyone was talking about it. Bakasura the Invincible, they call him. It seems that he has proclaimed that he will wrestle with any man in Ekachakra who puts up a hundred rupees as a deposit, and if he is defeated he will pay the winner five thousand rupees. All sorts of local *pahelwans* have tried, but he's thrashed them all. Bakasura's become richer by several hundred rupees, and the stake he's put up remains intact. There's even a drawing of a five-thousand rupee cheque on some of the posters.'

'I suppose we could use the money,' Yudhishtir said.

'Yes, come on, Bhim, go and have a crack at this Bakasura,' Arjun suggested, stretching a lazy leg.

'Not today,' the doting father replied, dandling his unpronounceable infant on his lap. 'Today I've promised to play with Ghatotkach and give him his bottle – eh, my Ghatotkachy-koo? Some other time, perhaps.'

'But today's our only chance,' Nakul protested. 'Bakasura's folding his tent and moving on to the next city in the evening. I heard them announce it. He always moves when he's run out of opposition anywhere.'

But Bhim, chucking his son under his arrowhead-shaped chin, could not be bothered.

'I'm planning to attend a lecture on the dharma of non-violence,' Yudhishtir said when they looked at him instead. 'Sorry.'

'And I've just discovered a library next door,' Arjun said. 'I want to catch up on my reading too. Life is not all physical activity, you know.'

'Oh, come on,' Nakul pleaded with his three elder brothers. 'If I hadn't twisted my ankle running here to give you the news, I'd do it myself.'

'Now that's a good idea,' Bhim said, briefly turning to them. 'Not you, Nakul, of course, but Sahadev. I mean, with what we've all learned and practised over the years, any one of us should be more than able to get the better of this Bakasura.' His words were met by a chorus of approval from three of his brothers. Even Ghatotkach gurgled his support.

'I don't know,' said Sahadev dubiously, but his hesitancy was drowned out by the unthinking enthusiasm of the others.

And so it was that the brave, the strong, the wise, the gifted Pandavas sent into the ring – against a cunning and brutal champion tested and tempered by his recent triumphs over the local wrestlers – their youngest brother, a boy who had never spoken for himself and who had never needed to act alone in a situation of any seriousness.

A cheer went up from the assembled crowds as Sahadev stepped diffidently into the ring, his slim, lithe and lightly muscled figure a startling contrast to the gleaming oiled barrel of solid flesh that was Bakasura. Sahadev turned to acknowledge the cheers and heard them become a roar – a roar, though he was to realize it only later, of fear and warning. He raised his hands in a grateful and graceful *namaste* and suddenly found himself being picked up from behind, spun above Bakasura's head like the blades of a human helicopter and flung bodily into the row of seats occupied by the judges of the contest. As he passed out amidst their screams and the splintering of chairs, the last word he heard was Bakasura's chest-thumping snarl: 'Next!'

'He gave me no warning,' Sahadev groaned later as he lay on a pallet at home and his mother applied compresses of turmeric on his rainbow of bruises.

'There are no *warnings* in wrestling, silly ass,' Arjun said.

'No one told me the rules.'

'You're supposed to guess them as you go along,' Bhim pointed out. 'If that Bakasura were still here I'd teach him a thing or two. I have half a mind to follow him to the next town and get our own back.'

'You'll do nothing of the kind.' Kunti's eyes blazed. 'Isn't one lesson like this enough for you? If I had been here when you discussed your stupid plan I would never have let poor Sahadev go in the first place. How could you allow it to happen, my sons? *How could you?*'

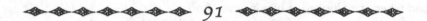

How could you have allowed it to happen? It was a question many of us in the Kaurava Party could not resist asking Dhritarashtra when the Chakars invaded, tossed our ill-fed, ill-clad, ill-shod *jawans* contemptuously aside and inexorably erased the Big Mac Line. By the time our panic-striken response could be organized the war was over; the Chakars had announced a unilateral cease-fire that we were in no condition to reject. In a few humiliating days they had achieved every one of their objectives: asserted their view of MacDonald's draughtsmanship, captured enough territory to permit the construction and protection of an all-weather road linking Tibia to Drowniang, and exposed the shallowness of our international pretensions to the world. They even shook the credibility of Dhritarashtra's non-alignment, for our blind Prime Minister panicked enough to welcome the offer of a squadron of fighter planes *and* pilots from the superpower whose alliances he had earlier consistently spurned. It was not, Ganapathi, a time at which we covered ourselves in glory.

Criticism in the party was vociferous and unrestrained: many of our MPs howled with the jackals of the Opposition for sacrificial blood. This time Dhritarashtra did not offer to resign, as he had so often done whenever the party had found fault with his approach to a multitude of lesser issues. He did not, because for the first time since Gangaji had brought him into politics he could not be certain that his offer would be unanimously and unhesitatingly rejected. He did the next best thing and presented the jackals with a hawk-faced head on a platter: his best friend Kanika's. The hero of Comea resigned and was relegated to the back benches in disgrace.

That was not the most important price the nation had to pay for its defeat by the Chakars. Dhritarashtra, the Dhritarashtra of the confident rhetorical flourishes and dazzling visual metaphors, the Dhritarashtra of the original international initiatives and the high priest of proud non-alignment, would never be the same again. The military humiliation not only shattered his self-esteem; it broke his heart.

His decline was gradual but decisive. He ate little, began denying himself more and more of the little comforts we all take for granted, resigned himself to acts of painful penance. He began to sleep on the bare floor and to invent new privations for himself. He replaced his regular massages with flesh-mortifying exercises. When he had no official appointments he would be found in the woods behind his prime ministerial residence, clad in tattered rags and penitential strips of bark. 'It is time for me,' he said to me when I approached him sympathetically, 'to take to the life of *Vanaprastha*.'

You know the ancient concept, Ganapathi, of the four ages of man: his youthful and celibate *Brahmacharya* when he learns what life has to offer him, his marital and parental *Grihastha* phase when he exercises his duties and responsibilities as householder and professional, his *Vanaprastha* of renunciation in the forest and, for a select few, the ultimate *Sannyas* of the sages. But to hear this traditionalism from the lips of the Cambridge-accented, agnostic Dhritarashtra was the final indication for me that his spirit had completely evaporated.

He did not last long after that. One morning he walked, thus attired, into the foliage of the woods. He breathed for the last time the honey-laden fragrance of the flowers, felt the warmth of the sun's rays on his faded skin and the sharp scratches of twigs and brambles against his emaciated legs. Then he sat down in the lotus position, his bare back to a tree, facing the east, where the dawn breaks for all of us but had never done for him.

I found him there hours later, immobile in the yogic posture, perfectly still. I did not need to touch his heart.

Gently, I removed the dark glasses from his lifeless eyes and let them face the sun. Then I took away the empty bottle he had dropped near his feet. He belonged to the ages, but the instruments of his failure did not.

THE FIFTEENTH BOOK:
THE ACT OF FREE CHOICE

92

'I'm afraid I have bad news for you,' said Draupadi Mokrasi's adoptive father. 'Dhritarashtra has left you nothing in his will.'

The girl looked at him with her large, untroubled eyes. She was beautiful now, and though her skin was not of the pale colour prized by upper-class India, she was delicately dusky, with the sun-ripened wheatfields of the Doab glowing in her complexion. Yes, Ganapathi, ours was inevitably a darker democracy, and all the more to be cherished for the Indianness of her colouring. The gleaming darkness of her skin lit up her beauty, so that she shone like a flame on a brass lamp. When she entered a room, everyone in it became a moth, drawn irresistibly to her. Yet her beauty did not intimidate or threaten. Draupadi's beauty attracted both men and women, both young and old. All sought to be part of her beauty; no man presumed to attempt its submission.

When I saw her, Ganapathi, I wanted the radiance of that flame to spread, to engulf everyone I knew within its warmth. For she was warm, our Draupadi. Hers was not a beauty that held itself aloof; it was not arrogant, nor withdrawn, nor self-obsessed, indeed not even self-sufficient. Other women nurtured their beauty privately, with their secret scents and oils and unguents; Draupadi's beauty was public, absorbing the beauty of the world around it, blossoming in the sunlight of popular adulation. With her it seemed that in isolation there would be nothing: this was not a beauty that sought confirmation in a mirror; nor was it a light that burned alone, eventually to flicker out untended. No, Ganapathi, Draupadi was like the flame of a brass lamp in a sacred temple of the people. Imagine it: a flame nourished by a ceaseless stream of sanctified oil and the energy of a million voices raised in chanting adoration. A flame at an evening *aarti*, at the end of the puja, a flame offered to the worshippers as bells tinkle and incense smoke swirls, and a hundred hands reach out to receive its warm benediction; a flame curling and moving towards these hands, glowing ever more brightly as it breathes their reverence. This was the beauty of Draupadi, a beauty that glowed in the open, that drew sustenance from the public gaze. The more people beheld her, the more beautiful she seemed.

This was the extraordinary woman who confronted the reality of her father's passing. 'He did so much for me when he was alive; must I expect him to sustain me even after his death?'

'My child, I have nothing,' her guardian replied. 'I gladly took you on for his sake, though God knows it has not always been easy. But now – you are of marriageable age, and what can I do for you? In my community it is not a custom to arrange marriages, and anyway, to whom could I marry off a girl of your uncertain parentage? Draupadi, I simply don't know what to do.'

'Don't worry, Papa,' Draupadi said, those still, round eyes completely calm. 'I shall find my own husband.'

It happened sooner than either of them expected.

Those were difficult days for the party. Dhritarashtra had been like the immense banyan tree under whose shadow no other plant could grow. There were a number of us who were leaders of some consequence in different parts of the country, but we had no one of truly national stature to succeed Dhritarashtra – except perhaps for me, and I was already far too old for the job. After long and inconclusive meetings we decided that the Kaurava Party would be run more or less by collective leadership, with the Working Committee effectively in command and the one who was least unacceptable to the others – the honest but limited Shishu Pal – as Prime Minister.

No one was at all certain how it would all work out, or even whether poor decent Shishu Pal would prove up to it. Nor could anyone be entirely sure that Indian democracy itself would not fall into the wrong hands. It had happened elsewhere, notably in neighbouring Karnistan, where a series of shambolic civilian administrations had been overthrown by a military coup.

It was amidst this state of uncertainty that I convened a training and consciousness-raising camp for the youth members of the Kaurava Party. Priya Duryodhani helped me run it. The Pandavas were there; the news of Dhritarashtra's death had brought them back to Delhi, since Vidur's reason for keeping them away was gone. Also present at the month-long event was the dark, captivating beauty whose origins only I fully knew, Draupadi Mokrasi.

The camp was a success. I organized, and sometimes gave, lectures on the history and philosophy of the Kaurava Party, the precepts of Gangaji and the contribution of its illustrious leaders from Dhritarashtra and Pandu to Rafi and Shishu Pal. Apart from the plenary sessions under an enormous *shamiana*, we sat together in smaller discussion groups, talking about the country's social and political problems in a more intimate atmosphere, often late into the night. The air those young people breathed was heavy with the warmth of ideas.

It was here that Draupadi Mokrasi met the Pandavas for the first time, and dazzled them, and all the other young men in the camp, with her radiance. For all my advanced years, Ganapathi, I am not insensitive to the impact of young beauty on the rest of my species. But I allowed myself to think that Draupadi's would be different – until the evening Priya Duryodhani stepped into my room wearing an elegant shawl and an inelegant scowl.

'You've got to do something about this.' She was direct as usual. 'The girl is becoming a positive nuisance. None of the boys are listening to anything that's going on – they have eyes and ears only for Miss Draupadi Mokrasi.'

I didn't think it was quite that bad, but I shrugged sympathetically. 'What do you expect me to do?'

'You've got to get her married,' she responded bluntly.

She herself had never married, sacrificing nuptial pleasure for service to her father as his official hostess. It was an improbable proposition for her to advance.

I'm afraid I was too taken aback to reply. 'Married?' I repeated stupidly.

'Yes, married.' Priya Duryodhani's tone was impatient. 'It's the only solution. She has no one to arrange her marriage, it would seem. And you're practically *in loco parentis* to all of them here, so there'd be no harm in your trying. Might tame the girl, and bring the boys under control. We can't have Miss Mokrasi running wild.'

Marriage! Yes, of course, Draupadi had to be married one day. But to tie that boundless spirit to any one man – it would be a crime; it would diminish and confine her, and all of us. It would be like imprisoning the rays of the sun in one room. And who could this exceptionally fortunate man be, who deserved the hand of Draupadi in his? To such a question there could be only one answer – Arjun. To many the pairing would mean wedding perfection to magic; it would unite democracy with the voice of the people. And yet I knew that could not be the whole answer. Arjun might prove worthy of her, but she would not be enough for him. His restless spirit would inevitably move on to other challenges; he would not always be faithful to her. Draupadi could not, should not, be given away to a man who would one day break her heart.

I needed time to think about this. 'You have raised an interesting question, Duryodhani,' I acknowledged. 'And, dare I say it, an important one. I must think about who might be suitable for the girl. Do you have any suggestions?'

'Certainly.' Her coal-black eyes seemed to shift away, to a point on the wall behind me. 'It should obviously be a young member of the Kaurava Party, who is bright, intelligent, well-informed. I can think of only one person who meets these requirements in all respects.' I sat back, waiting for the obvious name. 'Ekalavya.'

I tried not to show my surprise. Ekalavya! The boy who had once presumed to call himself a pupil of Drona, and been sent packing by his mentor in an act of dubious ethicality. Of course, I had noticed this repellent youth, with his pencil-line moustache and mocking voice, an intelligent but arrogant young man who had struck me throughout the camp as being far too clever for his own good. And it had been whispered, I knew, that there was hardly a girl at the camp who had been spared one variety or another of his amatory attentions. Why him?

Out of the mists of half-registered memories an image swirled into my mind — an image of Ekalavya emerging from Priya Duryodhani's room one night; a recollection of his stumbling into me and saying quickly in his cocky voice, 'I had hoped to borrow a copy of the sayings of Gangaji, but Miss Duryodhani isn't in her room. May I have yours?' At the time it had never occurred to me to wonder where Priya Duryodhani could have been at that hour of the night. Now, all of a sudden, it struck me. She *had* been in her room all along.

So this was how she consoled herself for the opportunities lost in filial devotion to her blind father: and was this the reward she had agreed for Ekalavya's services?

'He is bright and able, but suffers unfairly from the handicap of a low-caste birth,' Priya Duryodhani went on. 'In our country that means he will never be able to marry a woman worthy of him. Draupadi would be perfect: after all, she has a similar problem. You would be doing them both a favour.'

I tried to keep my voice steady. 'You seem to have thought it through,' I said. 'Then why do you need me? You' – and I was aware of the cruelty of my words, Ganapathi, but I rubbed them in deliberately – 'you are old enough to take them both by the hand and arrange it for them.'

She gave me a quick, suspicious look, but my expression had not changed. 'Who am I?' Duryodhani asked bitterly. 'Draupadi would never listen to me. There . . . there isn't the required . . . trust between us.'

'Then this is very selfless of you, Duryodhani,' I replied. 'But I am sorry, my answer must be no. I have never myself believed in arranging marriages. Draupadi needs a husband, but she must make her own choice. I will not force it, and' – I looked directly into those smouldering eyes – 'neither must you.'

Of what happened thereafter, Ganapathi, and of how it happened, I retain only the most confused of recollections. There was always something mystical about the daughter of Dhritarashtra and his British Vicereine, as if she walked on another plane from the rest of us, and my memory of her act of choice is inextricably entangled with the long and vivid dreams I later began to have about her life and times.

I seem to remember a competition. Yes, definitely: a competition for

Draupadi's hand. Was it at the Kaurava Party camp, or in some bejewelled palace from the depths of mythological memory? I cannot say. I have a vision of a vast canopied hall, filled to overflowing with teeming, cheering multitudes; of nobles and princes assembled in their finery to vie for the hand of our heroine; of Draupadi herself, resplendent in a simple cream sari with a striking red border, her long hair hanging loose to her waist, adorned by a solitary rose. She held a garland of white jasmine in her hands, fragrantly poised to be draped around the neck of the deserving victor.

Then the contest began, and this must have been a dream, for it was a contest unlike any I have ever seen in our land. A large wooden box, slit at the top, sat in the middle of the hall, and everyone in attendance moved forward, in a silent ethereal procession, to drop a folded slip of paper into it. This done, Draupadi approached the box, and I, with the expansive gestures of a magician at a fairground, elaborately placed her inside it, resting serenely on her bed of ballot-papers, white garland at the ready. I closed the lid with a click. Now it was the turn of Draupadi's suitors, each of whom had to try to open the box. The first to let Draupadi out of it would be garlanded by Miss Mokrasi as her husband.

In the mists of my dream, Ganapathi, a long line of contenders walked forward to claim the hand of Draupadi Mokrasi. There were rich men, men of title, commoners, kings. There were others from my dream: Heaslop in suit and bowler hat, clutching textbooks and commercial contracts; a strange, ugly American in a flowered shirt and Bermuda shorts, with a camera around his neck; a pug-nosed commissar in an astrakhan cap that still dripped the blood of the lambs slaughtered for its manufacture; even a clone of Chakra's inscrutably sinister Chairman. None of them could open the box. Draupadi sat within, breathing calmly through the slit at the top, betraying no sign of anxiety or expectation. Strong men, weak men, tall men, little men came to take their turn, and shuffled silently away in defeat.

Then Ekalavya strode to the box, but when he placed his fingers upon the clasp, he found his thumb would not move. He backed away in fear and wonder.

A figure from the past, a distant neighbour, emerged. It was Mohammed Ali Karna, his golden skin gleaming; but I barred his way, declaring his ineligibility with outstretched arm and pointing forefinger. He stopped short, his face losing the look of unsmiling confidence that had made him seem like a conqueror at his own coronation. He gave me a bitter grimace of comprehension, but went.

At last it was Arjun's turn. He rose from the ranks of the throng, and there was a collective gasp at his appearance, physical perfection dressed in simple homespun. Arjun stepped forward with the spring of youth in his step, and placed his hand on the clasp of the box. He looked steadily at me, sensing my anxiety at either result. Then, with no visible effort, he calmly lifted the clasp.

The lid of the box sprang open, and amidst the excited cries of the throng, Draupadi rose within, her graceful sari-clad body glowing like a white flame.

As she bent forward to place the garland around Arjun's neck, the hall erupted in prolonged cheers; the other Pandavas, watching amongst the crowd, leapt to their feet; and Arjun, the strength and suppleness of his limbs evident in each lithe movement, lifted Draupadi Mokrasi out of her confinement.

In my dream, through a corner of my mind's eye, I spotted Priya Duryodhani striding out of the hall. Draupadi's remarkable *swayamvara* was over, and I knew, even as I woke from the disorientation of my sleep, that one more of my desiccated grand-daughter's schemes had misfired.

 *93*

What followed was no dream.

Draupadi Mokrasi had made her act of free choice: and whether it was the way I remembered it, or in some more prosaic encounter at the local coffee-house or in a late-evening seminar on Modern Indian Institutions, it was as the betrothed of Arjun, and escorted by his four brothers, that she left the training camp.

The first thing the Pandavas did when the camp was over was to telephone their mother. The line was crackling and static-ridden, the kind of connection that makes conversation difficult, shortens tempers and sentences, and restricts communication to essentials. In the hands of Yudhishtir a brief, factual call might still have been possible. But it was, as always, the irrepressible Nakul who insisted on making the call, and who announced to Kunti in his usual fashion: 'You won't believe what we're coming back with! We have a surprise for you, Mother.'

Never would Nakul's singular choice of the plural prove so momentous.

'I don't need anything,' the matriarch responded across the echoing miles. 'Share whatever you have brought amongst the five of you – equally.'

'What did you say, Mother?'

'Share your surprise amongst yourselves.'

Share Draupadi amongst themselves! Imagine the consternation that remark caused, Ganapathi. How could the five ever forget they were committed, by their solemn oath, to obey every injunction of their mother's, however casual? Throughout the journey home, they discussed and debated, in growing confusion and anxiety, whether their oath could be interpreted to exclude Kunti's command. Yet for all the outrageousness of it, for all the risk of social disapproval and scandal, the idea of sharing Draupadi entered a corner of their minds and grew to thrilling immediacy.

It was Yudhishtir who first expressed the previously unthinkable.

'I didn't ever want to get married,' the eldest brother said in that solemn way of his, 'but now I think we shall all have to marry Draupadi, even Bhim who is already married. Otherwise it would be a violation of our sacred oath, and of the precepts of dharma.'

When they returned to confront her with the situation, Kunti seemed distraught at the dilemma into which her unthinking utterance had plunged the family. Arjun's features were overwhelmed by agonized uncertainty. Only Draupadi remained undisturbed. She stood erect and calm amidst the confusion, unquestioning, untroubled, reading each brother's mind, seeing through Kunti's ambivalence. In her self-possessed silence it was apparent that, though she had given her heart to the godlike youth who had won her hand, she realized that democracy's destiny, and hers, embraced his brothers too.

'There's only one thing we *can* do,' Kunti said at last. 'Nakul, since you started it all, run off and bring Ved Vyas. He's the only one who can tell us what would be – proper.'

So I came back into the lives of my grandsons. Kunti offered me a cushion on a golden carpet. Before I sat down, the boys all bent to touch my feet. I pushed them away before their fingers got anywhere near my dusty toes: that is one traditional custom with the insincerity and unsanitariness of which I have little patience. The gesture is supposed to symbolize that the bender considers himself as the dust beneath the feet he bends before: if anyone has as little regard for himself as that I don't want him to touch me at all.

The abortive ritual undergone, Yudhishtir gravely explained the problem.

'There's nothing in the *vedas* that would sanction one woman marrying several husbands,' I responded at my most ponderous, 'but there is certainly a great deal against violating a vow, especially a promise made to a parent. The real question is which would be a worse violation of dharma – breaking your oath to your mother or adopting polyandry. I am inclined to think our traditions would tolerate the second option more easily than the first. There is nothing in any of our ancient texts that extenuates the breaking of a promise – I can't even think of anyone, however villainous, who is described as doing so. Whereas in the *Puranas* one reads of Jatila, simultaneous spouse of seven sages, so polyandry's not wholly without precedent.' I paused, and softened my learned tone. 'But the sacred texts may not be the only place to look for an answer to our conundrum.' I looked deep into Draupadi's eyes. 'Strange, my dear, are the ways of the Lord. Did you, when you were anxious about your marital prospects, pray to Heaven to intercede?'

Draupadi lowered her lashes. 'Yes,' she admitted.

'Did you, by any chance, invoking Shiva, plead, '"Give me a husband"?'

'I prayed to Shiva,' Draupadi said, 'to Jehovah, to the Virgin Mother of my adoptive parents, to the Allah of the Muslims and' – she blushed in acknowledgement of her maternal faith – 'to the Archbishop of Canterbury.'

'Poor confused child,' I said. 'They have *all* answered your prayers.'

Once it was clear that Draupadi had brought her five husbands upon herself by her five prayers, all resistance to the multiple marriage melted.

Only Nakul had one last question: 'What about the . . . the law?'

'The law proscribes bigamy,' I admitted, 'but says absolutely nothing about polyandry. You will undertake five religious marriages, which I, as a Brahmin, will conduct; the law does not oblige you to register any of the five. Prosecution, in any case, is highly unlikely: the Indian police have far too many other things to worry about. This is not an offence – if offence it is – of which they will take cognizance.'

'And I thought I was the lawyer in the family,' Yudhishtir said admiringly.

So the weddings were solemnized and conducted with all due ceremony, one a night for five successive nights. For the last time in my long career I was able to put to good use the instruction of my father Parashar, so that Draupadi entered each of her nuptial beds a virgin. She was not a woman whom any single man could feel he was the first to possess.

And yes, Ganapathi, I see from your frown that you have sensed the one discordant note I have so far omitted to strike. Bhim's wife, the sylph-like sister of the monster Hidimba, left him and took with her his copper-muscled, spear-chinned son Ghatotkach.

'My brother,' she said sadly, 'needs me more than you do.'

This was true: the Pandavas, under their mother, were terribly self-sufficient, with the self-obsession that sometimes accompanies self-possession. It had not been easy for her to belong; perhaps the only way to belong in that family was Draupadi's.

It was ironic but true: one *swayamvara* drove out another.

And so, Ganapathi, Bhim's wife left our story, never to return. And – have you noticed? – we still don't know her name.

After the last of the wedding ceremonies, I took Kunti aside and thanked her. 'You played your part well, mother of Arjun,' I said solemnly. 'I realize it could not have been easy for you. But it was essential that you maintained your command to share her. Draupadi Mokrasi cannot be confined to one husband, however worthy: she needs them all.'

Kunti lowered her eyes in acknowledgement of our collusion. When she raised her head there was a fierce determination in the set of her jaw. 'I did as you said,' she admitted, 'but I only knew I was right when they all arrived home. I saw then that it was the only way. The beauty of this woman would have destroyed the unity of my family.'

'You did well, Kunti,' I said. 'Now she will bring strength to your sons, as she will derive strength from her husbands.'

Kunti smiled quietly and left me. I watched with grandfatherly affection as she rejoined her five sons and their common bride.

Once again, Ganapathi, I was playing my role.

 *94*

Shishu Pal was a good Prime Minister, in his decent and well-meaning way. But he was one of those whom Fate destines to the footnotes of history.

Almost from the first day his rule seemed stamped with the label 'interregnum'. The Karnistanis, too, saw the haze of transience around his eyes. They began their preparations soon after he had unassumingly assumed office, and seized the first tactical opportunity to make their second grab for Manimir.

But, like everyone else, the Karnistanis had underestimated Shishu Pal. He prayed from dusk till dawn, then gave the order for counter-attack. Our army had learned its lessons from the Chakra humiliation, and hit back so hard that our troops were just seven kilometres from Karnistan's most populous city, Laslut, when another cease-fire intervened. (The story of the subcontinent's recent wars, Ganapathi, is that of politicians shouting both 'Fire!' and 'Cease!' at the wrong times.)

Shishu Pal then sat at the conference table and meticulously gave back everything our boys had won on the battlefield.

'Peace demands compromise,' he murmured, as he signed away the very passes and bluffs and salients on which our best soldiers had earned their posthumous mentions in despatches. But he agonized over each square inch he returned, seeming to weigh the amount of Indian blood soaked into each clump of soil that he tossed back into Karnistan.

At last, the night that he signed the peace treaty, aware that at home the jackals were again baying, 'Betrayal,' but convinced that his dharma placed the preservation of life above the exaction of revenge, Shishu Pal tossed and turned his way into an eternal sleep. It was almost as if dying was the only means he had of showing the widows and cripples how intimately he suffered for their wasted sacrifice.

And so Shishu Pal passed from the nation's front pages as unobtrusively as he had entered them. If a war had broken Dhritarashtra's heart, a peace had broken his.

And so, too, we sat down together again in my house, the members of the Kaurava Working Committee, the collective husbands of Indian democracy, and asked ourselves a question we had hoped not to ask again so soon: 'What do we do now?'

Someone suggested the same formula: that one of us be elected to rule as *primus inter pares*, just as Shishu Pal had been. But as soon as names were broached it became apparent that no one could attract even the minimal 'no objection' consensus which had given that good man the job that had cost him his life.

At last I spoke the words that had lain dormant in me all those years, the words I had hoped I would be able to suppress when the time came, the words I knew I was fated to speak from the moment that Gandhari the Grim had rested her sweat-soaked head upon her pillow and refused to look at her new-born baby.

'There is only one possible solution to our dilemma,' I said, the words emerging by themselves from my vocal chords. 'Priya Duryodhani.'

'A woman?'

Imagine, Ganapathi, that was all they found to say; that was the principal objection of the guardians of our nation to the forces of destiny. 'A woman!' they said, as if they were not all born of them.

'Precisely,' I replied, speaking as I was willed to speak. 'We want a Prime Minister with certain limitations, a Prime Minister who is no more than any minister, a Prime Minister who will decorate the office, rally the support of the people at large and let us run the country. None of us can play that role as well as Priya Duryodhani can. She is easily recognizable, she is known as her father's daughter, and she will be more presentable to foreign dignitaries than poor little Shishu Pal ever was. And if we ever decide we have had enough of her — well, she is only a woman.'

What can you expect, Ganapathi? My irrefutable eloquence carried the day. Priya Duryodhani was sworn in as the third Prime Minister of independent India. And once again I had acted as the agent of forces stronger than myself, leaving my smudgy thumbprint on those pages of history that it had been my task to turn.

 *95* ◆◆◆◆◆◆◆◆◆

Do you, Ganapathi, know the story of Tilottama?

Tilottama was an *apsara*, the most ravishing of celestial nymphs, and she was sent down to earth to perform a task even the gods found impossible – the destruction of the invincible twin sovereigns Sunda and Upasunda.

The twins were absolute monarchs and absolutely inseparable; they ruled the same kingdom, sat on the same throne, ate off the same plate and slept on the same bed; and they enjoyed a boon that decreed they could die only by each other's hand. They were so close that this seemed an improbable prospect, but the gods knew a thing or two about men. They sent Tilottama down on her terrestrial mission, and within days – not to mention nights – she had the twins so maddened by jealousy of each other that they fought over her, fatally.

Imagine, Ganapathi: they had, in the modern phrase, everything going for them, and yet they killed each other for exclusive possession of a calculatingly desirable woman.

There are many lessons one can derive from this story, including the basic one that twins should beware of women called Tilottama, but the moral that the Pandavas took to heart from my recitation of the tale was more constructive: that when many men desire one woman they must take all possible precautions against the slightest risk of similar self-destruction. Accordingly the Five drew up elaborate schedules and procedures for the sharing of Draupadi, dividing their proprietary rights with due heed to the privileges of seniority and the inconveniences of her time of month. And they concluded with a rule as inflexible as the one that bound them to filial obedience: should any one of them interrupt Draupadi in the embrace of another, the intruder would be banished from the household for twelve months.

A remarkable rule, that, but they were a remarkable quintet, Ganapathi. Some day their lives and beliefs will be studied by bright young scholars across the country, so let us look at them now, in the early years of their adulthood, as a textbook might. A school textbook, for they personified the hopes and the limitations of each of the national institutions they served; a school textbook, with portraits drawn in clear simple lines, and accompanying text in large bold letters.

First, inevitably, would be Yudhishtir, clearly the inheritor of the Hastinapur political legacy. Maturely serious and prematurely bald, he qualified as a lawyer but made politics his only vocation, rising with steady inevitability up the party's ranks. The fact of seniority and the assumption of authority made him extremely sure of himself, to the point, indeed, where he did not always stay on the right side of the borderline between self-confidence and smugness. Oh, he was polite, courteous to elders, truthful, honest, dutiful. But certitudes came too easily to him, doubts almost never. Like many an eldest son in India, he believed he invariably knew what was best for his juniors and expected automatically to be obeyed by them. This meant that the older he grew, the fewer were those to whom he needed to defer, and the less accommodating he became. Secure in his integrity and righteousness, he was impervious to the corruption and injustice around him; he sought to be right rather than to do right.

Turn the page of our primer, Ganapathi, and you would find a large, muscular figure in battle fatigues. Bhim embodied the physical strength without which the new nation could not have defended itself. He joined the army; to many of us, he *was* the army. His pureness of heart and spirit, his courage and bravery, the depth of his convictions, were at the nation's disposal at the borders, and — in times of emergency — wherever it was needed within the country. Belying the profuse moustache whose bristles he proudly groomed, Bhim was gentle and considerate with those in his care, especially his mother and Draupadi Mokrasi. But he was as thick-skinned and unimaginative, as incapable of original initiative, as the strongest ox in a fertile field.

Our textbook would probably devote most space to the paragon of perfection, Arjun. There he would stand, straddling two pages, his shining gaze as steady as his strong legs. I thought of Arjun, with his paradoxical mixture of attributes, as the spirit of the Indian people, to which he so ably gave voice as a journalist. India could not be India without the loud, vibrant, excited babel of contending opinions that its free press expresses. Arjun, himself a man of contradictions, perfectly reflected both the diversity and the discordance of the Indian masses, whose collective heartbeat he heard and echoed. His gentleness of expression, his frequently troubled frown of reflection, mirrored the doubts and questions that were as much a part of his nature as the decisive flurries of action he undertook when circumstances generated their own certainties.

Madri's twins Nakul and Sahadev — can one ever speak of them separately? — were destined early for the twin pillars of India's independent governance: the administrative and diplomatic services. Nakul's quickness and agility kept him always a step ahead of his brother. He spoke with breathtaking speed, the words tripping out as if only the act of utterance could give them stability and coherence. Nakul was made, Yudhishtir drily said, for diplomacy, since he could speak a lot without saying anything. Sahadev was both opposite and complementary: quiet, reflective, willing to let Nakul speak for him – until and unless he was sure of his own view, in which case his diffidence quietly gave way to clarity and firmness. One might have imagined that, with these attributes, it would be Nakul who would articulate the glib banalities of diplomacy and Sahadev who would confront the agonizing dilemmas of administration. But Fate, and a shrewd Public Services Commission interviewing panel, willed otherwise, and each went into the profession seemingly suited for his brother.

These, then, were the five who shared Draupadi Mokrasi, who gave her sustenance and protection, and who guaranteed their unity by the rigid rule that punished any intrusion with a year's banishment.

It was a good rule as far as it went, but like all inflexible rules it suffered from the great disadvantage of leaving no room for exceptions. And so it happened that one day I stopped by and asked Arjun for the manuscript of a speech whose text he had been revising for me; I had to leave sooner than expected to deliver it and needed it immediately. I had no idea, of course, that Arjun had left it in the bedroom where at that very moment Yudhishtir and Draupadi were locked in connubial bliss. For a moment he weighed in the balance the certainty of the penalty against the certainty of letting me down, and made his dutiful choice. Perhaps he was, in some subconscious way, restlessly yearning for exile.

Arjun entered the bedroom quietly, not wishing to disturb his brother, and slipped the text off the bedside table unnoticed by the ecstatic couple. But when I had gone he waited for Yudhishtir to emerge and confessed he had violated their mutual undertaking.

'Well, in that case I guess you'll have to go,' Yudhishtir said righteously. 'Pity – it was going to be your turn tomorrow, since Bhim's away.'

'You can have my shift,' said Arjun, without resentment. 'Draupadi seems happy enough in your company.'

'That's dangerous talk,' his elder brother said sharply. 'In fact, I intend to rearrange everyone's schedule to share your turn equally amongst the others, if you must know. But Arjun – watch your tongue. Remember Sunda and Upasunda.'

'I know.' Arjun was instantly ashamed. 'I'm sorry.'

But despite everything – and though he fully appreciated the objective necessity for the arrangement they had made and the exile it now imposed upon him – Arjun could not help wondering, as he took his leave of a tearful Draupadi, whether Yudhishtir would have been able to win Draupadi's hand by himself.

And think of Draupadi: abandoned by the man she had loved and wanted to marry, because of his unavoidable violation of a rule that itself served only to limit his access to her. It was not that the others displeased her; but Arjun was always her favourite, the reason why she was a Pandava bride at all, and now she would have to do without him altogether for a year.

It is, Draupadi Mokrasi thought as she submitted again that night to Yudhishtir's studious caresses, a curiously unjust world.

96

Arjun embarked, on the rebound, on one of the great erotic sagas of our history. Travelling around the country to spend his exile as a roving corre-spondent for his paper, he restlessly sought an elusive fulfilment in the arms of a succession of remarkable women. Each dateline on the despatches he mailed or cabled back to the capital concealed a night, or a week, of passion.

In Hardwar, for instance, by the sacred Ganga, there was Ulupi, a Naga beauty who taught him underwater pleasures omitted in his adolescent swimming lessons. In Manipur, source of a story about the great indigenous school of classical dance, he found Chitrangada, a skilled *danseuse* who performed startling duets to his percussion instrument. At Khajuraho, from where he mused in print about the nation's most sensuous tourist attraction, he succumbed to the dusky Yaga, who practised on him the results of her extensive study of temple sculpture. At each halt he left behind something of himself, but he grew immeasurably as well. He moved on, driven by an urge he could not describe and did not fully comprehend, knowing only that he had not yet found what he was seeking.

Despite the women, Arjun's travels were not all pleasure. He saw the range and immensity of India and all its concerns. In rural Bengal he learned of the rage and frustration that led middle-class young intellectuals to throw bombs at lower-class old policemen — underpaid uniformed menials who were startled to find themselves branded by their betters as symbols of the injustice of an oppressive social order. He understood, in turn, the reciprocal ruth-lessness of the police, who felt closer to the proletariat than their highly educated assailants, and who beat and gouged and shot the Naxals on the principle of doing unto others before they did unto you. And then Arjun saw the tortured Naxalites languish in their cockroach-infested prison cells and did not blame them when they recanted, emerging to join commercial firms where they could dissolve their angst in the cocktails of a new con-formity.

In the urban Bengal of the Maoists' coffee-houses and second-hand book-shops and crowded theatres, Arjun met a young poet with piercing eyes and a goatee, who recited with painful intensity the refrain, 'Calcutta, if you must exile me, blind my eyes before I go.' Blind my eyes, Arjun understood, to the despair and the disrepair, the dirt and degradation, but also to the searing summer beauty of the *gulmohar* and cassia blossoms flaming insolent and tender along the dusty roadsides, to the awesome thunderclouds swallowing up the rooftops before a northwester storm, to the little boats gently bobbing on the Hooghly river at sunset against the shining steel frame of the massive Howrah Bridge. Blind my eyes to the rioters and the agitations and the human molluscs clinging to the outsides of smoke-spewing buses, but also to the kaleidoscope of brightly coloured kites leaping up at the blue sky, to the little boys playing cricket with makeshift gear in countless narrow lanes, to the compassion of students, housewives and nuns who strive to serve the city's victims. Blind my eyes, finally, to the flimsy sheet-covered forms of the homeless sleeping under the arcades of fashionable hotels, to the resigned despair in the unblinded eyes of the woman, a small infant balanced on her hip and two ragged children trailing behind, who begged for help in a thin, melancholy wail which clung tenaciously to the air long after she had silently received Arjun's alms and left.

Arjun left too, but each departure was a new beginning. In the foothills of the Himalayas he saw poor village women tying themselves to tree trunks in a defiant and life-saving embrace to prevent the saws of rapacious contractors cutting them down for commercial timber. In the deserts of Rajasthan he found how cheap it was to buy a woman for life at the district bazaar, and wrote savagely about his own purchase of such a girl for sixty rupees (when he told her she was free to go, she asked, 'Where to?'). In urban Madras he marched alongside slogan-shouting Tamil demonstrators whose protests against the imposition of that alien and barbaric northern tongue masquerading as a 'national' language – Hindi – soon disintegrated into riots in which buildings and vehicles otherwise innocent of linguistic preference were stoned and burned in the angry flames of Dravidian cultural assertion. He saw the devastation wreaked by cyclones in the lush green lands of the Coromandel coast, and he dragged himself above the floodwaters to travel to drought-ravaged Bihar. There he walked on the parched, sun-scorched clay oven that had once been part of the fertile Gangetic plain, feeling the earth cracking and crumbling underfoot, learning the meaning of famine in the hollow cheeks and sunken eyes of mothers whose babies sucked at breasts as dry as the area's riverbeds. Here too, in the cradle of Magadhan civilization that had ruled India more than 2000 years earlier, he watched a skeletal cow stumble and collapse by the side of a withered tree; and as he saw a village woman bend to pour the last precious drops of water from her own *lota* into the animal's mouth, the thought struck him with overwhelming intensity: 'This is my land'.

It was eye-opening, heart-rending — and exhausting. When the last sight and the last night had passed without either the event or the woman leaving an impression on him, Arjun realized he had seen and done too much. But he had to go on: the terms of exile were harsh.

It was thus a weary, jaded Arjun who arrived at the tip of the peninsula, at the last halt on his long traverse across the land, the obscure southern town of Gokarnam.

He did not, of course, know that it was to be his last halt. Arjun was looking for a young political giant-killer who was not well enough known outside the south, the man who had unseated the formidable local Tammany Hall boss, Kamsa, in his first election and had made himself something of a legend in the area since then. He was the Gokarnam Party secretary, and Arjun thought it would make an intriguing story to feature a local hero who had refused to seek national office. He could already visualize a quick, five-hundred word despatch: 'THE MAN WHO WOULD NOT BE KING'. Then he would move on.

The town's Kaurava Party office was a long, musty room in the rutted main street with a painted aluminium board outside proclaiming its purpose. Inside, the busiest sound was the hum of a fly amidst the dusty stillness of scattered files. A young man in white — clerk or functionary, Arjun did not know — sat beneath a black-and-red Malayala Manorama calendar idly fanning himself with a yellowing *Mathrubhoomi Azhichapadippu*.

'Secretary gone out,' he informed Arjun with pleasure. 'Some party work he is having in near-by village. If you are wishing to go there, I will explain you how.'

Arjun was indeed wishing to go there, having nothing better to do. He soon found himself stepping off a shuddering rural bus at an enormous family-planning hoarding that dominated the centre of the village of Karink-olam. Tea drinkers at the rickety stall near the bus stop, their *mundus* tucked up around their knees, grinned at his attempts to communicate the object of his search in English, Hindi and the universal language of signs.

'Krishna, party secretary? From Gokarnam?' the *chaya-kadakaran*, the stall-keeper himself, finally put Arjun out of his misery. 'You will find at Ottamthullal — that way.'

Arjun followed the pointing finger down a dusty track that led from the village centre towards, and then through, the paddy-fields that covered most of Karinkolam. He paused at the crest of the road, overwhelmed by the breathtaking simplicity of the sight. The beauty of the Kerala countryside was the beauty of the commonplace: of the green of the rice stalks and the green of the palm fronds, of the glow of the sun and the freshness of the air, of the sweat of labour and the miracle of grain. Arjun walked on past the busy figures of *thozhilalis*, ankle-deep in muddy water, bending over the breeze-stirred plants, and he slowed his pace occasionally for a gaggle of giggly schoolgirls or a trundling bullock-cart. He was now walking through the fields themselves, on a narrow path of earth, in places barely a footstep wide. As he picked his way gingerly over an unexpected dip in the path, the rhythmic throbbing of an unfamiliar drum floated across the paddy-fields. Clearly something was going on, a local event at which he might find someone to lead him to Krishna.

The path turned a corner and Arjun suddenly found himself facing a rudimentary stage, sheltered by palm fronds. Over a hundred people had gathered before it, and were intently watching a performance of an art form Arjun had never seen before. A dancer, his head topped by a vividly painted papier-mâché crown, bells dangling from a string around his waist and tinkling at his feet, was jumping — there was no other word for it — in large, flowing steps to the rhythm of the accompaniment of three musicians. There were also, on stage with him, three expressionless men with bare chests and *mundus* trailing to the floor, one banging vigorously at the taut sides of a *madallam*, one striking a kettle-drum with the flat of his palm, the third clashing tiny cymbals in time with the crashing of the dancer's feet. A song, incomprehensible to Arjun but unquestionably of solemn, possibly religious, significance, droned on in the background.

Arjun looked round the appreciative crowd, then selected a bespectacled man attired in a Terylene shirt, with a pen in his front pocket.

'Excuse me,' he asked in English, 'but can you tell me where is . . . er . . . Ottamthullal?'

The man turned and looked at him with interest. 'What do you mean, where is Ottamthullal?' he asked.

'I'm a stranger here, and I may not be pronouncing it right, but I'm looking for a place, or house, called Ottamthullal. I'm hoping to meet someone there.'

'You have found your Ottamthullal, but it is not a place or a house. It is a dance. This dance.' The man gestured toward the stage, from which the dancer, to loud applause, was just descending. 'Which seems now to have ended.'

But not quite. As Arjun looked in dismay at his informant and at the applauding audience, a white-shirted figure — apparently at the urging of a section of the crowd – rose from the audience and leapt on to the platform. The crowd greeted his appearance with a thunderous roar. Even the expression-less musicians smiled briefly to acknowledge their new companion, and thumped their instruments with celebratory verve. A few young men in the audience whistled in loud excitement. Grinning unselfconsciously, the in-truder pulled off his immaculate shirt, revealing a dark, gleaming and un-deniably pudgy torso. He tossed the garment into the crowd and deftly caught the gaily coloured dancer's head-dress and bells that were tossed back to him. As he tied them on, the music built up into a steady rhythm, clearly more cheerful than the dirge that had preceded it. Arjun found himself waiting to see what would happen: the happy expectancy of the crowd had infected him too.

The man on the stage stepped forward, knees apart and bent, feet pointing in opposite directions. His right foot came down in a decisive thrust; the crowd cheered. His body swerved, his feet pounding the stage, the tempo of the music accelerating. Then he began to sing. Arjun could not understand the words, but it was a strange, droll lyric, the man's almond eyes widening and shrinking expressively with each turn of phrase, his hands turning and flowing in gestures of mock classicism, his every movement punctuating the verse with bursts of laughter from the ground. Arjun turned in puzzlement to his informant.

'It is very funny,' the man in the Terylene shirt explained. 'You see, the Ottamthullal is normally a dance that illustrates songs from our *Puranas*, especially the *Ramayanam* and the *Mahabharatam*. But what this man is doing is a very good parody. A very good dance, with very good lyrics written by T. Chandran, a Malayali immigrant in England. It is all about learning English manners and ways of behaviour. Very funny.' The man chortled. 'But, ah, of course, you do not understand Malayalam. Naturally, naturally. How foolish of me. But wait – if you listen carefully, you will find it is not so difficult, after all.'

Arjun strained dutifully to catch the words chanted by the dancer, and by many members of the crowd in ragged unison, but they seemed to have little in common with the languages of the north that Arjun knew. One refrain stuck tantalizingly in his ear:

> *Thottathin ellam 'Thank you, thank you',*
> *Ottu mushinyal 'Sorry, sorry' . . .*

He gave up, and concentrated on the dance. The man on the stage, his body glistening with sweat, was executing ever more vigorous steps. His feet pounding, his trunk swaying, his hands and legs flailing the air, bells ringing furiously with each movement, the dancer twisted and turned, leapt and flew, rose and fell.

There was neither beauty nor elegance in the dance. Its cadences, its vigour, were wholly foreign to Arjun's experience. Yet Arjun felt an involuntary stirring within him, a quickening of his spirit in response to the movements of this strange, magical man. The drums throbbed, and the dancer strode and jumped and sang, his arms and legs moving to the tempo of the rhythm of life. Arjun was suddenly seized by the sense that everything he had seen around him in Kerala that day was embodied in this man: the surge of the sea at the shore, the swaying of the palm trees, the rippling green of the sun-drenched paddy-fields, the laughter of the children running in the village street. The dancer's energy flowed into him: Arjun felt his earlier satiety and tiredness lifting.

On stage, the dancer's movements accelerated in a fast, flowing piston-burst of motion till, with an enormous crescendo that seemed to shake the platform, he swivelled, back arching, to a feet-scudding stop. The audience rose to its feet and applauded, cheering him loudly. Grinning in open delight, the dancer waved at them and stepped off the stage.

'How did you like it?'

'Very much,' Arjun answered truthfully. 'I've never seen anything like this before. Is that man your village Ottamthullal expert?'

'Not at all,' the man in the Terylene shirt replied. 'He is not even from here. In fact, he is the local MLA, and the Kaurava Party secretary for the *taluk*. His name is D. Krishna Parthasarathi.'

And Arjun knew that he had at last come to the end of his search.

 97 ❖ ❖ ❖ ❖ ❖ ❖ ❖

'Call me Krishna.' The party secretary smiled. 'Everyone does. Dwarakaveetile Krishnankutty Parthasarathi Menon is a bit of a mouthful even in these parts.'

'Thanks, Krishna. I'm Arjun.'

Krishna smiled again as he acknowledged the easy assumption of familiarity. He was dark, of medium height and build, with long, slightly curly hair and brilliant white teeth which shone like pearls against the velvet of his skin whenever he smiled, which was often. He smiled at everyone he met as he walked with Arjun to the bus-stop, picking up one fold of his spotless white *mundu* to facilitate his stride. The villagers all seemed to know him, and he was greeted affectionately by young and old, male and female alike — a joyous, radiant being with God's own mischief in his eyes.

The jolting bus ride back to Gokarnam was the beginning of a friendship that would transcend time, space and distance, and give meaning and purpose to Arjun's life.

Krishna was, despite his relative youth, a political veteran. He had entered politics earlier than anyone else in the Kaurava Party: his parents, both freedom fighters, were in jail when he was born, the youngest and decidedly the most vocal prisoner of the Raj. With his parents continuing active electoral careers, Krishna's largely unsupervised childhood had given him a reputation both for mischievous pranks and political precocity. The youngster's playgrounds were often the *maidans* of party rallies; he was reading Gangaji's abstruse autobiography when his classmates were coping with comics; and he was arguing with adults when he ought to have been speaking to them only when spoken to.

His political opportunities came correspondingly early. He was a popular and successful election campaigner for the party, with almost no competition for the women's vote. From an early age Krishna had the rare talent of being able to talk to people at their own level. He was equally at home teasing the milkmaids while they bathed in the river as when debating the theory of permanent revolution with the local Mau-Maoists. He would disarm them all with his laughing good nature, then resolve the point at issue through the utterance of a perception so startling in its clarity and simplicity that it made all further argument otiose. And he would invariably get his way with members of either group.

This was not surprising, for the most striking thing about Krishna was his joyousness. He was always relaxed, always laughing, full of innocent mischief that never quite obscured his deep, instinctual wisdom. The wisdom was always apparent, despite the laughter, and it was not a wisdom acquired through learning or even through experience, but something that arose from deep within himself, as if from the very earth he stood on. Yet Krishna wore his wisdom lightly: he expressed it with a simplicity so profound that it did not seem to recognize the depths from which it sprang.

Arjun found himself entranced. In Krishna he found qualities he had never seen in any man nor sought in any woman. He was irresistibly drawn to Krishna's almost magical combination of self-possession and extroversion, mischief and maturity, joy and judgement, and his rare gift of the common touch. Days after he should have filed his story and left, Arjun stayed on at Gokarnam as Krishna's guest and disciple.

He followed the Gokarnam Party secretary on his daily round of meetings and speeches; watched him squat on his haunches in a paddy-field with a stalk between his teeth, talking about irrigation to a calloused peasant; helped him hide the *davanis* of bathing milkmaids in the bushes by the river. And at night after a late meeting or a working dinner, Arjun sat alone in the swift-falling darkness and surrendered himself to the haunting strains of Krishna's flute floating across to him on the still night air. Each pure clear note on that magical instrument seemed marinaded in mystical meaning, yet when Arjun first tried to express his admiration, Krishna laughingly dismissed the topic. And Arjun understood that even the highest praise would only diminish what the music of that flute meant to his friend.

Krishna's words, like his music, were those of a soul at peace on this earth. But Arjun learned that not all had been tranquil in his friend's life. Stories he heard suggested that when Krishna was young, jealous relatives — led by his maternal uncle, the dread patriarch in Kerala's matrilineal *marumakattayam* system — had coveted his inheritance and sought to destroy him. But Krishna's surging vitality had triumphed, and in his first election Krishna had toppled his own uncle, the formidable local party boss, Kamsa. Yet as a popular hero and a secure Member of the Legislative Assembly, Krishna had been too satisfied with his life in Gokarnam to seek a place in the national Parliament. As someone who knew national politics too well, Arjun found this appalling.

'You've got to let me persuade you,' he told his friend, 'that the country needs people like you in the mainstream of national politics.'

'I'm quite happy with my local river, thanks,' Krishna laughed. 'If you were to stay a little longer here, see my life, my place in the lives of the people, you would understand.'

'But what a waste,' Arjun expostulated, warming to his theme and his friend. 'You could find a place in the hearts of the entire country, not just one part of it.'

'I should quote you to Radha,' Krishna said. 'You see, Arjun, I'm very content with the part I have.'

'Are you married?' Arjun asked gauchely.

'No,' Krishna replied, flashing those white teeth of his, 'but my wife is.'

Arjun deeply pondered that remark. Krishna, though always warm and candid, was a master of the art of being elliptical without sounding evasive.

Yet his friend's ellipses never aroused the slightest doubt or anxiety in Arjun. Krishna must have had good reasons; Krishna had to be right. True, he avoided making a national commitment; but so what? His very being was a celebration of life; he could not possibly be accused of evading its challenges. Krishna could, after all, have lived on his inheritance, enjoying prestige and status without effort, but he had entered the lists and toppled Kamsa. He would swim out of his chosen backwater when he considered it necessary, and not before.

Arjun found his article impossible to write. It was intended to be simple and short, but nothing about Krishna could be either.

 *98*

For a man so completely in tune with India's ancient harmonies, Krishna was startlingly liberal.

'Who is that stunning girl?' Arjun asked as they strolled outside his host's parental home one evening, past a group of laughing collegians who smiled and waved and called out to Krishna.

'Which one?' Krishna looked at him shrewdly. 'There were seven girls in that group, unless my buttermilk had fermented more than I realized.'

'I only noticed one,' Arjun replied. 'It was as if the other six were her maids in a traditional painting, gathered to do her honour. The fair girl in red, with music in her voice and sunrise in her hair.'

Krishna's laugh bellowed across the road. 'I hadn't heard the music or been blinded by the sunrise, but there was only one girl in red,' he chuckled. 'My sister Subhadra.'

Arjun stopped still, the shock of recognition coursing through him. Of course! That was what had caught his eye — the startling similarity of the fair girl to his dark friend. He had noticed it subconsciously as they approached the girls and as they walked past, but he would not have been able to define what it was about the girl that so captivated him. Now he knew. Despite the astonishing difference of colour — not so uncommon in Kerala families — the girl's every gesture, every turn of the head or movement of the hands, was Krishna's. He found himself looking back at her, and reddened. 'Your sister! I say — I hope you don't mind.'

'Not at all,' Krishna laughed. 'I don't often find myself in this position. Now if it was one of the other six . . . So you like the look of Subhadra, do you?'

'God, yes,' said Arjun fervently. He looked at the merry face before him and recalled its smiling female version. 'I'd want to woo her immediately, if you'd only tell me how.'

'I thought you said you were married.'

'Yes and no. I mean, I'm married but not all the time,' Arjun assured him hastily. 'Four fifths of me is still available, and I'd like to offer that to Subhadra. If you will allow me.'

'Allow you? My dear Arjun, what age are you living in? I do not dictate to Subhadra whom she should allow to woo her. Besides, she is somewhat difficult to woo. Like many of these modern girls, she thinks herself too good for a mere man, but unlike most, she won't let any man get close enough to prove otherwise.'

'Then tell me, Krishna, what should I do? How can I seek to win her?'

'You *are* one for medieval chivalric conventions, aren't you? Subhadra has always said she'd choose her own husband, but from what I've seen of her I doubt very much she'd be able to judge what was for her own good. My advice would be quite simply to give her no choice. Be Valentino, not Valentine. Kidnap her. Take her away on a white charger!'

'You mean – elope?'

'You make it sound so prosaic, Arjun,' Krishna sighed in eye-twinkling resignation. 'But yes, I suppose I do mean elope. Except that if eloping involves the consent of both parties, abduction might be a lot more effective.'

Startled, Ganapathi? Not quite the way for a good Indian elder brother to behave, eh? If you thought that, I suppose you'd be right, but this was just one more instance of Krishna's innocently instinctual amorality. He lived by rules which originated in an ancient and ineffable source, a source that transcended tradition. Unlike the rest of us, even unlike Arjun, Krishna found his basic truth within himself. No conventional code could confine the joyous surging force of vitality, of essential life, that he embodied.

And so the plans were laid; Arjun borrowed a white Ambassador car to serve as his charger, and lay in wait after dark along the route Subhadra used on her way back from her evening classical-music lessons.

A little later than expected, he saw her emerge from a building across the road with a small group of fellow students. They stood in a little knot on the front steps, but in a moment the knot unravelled and the girls strolled away in different directions.

Subhadra was walking alone.

Arjun felt the palpitations in his chest as he turned the key. The car did not start. His heart was beating more vigorously than the motor.

He turned the key again, cursing. The girls were disappearing one by one down several streets.

The Ambassador car is, of course, Ganapathi, the classic symbol of India's post-Independence industrial development. Outdated even when new, inefficient and clumsy, wasteful of steel and petrol, overpriced and overweight, with a steering mechanism like an ox cart's and a frame like a tank's, the Ambassador has dominated India's routes since Dhritarashtra's ascent to power, protected and patronized by our nationalists in the name of self-reliance. Foreign visitors have never ceased to be amazed that this graceless contraption of quite spectacular ugliness enjoyed two-year waiting lists with all the dealers.

What they don't realize is that if they had to drive on Indian roads in Indian traffic conditions, they would prefer Ambassadors too.

Arjun sighed, then opened the boot and pulled out one more evidence of the Ambassador's appropriateness to Indian conditions – the crank. He took the L-shaped iron bar to the front of the vehicle, inserted it and turned it vigorously. The engine cranked, wheezed and spluttered into life. Arjun was back in the running.

He returned to the driver's seat and anxiously scanned the road. The girls had all disappeared. But he was fairly sure he knew which road Subhadra would take to walk home. Amidst the blaring of offended horns, he eased his car into the traffic.

That was it – the turning – and surely that was her, just beyond the last flickering street-lamp? Arjun began to turn, then realized it was a one-way street. This is not a consideration that always impedes Indian drivers, but in this case the entrance to the street was blocked by an enormous lorry prevented from heading the right way by a homesick cow yoked to an unattended cart. The impasse appeared likely to last: certainly the truck driver had resigned himself to the situation, for he had placed his prayer-mat on the bonnet and had begun performing his *namaz*. Arjun drove on. He would try the next street.

This time the turn was easier to execute. He proceeded slowly, looking for the first left turn that would bring him back to the street on which he had spotted Subhadra.

There wasn't one.

Arjun felt the sweat on his palms and the frustration higher up. He *had* to get her! He turned right, hoping to find two lefts later. The roads all seemed to curve away at impossible angles from the direction in which he wanted to go. Whenever he found a left, it seemed to be succeeded by a street with a no-entry sign or a cul-de-sac. He turned; he swerved; he reversed down one-way streets; he retraced his route and did the opposite of what he had done before. Finally, dizzied by seventeen left turns and thirteen unintended rights, he emerged on a quiet unlit street that seemed vaguely familiar. As familiar, in fact, as the skirted figure walking hip-swayingly ahead into the shadows.

Subhadra!

Amidst the darkness and the shadows of confusion in his own mind there shone a clear beam of determination. He was at last going to be able to do what he had set out to do.

He swung the car around and accelerated past the girl. The street was deserted; its lamps, which blinked half-heartedly at the best of times, had given up the attempt and were completely extinguished. He drew up at the edge of the pavement and waited.

The footsteps approached, the soft flapping of leather *chappals* accompanied by the light tinkle of *payals* at her ankles. Arjun's heart thudded in unbearable anticipation.

As the girl neared the car, Arjun flung open the door, grasped her by the waist and, with one hand over her mouth to prevent a scream, pulled her on to the back seat.

His victim gave a startled gasp and then began to fight, kicking, lashing at him. Arjun realized there were limits to the effectiveness of the abduction technique as a means of promoting his cause.

'Don't,' he begged. 'I will not harm you. I do this out of love! I desire you as the bee desires the flower, as the minute desires the hour, as the *sannyasi* desires moksha!' The girl's resistance seemed to subside with his protestations. Arjun followed his words with a flurry of kisses that effectively silenced all opposition.

She was responding! As Arjun used his one free hand – the other still prudently covered the girl's mouth – to caress his companion, he found his ardour reciprocated. The hands that had been attempting a moment earlier to scratch and hit him now stroked their ravisher. The girl's body arched, and her fingers fumbled in the dark for his malehood.

Arjun was lost. He freed himself, raised his companion's skirt, and expended an hour of anxiety, anticipation and hope in a minute's frenetic release.

'I love you, Subhadra,' he breathed afterwards, dropping his head on to the gentle swell of her breast.

His partner laughed, a harsh, guttural sound. 'Gosh, you really were in a hurry, weren't you? I've never done it this way before.'

The voice was coarse, and Arjun, realization pouring on him like iced water on a cold morning, reached up to switch on the car light.

'That'll be forty rupees,' said a rouged and painted woman, blinking into his face. 'And my name isn't Subhadra, it's Kameswari.'

She swung thick legs off the back seat. 'Though you can call me Subhadra if you like, sweetie.' She shook her head. 'How impatient you young boys are! Couldn't you have waited to find a room in a hotel?'

 *99*

Crass, Ganapathi? Of course it was. But this is one memoir which will not conceal the crassness of its heroes. No more than it will be embarrassed by their greatness.

The next morning Krishna gently mocked the shame-faced Arjun. 'I must take lessons from you,' he laughed. 'What subtlety of technique! Your victim didn't even realize she'd been abducted!'

'Watch me next time,' said Arjun defiantly. And indeed, when Subhadra was returning one morning from the temple, with the sun's rays weaving delicate patterns of light and shade in her hair (and doing so brightly enough to leave no doubt as to her identity), Arjun swooped down and swept her, in every sense, off her feet.

The elders of Gokarnam were furious, and rose with inflamed faces to demand Arjun's arrest. It was Krishna who calmed them down by pointing out to his father Vasudevan: 'Subhadra couldn't have found herself a better husband, and she might easily – you know how women are – have done a lot worse. We had decided long ago we weren't going to subject my sister to the humiliation of being inspected like a chicken at a market by a succession of prospective fathers-in-law, who would base their final decision on the size of the dowry we could offer them to take her off our hands. In the circumstances, isn't what Arjun has done the best thing that could have happened, from our own point of view?'

'And what about Subhadra's?'

'Does any woman of spirit allow herself to be abducted without at least some degree of acquiescence? Had she disliked Arjun, she would have made his life so miserable he would have returned her to us in hours. Let us call them back, and we shall see how happy Subhadra is.'

They did, and she was. A lavish wedding was quickly arranged, and Arjun spent the remainder of his exile in Gokarnam enjoying his honeymoon and the companionship of Krishna. When it was time for him to return to Delhi, he made one last appeal to his new friend.

'Come back with me, and let me introduce you to the party elders,' he said. 'Your future is in Delhi.'

'No, Arjun. I'm sorry, I can't. Not now, not yet. But I promise to come and visit you before long, and to give you my advice whenever you need it.' Krishna placed his hands on Arjun's firm shoulders, and looked intently into his eyes. 'It is *your* future that beckons in Delhi, and you must go to it. As for myself, I shall be happy to remain behind the scenes here in Gokarnam and guide you when I can.'

Wise guidance from a detached distance: that was all that Krishna would offer Arjun, and India. It was maddeningly inadequate, yet it seemed impossible to change his mind. Just as well, perhaps, Arjun thought: it might have been worse to try to confine this gloriously free spirit in the concrete chrysalis of the capital.

And so the friends parted, and Arjun returned home with Subhadra. How would she be welcomed into the home from which he had been exiled, twelve long months earlier? Despite himself, Arjun worried about this. He had, quite simply, lied to Draupadi, with an inland letter-card telling her he was bringing her a new maid. He knew she would not believe him, and it almost did not matter that she would not. What he wanted was for the lie to hold until the women met, when he knew it would all resolve itself, one way or another.

Do not rush to condemn our bigamist hero, Ganapathi. He was faithful to Draupadi in his fashion, but fidelity was not the touchstone of their relationship. Arjun was bound to Draupadi by the very essence of their complementary natures, by the inexorabilities of destiny, *par la force des choses*. His relationship with Subhadra was of a totally different texture, one of lightness and joy; within it he had a sense of responsibility for his choice and for his love, an awareness that the bonds were willed by him and not by events over which he had no control. He needed her, whereas he and Draupadi responded to a need that was greater than themselves.

After anxiety, bathos. When she had touched Kunti's feet and been embraced in welcome by her mother-in-law, Subhadra turned to Draupadi Mokrasi.

'I've really been looking forward to meeting you,' she said, the sincerity glowing in her eyes. 'I've heard so much about you.'

'I wish I could say the same,' Draupadi replied.

The situation was, in a word, fraught. The two women eyed each other for a moment in – Ganapathi, I cannot resist the phrase – a pregnant silence. Then, almost simultaneously, they both rushed to the kitchen sink and were sick.

Subhadra's son Abhimanyu and Yudhishtir's heir Prativindhya were born less than nine months later. And from the moment their foreheads met painfully over the kitchen sink, the two women became the best of friends. It was, in its own way, only natural; for they shared more, Ganapathi, than the closest of sisters ever could.

And it was no accident, after all, that Sunda and Upasunda had been men. It would have taken the gods a good deal more than a male Tilottama to break the elemental bonds of sisterhood.

THE BUNGLE BOOK —
OR, THE REIGN OF ERROR

100

A nd as with our heroes and heroines, so too our nation's politics were subject to the confusion, the misunderstandings, the casual couplings and startling intimacies of our story. After an undistinguished and diffident first year in office – during which Priya Duryodhani seemed far more conscious of what she did not know than of what she could find out – the country went to the polls in its fourth general elections. We should not have been surprised at what happened, but we were: though the Kaurava Party retained power thanks to the absence of any real alternative, we lost seats all over the country to a motley array of opposition groups. In half a dozen states non-Kaurava majorities had a chance to form governments, something which had not occurred since Karna took his Muslim Group out of the country. They seized their chance as best they could, cobbling together opposition coalitions based more on arithmetic than principle. From the first day it was apparent that their political miscegenation could not last, but the very fact that these parties had got into bed together at all, and penetrated so far into our citadels of power, was deeply galling.

'If we had stronger leadership,' said Yudhishtir bluntly at the post-election meeting of the Kaurava Working Committee, 'this would not have happened.'

He had grown into a severe, almost ascetic figure, his thinness and baldness reminiscent of Gangaji's. He was beginning, too, to be known for fads that rivalled the Mahaguru's, his interest in micturition mirroring Gangaji's obsession with enemas. But there the resemblance ended. For Yudhishtir's self-denial did not extend to his conjugal entitlements with Draupadi; his vegetarianism, which included a taste for walnuts, pistachios and Swiss chocolate, could hardly be considered Spartan; and his sense of righteousness gave him a look of perpetual self-satisfaction which contrasted sharply with the doubt-lined wisdom of the Mahaguru's face.

'What are you suggesting?' Duryodhani asked sharply.

'I'm not *suggesting* anything, I'm saying it quite clearly,' Yudhishtir retorted. 'I think this party needs to be led from the front if it is not to go on losing elections and state governments.' He glared at her balefully. Yudhishtir had won his own re-election from Hastinapur quite easily; Priya Duryodhani, though standing in the safe seat her father had arranged for her in his electoral heyday, had witnessed an erosion of her majority.

'I think that if the elections have shown anything, it is that the people want a change,' Priya Duryodhani said. 'I represent that change. The Kaurava Party can't do without me.'

'I'm willing to put that to the test,' Yudhishtir responded.

'Now, now, calm down, we can't go on like this,' I intervened. My own position as the party's elder statesman had taken a bit of a knock in the elections, for I had been comprehensively defenestrated by a firebrand trade unionist who must have been in short trousers when I first became a minister. But then I was not the only one to have lost his seat by having it pulled out from under a complacent behind. And I had a duty to prevent the party tearing itself apart. 'There is merit in what both of you are saying.' I was rewarded by resentful glances from both. 'We have lost seats, that is an undeniable fact; and as a member of the party's leadership, it is clear to me that the leadership should accept its responsibility for the defeat.' I directed these words at Yudhishtir, knowing that steam was issuing from Duryodhani's ears. 'At the same time' – now I turned to our Prime Minister – 'it is equally true that most of us who have lost are those who have come to be known as the Kaurava Old Guard. Priya Duryodhani is certainly not part of this Old Guard and cannot be associated with its seeming unpopularity.'

'I should think not,' the Prime Minister concurred. Scant thanks for my deliberately having omitted to point out that she was, instead, widely regarded as our creation.

'Dhritarashtra taught us,' Yudhishtir said self-servingly, 'to respect the institutions of democracy and the will of the majority. I suggest that we follow the same precepts within the party. It is time we really elected the party leader, instead of leaving it to a small group of elders.'

'What are you saying, Yudhishtir?' I was frankly aghast. 'Are we now to parade our internal differences before the world? Democracy, as you put it, if carried too far in the wrong places, can only jeopardize democracy where it ought to exist. If we reveal dissension in our choice of a leader we shall only strengthen the hands of our enemies. A political party is like a family, Yudhishtir. A family does not decide in the street who will cook its dinner tonight.'

'So democracy, unlike charity, does not begin at home?' Yudhishtir asked, his lip curling.

'If you want to put it that way, yes.'

'But it's you who put it that way, VVji.' Yudhishtir took care to keep his tone mild. 'And yet, you couldn't really know, could you, never having had a family yourself?'

That hurt, Ganapathi, I don't mind telling you. And yet, my pale son's enforced celibacy had effectively removed the direct genealogical link between Pandu's heirs and me. Yudhishtir was less my family than Priya Duryodhani was.

'*I* don't mind,' Duryodhani said. 'Let us by all means elect a Prime Minister. It may not be such a bad thing to free the Prime Minister from dependence on a small group of unelected elders.'

Her words sent a shiver through me. I heard in them a portent of all that was to come.

'Yudhishtir, Duryodhani, listen to an old man and be reasonable,' I pleaded. 'This is not the time for the Kaurava Party to tear itself apart over an election, whatever be the merits of the argument in favour of one. When we are weak, when we are reeling in pain from the body blows of our opponents, we cannot take a step that might bring us crashing to the ground. There *is* a compromise possible, and I plead with you both to accept it.'

'What is your compromise?' Priya Duryodhani asked suspiciously.

'There will be no change of Prime Minister,' I said, 'because at this time it is imperative we show complete loyalty to Duryodhani and faith in our original choice of her.' I raised a hand to forestall Yudhishtir, who already seemed about to speak. 'But, in order to accommodate those of a contrary view, I propose that a new post be created, that of Deputy Prime Minister – and that it be offered to Yudhishtir.'

Once again, Ganapathi, I had acted for the greater national interest. But this time I was only to delay the inevitable course of history, not to facilitate it.

Both putative parties to the compromise demurred. But after many hours of argument, everyone else in the room came to the conclusion that the arrangement I had proposed was the least undesirable of the available options. In the end, Duryodhani and Yudhishtir had no choice but to agree. They did so like actors obliged to perform what our Bombay film-wallahs call a love-scene, concealing their mutual detestation only when the cameras roll. At the press conference held afterwards to defuse the prevalent rumours of inter-necine conflict, Yudhishtir was his unsmiling but correct self. A journalist asked him what exactly his new and unprecedented designation meant. Would he be a sort of functioning chief executive while the Prime Minister presided over the Cabinet like a Chairman of the Board?

'You can look it up in the dictionary,' Yudhishtir said humourlessly. 'A Deputy is a deputy.'

'I couldn't have put it better myself,' concurred Duryodhani, relieved.

*

And Draupadi Mokrasi, still beautiful, began to appear plump, her instinctive smile creasing the flesh of her face in the slightest suggestion of a double chin . . .

101

Of course it could not last. Priya Duryodhani, confirmed in power with the next elections five years away, decided never again to endure the humiliation of having her position determined by others in this manner. She had seen and learned too much over the years to need to be subjected to this.

And she realized, too, that having reconfirmed her as the Prime Minister, the party elders would not proceed against her in a hurry. Her task would be to shore up her position so that by the time they did, she would be ready for them.

Determination had always been Priya Duryodhani's greatest asset. Once she had made up her mind and realized the strength of her post-election position – there was, after all, only one Prime Minister, and she was it – the change in her style was dramatic. She shook off her uncertainty as a palm tree casts off its fronds. Her public diffidence turned into assertiveness; her insecurity she converted into arrogance.

'I saw how my mother was hurt,' she said once to a foreign interviewer, 'and I was determined not to let that happen to me.' She allowed no one to acquire enough power or influence over her to be able to hurt her one day. Strange, Ganapathi, is it not, how the lessons learned by little girls so often go on to defeat the biggest of men.

With the party elders, whose compromise had both saved and embarrassed her, she was increasingly cold and distant. She began to let it be known that she believed it was our traditionalism and conservatism that had reduced the party to its present state.

As for her Deputy Prime Minister, the stiff and straight-backed Yudhishtir, she simply ignored him.

'I can't take this much longer,' he confided to me one monsoon day, as the rain stormed down on to the streets like liquid buckshot. 'She treats me like a stranger, disdains to respond to my every suggestion. The most I can get out of her is one raised eyebrow, like this.' He attempted to imitate the arched facial gesture for which Duryodhani was already famous, and succeeded only in giving himself a twitch. 'I'm Deputy Prime Minister but I know less about what's going on than my own *chaprassi*. Hardly any files reach me, and my annotations on the ones that do are never acted upon. What a wonderful "compromise" you got me to agree to, VVji.'

And then one day Yudhishtir found out a Cabinet meeting had been held without his even being aware of it. The Prime Minister's Office said the usual notification had been sent; his staff swore they had never received one. He demanded an appointment with the Prime Minister to discuss the matter. When after three days she had still failed to grant him one, he did the only honourable thing open to him: he resigned.

'You're a fool,' I told him, echoing Vidur's advice to Dhritarashtra at the beginning of the global war, advice which if heeded then might have prevented the partition of the country. 'An empty seat never benefits the one who has vacated it.'

'It was a question of honour, VVji,' Yudhishtir said stodgily.

They say Priya Duryodhani opened a bottle of champagne at home that night. But these days, Ganapathi, you can never rely on the servants' gossip as you could when their masters were British.

*

And Draupadi Mokrasi, running a fever, took to bed, complaining of alternating hot flushes and chills . . .

 *102*

With her most visible rival out of the way, Duryodhani began openly to promote her own cause within the party. She made speeches about the immense sacrifices made by her father and family for the cause of national independence. She spoke of Dhritarashtra's socialist ideals, and how they had been betrayed by the 'reactionary' elements among the Kauravas. The Kaurava Party, she averred, had to find itself again under her leadership. She appealed to all 'progressive' and 'like-minded' people outside the Kaurava Party to join her effort.

One of the first to heed her appeal was Jayaprakash Drona's bearded and populist son, Ashwathaman.

Since their days in the countryside agitating for rural reform with the

Pandavas, Drona and his son had disappeared from political prominence. The sage himself had retreated into the honourable obscurity that our country accords to those who have performed their good deeds and voluntarily retired from the fray. Whether it was disillusionment with the slow pace of change that demotivated him, or a simple reluctance to attempt to repeat his unhappy experience in government, Drona set himself up in an ashram with very few followers and devoted himself to detached reflection on the nation's ills. Though he was still fit and well and his 'special skills' had not entirely rusted with disuse, his was a respectable and singularly unthreatening activity. So Drona was left in peace by everyone, surfacing occasionally – very occasionally – in the press with a pious utterance about peace, Gangaism (Drona was a post-Independence convert to the Mahaguru's dogma of non-violence) or land reform. Every year in May there would also be a small, three-line item buried on the inside pages of the newspapers, sometimes under the rubric 'NEWS IN BRIEF' and sometimes, if space was available, under the heading 'JD CELEBRATES –TH BIRTHDAY'. It was a dutiful acknowledge-ment of the historical stature of a man who had not yet passed into history, precisely the sort of treatment, Ganapathi, that I am accorded today. And it served then, as it serves now, as an annual reminder to the politicians and the editorialists to brush up their elegies for the day when Yama's inexorable countdown reaches its predictable end.

Ashwathaman, the inheritor of his father's political mantle and equally, it seemed, of his distrust for power, grew a beard and joined a small splinter socialist grouping that was remarkable only for the energy with which it maintained its irrelevance. His decision to respond to Priya Duryodhani's appeal and join the Kaurava Party put his rough, attractive face and sad eyes on the front pages of the newspapers. With his childhood poverty, his impeccable political pedigree and the idealism of his recent career on the socialist fringe (which distinguished him from the rampant opportunism of the office-seekers flocking round the Kaurava Party central office in New Delhi), Ashwathaman's credentials could not have been better. Duryodhani welcomed him to the party and, while being careful not to find him a seat in government, nominated him to the Kaurava Working Committee.

There Drona's son became a one-man ginger group, loudly advocating a more socialist direction to party policy. The more the party elders explained why his proposals could not immediately be adopted, the more Ashwathaman insisted upon them, the Prime Minister encouraging him with her silence, and sometimes with her support.

'Why should we continue to give privy purses to our ex-maharajas?' he asked. 'Why should the likes of Vyabhichar Singh be subsidized to the tune of crores of rupees in taxes pressed from the sweat on the brow of the toiling peasant?'

'The toiling peasant, Ashwathaman,' Yudhishtir pointed out drily, 'doesn't pay any taxes.' They had agitated together, all those years ago, for the abolition of agricultural taxation, and Shishu Pal had finally granted it in the last budget before his death.

'But he could benefit from those taxes being spent on him, instead of being paid to these filthy rich oppressors of the people in exchange for their indolence.'

'It was actually in exchange for their accessions, Ashwathaman.'

'That was twenty years ago! They have been compensated more than enough. I say we should not pay them another paisa. As from now.'

'Who is to decide when we have given them more than enough? They gave up their kingdoms to join a republican India. Their privy purses don't even make up for the revenue they lost by doing so.'

'Spoken like a true prince, Yudhishtir.'

Yudhishtir's eyes flashed. 'I don't need to remind *you*, Ashwathaman, that since Hastinapur was annexed by the British *before* Independence, my family receives no privy purse.'

'I wasn't suggesting that you did. But it's clear where your sympathies lie.'

'It's not a question of sympathies!' Yudhishtir banged the table with a trembling fist. 'It's a question of promises. We made a solemn promise as a nation to the princes who joined us that we would pay them an agreed compensation, in perpetuity, for their sacrifice. It's in our Constitution – a document, Ashwathaman, that I would urge you to read some day.'

'How dare you suggest I don't know the Constitution!' Now it was Ashwathaman's eyes that blazed. 'The difference between us, Yudhishtir, is that you quote the letter of the Constitution while I cite its spirit. What about the Directive Principles of the Constitution, eh? What about equality and social justice for all?'

'What about the credibility of a solemn national undertaking? Is it right to help the poor by breaking your promises to the rich?'

'Breaking promises? This is not a moral exercise, Yudhishtir. The Kaurava Party is supposed to improve the lot of the common man, not strive for a collective place in Heaven.'

'I think Ashwathaman is right.' Priya Duryodhani intervened at last. 'I am in favour of adding this clause to the party programme. We should introduce legislation to this effect at the next session of Parliament.'

The majority of the Working Committee went along with her. They took their stances with one ear to the ground, and they interpreted the rumblings correctly: it was better in the popular eye to be associated with a broken promise than with the defence of privilege. Ashwathaman's resolution was passed overwhelmingly.

So what could Yudhishtir do? He resigned from the Working Committee as well.

*

And Draupadi Mokrasi, bolstered with vitamins and tonics, returned a little unsteadily to her household chores . . .

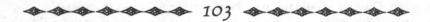

Matters came to a head over an issue which today, all these years later, seems almost too banal to have provoked such an earthquake. It was the issue of bank nationalization.

Do I hear you snort, Ganapathi? And well you might. Today we all realize what some of us realized even then, that nationalization only means transferring functioning and successful institutions from the hands of competent capitalists to those of bumbling bureaucrats. The prevalence of nationalization in the face of widespread evidence of its shortcomings, inefficiencies and failures only affirms the characteristic Indian credo that public losses are preferable to private profits. But in those days our Ashwathamans did not speak of profit or loss: they spoke of service. Nationalized banks, they argued, would serve public purposes that private banks would not. Nationalized banks would go out into the rural areas and give loans to poor peasants, while private banks would ask for security they couldn't provide. (If anyone suggested that that was why private banks were safer to deposit your hard-earned savings in, he was only being selfish, of course.) Today we know that the good nationalized banks are just as wary of unsecured loans as anyone else, but they have to function in an environment where success is judged by how many debt write-offs you can proudly attribute to the promotion of social uplift. (Again, should anyone suggest that if the bad loans had really served their social purpose they would have been paid back by the uplifted borrowers, he would be considered churlish. Especially by those bank managers into whose capacious pockets some of the irretrievable funds have been siphoned.)

But, yet again, I digress, Ganapathi. Bank nationalization was elevated by Ashwathaman and Duryodhani and others of their ilk alongside motherhood and *dal-bhaat* as an unquestionable national good. Before the rest of us knew it, Ashwathaman had introduced a private member's bill on the floor of

Parliament. Duryodhani – failing this time to carry a majority of the Working Committee with her – gave it her *personal* support and called for a free vote in the House. In the absence of a party whip (it had been impossible to agree on one) and with the support of the leftist Opposition parties, woolly-headed socialists and clear-thinking Communists alike, the Bank Nationalization bill was passed.

As the party and the nation erupted in debate on the issue, all eyes turned to the President of the country, the gentle Muslim academic who now occupied the palace where Lord Drewpad's investiture had taken place. His role was now that of the monarch his predecessors in residence had represented: as the country's constitutional head, his signature would make the bill an Act. What would he do? The media, politicians, friends, fellow academics and Priya Duryodhani all gave him their advice. All – especially the Prime Minister – did so in the strongest possible terms.

Beset by conflict and controversy, heated by the fieriness of his interlocutors' convictions and sizzled in the unaccustomed glare of publicity, poor Dr Mehrban Imandar did – as usual – the only decent and dignified thing possible. He died.

*

And Draupadi Mokrasi felt her head swim as one spell of dizziness succeeded another . . .

 *104*

The presidential election that immediately followed now became crucial for India's political future. The Kaurava Working Committee quickly met to choose the party's candidate for the post. Since the President was elected by the members of the national Parliament and the state Legislative Assemblies – an electoral college in which the Kaurava Party still enjoyed, despite its recent setbacks, a safe majority – the choice of the Kaurava candidate should normally have settled the matter. But it was clear that would no longer necessarily be the case.

For one thing, the Kaurava Old Guard – they had even begun calling themselves that, so used were they to the term of abuse – were determined to use this opportunity to regroup. In Priya Duryodhani they had a Frankenstein's monster who was suddenly growing out of control. If they could impose a

President on her who would not stand too much of her nonsense – who would, for instance, refuse to sign her Bank Nationalization bill – they could rein her in a bit. If, on the other hand, she succeeded in getting herself a sympathetic Kaurava candidate, the Old Guard could bid farewell to their last chance of control, and reconcile themselves to the complete loss of the authority that was already slipping away from their loosening grasp.

That Working Committee meeting was the stormiest I have ever attended, and believe me, I have attended a few. Priya Duryodhani put forward the name of one of her ministers – a son of God with a long record of serving the interests of the downtrodden, especially if they were related to him. The Old Guard balked and proposed me instead. Duryodhani lost.

My adoption as the official Kaurava candidate for President gave me my last chance to play a direct role in the nation's history. For about twenty-four hours I thought I would be able to end my career as a symbol of national reconciliation and Kaurava unity. Duryodhani appeared to have accepted my nomination with good grace.

Then, on the last day that nominations were to be filed, a young man, a member of our own party barely past the minimum age limit for the presidency, filed his papers as an Independent candidate. There were normally at least a dozen such Independent candidacies, ranging from the local butcher to the surviving flag-bearer of the Society for the Restoration (as it was now renamed) of the Imperial Connection, candidacies which gave journalists amusing copy to submit before a predictable ballot. I idly scanned the list for a laugh and stopped short at the last name.

It was not the name of just another irrelevant Independent. It was the name of Ekalavya.

And his candidacy had been proposed by the incumbent Kaurava Prime Minister.

*

And Draupadi Mokrasi, blinking her eyes, did not know why she felt faint . . .

105

Duryodhani's strategy began smoothly, almost predictably, to unfold. When the horrified party elders asked her to explain her sponsorship of a candidate who was intending to oppose the official party nominee, she said it was only an act of personal loyalty to an old friend. It did not necessarily mean that she would vote for him. In fact she was hoping, she said, to come to an understanding with the official Kaurava candidate about his perception of his role.

Oh? asked the Old Guard. What sort of understanding?

A general sort of understanding, she replied vaguely. About the ceremonial nature of his functions. About his commitment to upholding the will of the people, as expressed through Parliament.

You mean, I asked, you want him to agree in advance to sign every bill you submit to him?

Not really, she said. Not exactly. Well, yes.

You can't seriously expect me to give you this kind of undertaking, I said.

I do, she replied. What a pity.

The next day the papers carried two simultaneous announcements: the Kaurava Party had issued an official notice to Shri Ekalavya asking him to show cause why he should not be expelled for breach of party discipline, and the Prime Minister had stated that the time had come in India, too, for the torch to be passed to a new generation.

Ekalavya, cocky as ever, replied to the 'show-cause notice' with a letter he released simultaneously to the press. 'When the Kaurava Party, at this hour of national crisis, confronted with the responsibility of naming a helmsman to stand at the bridge of the ship of state to assist its captain, our dynamic young Prime Minister, to steer it through the muddy waters of communalism, capitalism and casteism, takes refuge behind the nomination of its oldest member for this arduous task, one wonders toward which century the party intends the ship to be steered,' he read aloud, to appreciative laughter from the whisky-plied hacks at the press conference. Mind you, what I'm quoting is only part of one sentence of his letter, and the other sentences were even longer, but I think you can get the drift of his ship of state from that specimen.

That warning shot across our bows indicated very clearly what their ammunition was made of. The reference to the three c's that constituted the pet aversions of the Ashwathaman left, the attack on my age and presumed conservatism, the interpretation of the role of the President as one who was supposed to 'assist' the Prime Minister, all pointed very clearly to the nature of their electoral message. The point was, how many in the Kaurava Party would listen?

The Working Committee of the Kaurava Party expelled Ekalavya from its primary membership and called upon all its members to desist from lending support to any other than the party's official candidate for the presidency.

The Prime Minister then called for a 'conscience vote' in the presidential election. The issues at stake, she declared, were far too serious to be brushed under the carpet of party discipline.

The Working Committee took strong exception to her statement and asked her to explain herself.

The Prime Minister said it was not exactly unconstitutional to uphold the sanctity of the secret ballot.

The Working Committee met for six hours and was unable to come up with an agreed statement in response.

The Prime Minister urged all 'modern and progressive forces' in politics to vote for Shri Ekalavya for President. The Communist and socialist parties endorsed her call, and pledged their votes to him.

The Kaurava Party asked Priya Duryodhani to show cause why she should not be expelled for breach of party discipline.

Priya Duryodhani did not reply.

The Kaurava Party repeated its question, and gave her forty-eight hours in which to reply.

Priya Duryodhani ignored them.

At the end of the forty-eight-hour deadline, the Working Committee met to discuss her reply, found there was none to discuss, and scheduled a meeting for the following week to discuss the issues arising from the lack of a reply.

The day before this meeting was to take place, the presidential election was held. It resulted in a narrow victory — half a percentage point — for Shri Ekalavya, who thus became the youngest President in independent India's brief history, and the first one not to have been the official nominee of the Kaurava Party.

The next day, the Working Committee of the Kaurava Party, meeting with several empty chairs, voted to expel Prime Minister Priya Duryodhani from the primary membership of the party.

An hour later, a group of people calling themselves the 'real Working Committee of the Kaurava Party', meeting at Priya Duryodhani's house and under her chairmanship, voted to expel all those who had attended the first meeting from the primary membership of the 'real' Kaurava Party — all, that is, except the three or four who had changed their minds in time and gone from the first meeting to the second.

And thus, over the essentially trivial issue of the election of a national figurehead, the political equivalent of the dragon on the bowsprit of a Viking ship, and ostensibly provoked by the even more trivial question of whether the fattest bankers in the country should draw government salaries or private ones, the great Kaurava Party, the world's oldest anti-colonial political organization, sixteen years away from its centenary, split.

The majority called themselves the Kaurava (R), the R standing for Real, or Ruling, or Rewarded by Priya Duryodhani, depending on your degree of cynicism. The rest of us, at first a not insubstantial rump, were dubbed the Kaurava (O), the O standing for Official, or Old Guard, or Obsolete, depending on the same thing. For the first time, the Prime Minister of the country represented a party which did not have an overall majority in Parliament. But the short-sighted ideologues of the Opposition Left supported her in the House, thinking this would give them some influence over her. It did – in her rhetoric: the very rhetoric which would then enable her to capture their seats at the next general election.

The poor idiots. It was, I declared with feeling, the first time I had seen goats opting for an early Bakr-Id. When they were no longer useful to Priya Duryodhani, there would be no one to hear their bleats as they were led off to the electoral slaughterhouse.

What more is there to say, Ganapathi, about this phase of my eclipse into irrelevance? Let us draw a discreet veil over the gradual but steady haemorrhage from the Kaurava (O) to the Kaurava (R), the self-serving prime-ministerial attacks on big business and 'monopoly capital', the increasing unproductive frustration of the Old Guard, the brilliant manoeuvre of calling a snap general election that caught all of us at our unready worst, the even more brilliant campaign slogan 'Remove Poverty' (as if she hadn't had the power to do anything about poverty so far) to which we were stupid enough to retort 'Remove Duryodhani' (as if we cared less about poverty than power). At the end of it all, Priya Duryodhani stood alone amongst the ruins of her old party, having smashed to pieces all the pillars and foundations that had supported her in the past. Alone, but surrounded by the recumbent forms of newly elected supplicants prostrating themselves amidst the rubble, the ciphers whose empty heads collectively gave Duryodhani a bigger parliamentary majority than even Dhritarashtra had ever enjoyed.

How had she done it? We were all too much in a state of shock to answer the question coherently, but there was no lack of random theorizing. It was her father's magic, some said; but then to anyone who knew the family it was obvious she took not after Dhritarashtra, but after the undeservingly unknown Gandhari the Grim. It was the privy-purse question and bank nationalization, others suggested; but then how many of the country's electorate understood what was involved in these issues, or cared? No, Ganapathi, I think it was innocence. Not hers, for what little she had been born with had dried with the sweat on Gandhari's satin blindfold, but ours, India's innocence. She had tapped the deep lode of it that still ran through our people, the innocence which had led 320 million voters to cast their ballots for a slogan ('Remove Poverty') devoid of sincerity, merely because for the first time a Prime Minister had bothered to imply that their votes served a purpose and, even better, that they could actually make a difference to the fulfilment of that purpose. 'Remove Poverty' indeed! Priya Duryodhani could as well have declaimed 'Invade Mars' for all the difference it made to her real intentions; but she did not, and in 'Remove Poverty' she found the two words that innocent India took to its heart and into its polling-booths.

So India had a new Queen-Empress, anointed a hundred years after the last one. And for a year, maybe two, the Empress's new clothes shone so brightly, so dazzled the eyes of her observers, that it was impossible to tell what they were made of or whether they were made of anything at all. But then, Ganapathi, they began to unravel.

*

And Draupadi Mokrasi was diagnosed as asthmatic, her breath coming sometimes in short gasps, the dead air trapped in her bronchia struggling to expel itself, her chest heaving with the effort to breathe freely . . .

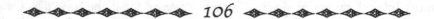 *106*

But before then, before Duryodhani's raiment, and the nation's hopes, began to come apart at the seams, there was the brief moment of national glory that came to be known as the Gelabi Desh War.

When Karnistan was hacked off India's stooped shoulders by the departing Raj's pencil-wielding butchers, it was carved like two pieces of prime human meat from the country's two Muslim-majority areas, choice Islamic cuts for the carnivorous Mohammed Ali Karna. But even if the appropriate Koranic verses were chanted during the operation and the resultant bleeding mess was undoubtedly halal, in the matter of economic and political development – the seasoning, as it were, of Karna's consecrated cuisine – the two halves were not treated the same way on the national cooking-range. They may both have had their steaks in the Islamic roast, but as far as development went, one was well-done and the other decidedly rare.

The half that did well was – inevitably – West Karnistan, where Karna had settled during his brief life as a Karnistani. It boasted the best infrastructure, the most important roads, canals and factories. It even had the most vigorous people – the perpetrators and survivors, indeed, of the bloodiest carnage at the time of Partition. The other half of Karnistan, the half where economic bounty was rare, lay in the swampy, humid east, where paddy-fields ripened gradually under an ageless sun, where ancient boats ferried people across terrain so wet the roads had sunk, where art, and music, and song, and culture and – why not admit it? – sleep were valued more highly than energy and industry and killing. The land that became East Karnistan had, in fact, been the site of one of Gangaji's few successful attempts at communal peace-making before Partition.

For nearly two and a half decades the people of East Karnistan, who were all ethnically Gelabins (a name that happened to be an anagram, as the West Karnistanis ever hastened to point out, of those notoriously stupid and lazy people, the Belgians) had put up with being despised, neglected and exploited as a concomitant of their shared Islamic nationhood. They had seen the profits of their jute exports pay for luxury car factories in the western half of their country, the bulk of their taxes swell the coffers of western provincial governments, the bodies of their women fill the brothels of the western cities, and the boots of western soldiers tramp their fields and streets in defence of a legal and constitutional order imposed by West Karnistan. They had honoured their moral and economic share of the national loans taken to finance the increasing prosperity of that better half. They had accepted the marginalization of the Gelabin language (which no West Karnistani ever learned, but which several imitated by pouring half a glass of water into their mouths and making bubbling round-lipped sounds, like the fish on which the Gelabins thrived). They had even patiently resigned themselves to the jibes that the West Karnistani creators flung at the eastern procreators. (Sample: 'When is the only productive period in East Karnistan? Night.' 'What is the difference between rabbits and Gelabins? Gelabins are browner.' 'Why should electricity never come to East Karnistan? Because if you could put the lights on after dark you would curtail the Gelabins' principal activity.' And so on.)

But suddenly, indeed unexpectedly, after two decades of military rule – stripes and stars on starched uniforms having been the Karnistani equivalent of the electoral tallies that determined India's political dispositions – the jaded general in power at the time of Duryodhani's triumph in the battle of the hustings, Jarasandha Khan, decided to call elections. Not having been entirely sober at the moment the decision was made, Jarasandha had omitted to figure out that elections were inconveniently based on the computation of votes, and that therefore the leaders with the most followers came out on top. Since the one inequality in Karnistan that could not be denied was its population balance, and since there were inescapably more Gelabins in Karna's bifurcated new country than any other group, the attempt at giving Karnistan electoral legitimacy meant that the biggest disadvantage of East Karnistan – its over-population – became suddenly its biggest asset. If its people played their electoral cards right, they could win a majority of seats in the new Karnistani Parliament, and they could rule all of Karnistan.

They did, they did, and they couldn't.

They voted overwhelmingly for the Gelabin People's Party, which won all but one seat in East Karnistan and thus, by sheer arithmetic, a numerical majority in the Karnistan Parliament. The prospect of being ruled by their chattering brown compatriots, however, so appalled the politicians of West Karnistan – and in particular the mercurial Zaleel Shah Jhoota, a procacious autocrat who had managed to convince a majority of West Karnistani voters that he was really a precocious socialist – that they persuaded Jarasandha Khan to declare the election results null and void, declare martial law in the East and lock up all the Gelabin politicians the Karnistani Army could lay their hands and batons on. The few who escaped incarceration promptly reacted by declaring the secession of Gelabi Desh from Karnistan.

India had no choice but to be involved in the business from the start. For one thing, it separated the two halves of Karnistan the way a surfacing whale separates waves. For another, the repression of the Gelabins following the imposition of martial law sent a panic-stricken flood of brutalized humanity flooding across our borders to create, on Indian soil, the biggest refugee problem the world has ever known.

I do not know if they moved Priya Duryodhani, those millions of ragged men, ravaged women and ragtag children who with tragic dignity suffered and trudged and struggled their way into the world's consciences. I do not know if it made her sad or angry to see them huddled under trees, in tents, in enormous lengths of unused piping, wherever they could find shelter from the relentless monsoon and the unrelenting humanitarianism of Occidental zoom-lenses. I do not know if she raged as the world showered platitudes and offers of charity at her while the refugees kept flowing from the bleeding wounds inflicted by Karnistan's Western Army. I do not know if it was with bitterness or contempt that she spurned these Band-Aids and tranquillizers the world proved more willing to give than the tourniquet she sought, the strong international pressure that alone might force Jarasandha Khan to withdraw his bayonets from the soft Gelabin flesh in which they were so grotesquely stuck. I do not know, Ganapathi, what she felt. But we all know what she decided to do.

Priya Duryodhani may not have meant it when she declared that all she wanted was for Jarasandha Khan to restore to the Gelabins the basic human decencies that would, above all, prevent more of them fleeing their homes and, in due course, encourage those who had fled to India to return. Her enemies outside the country and her admirers within it suggest these were merely time-buying pieties meant to lull diplomatic opinion while the troops prepared for war. Whatever the truth of the matter, it soon became apparent that Jarasandha, with the menacing figure of Zaleel Shah Jhoota hissing behind him like an under-age Rasputin, had no intention of relaxing his grip on what the Americans so charmingly call the short and curlies of his eastern compatriots. If India wanted to resolve the deadlock, ease the refugee burden on her soil and in the process teach Karnistan the kind of lesson India itself had had to learn not so long ago from Chakra, it would have to march in.

It did. Priya Duryodhani was no angel, but she ordered the Indian Army to strike in what was, in my view, one of only two wars in this century of carnage that can be morally justified. Seventeen days was all it took to sweep across the fields and rivers of East Karnistan and give the miserable millions their Gelabi Desh. For a short while it was to make them less miserable, and for a slightly shorter while it made Priya Duryodhani a national heroine.

Yes, Ganapathi, India accorded Duryodhani its ultimate accolade: she was not just deified, she was maternalized. This woman who had never married, and who looked incapable of producing or sustaining human life, became known as 'Ma Duryodhani' and 'Duryodhani Amma' to a people who saw in her the embodiment of the female principle of Shakti, the power and the strength of a national Mother Goddess.

It was about this time that my dreams started. They were extraordinarily vivid dreams, in full costume and colour, with highly authentic dialogue delivered (for they were clearly set in the epic era of our national mythology) in Sanskrit. Yes, Ganapathi, I dreamt in Sanskrit, and I dreamt of our traditions. Yet my dreams were populated not by the Ramas and Sitas of your grandmother's twilight tales but by contemporary characters transported incongruously through time to their oneiric mythological settings.

I dreamt, for instance, of Karnistan's Jarasandha coming into being like the son of our mythical king Brihadratha – the fruit, quite literally, of his twin wives. Brihadratha's wives had conceived after years of childlessness by each eating half of a mango given as a boon to their husband by the sage Kaushik, and each had produced half a boy. The two halves had fused into the strong and independent Jarasandha, whose great physical prowess was limited by one fatal flaw – the fact that his body, being a fusion of two separate parts, could, one day, be broken into two again.

And in my dream Duryodhani was a queen who resolved to conduct the

Rajasuya sacrifice and crown herself Empress. She could not do so, however, as long as the wicked and powerful Jarasandha reigned in his twin kingdom; so she sent an expedition, consisting of Bhim the soldier, Arjun the spy and Krishna the thinker (no, Ganapathi, don't pause, there is no thailor to follow) to destroy Jarasandha.

Entering his kingdom in disguise, our trio, after the inevitable moments of deception and temporizing diplomacy to put Jarasandha at ease, finally confronted the tyrant. Bhim challenged him to a duel.

Jarasandha fought bravely, but he was no match for the immense Bhim, who twice tore him apart in the middle and flung him in two to the ground, only to find the pieces fusing together again and Jarasandha returning refreshed to the fray. At last Krishna, the political advisor, caught the dismayed Bhim's eye, picked up a straw, broke it in half and cast the two pieces in opposite directions. Bhim, catching on immediately, seized Jarasandha with a cry, wrenched him apart and flung the two bits away on either side, making it impossible for the halves to reunite.

Thus, Ganapathi, was Jarasandha slain in my dream, and thus, when I opened my eyes, was Karnistan, the Hacked-Off Land, itself hacked in two.

*

And Draupadi Mokrasi knew moments of good health, entire periods when her breath came sweet and clear into her lungs and the radiance of living reddened her cheeks . . .

 *107*

My dreams continued, while in the real world around me, Duryodhani dissipated her goodwill, her adulation, her position by revealing she did not know what to do with any of it. Nothing changed in the daily lives of ordinary Indians, who still tilled and toiled to scratch an existence from the country's exhausted soil or sought pitiable betterment in the foetid city slums. The majority of our people remained illiterate; an overlapping majority remained below a poverty-line drawn lower and lower by Duryodhani's experts; and an overwhelming majority resigned themselves to being over-whelmed — by their fate, by disease and malnourishment and exploitation, and by the heartless ineptness of the one in whom they had placed their trust.

It angered me then, as it angers me now, to read Western accounts of

Indians 'starving to death'. If they starved to death, Ganapathi, there wouldn't be a problem, for they wouldn't survive to constitute one. They didn't starve to death, because they slaved and swept and sowed and stood and served and scratched in order to slake the hunger in their bellies, and found just enough to keep alive – underfed, undernourished, undergrown, underweight, underclad, undereducated, underactive, underemployed, undervalued and underfoot, but alive. Yet how sympathetically their underdevelopment was understood by Duryodhani's underlings! Her speech-writers peppered her rhetoric with dutiful obeisance to the wretched of the Indian earth, she proclaimed her democratic pedigree and socialist convictions from every lectern and platform – and she acquired more and more power in their name.

Ah, Ganapathi, the causes the poor of India lent themselves to in her hands! She squeezed the newsprint supplies of the press because they were 'out of touch' with the masses (you see how she remembered Kanika's conversation with her father), she fettered the judiciary by demanding they be 'committed' to the people (whose true needs she, of course, and she alone, represented), she emasculated her party by appointing its state leaders rather than allowing them to be elected (for she alone could judge who best would serve the people). And all this, Ganapathi, while the poor remained as poor as they had ever been, while striking trade unionists were beaten and arrested, while peasant demonstrations were assaulted and broken, all this while more and more laws went on to the statute books empowering Priya Duryodhani to prohibit, proscribe, profane, prolate, prosecute or prostitute all the freedoms the national movement had fought to attain during all those years of my Kaurava life.

And I dreamt then, Ganapathi, of the great forest fire of our epic. Of Arjun and Krishna, seated by the banks of the Jamuna, being approached by a resplendent figure taller than a coconut tree, his golden skin glowing like a sacrificial flame, his eyes flashing sparks. 'I am Agni, God of Fire,' he announces in a portentous voice. 'Help me consume this forest.' And our two heroes, the one dark like the night sky, the other fair like the stars, stand at each end of the wood as Agni rages within, preventing the Fire God's victims from fleeing, slaughtering those who stumble their agonized way towards them, their weapons swinging, scudding, scything through their victims in a blur of light and motion, as Agni burns and crackles and devours each branch, each tree, each jungle creature, and the smoke rises and the trunks fall and the jungle streams boil, and the animals wail as homes become pyres, mynah birds shriek as their singed wings strangulate their song, tigers roar as the flames lacerate their stripes, deer close their gentle eyes and leap in graceful thanatopsis into the swelling furnace, and Arjun and Krishna, Krishna and Arjun, doing their duty to divinity, refuse to permit escape, turn back the snakes slithering away from the sizzling grass, bar the way to the bears whose charred tails propel them screaming from the cinders of their lairs, kill the howling jackals who try to bound out of the searing circle of heat that engulfs them. And at last, at the end, when Agni is satisfied, and all that remains of the forest is a pile of faintly smoking ashes smouldering blackly amidst the devastation, the Fire God turns to our heroes and thanks them for their faithful defence of his slaughter.

'Tell me what you want,' he says, 'ask me for a boon, and you shall have it.'

It was Arjun who spoke, but Krishna, I believe, who inspired the thought.

'Give us, Agni, the power to create as we have the strength to destroy,' he said.

'You shall have it,' Agni responded, 'but not yet.'

And then the shining figure of the Fire God shimmered away from them, and my dream was over.

THE SEVENTEENTH BOOK:

THE DROP OF HONEY – A PARABLE

108

At last the people rose. Or, as always in India, some of the people rose, led by an unlikely figure who had stepped from the pages – so it almost seemed – of the history books. Jayaprakash Drona emerged from his retreat and called for a People's Uprising against Priya Duryodhani.

It was a shock, not least because JD's son Ashwathaman was still in the Kaurava camp, though increasingly on the margin of it. And for the Prime Minister it was a particularly rude shock, since Priya Duryodhani had done nothing to prevent Drona's name and image from being kept quietly alive, like a musty heirloom on a darkened mantelpiece. Drona had even been allowed a brief recent return to the headlines when he was pressed into service by the government to persuade the fiercely moustachioed dacoits of the wild Chambal ravines to give up their violent ways, just as he had renounced his. Drona's sincerity was so transparent, his own example so transcendent, that many of the dacoits, men with twenty and thirty murders, rapes and abductions each to their name, had actually listened and been converted. Drona had brought them out from their underground hideouts in mind-boggling ceremonies where they had dropped their rifles and gun-belts at his feet before an applauding audience of their victims' families – and in exchange for nothing more than the promise of a fair trial.

This, then, was the Drona who rose one day, bathed his feet in the sacred Ganga, and proclaimed that he could not take it any more. He had converted the petty criminals, but the biggest were the ones running the country – and they would not listen to him. The dishonesty and cynicism of the government of Priya Duryodhani was an affront to his conscience that Drona could no longer abide. It was time, he declared, for a People's Uprising which would restore India's ancient values to its governance.

Where were all our protagonists at this time? You may well ask, and you would be right, Ganapathi, to do so. The trouble with telling a tale on an epic scale is that sometimes you neglect the characters in the foreground as you admire the broad sweep of the landscape you are painting, just as the overall picture fades occasionally from sight when you focus closely on the smudgy details of individual impressions. Let me, Ganapathi, make amends.

Shall we begin at the top of the ladder of righteousness, with the son of Dharma? Yudhishtir was now a respected leader of the Opposition, sternly adopting the mantle of elder statesman which I was now too inactive to hold (yes, Ganapathi, you can be too old even to be an elder statesman). His earlier criticisms of Duryodhani, his principled resignations, gave him the saintly aura of one who has been right before his time – even though many would have preferred him to be more preoccupied with political, rather than urinary, tracts.

Bhim was still in the army, which he had served so well in the war that destroyed Jarasandha and broke up Karnistan. He had his limitations, but below the neck there was still no one in India or its environs who could stand up to him.

Arjun, perfect Arjun, had at last revealed a major imperfection: indecisiveness. When the Kaurava Party split he could not find it within himself either to support his increasingly priggish elder brother or to endorse the view of the idealistic, bearded Ashwathaman. On this his self-contented brother-in-law gave him no advice except to do what he thought best. 'If I knew what was the best thing to do,' Arjun expostulated to the untroubled Krishna, 'I wouldn't be asking you, would I?' But Subhadra's brother smilingly declined to go any further in his counsel.

Krishna himself seemed to find in the national convulsions a vindication of his preference for local politics. 'Your national mainstream,' he said to Arjun, 'isn't clean enough to swim in.' He remained with the Kaurava Old Guard, one of our few supporters who did not need the blessings of Dhritarashtra's daughter to retain his seat and who could therefore afford to keep his distance from her both geographically and politically. But Krishna's opposition to Priya Duryodhani was not active enough to prompt Arjun to emulate him. Nor could Ashwathaman's increasing irrelevance in the Kaurava ranks inspire Arjun to endorse his friend's radical idealism. Priya Duryodhani seemed happy enough to keep Drona's son on her Working Committee to let off occasional bursts of socialist steam, which she continued to ignore in practice as she fuelled her political gas-flames under blacker kettles. So Arjun ignored politics altogether and devoted himself – with great competence, but no greater consequence – to Subhadra, Draupadi and non-political freelance journalism.

Our supporting cast did not benefit from any larger unity of purpose than the principals. Kunti, her hair now almost as white as the widow's saris she had at last begun to wear, presided over the joint Pandava ménage like a dignified Mother Hubbard. She had given up the Turkish cigarettes of her insecure loneliness and now chewed Banarsi pan with as much red-stained confidence as any other Indian matriarch. Nakul, with his gift for speaking in the plural, had entered the national civil service from which Vidur had at last retired (while retaining enough governmental consultancies not to notice the difference). Sahadev, his silent twin, took his reserve and his gift for allowing himself to be told what to say into the foreign service. And I, Ganapathi, chomping reflectively on the new reality with my toothless gums, watching the few wisps of white on my scalp curl in dismayed betrayal, I sat, and aged, and saw, and dreamt.

 109

Drona's uprising was, of course, a peaceful one, so it was not really an uprising but a mass movement. It was, however, a movement that rapidly caught the imagination of the people and ignited that of the Opposition. Drona preached not only against Duryodhani but against all the evils she had failed to eradicate and therefore, in his eyes, had herself come to represent: venality and corruption, police brutality and bureaucratic inefficiency, rising prices and falling stocks in the shops, adulteration and black-marketing, shortages of everything from cereals to jobs, caste discrimination and communal hatred, neglected births and dowry debts – the whole panoply of national evils, including the very ones against which the Prime Minister had campaigned in the elections. Priya Duryodhani was being held accountable for the pledges she had failed to redeem, the hopes she had betrayed and the miracles she could not possibly have wrought. The sharpest focus of the movement was on herself: she was finally paying the price for her party's complete identification with its Leader.

Within months the movement had rocked the government to its unstable foundations. It did so by making the country ungovernable. In villages and towns, Drona preached a new civil disobedience, urging students to boycott classes, clerks to withhold their taxes, workers to strike at government-owned plants, legislators to resign from the assemblies to which they had been elected and the police to disobey orders to arrest the disobedient. It became clear that, for all their jingoistic hubris at the breaking in two of Karnistan, the people were judging the Prime Minister by the domestic goods she had failed to deliver rather than the strategic international stature she had diverted the government's energies to attain.

The Opposition parties quickly jumped on the Drona bandwagon. They gave it some of its lung-power, much of its muscle, and a great deal of its political thrust. With the Kaurava (O) and other parties in its ranks, the People's Uprising soon turned its attention to specific targets, the most vulnerable of which were the Kaurava (R) state governments. These were led largely by inept minions hand-picked by Duryodhani solely for their loyalty; they were thus easily attacked. In Drona's home state, the government was so completely paralysed by the need to contain his movement that its police spending reached the colossal sum of 100,000 rupees a day – yes, Ganapathi, one lakh of rupees, or enough to feed 20,000 Indian families and have something left over for dessert. In Hastinapur, after weeks of popular agitation culminating in a highly popular march by housewives banging empty pots and pans outside his residence, Duryodhani's Chief Minister resigned. When New Delhi showed no inclination to hold elections for a new state assembly – preferring to control Hastinapur directly under 'President's Rule' – Yudhishtir, the state's most famous political leader, undertook a fast unto death. He hadn't even lost a kilo before Duryodhani caved in and called new state elections – which her party comprehensively lost. The political tide seemed to be turning decisively away from the Prime Minister.

I watched all this, Ganapathi, in increasing gloom. I was no admirer of Priya Duryodhani or what she stood for, but I was equally distraught about Drona's Popular Uprising and where it was leading the government. For the independent India that I had spent my life trying to achieve to be wasting itself in demonstration and counter-demonstration, mass rallies and mass arrests, was pitiable. For the government to be devoting all its attention to policing opposition rather than developing the country was tragic. For our precious independence to be reduced to anarchy, betrayal and chaos was downright criminal.

If only they had waited, Ganapathi! The next elections were not so far away; Drona and Yudhishtir could have rallied the Opposition around them, consolidated their organization and swept Duryodhani from power at the hustings. Instead they clamoured for her removal, and that of her party's state governments, now; and they did so not in the assemblies, where the post-Gelabi Desh electoral wave had left them clinging to the jetsam of just a few seats, but in the streets.

Priya Duryodhani had her back to the wall, and that was the position from which she always fought the hardest. Especially when the wall itself appeared on the verge of crashing down behind her.

Yes, Ganapathi. For right in the midst of this political crisis, an upright if excessively legalistic provincial court found the Prime Minister guilty of a corrupt electoral practice' for making a campaign speech for her parliamentary seat during the last elections from a platform shared with President Ekalavya. The President being a non-political national figure, Priya Duryodhani should not have 'exploited his presence for partisan ends'. I don't know what was more laughable, the suggestion that the Prime Minister stood to gain in the slightest from the President's political lustre (all of which was reflected from her in the first place) or her conviction for an offence whose triviality was underscored by the far greater crimes perpetrated and perpetuated all around her and her government.

The conviction – which deprived her of her parliamentary privileges pending appeal – gave the Popular Uprising just the spark it needed. They turned their movement into a massive orchestrated cry for her resignation, threatening to court arrest outside her home every day until she quit. More ominously for her, Drona began to talk to a faction within her own party, led conspicuously by his son Ashwathaman, which was calling for her to step down 'temporarily' in order to quieten the Opposition demands and give the judicial process time to work.

But if there was one thing Priya Duryodhani had learned from her mother's wasted sacrifices, it was never to put anything, anything at all, ahead of self-interest. She would not allow anyone to place a blindfold on *her* blazing eyes. And her instincts were confirmed by her closest advisor, the hand-picked President of the Kaurava (R) Party and the man known as 'Duryodhani's Kanika', the Bengali lawyer Shakuni Shankar Dey.

Shakuni was an immense mountain of a man, oily and slick, with a gleaming bald pate, gleaming gold buttons on his immaculate silk *kurta*, and gleaming white enamel in place of the teeth he had lost at the hands of a grieving mob (which had expressed its grief with its fists after he had got a murderer off on a technicality). 'Duryodhani's Kanika' flicked a stray speck of lint off his spotless sleeve and turned to the Prime Minister.

'Don't resign, even for appearances' sake,' he said firmly. 'Why gratify the howling jackals outside and give time for the opportunists within the party to wrest control from you?'

'But do I have a choice?'

Shakuni frowned his disapproval of the question. 'The Prime Minister always has a choice,' he growled. 'You don't have to do anything merely because it's expected of you. But there is something else you can do,' he added meaningfully.

'What?'

Shakuni rested manicured fingers on the prime-ministerial table in front of him. 'Hit back.'

The Prime Minister looked at him like a schoolmistress whose favourite pupil has given too pat an answer. 'Obviously,' she said. 'But how? I can't just lock up all those I'd love to put behind bars.'

'You can.'

'Oh, of course I *can*,' Duryodhani said in exasperation. 'But I wouldn't last a day afterwards if I did that.'

'You might not, if things were allowed to continue as at present,' Shakuni said carefully. 'But you could change the rules of the game. You could declare a Siege.'

'But we already have.' This was true: the state of Siege declared in the country at the time of the Gelabi Desh war had never actually been lifted.

'Yes, but *that* Siege was declared to cope with an external threat which everyone knows has long since passed,' replied the lawyer. 'What you could do now is to declare an *internal* Siege. A grave threat to the stability and security of the nation from internal disruption.'

'Which is true enough,' Priya Duryodhani nodded reflectively.

'No one has ever defined the permissible procedures under an internal Siege, which leaves it more or less up to us to define them,' Shakuni added. 'I think they could very safely include the preventive detention of some of our more obstreperous politicians . . .'

'All of them,' the Prime Minister said firmly.

'Or, indeed, of all of them,' Shakuni affirmed. 'Not to mention censorship of the press, which is nowhere explicitly ruled out in the Constitution, suspension of certain fundamental rights – free speech, assembly, that sort of thing – and measures to put the judiciary in their place.'

'Go on,' Duryodhani said, her anxious pinched face brightening. 'I like the sound of this.'

'Of course, this plan will need the cooperation, or at least the signature, of the President.'

The Prime Minister's face took on its famous determined look. 'It is time,' she said pointedly, 'that Ekalavya earned his keep.'

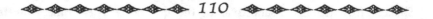 *110*

While this conversation – or something very like it, Ganapathi, for my sources were no longer as good as in the old days – was taking place, Yudhishtir, flanked by Drona and the assembled luminaries of the Opposition, was addressing a mammoth mass rally at the Boat Club lawns convened by the People's Uprising movement to call for the exit of Priya Duryodhani.

'As I get up and stand at this microphone,' he declaimed, 'as I stand here and look upon the hundreds and thousands of you gathered here before me, the lakhs of men and women who have come to *see* us all on the same platform, who have come to *sense* and *feel* our unity, our confidence, the strength of our commitment to freedom and justice and change, who have come to *hear* us because for once we represent your hopes instead of merely your dissatisfactions, as I see all this, I feel a *surge* in my heart.' The crowd roared its approval at each pause, its excitement rising as Yudhishtir added clause to heady clause to bring his audience to a crescendo of vocal adulation. 'I know,' Yudhishtir declared, 'I *know*, standing here, that change is at hand. I *know* that India can no longer be the same. I offer my respectful salutations in your name to our guru Drona.' Enthusiastic applause. 'I look from you to my colleagues on this platform' — a broad sweep of his hand encompassed his former rivals and critics in other opposition parties and he named some of them, receiving a lusty cheer from each politician's supporters in the crowd — 'and I know that from now on there is *no* looking back' — roars from the crowd — 'that our differences are over' — another roar — 'that together we are going to seek and attain our *supreme* goal, the bringing down of this corrupt and iniquitous government.' Another roar, this time louder than all the rest; the crowd on its feet; slogans raised by Kaurava (O) workers judiciously scattered amongst the throng — 'Down with Priya Duryodhani! Yudhishtir, *Zindabad*! Long Live Opposition Unity! People's Uprising, *Zindabad*!'

And so it went on, with even stiff-necked Yudhishtir provoking the exhilaration of the rallied mass, but there was still something staged, unreal, about this piece of political theatre. The court verdict had, inevitably, stirred the Opposition movement to greater boldness, just as the Hastinapur elections had prompted them towards greater unity. (There the disparate followers of Drona's Uprising had banded themselves together in a Janata Morcha or People's Front, which with the linguistic eclecticism of Indian politics had quickly become known as the Janata Front.) The Prime Minister's court-directed loss of her parliamentary privileges now gave them the one thing they needed: a clear-cut issue on which they could unite.

But their unity seemed purely expedient, their programme severely limited and their theatre all the more unreal. For several days now they had been calling on the Prime Minister to resign without the slightest thought of who or what might take her place. Demonstrations took place in every significant stretch of ground in the country to condemn the government and demand that the Prime Minister step down. To counter them, Shakuni had had busloads of rural peasants wheeled into Delhi from neighbouring farmlands on diverted public transport to express their support for the government in raucous rallies outside the Prime Minister's residence. Sometimes the two groups had clashed; sometimes the innocent farmers had lent their vocal chords to the wrong cause. But they were not the only ones who had no idea of the rest of the script.

It was, I suppose, heady stuff, grist for the foreign news-magazines which reported on wars and political conflict in the same tone that they reported the goings-on in Hollywood bedrooms, but my own view of it was entirely ambivalent. I knew that in India there were really no blacks and no whites; nor was there a uniformly dingy grey. Instead, political morality and public values were a mystical, blurred, swirling optical illusion of alternating blacks and whites in different shades of depth and brightness. The Prime Minister ruled like a goddess: black to liberal democrats, black to her political opponents (who were not all liberal democrats), white to adoring impoverished *sansculottes* at rural public meetings, white also to contented corpulent capitalists who shrugged off her strident socialist rhetoric and fuelled her party's electoral machine with the profits they made through her less-than-socialist policies. An honest judge had disqualified her from office by an impartial (if un-imaginative) reading of the statutes: white to those who believed in the rule of law, white to her critics and enemies (who did not all believe in the rule of law), black to those who believed her hand at the helm was essential to steady India's ship of state, black also to those sycophants and hangers-on who stood to lose personally from her downfall. It was a complex spectrum of blacks, whites and fluid greys; Brahminical ambivalence was therefore nothing to be ashamed of.

My ambivalence, Ganapathi, was to become less and less tenable with time.

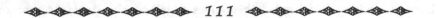 *111*

Yudhishtir's grand show at the Boat Club received a rousing curtain-call, but there were to be no repeat performances. Later the same night Shakuni's plans were put smoothly into motion, and teams of red-eyed policemen knocked before dawn at the doors of the Uprising's leaders to take them away to the prisons and the 'rest houses' that would be their home for months to come.

I do not know what saddened me more, the fact of the Prime Minister of free India arresting her political opponents, or the fact of their surprise at their own arrest. Drona's astonishment at being taken away confirmed the extent to which he was living in the past. All he could bring himself to say was a Sanskrit phrase that had been coined two thousand years earlier, the same phrase that had sprung to Gangaji's lips at the Bibigarh Gardens all those years ago: 'Vinasha kale, viparita buddhi.' You may remember from that occasion, Ganapathi, that the Greeks had an equivalent: 'Whom the gods wish to destroy, they first make mad.' Questioning the sanity of the victor is the only course open to any civilization defeated by forces it cannot understand.

I was not honoured with a pre-dawn knock on my door. Priya Duryodhani evidently considered me too old to be worth locking up. But that was not why I failed to join the chorus of condemnation that was raised in the Western press and in Indian drawing-rooms about what had happened. You see, Ganapathi, I was sensitive to the excessive formalism of some of the attacks on the Siege: the critics seemed to think that democracy had been overthrown, without paying much heed to the content of that democracy or the results of its abrogation. I could not, at that stage, think of the issue simply as one of freedom versus tyranny. Yes, Duryodhani's motives in proclaiming a state of Siege, arresting a number of opponents and imposing censorship on the press were primarily cynical and self-serving: without these steps she would not have been able to contain the mounting pressures on her to resign. But I still believed that the political chaos in the country, fuelled by Drona's idealistic but confused Uprising which a variety of political opportunists had joined and exploited, could have led the country nowhere but to anarchy.

The Siege was accompanied by the declaration of a twenty-point socioeconomic programme which the government seemed determined to implement. With strikes and political demonstrations banned, there was a new sense of purpose where earlier there had been drift and uncertainty. In the slothful, yet oh-so-vital world of officialdom, the officialdom in whose hands rests the hope of progress for so many of our helpless poor, habitual absentees were reporting for work all over the country; in some government offices they suddenly discovered a shortage of chairs, so long had it been since they were last all occupied. I felt (and said openly to an anxious Arjun, whose very expression in those days betrayed the discomfort of his posture on the horns of this dilemma) that if the Siege, however base its basic motive, was going to permit the government to serve the common man far more effectively than before, then people like us, who had lost the freedoms we alone knew how to exercise, had no right to object. The purpose of democratic government was the greatest good of the greatest number, and I had no doubt that more Indians would benefit from the abolition of bonded labour and the implementation of land reforms than would suffer from the censorship of articles, however well Arjun could write them.

And then, Ganapathi, I had the old politician's regard for the wishes of the people. The declaration of the Siege, the arrests of the agitators, the silence in the streets, had been accepted by non-political India without a murmur. The only sound that replaced the months of clamour appeared to be the deflating hiss of a long public sigh of relief.

'It's strange, VVji, this silence,' said Arjun. 'Even as a journalist I had come to think that India without politics would be like Atlantis without water.'

'Why "even"?' I leaned back comfortably on my bolsters. 'It's precisely you journalists who've contributed to that feeling. Is there any limit in your newspapers to the amount of space you allocate to politics? Your news columns, and much of your editorial pages, are inundated with reports of speeches, clashes, accusations and counter-accusations, by-elections, resignations, defections, appointments, walkouts, rallies, *padayatras*, satyagrahas, fasts, demonstrations, attempts to court arrest, charges of breaching party discipline, show-cause notices, expulsions, party splits. Every other day there is at least one account of a provincial political "leader" with several hundred followers (it is always "several hundred") crossing over to another party and swearing allegiance to his former rivals in the presence of one of its national *neta*s. To someone like me, who can't get out of this room as often as I used to and who must depend more and more on what the newspapers tell me about the world outside – though, thank God, they are not my only sources – it would seem from the newspapers that Indian life consists almost exclusively of a bewildering variety of forms of political behaviour.'

'It's what the readers want,' Arjun said defensively. Defensiveness had become something of a second nature to him these days.

'Nonsense,' I barked cheerfully. 'Most Indian readers have learned to skim through such accounts, though they provide considerable fodder for the likes of me. The truth is that surfeit has bred cynicism: we have all read and heard too much for too long to take it very seriously.'

'It wasn't always like this, was it, VVji?'

'Not in the nationalist movement. Then, everybody cared.' I caught myself slipping into the righteousness of the terminally nostalgic, and changed my tone. 'Of course, the issues were different then. But when we were fighting for independence we were fighting also for participation in the parliamentary democracy from which we felt excluded. When we won freedom it was almost axiomatic that we had won ourselves a parliamentary democracy too. For all Dhritarashtra's sins and limitations that was one conviction he never betrayed. Even though – or perhaps because – he let no one else come near to being Prime Minister, he constantly reaffirmed and encouraged the institution of parliamentary democracy in the country. But the poor boy couldn't see that behind the solid façade of the edifice, the rooms were empty.' I shook my head. 'We Indians, Arjun, are so good at respecting outward forms while ignoring the substance. We took the forms of parliamentary democracy, preserved them, put them on a pedestal and paid them due obeisance. But we ignored the basic fact that parliamentary democracy can only work if those who run it are constantly responsive to the needs of the people, and if the parliamentarians are qualified to legislate. Neither condition was fulfilled in India for long.' I smiled a humourless and toothless smile. 'Today most people are simply aware of their own irrelevance to the process. They see themselves standing hopelessly on the margins while the professional politicians and the unprofessional parliamentarians combine to run the country to the ground.'

I paused, fatigued by my own dismay, and poured myself a tumbler of water from a pitcher beside me. Arjun got up to help me, but I waved him away and went on.

'What we have done is to betray the challenge of modern democracy. You have to understand, Arjun, that the political and governmental process in our country has always been distant from the vast mass of the people. This has been sanctified by tradition and reinforced by colonialism. The picture of political power portrayed in the *Arthashastra* is that of a remote authority no more accessible to the common man than the institutions of later imperial rule. Two hundred years of the British Raj underscored the detachment of ordinary Indians from the processes of their own governance. Perhaps Gangaji's greatest achievement was that he made the people at large feel they had a stake in the struggle for freedom. Under him the nationalist movement inspired a brief surge of enthusiasm which overcame the general apathy, but it has all faded away.' I shrugged. 'Indians learned to talk about politics like Englishmen about the weather, expressing concern without expecting to do anything about it.'

'And now they accept the loss of their politics without demur,' Arjun mused.

'Exactly. Not so surprising after all, is it?' I laughed, without either amusement or bitterness. 'But Arjun, we Indians are notoriously good at being resigned to our lot. Our fatalism goes beyond, even if it springs from, the Hindu acceptance of the world as it is ordained to be. I must tell you a little story – a marvellous fable from our *Purana*s that illustrates both our resilience and our self-absorption in the face of circumstance.' I sat up against my bolsters and assumed the knowingly expectant attitude of those who are about to tell stories or perform card tricks. 'A man, someone very like you, Arjun – a symbol, shall we say, of the people of India – is pursued by a tiger. He runs fast, but his panting heart tells him he cannot run much longer. He sees a tree. Relief! He accelerates and gets to it in one last despairing stride.

He climbs the tree. The tiger snarls below him, but he feels that he has at last escaped its snapping jaws. But no – what's this? The branch on which he is sitting is weak, and bends dangerously. That is not all: wood-mice are gnawing away at it; before long they will eat through it and it will snap and fall. The branch sags down over a well. Aha! Escape? Perhaps our hero can swim? But the well is dry, and there are snakes writhing and hissing on its bed. What is our hero to do? As the branch bends lower, he perceives a solitary blade of grass growing on the wall of the well. On the top of the blade of grass gleams a drop of honey. What action does our Puranic man, our quintessential Indian, take in this situation? He bends with the branch, and licks up the honey.'

I laughed at the strain, and the anxiety, on Arjun's face. 'What did you expect? Some neat solution to his problem? The tiger changes its mind and goes away? Amitabh Bachhan leaps to the rescue? Don't be silly, Arjun. One strength of the Indian mind is that it knows some problems cannot be resolved, and it learns to make the best of them. That is the Indian answer to the insuperable difficulty. One does not fight against that by which one is certain to be overwhelmed; but one finds the best way, for oneself, to live with it. This is our national aesthetic. Without it, Arjun, India as we know it could not survive.'

But for all my certitudes, I knew, and I knew Arjun knew, that what I had said wasn't really an answer to his dilemma. He looked at Priya Duryodhani's Siege and felt the need to make a choice, while I could only explain how to avoid one.

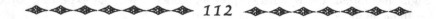

112

And so we talked; and I can tell you, Ganapathi, that we were not the only ones. Duryodhani censored the press, stifled public debate, and placed restrictions even on the reporting of the speeches of the few Opposition stalwarts left in the House to criticize the new laws she was bulldozing through Parliament like the steel-rimmed *chakra*s of an invincible juggernaut. (Yes, spell that the British way, Ganapathi. The juggernaut of their dictionaries has only a distant connection to the Jagannath of our devotees.) Yet everything that it was illegal to say in public was now said in private. Opinions flowed from Indian tongues like the Ganga through Benares: profuse, stimulating and muddied with other people's waste matter. From village tea-shops to urban coffee houses, Indians gave whispered rein, sometimes punctuated by prophylactic glances over their shoulders, to their imaginations.

Often these opinions, like the people who expressed them, had no visible means of support, but then Indian opinions are rarely founded on any sense of responsibility or any realistic expectation of action. For all her canny cynicism, Duryodhani had failed to make one simple discovery about the people she ruled: that you could let them say what they liked without feeling obliged to do something about it. There was no need for the censorship she had clamped upon the political commentaries of the élite. In India, the expression of private opinions was no proof of the existence of a viable and demanding public opinion.

Yes, Ganapathi, that was one of the ironies of Duryodhani's experiment with authoritarianism – it was more authoritarian than it needed to be. She could have let the newspapers write what they wanted, and it would have changed nothing. Instead, the very fact that they could no longer write what they wanted became a burning issue to those for whom conversation was now the only outlet.

And as so often in Indian life, Ganapathi, indeed as so often in this story, the really important issues were worked out not in action but through discourse. That is how we seek to arrive at objective perceptions in a land whose every complex crisis clamours for subjectivity. If we were to try to find our ethics empirically, Ganapathi, we would for ever be trapped by the limitations of experience: for every tale I have told you, every perception I have conveyed, there are a hundred equally valid alternatives I have omitted and of which you are unaware. I make no apologies for this. This is my story of the India I know, with its biases, selections, omissions, distortions, all mine. But you cannot derive your cosmogony from a single birth, Ganapathi. Every Indian must for ever carry with him, in his head and heart, his own history of India.

How easily we Indians see the several sides to every question! This is what makes us such good bureaucrats, and such poor totalitarians. They say the new international organizations set up by the wonderfully optimistic (if oxymoronic) United Nations are full of highly successful Indian officials with quick, subtle minds and mellifluous tongues, for ever able to understand every global crisis from the point of view of each and every one of the contending parties. This is why they do so well, Ganapathi, in any situation that calls for an instinctive awareness of the subjectivity of truth, the relativity of judgement and the impossibility of action.

Yet one day, at the end of another intense conversation with an increasingly troubled Arjun, I found it impossible to sustain my comfortable ambivalence.

I was in full flow about the state of Indian politics, trying to convince my-self as much as Arjun that what had been lost was not worth keeping – that

Indian democracy had become so atrophied and the people so divorced from it that Priya Duryodhani's Siege didn't really deserve to be condemned. (It was, Ganapathi, a typical case of mind over matter — if you don't mind, it doesn't matter.) Then, suddenly, Arjun spoke in a tone of greater conviction than he had ever used in the preceding months of one-woman rule. 'You've got to be wrong, VVji,' he said with infinite sadness. 'You've got to be wrong, or the whole world wouldn't make sense any more.'

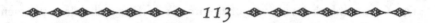 113

The whole world wouldn't make sense any more. I think it was those words, spoken in soft sincerity by the purest of the Pandavas, that penetrated my conscience so deeply that they shattered the careful equilibrium I had constructed there, fragmented my complacency like a breaking mirror. Did my world, I found myself silently asking, make sense any more? Had I, in my Brahminical ambivalence, twisted and turned so cleverly that I had failed to stay in the same place, slipping unnoticed to a different mooring? Had I not seen, or worse, pretended not to see, that the sun and the moon and the stars of my world were no longer shining where they had always shone before?

Oh, Ganapathi, there was no escaping from these questions! I tried to tell myself that the answers were irrelevant, that the questions simply had to be asked differently. But I knew, as you too may well have guessed, that however flexibly I had sought to define the truth, however safely I had delimited my world, I had spent too long avoiding all thought of one facet of my world, one shining visage, one person. Yes, Ganapathi, you are right, you have caught me in my self-deception: for too many hours now, and too many pages, I have failed to make any reference to Draupadi.

What can I tell you, Ganapathi? Can I look into the hurt in her eyes and claim it didn't matter? Can I acknowledge the little cuts and bruises and burns I had spotted on her arms and hands and face at each visit to her home and dismiss them, as Kunti did, as minor kitchen mishaps? Can I admit the terrible suspicion that her own husbands were ill-treating her, exploiting her, neglecting her, even ignoring her, and still excuse myself for having done nothing about it? Can I recall the sagging flesh that had begun to mask her inner beauty, the lines of pain that had begun to radiate from those crystal-clear eyes, the tiredness in the normally firm voice, and allow myself to pretend that I had noticed none of it, that none of these things, perhaps not even Draupadi herself, was real?

I cannot, Ganapathi, and yet I must turn away from reality. Because when Arjun's gentle words smashed my mental equipoise and forced me to think of Draupadi, I began again to dream.

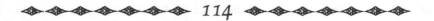 *114*

I dreamt once more of legends past, of shimmering palaces and moustachioed men in shining brass armour and princesses glowing with gold bangles and scented garlands; of glorious Hastinapur, home of my ancestors. I dreamt of long-dead Dhritarashtra, restored to unseeing life, on a kingly throne; of sharp-faced Duryodhani, his crowned heiress; of righteous Yudhishtir and the Pandava brothers; and of the beautiful, fresh-faced Draupadi, their common wife.

I dreamt, too, of Karna, the Hacker-Off, strong and proud; of his un-acknowledged mother, the widowed Kunti; of the brilliant smile of Krishna, still distant in Gokarnam, but with his far-seeing eye never straying from the events in Hastinapur. And I dreamt of the sinister slimy Shakuni, rubbing hands from which a profusion of rings gleamed, as he approached the Princess Duryodhani in a sibilant whisper.

'I have a plan,' he breathed. 'A plan that will trap the Pandava brothers like five fish in a net.'

'Oh, tell me, Shakuni,' Duryodhani responded eagerly.

'You want to defeat Yudhishtir, but he cannot so easily be beaten on the battlefield. For this reason we have been searching for another stratagem. I believe I have found it.'

'Yes?' Duryodhani could have been a maiden waiting for the announcement of a suitor's name, so excited did she sound.

'Yudhishtir likes to play dice.' Shakuni saw the blank look on the princess' face and spelt the word for her. 'Dee – eye – she – eee, dice. You know, the little ivory cubes with dots on them.'

'Ah, yes. But what has his playing dice got to do with . . .?'

'Everything. As a noble of Hastinapur, he cannot in all honour refuse to accept a challenge from me to play dice. For stakes. Very high stakes.' Shakuni's eyes rolled heavenwards.

'I think I'm beginning to understand.' Duryodhani's voice took on a girlish tremor. 'I suppose you play dice rather well, Shakuni.'

'Rather well!' Shakuni giggled incongruously, his jowls trembling with pleasure. 'I am unbeatable. Simply unbeatable. I have,' he explained, lowering his voice to a confidential croak, 'a very special pair of dice. And in our traditional rules, it is the challenger who has to provide the dice.'

'Bless the traditional rules,' Duryodhani said. 'I'm delighted, Shakuni. I'll give you whatever support you need.'

'First there is your father to be thought of,' Shakuni pointed out. 'Will Dhritarashtra permit the game in his palace? That is the only location which would make the challenge respectable, and where Yudhishtir would not be able to refuse, even if he were advised to.'

'Hmm,' Duryodhani said. 'I'll try.' And she hurried, floating through my dream like an animated wraith, to her father. Dhritarashtra was seated on his golden throne, the white umbrella of kingship wobbling unsteadily above his thinning hair.

'A game of dice?' Dhritarashtra asked. 'I'm not sure that's entirely in the spirit of the rules I've drawn up for the kingdom, Duryodhani. There's nothing explicitly against it, though. I'll tell you what, my dear one. This is the sort of thing on which I normally consult the officials. Let me ask Vidur and see what he has to say.'

'Don't!' Duryodhani pouted. 'He will be against it, I know. You know how these bureaucrats are – they don't like anybody to have fun. Why not let it remain a matter for your ministers? Shakuni thinks it's all right, and he's a minister.'

The blind king sighed, as he often did in the face of his daughter's insistent demands. 'All right, then,' he said at last, the words echoing hollowly in my suspended mind. 'Have it your own way.'

The jackals howled again, Ganapathi, the vultures wheeled overhead and screeched, the crows beat their black wings against the window-panes of the palace, and the sky turned grey, the colour of ashes on a funeral pyre. Priya Duryodhani skipped happily to Shakuni and announced the king's consent.

'You can leave the rest to me,' the minister said.

In my dream it was Vidur who arrived at Yudhishtir's palace to invite him for the game.

'I don't like the sound of it one bit,' the civil servant said. 'But I'm afraid it's my duty, Yudhishtir, to ask you to come.'

'Oh, I'll come,' Yudhishtir said impassively. 'It is my duty, too, in all honour, to accept Shakuni's challenge. Besides, I'm not too bad at dice myself.'

And so the five brothers and wife set out for Hastinapur, to the tune of a farewell song which rang arhythmically in my mind:

Yudhishtir said, 'It's time to go
To keep a date
With Fate;
Fate beckons; we mustn't be slow
Or hesitate –
We'll be late!

I realize that in this thing
I have no voice,
No choice;
We're just puppets on a string,
To be thrown thrice –
Fate's dice.'

They reached Dhritarashtra's palace, and bent before his throne to touch his feet in ritual homage. Mynahs chirped in the trees as they entered, and the sweet fragrance of frangipani blossoms wafted before Draupadi with each tinkling step of her hennaed feet.

'Welcome,' Dhritarashtra said. 'I understand, Yudhishtir, that you have accepted Shakuni's challenge.'

'It is my duty,' Yudhishtir said simply.

'You don't have to, you know,' the aged king responded sharply. 'You can leave now, if you prefer.'

'My honour obliges me not to flee from a challenge,' Yudhishtir replied. 'Besides, I am in the hands of Fate, as are we all.'

'Not me,' said Priya Duryodhani, the ultimate beneficiary of Shakuni's skills. 'I'll watch.'

'I really don't think this is a good idea,' Vidur said from behind the throne. 'When we drew up the rules of the kingdom, Dhritarashtra, we did not envisage anything like this.'

'Go ahead, Yudhishtir!' blazed old Drona, standing up at the sidelines. 'Defeat rotten Shakuni and win his treasures in the name of the people! You can do it.'

'I think so too,' agreed Yudhishtir, seating himself before the bald and gleaming minister. 'Throw the dice, Shakuni.'

And in my dream, the clouds, which had lifted for Draupadi's entrance, closed in once more, and the skies darkened again. And Shakuni boomed, 'What do you wager?'

'I wager my palace, my position, my share of the Kaurava kingdom,' Yudhishtir responded, throwing the dice.

Shakuni threw, and announced, 'I win.' A great wail rose in the distance, like the lowing of a thousand wolves in a moonlit forest. The players remained oblivious of it. 'And what do you wager next?'

'I wager the Constitution, the laws, the peace of the people,' Yudhishtir proclaimed stiffly, and threw.

'I win. Next?'

'I wager my own freedom, together with that of ten thousand faithful party workers, the support of the press and the prospect of the next elections,' he said.

Shakuni threw again, and the pockmarks on the ivory cubes gleamed dully at Yudhishtir, like the scabs of a virulent rash. 'I win.'

The eldest Pandava sat very still, looking straight into the eyes of his victor. 'I am ruined,' he said evenly. 'I have nothing else to wager.'

'Oh, yes, you do.' The massive bald pate inclined towards the five figures of Yudhishtir's appalled family along the wall. 'You have them.'

A thin line of perspiration, like a row of transparent beads, appeared on Yudhishtir's upper lip. He seemed about to say something, then stopped.

'I stake my brothers,' he said in a strained voice.

'You've got to stop them, sir,' Vidur pleaded with his blind half-brother. 'Dhritarashtra, this mustn't go on. Damnation will visit us all. Shakuni is not playing an honest game. Yudhishtir is trapped. You must stop it, or the whole country will be ruined.'

But Priya Duryodhani was within earshot. 'Don't listen to him, Daddy,' she urged. 'He's always been on their side, even when he pretended to be helping you. Shakuni knows what he's doing. And as for the country, we can manage it just as well without the Pandavas. Probably better.'

Dhritarashtra was too absorbed in the contest to reply to either of them. Vidur lapsed into a sullen silence, his arms folded across his chest, disassociating himself from the proceedings his invitation had initiated.

'I throw for your brothers.' Shakuni flung the dice, which landed mockingly at Yudhishtir's feet, their unbeatable dots face up.

'They are now your prisoners,' Yudhishtir conceded, his staring eyes downcast, avoiding the looks of impotent betrayal his brothers were directing at him from their hopeless places on the sidelines.

'There is still,' Shakuni said pointedly, 'Draupadi. Wager her, Yudhishtir, and you might win your own freedom back. Who knows how the dice will fall?'

At these words the howling started up again, Ganapathi, the fluttering resumed outside, and thunder rolled in the heavens. 'Close the windows,' Duryodhani commanded.

In my dream Yudhishtir never looked at his wife as she cowered at the wall. He spoke in a hoarse low voice. 'My wife Draupadi, most desirable of all women, in the full flower of her youth, pride of our nation and mother of our fondest hopes – I stake her.' And Karna's golden face, the half-moon throbbing on its forehead, parted in a mirthless ghostly laugh that echoed around the room.

The dice flew from Shakuni's fingers in a flash of his wrist. 'I have won!' he exclaimed. 'Draupadi is mine.'

As the howls rose again in the distance, a streak of lightning at the window illuminated the glee on Priya Duryodhani's pinched face, lit up the horror on the faces of the Pandava brothers and threw a shadow on to Draupadi, cringing against Arjun's shoulder.

'Go and bring them to the centre of the room,' Duryodhani said to Vidur, who was sitting near the throne with his head in his hands. 'Let everyone see what Yudhishtir has lost.'

'No,' he groaned in the only refuge of bureaucrats. 'It is not my job to do that.'

A guard instead went forward to summon the Pandavas. Draupadi alone stayed where she was, refusing to move.

'Ask Yudhishtir,' she said, 'by what right he staked me as his wager, when he had already lost himself? Can a fallen husband pledge his wife when he himself is no longer a free man?'

The guard repeated the question before the hushed gathering.

'How dare she waste our time with such questions!' Duryodhani snapped. She turned to a faithful retainer, the organizer of the palace fairs, a man of unquestioning loyalty and unquestionable coarseness. 'Go, Duhshasan, and bring her to us.'

Duhshasan, with his red eyes and Pathan nose, his cruel moustache and vicious tongue, strode towards Draupadi Mokrasi, who with a terrified gasp ran towards the women's quarters. But the villain was too quick for her; with a lunge he caught her by her long dark hair and began dragging her to the centre of the room.

'Leave me alone,' she pleaded. 'Do not humiliate me. Can't you see I'm bleeding?'

'Bleeding or dry, you're ours now, my lovely,' the Pathan snarled, still tugging, as Draupadi's tinkling silver *payals* broke and cascaded to the floor.

'How can you all allow this to happen?' she screamed despairingly, and her words struck Yudhishtir and echoed round the room, hurtling in rage against the unseeing Dhritarashtra, the irresolute Arjun, the fist-clenching Bhim, the shaking Vidur, the broken Drona. But none of them replied; none of them could reply.

'This is wrong.' It was Ashwathaman, stepping forward for the first time. 'I have supported you so far, Duryodhani, but common decency –'

'Guards, arrest this man.' Priya Duryodhani's command cut through the bearded figure's voice, amputating his hoarse plea. Ashwathaman was dragged away, too shocked to resist.

'How can you?' It was a last desperate cry, for Duhshasan was now rolling Draupadi's hair up in his hands, winding the wife of the Pandavas inexorably closer to him as her five husbands stood gritting their teeth in impotent fury.

'They can,' Shakuni said, 'because I have won you, my dear. On behalf of everyone assembled here. You, Draupadi Mokrasi, are our slave.'

A shout rose from Duryodhani's men in the court, almost loud enough to drown the insistent howling of the jackals outside.

'No!' Draupadi implored, as Duhshasan's arm snaked round her waist. 'Yudhishtir didn't know what he was doing. He was playing by his old code, and he was cheated.'

'Silence!' Priya Duryodhani snapped. 'How dare you accuse our distinguished minister Shakuni of cheating! Silence, slave!'

And in my dream the weeping Draupadi turned to the blind king and his assembled court, extending her fair bruised arms in tearful supplication. But Dhritarashtra could not see, and the others, especially after what had happened to Ashwathaman, dared not intervene.

'Please,' she whimpered, as Duhshasan's fingers spread across her midriff. 'They entrapped him.'

A roar of fury from Bhim stopped even Duhshasan for a moment. His red eyes bulged from their rage-suffused sockets. Bhim's hate-knotted muscles stood out in places where other men don't even have places. 'Even a whore would not have been risked in so shoddy a wager. How could you do this, Yudhishtir, to our precious Draupadi Mokrasi? We have always considered you to be right in anything you did, but this was wrong, unforgivably wrong! You should have done nothing that could put Draupadi in such a position. Bring me fire, Sahadev, and I shall burn those piss-holding hands that lost Draupadi!'

Sahadev blanched, but he did not need to interpret his brother's command too literally, since he was as much a prisoner as Bhim was. And Arjun was already speaking soothingly to his burly brother, as Bhim trembled to control his fury.

'You mustn't shout like that. Yudhishtir was only doing what he has been brought up to believe is right. He played of his own free will, and honestly. What is there to reproach him for? Fate decided the rest.'

With an effort that shook his mountainous frame like a palm tree in a breeze, Bhim remained silent.

Karna it was who spoke now, the half-moon on his forehead throbbing with an eerie glow. 'How is it that these slaves, defying custom, stand fully clad before their betters? Their clothes too are lost, and belong to Shakuni. Duhshasan, take them off.'

Duhshasan moved forward to execute the command.

'There is no need,' Yudhishtir spoke. 'We know the customs, and do not need help.' The five brothers proudly, in honour, removed their upper garments and flung them at Shakuni's feet.

Draupadi alone stood still, dismay and disbelief battling with each other on her face.

'It seems Draupadi Mokrasi needs your help, Duhshasan,' Karna said in my dream.

The Pathan grinned evilly, and reached for her blouse.

'No!' she screamed, a cry that rent the air, as the fleshy paw of her tormentor tore hook and material off in one savage gesture, baring Draupadi's pale breasts to the court.

'No – please – don't do this to me,' she wept, shame flowing down her cheeks. 'I am your slave, but do not . . . humiliate me like this.'

'Humiliation?' It was Karna again. 'Fine word, from the much-savoured lips of a woman with five husbands! You are no chaste innocent, Draupadi Mokrasi, but an object of many men's pleasure. Well, you are our pleasure now. Strip her, Duhshasan!'

And the jackals howled again, Ganapathi, the wolves bayed, the braying of donkeys rose above the clamour, the vultures screeched outside as their wings resumed their insistent beat on the window-panes, the claws of unknown creatures scratched gruesomely on the glass, but inside the court there was only the deathly unnatural silence of spectators at a public flogging as Duhshasan caught hold of the *pallav* of Draupadi's sari and wrenched it off her shoulder.

Draupadi cried out as she twisted away from his evil grasp: 'Krishna! I need you now, Krishna! Come to me!'

And then she was running, trying to escape her pursuer, but Duhshasan was pulling at the unravelling sari. Draupadi slipped and fell on to the floor. Duhshasan laughed maliciously, continuing to pull, and the sari unwound as Draupadi rolled away from him . . .

'It's a bloody long sari,' Duhshasan said.

And indeed there were already yards of material in his hands, certainly more than the regulation six, but Draupadi was still rolling, and the sari was still unwinding, and in my dream the whole court swam before my eyes, Duhshasan with his pupils popping as the material flowed into his fingers,

Dhritarashtra's ears cocked like a spaniel trying to identify a distant sound, Duryodhani's thin lips bared in a chilling smile of excitement, Karna's half-moon glowing, pulsating as he watched the slow disrobing, and the sounds outside echoed in my mind, mixed with the hoarse cackle of a thousand demented geese, the bleating of a lakh of tortured lambs, the mooing of a million milkless cows, as Draupadi's breasts swung tantalizingly in and out of view as she turned, and the sari continued to unravel, and faces leapt off the walls to look at her in my dream, Lord Drewpad pointing, Sir Richard, florid as ever, with a large black camera on his shoulder, Heaslop laughing with his head tossed back, Vyabhichar Singh grinning beneath a halo as a brown behind bobbed between his legs, Vidur placing his palms across his eyes and then parting two fingers for a peep, Drona shaking a sad head as if to drive the scene out of his vision, Ashwathaman in manacles weeping his self-reproach, the five brothers powerless in their anger, as Duhshasan kept pulling, and the material of the sari was strewn all over the floor, and Draupadi kept twisting and turning and rolling away from him, and in my dream her cry was no longer for Krishna, but for me . . .

Duhshasan stopped, exhausted. The walls swam slowly back into focus. My sleeping mind cleared. The court stood back in silence as Duhshasan looked stupidly at the end of the sari still in his hands and the flowing, multi-coloured cloth that littered the marble ground. He stared again disbelievingly at the half-naked figure of the recumbent Draupadi, her bleeding womanhood still not uncovered, and surrounded by enough resplendent material to clothe her for years. Shamed, he sat down heavily amidst the pile of clothes.

Yudhishtir smiled in vindication.

'By all the oaths of my ancestors,' Bhim swore, 'I'll get you for this, Duhshasan.'

And then Krishna's face appeared on the ceiling, just above Duryodhani's startled eyes. His dark face shimmered against the light from the chandelier.

'However hard you try, Priya Duryodhani,' he said in a calm, deep voice, 'you and your men will never succeed in stripping Draupadi Mokrasi completely. In our country, she will always have enough to maintain her self-respect. But what about yours?'

And then he was gone. But his message had been heard by every pair of ears in the room, including a chastened Duryodhani's.

This time, to my surprise, it was Arjun who spoke.

'One more dice game will give us a last chance to regain our self-respect and freedom,' he said evenly. 'You owe us that much, in the name of honour.' He addressed himself to Dhritarashtra, silent upon his throne.

'I agree,' the king said, before his daughter could raise her voice.

'Yudhishtir has lost to Shakuni. But I ... I wish to play your heir, Duryodhani.' Arjun's voice was firm.

'I agree,' Dhritarashtra said. Duryodhani shook her head, but it was too late.

Karna snorted. 'Fine specimen of the Kaurava race,' he said. 'Playing dice with a woman.'

'I shall play you, Arjun,' Duryodhani said quietly, as if sensing one last way to restore her credibility. She moved forward to pick up Shakuni's pair of dice, which the minister leaned forward to give her.

'Not with those dice,' Arjun stopped her. 'It was my challenge, remember?'

Duryodhani stopped, and dropped the loaded weapons with a clatter on to the floor. Sixes blazed uselessly from their polished surfaces.

'We have brought no dice with us,' Arjun said. 'King Dhritarashtra, could you call for dice from within your palace?'

'I'll attend to it,' responded Vidur, the guardian of conventions, disappearing indoors. He emerged with two new cubes, large-sided, their markings highly visible. They looked as if they had been made with paper, the material of ballots, but when Vidur tossed them in a trial spin they exuded an air of solidity – and landed with a highly promising thud.

'Let me throw them first,' Duryodhani said.

She picked up the dice, then looked at them, at Arjun, and at the silent faces around the room. And as she prepared to throw them, Ganapathi, I realized, even in my sleep, that I didn't need to dream any more. Her strained face, her staring eyes, the trembling of her hands as she picked up the instruments of her fate, told their own story.

She was going to lose.

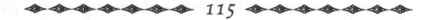 115

When I woke up my ambivalence had gone.

Sometimes, Ganapathi, dreams enable you to see reality more clearly. I looked around me and found the evidence everywhere I had failed to search. I sent Arjun to speak to Krishna. I summoned Nakul from the Home Ministry to give me the information he was paid to conceal; I wrote to Sahadev in Washington for the information he was paid to rebut. Even lying in my Brahminical bed, I realized how Duryodhani and her minions had been stripping the nation of the values and institutions we had been right to cherish.

The picture that emerged, Ganapathi, was sickening. The Siege had become a licence for the police to do much as they pleased, settling scores, locking up suspects, enemies and sometimes creditors without due process, and above all, picking up young men at the village tea-shops to have their vasa cut off in fulfilment of the arbitrary sterilization quotas that Shakuni had persuaded the Prime Minister to decree. As it wore on, it became painfully apparent, even sitting in my room as I was, that the reason for which I had been willing to suspend my criticism was simply not tenable. The poor were not getting a better deal as a result of the suspension of the freedoms of the relatively privileged; if anything, they were worse off than before. They were now subject to random police harassment, to forced displacement from their homes in the interests of slum-clearance and urban renewal, to compulsory vasectomies in pursuance of population-control campaigns on which they had never voted. Even the abolition of bonded labour had simply added to the pool of the floating unemployed. The slave who had toiled for no reward but a roof over his head and two square meals a day found he was free to sleep in the streets and starve.

And throughout it all there was no outlet for the frustration and humiliation of the disinherited. They could not seek redress for injustice in the courts (which had even declared that habeas corpus was not a fundamental right) and they had no recourse to the polling-booths. Nor could the silenced media reflect their grievances. By the time Arjun and Krishna turned decisively against it, when it had lasted a year, it was clear beyond all doubt that the Siege could no longer be justified in their name.

Duryodhani had made Parliament supreme because she could control it, and claimed that this was in the British political tradition we had inherited. She did not realize that the concept of the primacy of Parliament came from a very superficial reading of British constitutional history. It is not Parliament that is supreme, but the people: the importance of Parliament arises simply from the fact that it embodies the supremacy of the people. Duryodhani did not understand that there is no magic about Parliament in and of itself, and that it only matters as an institution so long as it represents the popular will. The moment that connection is removed, Parliament has no significance as a democratic institution. A Parliament placed above the people who elected it is no more democratic than an army that turns its guns upon the very citizens it is supposed to protect. That is why Priya Duryodhani's parliamentary tyranny was no better than the military dictatorships of neighbouring Karnistan.

It took me some time to realize this, but ironically, Ganapathi, Indians like myself were changing our Brahminical minds at just about the time that the Western, and specifically the American, media were beginning to change theirs – in the opposite direction. When we were willing to give the government the benefit of the doubt the American analysts had no doubt at all; they condemned the abrogation of constitutional rights, the arrest of opponents, the end of press freedom. These were concepts they understood and on which there could be no compromise. But as they got used to the Siege regime they began to see virtues in it: industrial discipline, more openings for US business, decisive action on the population front, no more of the stultifying slowness of the 'soft state' that developing India had been. And when the jailed opponents were gradually released, the press allowed to censor itself and the Constitution reconciled to the new situation, American reporters came to see India as no different from other autocratic non-Communist regimes which they had covered without outrage. Vital though I had found the American news sources about India that came to me through Sahadev, this was a pointed lesson in the limitations of the neutral and objective foreign correspondent.

No, Ganapathi, Draupadi was Indian; she was ours, and she had to wear a sari. We could not place her in universal beauty contests to be judged as her Occidental sisters were, by the shape of her legs or the cut of her costume. If she had been like the others, if she had been wearing the skirts or dresses or even the trousers of Western democratic women, she might have been far more easily disrobed.

Krishna rose against what Duryodhani was doing, and his firm and decisive opposition at last converted the irresolute Arjun. When a chastened Yudhishtir and a mortally ill Drona were released from jail, Krishna counselled against rash conduct, urging them to bide their time. Bhim spoke of leaving the army with enough explosives in his kit-bag to send Duryodhani back to her ancestors. Both Arjun and Krishna had to calm him down.

'Sooner or later,' Krishna said, 'our time will come.'

THE EIGHTEENTH BOOK:
THE PATH TO SALVATION

116

It came sooner rather than later. At the peak of her regime of repression, with the press tamed, the sterilizations mounting, the workers terrified and the poor terrorized — *and* the trains still running on time — Priya Duryodhani surprised the world, if not Krishna, by suspending the Siege and calling free general elections.

No one knew what had prompted this change of heart. Throughout the country, imaginative theories were woven with enough material to make Draupadi a new sari. It was said that Priya Duryodhani had received the visit of a political sage, a dark man from the south. Another suggested she had consulted an astrologer named Krishna, who had prophesied great success if the polls were held on a certain date. (You know, Ganapathi, how in our country marriages are not arranged, flights not planned, projects not inaugurated until astrological charts are drawn up and consulted. An Indian without a horoscope is like an American without a credit-card, and he is subject to many of the same disadvantages in life. Few politicians make their major career decisions without checking on what the stars foretell, so it was not such an improbable theory after all.) Somebody else gave the credit (and later the blame) to the Intelligence agencies: they had told her what she wanted to hear, which was that she was so popular she could sweep the polls. (A lesson to our future rulers, Ganapathi: if your spies only give you good news, something's terribly wrong.) And then there was the mischievous theory that what really got Priya Duryodhani to turn to the Indian people was the announcement by Zaleel Shah Jhoota across the border in Karnistan of elections in his little tyranny. That Karnistan, whose only political institutions were the coup and the mob, and where Zaleel had ruled since Jarasandha's death with the liberal use of black handcuffs and white lies, could put on an electoral show for the rest of the world while the 'world's largest democracy' transformed itself into the world's largest banana republic, was unbearably galling for Dhritarashtra's daughter. Karnistan was a country whose rulers usually overwhelmed the popular will with their unpopular won't, but Jhoota would still get international credit for holding an election. And international credit was beginning to matter now to Priya Duryodhani, who didn't like what foreign cartoonists were doing to her fine Hastinapuri features in their more-black-than-white caricatures of Siege rule.

So elections were called, the stragglers in prison released, the fetters taken off the press. Indians breathed the now unaccustomed air of freedom, and it tickled their lungs sufficiently to provoke them to shout. It was then that they realized they would not be able to shout again after five weeks, if Duryodhani, as she clearly expected to, retained power. That was when a large number of Indians who had not taken the slightest interest in politics – the readers of the newspapers Arjun and I had spoken about – decided there was too much at stake for them to stay on the sidelines. The most participative election campaign in Indian history began.

Elections, as you well know, Ganapathi, are a great Indian *tamasha*, conducted at irregular intervals and various levels amid much fanfare. It takes the felling of a sizeable forest to furnish enough paper for 320 million ballots, and every election has at least one story of returning officers battling through snow or jungle to ensure that the democratic wishes of remote constituents are duly recorded. No election coverage is complete, either, without at least one picture of a female voter whose enthusiasm for the suffrage is undimmed by the fact that she is old, blind, unlettered, toothless or purdah-clad, or any combination of the above. Ballot-boxes are stuffed, booths are 'captured', the occasional election worker/candidate/voter is assaulted/kidnapped/shot, but nothing stops the franchise. And for all its flaws, universal suffrage has worked in India, providing an invaluable instrument for the expression of the public will. India's voters, scorned by cynics as illiterate and ignorant, have adapted superbly to the election system, unseating candidates and governments, drawing distinctions between local and national elections. Sure, at every election someone discovers a new chemical that will remove the indelible stain on your fingernail and permit you to vote twice (as if this convenience made any great difference in constituencies the size of ours); at every election some distinguished voter claims his name is missing from the rolls, or that someone has already cast his vote (but usually not both). At every election some ingenious accountant produces a set of figures to show that only a tenth of what was actually spent was spent; somebody makes a speech urging that the legal limit for expenditure be raised, so that less ingenuity might be required to cook the books; and everyone goes home happy.

But these elections were somehow different. The high spirits were there – Yudhishtir's campaign workers made it a point to ask Duryodhani's candidates to produce their own vasectomy certificates before asking for votes, which raised a few laughs and not a few hackles in the Kaurava (R) camp – but there was a deadly earnestness beneath, as if everyone realized that they were being given a chance no other nation had ever enjoyed. A chance to choose, in a free election, between democracy and dictatorship. Indeed, some even said, between dharma and adharma.

But this facile equation with India's traditional values troubled me. And when a journalist – one of the very few, Ganapathi, who still thought this battle-scarred old dodderer a likely source of usable copy at this time – asked me, in an allusion to the great battle of the *Mahabharata*: 'Don't you think this election is a contemporary Kurukshetra?', I erupted.

'I hope not,' I barked, 'because there were no victors at Kurukshetra. Except in the childish popular versions of the epic. The story of the *Mahabharata*, young man, does not end on the field of battle. What happens afterwards is tragedy, suffering, futility, death. Which underlines the only moral of that battle, and that epic: that there are no real victors. Everyone loses at the end.'

'But – but what about the great conflict between the Pandavas and the Kauravas, the battle between dharma and adharma, between good and evil?'

'It was a battle between cousins,' I snapped back. 'They were killing each other's flesh and blood, shooting arrows into their own gurus, lying and deceiving their elders in order to win. There was good and bad, dishonour and treachery, betrayal and death, on both sides. There was no glorious victory at Kurukshetra.'

I saw his bewildered expression and took pity on him.

'Young man,' I said, my severity relenting, 'you must understand one thing. This election is not Kurukshetra; life is Kurukshetra. History is Kurukshetra. The struggle between dharma and adharma is a struggle our nation, and each of us in it, engages in on every single day of our existence. That struggle, that battle, took place before this election; it will continue after it.'

He stumbled away, and wrote no story. I do not know what he told his colleagues at the Press Club, but no other journalist sought to interview me during the campaign.

Just as well, Ganapathi, because in that particular election the issue was indeed an inconveniently non-traditional one: the rout or the restoration of democracy.

Democracy, Ganapathi, is perhaps the most arrogant of all forms of government, because only democrats presume to represent an entire people: monarchs and oligarchs have no such pretensions. But democracies that turn authoritarian go a step beyond arrogance; they claim to represent a people subjugating themselves. India was now the laboratory of this strange political experiment. Our people would be the first in the world to vote on their own subjugation.

Ah, what days they were, Ganapathi! Bliss was it in that spring to be alive, but to be old and wise was very heaven. I saw the great cause of Gangaji and Dhritarashtra and Pandu thrillingly reborn in the hearts and minds of young crowds at every street-corner. I saw the meaning of Independence come pulsating to life as unlettered peasants rose in the villages to pledge their votes for democracy. I saw journalists younger than the Constitution relearn the meaning of freedom by discovering what they had lost when the word was erased from their notebooks. I saw Draupadi's face glowing in the open, the flame of her radiance burning more brightly than ever. And I knew that it had all been worthwhile.

Through the clamour and confusion of the election campaign Krishna moved with secure serenity. Both sides came to him at the start: the Kaurava Party of Priya Duryodhani, of which he had never ceased to be a member, and the Opposition, in its quest for illustrious defections from the ruling party's ranks. To both, he reiterated his refusal to contest a seat in Parliament, insisting that his place was in his local legislative assembly, representing his neighbours. Since that was not, however, at stake in the coming election, he was available to campaign in the national contest, and both contenders came back to seek his active support and that of the dedicated party cadres he had so effectively trained. The need of the hour was too great: Krishna could not remain on the sidelines.

'Both of you say that the other's victory will be a disaster for the country,' he mused aloud. 'Perhaps you are both right. Disaster does not approach its victims wrapped in thunderclouds, dripping blood. Rather, it slips in quietly, unobtrusively, its face masked in ambiguity, making each of us see good in evil and evil in good. There is good and evil in both sides of this argument. Some say that under Priya Duryodhani India faces extinction: others point out that the majority of Indians have never been happier. I have my own views, but who is to say they are right for everyone?' He turned calmly to the two party representatives before him. 'It is not easy for me to take sides. I have been the Kaurava Party secretary here for too long to renounce it, but I have also stood for certain principles in my political life too long to renounce them. So let me propose this: one side can have me, alone, not as a candidate, with no party funds, but fully committed to their campaign; the other can have the massed ranks of my party workers, disciplined and dedicated men and women who will heed my instructions to work with undiminished vigour even if they see me on the other side. A fair division? Perhaps not, but I leave it to each of you to choose: which will it be? Me alone – or my cadres, with their experience, their vehicles, their skills?'

The Kaurava Party representative and the Opposition's aged envoy looked uncomfortably at each other. It was Krishna himself who broke the silence.

'In deference to your seniority, VVji, I must invite you to choose first,' he said. 'For the Opposition.'

I responded without hesitation. 'I choose you,' I said.

And so it was that both Duryodhani and Yudhishtir thought they had done the better out of the division, as the Kaurava Party workers remained true to their allegiances while Krishna went on to animate the Opposition's national campaign. With his pearly white teeth shining between violet lips and his deep eyes smiling beatifically at the electorate, Krishna brought to the loudspeaker-led hurly-burly of the contest the spirit of an older India, an India where the lilt of the flute called the milkmaids to the river to wash away their innocence before the laughter of their Lord.

Krishna's most difficult task undoubtedly came when Arjun, on the verge of filing his nomination papers for the Opposition, was assailed afresh by the doubts that had bedevilled his years in journalism. 'Is it right – should I fight – or if I just write, won't I cast more light?' was the nature of his misgivings. 'If you don't fight now,' his brother-in-law told him bluntly, 'you won't have anything to write about afterwards.'

I heard something of their exchange when they stopped for a reflective cup of tea at the Ashoka Hotel and failed to notice me at the next table. Ashoka, the great conqueror-turned-pacifist of the third century BC, is the one figure of our history who has most inspired independent India's schizoid governmental ethos. His tolerance and humanitarianism, his devotion to peace and justice, infuse our declarations of policy; his military might, his imposition of a Pax Indica on his neighbours, inform our practice. Our national spokesmen inherited his missionary belief that what was good for India was good for the world, and in choosing a national symbol our government preferred his powerful trinity of lions to the spinning-wheel advocated by Gangaji. Typically, though, the only institution to which they saw fit to give his name was a five-star hotel. And appropriately enough, it was here that the dialogue took place that was to change Arjun's life for good, if not for better.

Let us follow it, Ganapathi, in the form that seems most apt for these near-celestial sonnets of sophistry and sense. It is time for one last lapse from prose in this memoir; should we, too, not genuflect at the golden gate of contemporary taste, and pay iambic tribute to the tetrameter?

117

Arjun saw fathers, uncles, cousins
Teachers, preachers, grandsons, friends
Arrayed before him in several dozens
Convinced their means justified their ends.
Pity filled him. He spoke with sadness:
'Krishna, this is simply madness.
All these foes are our own kinsmen;
Who will wash away their sins, then?
My will fails me. My throat is parched.
I think of it, and feel a shiver.
I've always been for life – a liver.
Though I was ready; my bow was arched,
My mind's in a tumult. I can't continue.
My resolve trembles in every sinew.

'I can't attack them for doing their duty.
Duryodhani is Dhritarashtra's daughter.
She may not be a thing of beauty
But she's PM, she's earned her hauteur.
I admit her rule was not always just –
She betrayed some of us, abused our trust –
But still she is our nation's Leader:
India's masses have shown they need her.
If we attack and destroy our queen,
Breaking the traditions of our ancient line,
Won't it seem acceptable, even fine
To be disloyal to the next one seen?
And then has not the Mahaguru taught us
To hold our peace like the petals of a lotus?'

Krishna took a deep long breath.
'Why falter now, when we are ready?
Why grieve before a single death?
Why tremble when your grip is steady?
The wise grieve not for the living or dead.
Our selves are more than hands or head.
You, and I, have always been;
Our souls, our spirits, were ever keen;
And we shall never cease to be.
For one soul passes into another.
Death is only rebirth's brother.

Don't think too much of what you see.
Transcend; and realize this is meant:
What's on this earth is transient.

'Great heat, bitter cold, pleasure and pain,
Victory, defeat; indulgence or fasting;
All come and go like a burst of rain.
None is permanent, none is lasting.
That which is not, shall never please;
That which is, shall never cease.
The Spirit which moves both you and me
Is immortal; it will always be.
The Spirit exists, it does not destroy.
Nor, indeed, is it ever destroyed.
It was not born, nor made like a toy;
It does not feel, it is never annoyed;
Unborn, enduring, omnipresent,
Only the Spirit is permanent.

'But the Unchanging Spirit ne'ertheless does change.
Like a cloud that travels amidst great storms,
It spans an enormous physical range,
Altering, discarding its bodies and forms.
The Spirit appears and disappears.
It comes, it goes, it reappears.
The persons and causes it does infuse
(And the Spirit is all-pervasive, diffuse)
Rise and fall, glow and fade, live and die.
But the Spirit goes on, immutably.
Its nature must be treated suitably.
Respect it, Arjun; there's no cause to cry.
You need not fear knocking your kin to earth:
For birth follows death as death follows birth.

'In other words, Arjun, don't waver.
It's unworthy to neglect your duty.
Duryodhani is the country's enslaver:
She's no village belle or city cutie.
You must take a grip on yourself,
Not flap like a maid on the shelf.
Arise, stand, fight like a man;
The police have lifted the ban
On opposing Duryodhani's government.
So what if you help bring it down?

It's not the only show in town,
While the Soul of India is permanent.
Others will come and take its place
And they too will soon fall from grace.

'Of course there will be many fumbles:
Some will run, some will fall, some fail
But that's the way, lad, the *laddoo* crumbles.
You don't have to shudder and wail.
Moral doubts are often an excuse
For those who wish to refuse
To join the fight or the fray;
But I'm telling you, today
You can't let us down, Arjun.
Victory and defeat don't matter.
Non-involvement's just idle chatter.
We need action, and we need it soon.
(Just as a pilot can fly any airbus,
So scripture can be quoted for any purpose.)

'Put aside gospel, banish all doubts.
Our philosophy holds no attraction
For those who don't heed the shouts
Of their friends who call them to Action.
Accept good and evil alike;
Acknowledge the real need to strike;
Give up all attachment,
Flow like rain through a catchment
And join the election campaign.
It's a question of your self-respect.
And Draupadi's, which you're sworn to protect:
So don't let your scruples cause pain.
Think of this as working for peace.
Do right, and your torment will cease.

'So Arjun, abandon all hesitation.
This is not a cause you can shirk.
You can do just two things for the nation:
Meditate, or take up good work.
In our classics, it is clearly inscribed:
"Arjun, do the duty prescribed."
Dutiful action, without care of reward
Is the first step you can take toward
Eternal bliss; for what you do

Others will imitate; and thus uplift
Your cause, yourself, and your great gift
For initiating Action in others too.
Look at me; there's nothing I need to attain,
Yet I act, and inspire this election campaign.

'It is better to do your own duty, Arjun,
Than another's. But do it without desire.
The course of Right Action confers a great boon;
But as a womb wraps a babe, as smoke shrouds fire,
The universe is enveloped in sick desire
And the unselfish do-gooder's often a liar.
To surrender all claim to the result of your deeds
Is the greatness of one who transcends his own needs,
And that's what we need in a man of right action.
Someone to act in true selflessness,
And restore order to our national mess.
A disinterested sage rising above faction.
Who'll work, sacrifice, revitalize the nation.
The reward of his action? True realization.

'No misgivings need beset such an actor
Who acts for the Spirit, not for personal gain;
Who untouched by attachment, or any other factor
Acts for the nation in this election campaign.
He will no more be tainted by the sin of the Daughter
Than the fresh water-lotus is wetted by water.
As for whether Priya is adored by the masses,
Don't worry – too often, the masses are asses.
He who acts for the Spirit must aim much higher,
Knowing his action will purify the soul;
Content that salvation will come from his role,
As the act of flying fulfils the flyer.
It is not right in this to shirk obligation.
To avoid action through pity is wrong renunciation.

'So Arjun, stop doubting; rise and serve India.
Serve me, the embodiment of the Spirit of the nation.
I am the hills and the mountains, Himalaya – Vindhya;
I am the worship, the sacrifice, the ritual oblation;
I am the priest, the *sloka*, the rhythmic chant;
The do and the don't, the can and the can't.
I am the ghee poured into the fire, I am indeed the fire;
I am the act of pouring, I am the sacred pyre.

I am the beginning and the end,
The aimer and the goal;
The origin, the part, the whole,
The bender and the bend.
I am lover, husband, father, son, Being and Not-Being;
I am nation, country, mother, eye, Seeing and All-Seeing.

'Serve me, Arjun, like the warriors of yore.
If you can treat both triumph and disaster
As impostors (but someone's said this before)
You will have acted like a true master.'
Arjun turned, and his eyes were bright:
His jaw was firm, for he'd seen the light.
'You're right,' he said, 'Thanks, dear Krishna!
For playing vicar to my weak parishioner.
I was silly to be so irresolute.
Instead of thinking of the Spirit
And acting without heed to merit,
I'd wept and whined like a broken flute.
That's all over now! I'm ready to act —
Let's get the Opposition into an electoral pact!'

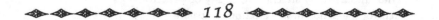 *118*

They did; as in Hastinapur before the Siege, the various Opposition factions got together in a People's Front. They were joined soon enough by the rats (and the Rams) deserting Priya Duryodhani's sinking ship, as well as by those of her erstwhile supporters, like Ashwathaman, whom she had mistreated and jailed during the Siege. The electoral battle raged intensely. Even I rose from my bed to deliver speeches in the hoarse voice of wisdom that age and late passion had given me.

Everyone took sides: there were few abstainers. Only the bureaucracy hesitated. This was, of course, in the fitness of things. Bureaucracy is, Ganapathi, simultaneously the most crippling of Indian diseases and the highest of Indian art-forms. No other country has elevated to such a pinnacle of refinement the quintuplication of procedures and the slow unfolding of delays. It is almost a philosophical statement about Indian society: everything has its place and takes its time, and must go through the ritual process of passing through a number of hands, each of which has an allotted function to perform in the endless chain. Every official act in our country has five more stages to it than anywhere else and takes five times more people to fulfil; but in the process it keeps five more sets of the potentially unemployed off the streets. The bureaucratic ethos dictated our administrators' roles in the campaign as well. They stayed in their offices and waited for the outcome.

Nakul and Sahadev, like their peers, took no part in the political conflict. Both had been requested by Krishna, for reasons very similar to the Mahaguru's in respect of Vidur all those years ago, to remain in their functions, but unlike Vidur our bureaucratic twins had not leapt to submit their resignations. Nakul, if truth be told, was still far from certain his resignation was warranted; he was cynical, or sophisticated, enough to think things could be worse. Sahadev's honest rejection of the government's domestic policies fell afoul of his diffidence. (Our diplomatic corps, Ganapathi, is full of sincere people who feel they are so out of touch with the masses they can only speak for them abroad.) Both agreed, therefore, with alacrity to stay cool in their jobs as the electoral flames blazed and crackled around them.

As for Bhim, there was a rumour at one stage that he might be tempted to intervene; but everyone urged against it, even Yudhishtir, and he remained in his military cantonment, keeping a baleful eye on the Kaurava campaign. I suspect, though, that he managed at least one leave. One morning when popular wrath against the excesses of the Siege was at its highest, Duhshasan was found tied to a tree not far from Delhi's most famous red-light area. His pyjama trousers were down to his ankles, and the remainder of his elegant *kurta-sherwani* ensemble hung in tatters from his drooping shoulders. His bare behind was criss-crossed with the livid stripes of swelling red weals. He had, apparently, been mercilessly flogged just before dawn with a wet knotted sari whose *pallav* had then been flung derisively on to his genitals, to provide him with a shred of incongruous modesty.

The Duryodhani camp emitted muted howls of outrage. The Prime Minister even spoke darkly of assassination attempts by the forces of violence and anarchy upon her supporters. But Duhshasan himself proved singularly unwilling to press charges, or even to identify his aggressor. Nothing similar recurred, and the episode was soon forgotten. It left its only trace in the smile of Draupadi Mokrasi, the smile of a woman who knows she will not easily be tampered with again.

On election night I had another dream.

This was a dream of Arjun: of Arjun, perhaps, on his Himalayan wanderings during those months of self-imposed exile that had brought him his mentor and his wife. And in my dream Arjun sat on a rock, clad in the loincloth of penitence, his hair long and matted with neglect, his ribs prominent with starvation, his eyes red with ascetic wakefulness. Prayer and self-denial on the mountaintop, Ganapathi: how many of our legends have not portrayed this scene, as a hero seeks an ultimate boon from the gods?

But in my dream, no god appeared to disturb Arjun's meditation. Instead, an animal shimmered across his consciousness, a Himalayan deer, dancing playfully before him as if offering herself to the starving man. The Arjun of my dream picked up his bow and shot the deer, but before he could pick up his trophy, a strange apparition interposed itself — a primitive hunter, dressed in bearskins, also bearing a bow. Before an astonished Arjun, the hunter picked up the deer, heaving it lightly on to his immense shoulders. Arjun protested, laying claim to his animal: in the clear wordlessness of the dream, the hunter spurned his imprecations. Arjun, enraged, shot his arrows, but the hunter contemptuously side-stepped them, and when the young hero flung himself bodily on the intruder, he found himself spinning back in my dream to crash senseless on to the ground. The hunter laughed. Arjun awoke, returned to his prayers, and invoked the name of the god to whom he had been offering his austerities: Shiva. And then, in the kind of transformation only a miracle or a dream can bring about, the hunter turned into the god. Shiva himself, most powerful of the gods, blue-skinned Shiva clad in gold instead of bearskin, with his hunter's bow metamorphosed into a trident.

Arjun prostrated himself in my dream, begging forgiveness for having fought with no less a being than Shiva in his ignorance. And the god, victorious, pleased with the ascetic privations of his supplicant, forgave him and asked him to seek his boon. Arjun raised his head, all the power of his spirit shining through his gaze, and asked for the one favour Shiva had never before been called upon to grant — the use of Pashupata, the ultimate weapon, the absolute.

The god tried not to show his surprise: no one had dared to ask for such a potent instrument of destruction before, one which required no launchpad or silo, no control-panel or delivery-system, but could be imagined by the mind, primed with a thought, triggered by a word, and which flew to its target with the speed of divinity, inexorable, invincible, irresistible.

And Arjun said: 'I know all this, but still I ask, O Shiva, for this weapon.'

And Shiva replied, his third eye opening, 'It is yours.'

In my dream, Ganapathi, the very Himalayas shook with the gesture, the mountain ranges trembled as the knowledge of Pashupata descended to mortal hands, whole forests swayed like leaves, the wind howled, tremors passed through the earth. The figure of Shiva ascended to the heavens, atop a blazing golden chariot, emanating shafts of fire, dispersing singed clouds, and as the circle of flame made a halo for the chariot, Arjun rose to mount it. The stars shone in the lustre of the day, meteors fell and shot their sparks in fiery trails across the sky, the planets were illuminated, flaming spheres of transcendence, and still Arjun rose with the chariot, his unblinking gaze fixed on a spot on earth far below him. And just one word resounded like the echo of a thousand thunderclaps through the firmament: 'Destroy! Destroy! Destroy!'

 *119*

Sahadev pushed his way through the milling crowd outside the newspaper office. The noise was deafening: shouts, exhortations, muttering, even prayers, rose from the throng. The election results were filtering in, and this was the place to get them as they came. No one believed the radio any more.

Now there, Ganapathi, lay a sad irony. Despite being controlled by the government, Akashvani — the voice from the sky — was also the voice of millions of radio-receivers, transistors and loudspeakers blaring forth from puja *pandals* and tea-shops. Its ubiquitousness reflected the indispensability of radio in a country where most people cannot read, its content — despite the often heavy hand of bureaucracy on its programmes — the range of the nation's concerns. From the anodyne cadences of its newsreaders to the requests for film-songs from Jhumri Tilaiya and other bastions of the country's cow-belt, All-India Radio mirrored the triumphs and trivialities that engaged the nation. But its moderation also meant mediocrity, and during the Siege it came to mean mendacity as well. It is Priya Duryodhani's legacy, Ganapathi, that today when an Indian wants real news, he switches on the BBC; for detailed analyses, he turns to the newspapers; for entertainment, he goes to the movies. The rest of the time, he listens to Akashvani.

A small peon in khaki shirt and white pyjamas, standing on the top rung of a rickety ladder, was putting up the letters on the display board with excruciating slowness. 'D – H – A – N – I.' That made Priya Duryodhani. What next? People at the front of the crowd were yelling to the man to let them know the news first, orally, before he put up the remaining letters. He remained impervious to their pleas. Perhaps he couldn't hear them above the din. He had the aluminium letter-boards he needed to hang up: maybe he wasn't sure what they meant himself. It was possible that he knew just enough of the English alphabet to put up the headlines on the 'Spot News' board every day without understanding what the newspaper was announcing through him.

'W,' Nakul said next to him. 'W for Wins.'

'D,' Sahadev replied as the letter went up.

'Declares Victory?' Nakul asked. All-India Radio had been announcing substantial wins for Duryodhani's party in some states.

D. E. Then, as the crowd seemed to hold its collective breath, F.

An immense cry of exultation rose from the crowd.

'Could be "Defeats Opponent,"' Nakul ventured. 'You know, in her constituency.'

'No way, *bhai-sahib.*' Sahadev was grinning from ear to ear: he had suddenly realized what he had wanted all along. 'He doesn't have enough letters with him for that.'

The crowd was already roaring its approbation. Scattered cheers rent the air. People were slapping each other's backs in delight. E. A. T. Then, finally, the khaki-skirted *meghdoot* speeding up his pace as the task neared completion, E and D. DEFEATED. Priya Duryodhani had been defeated.

'Janata Front!' somebody shouted. '*Zindabad!*' Came the answering roar: 'Janata Front, *Zindabad!*' The chant picked up variety, and rhythm. 'Drona, *Zindabad!* Yudhishtir, *Zindabad!* Janata Front, *Zindabad!*'

'I knew it, I knew it,' Sahadev found himself squeezing Nakul's shoulders in triumph. 'Oh, I'm so glad I took my home-leave now, Nakul. This is great! It's simply great!'

Nakul still seemed to be absorbing the news. Around them, the chant was vociferous; some energetic youths had begun dancing an impromptu *bhangra*. Members of the crowd were flinging coins and rupee notes at the peon who had put up the headline. The little man in the khaki skirt was catching them in dexterous ecstasy.

'I was wrong,' Nakul said slowly, abandoning the plural for perhaps the first time. 'It's all over.'

'No it isn't, brother,' his twin contradicted him with uncharacteristic confidence. 'It's only just begun.'

 *120*

They were both wrong. Something had passed whose shadow would always remain, and something had begun that would not endure. For it is my fate, Ganapathi, to have to record not a climactic triumph but a moment of bathos. The Indian people gave themselves the privilege of replacing a determined, collected tyrant with an indeterminate collection of tyros.

I was partially responsible, but only partially. When the elections were over there was a general desire to avoid a contest among the victorious constituents of the Janata Front. It was resolved that Drona and I, the Messiah and the Methuselah, would jointly designate the nation's new Prime Minister, who would then be 'elected' unanimously by the Janata legislators. At the time this seemed a sensible way of avoiding unseemly conflict at the start of the new regime. Only later did I realize the irony of beginning the era of the restoration of democracy with so undemocratic a procedure.

And it was not just ironic. In our ageless wisdom Drona and I had failed to realize what most college students know: that if you begin an examination by avoiding the most difficult question it raises, it is that very question that will eventually guarantee your failure.

The two of us spoke individually with the leaders of each of the political parties that made up the Front. There were several of them, each with his claims to overall leadership: political parties, after all, Ganapathi, grow in our nation like mushrooms, split like amoeba, and are as original and productive as mules. Most of these leaders had at one time or another been in the Kaurava Party, but had left – or been pushed out – at various stages of the party's takeover by Priya Duryodhani. Drona and I surveyed the unprepossessing alternatives and decided to go for the only one among them whose honesty and sincerity was as unquestionable as his seniority: Yudhishtir.

I made the suggestion knowing only too well how little these very qualities suited my grandson for kingship. Drona agreed because, typically, he was more anxious to make a moral choice than a political one. Yet we were political enough to make a gesture of appeasement to the many who disagreed with the conservatism of the new Prime Minister: almost immediately after announcing our view that Yudhishtir would be the Front's consensual choice for the nation's leadership, we asked the populist Ashwathaman to preside over the Front's party organization.

There was, Ganapathi, one brief shining moment of hope, when the Front's leaders, the euphoria of their unprecedented victory still mollifying their egos, gathered together before that symbol of the nation's enduring greatness, the Taj Mahal, and swore a collective oath to uphold India's glory and its traditional values. Draupadi was present that day, as an honoured guest, and her skin glowed with a health and inner beauty that it had lacked for many years. She smiled then, dazzling onlookers with the strength and whiteness of her teeth. Even I could not guess how weak the roots were under that sparkling display of oral confidence.

It seemed strangely appropriate, Ganapathi, that the Front had chosen the Taj for this public reaffirmation of their democratic purpose. The Taj Mahal is the motif for India on countless tourist posters and has probably had more camera shutters clicked at it than any other edifice on the face of this earth. Yet how easily one forgets that this unequalled monument of love is in fact a tomb, the burial place of a woman who suffered thirteen times the pain of childbirth and died in agony at the fourteenth attempt. Perhaps that makes it all the worthier a symbol of our India – this land of beauty and grandeur amidst suffering and death.

I stayed on after the ceremony, after the shamianas had been dismantled and the shamas, their songs over, had flown away. I sat before the marble whiteness of the monument, already yellowing with the sulphur dioxide from the fumes of a near-by oil refinery, and watched the darkness drape itself round the familiar dome like an old shawl. Night had fallen many times upon the Taj; many times had dawn broken the promises of the last sunrise. But it had endured; chipped and vandalized and looted and trampled upon and scrubbed and admired and loved and envied and exploited, it had endured. And so would India.

The hopes raised by that moving ceremony were soon betrayed. Krishna went back to his southern district and it was almost as if he had taken with him Agni's boon of creative accomplishment. The Front began rapidly to dissipate its energies in mutual competition and recrimination. Yudhishtir was as stiff and straight-backed and humourless as his critics had always portrayed him, and his colossal self-righteousness was not helped by his complete inability to judge the impression he made on others. As the 'strongmen' of his Cabinet – a term they assiduously encouraged the media to employ – quarrelled querulously at every meeting, the Prime Minister remained tightly self-obsessed, seemingly unaware that half of those who sat on the executive branch with him were busily engaged in sawing it off.

Yudhishtir suffered particularly from the failing of expecting everyone to take him as seriously as he took himself. When, in response to a question from an American television interviewer, the first journalist indiscreet enough to ask in public what her peers had cheerfully confirmed in private – 'Mr Prime Minister, is it true that you drink your own urine every day?' – when, Ganapathi, before a prime-time audience of 80 million incredulous Americans, quintupled by satellite newsfeeds to every television channel in the world with the money and the lack of taste to broadcast it, when, with the same lack of reflection he had shown in accepting Shakuni's challenge, Yudhishtir launched into a sanctimonious homily on the miraculous properties of auto-urine therapy, he dropped the dice of government back at the Kauravas' feet.

His positive response was quoted in every one of India's resurgent newspapers. Cartoonists and cocktail-party wags combined Yudhishtir's confession with his well-known stance in favour of Prohibition ('If I drank what he drinks, I'd be for Prohibition too'; 'Would you ever invite the Prime Minister to a Bring-a-bottle party?'). Graffiti appeared on public lavatories across the country, more than one entrance signboard being repainted to read 'Yudhishtir Juice Centre'. As the Prime Minister unsmilingly continued to make himself the laughing-stock of the nation, his coalition gradually unravelled beneath his feet. Write it on his epitaph, Ganapathi: our Hero piddled while home burned.

Not that the unravelling Front had ever been very tightly knit. Within weeks of its assumption of office it had become the vehicle for the personal ambitions of at least three veteran politicians besides the Prime Minister. With their adeptness at camouflaging petty self-interest under wordy speeches on the uplift of (depending on the precise nuances of their electoral bases) the 'backward classes', the 'backward castes' or the 'backward strata of society', they rapidly acquired for their party the sobriquet 'the Backward Front'. As they stumbled from argument to argument, lawlessness erupted, prices spiralled upwards, government offices sank beneath dusty cobwebs of red tape, and every policy decision was hamstrung by factional disagreement. Their ineptness helped Priya Duryodhani rapidly to recover from the shock of her ouster. 'The Backward Front government can move the nation neither backward nor forward,' she was able to declare to uneasy applause at surprisingly well-attended public meetings. 'It is merely awkward.'

That she was free at all to lavish such scathing contempt on her conquerors was one more instance of the weakness of the Front's combination of virtue and avarice in the face of so formidable an adversary. Just across the border, chaos following charges of intimidation, ballot-stuffing and vote-rigging in Karnistan's show election had led to Zaleel Shah Jhoota's being toppled and jailed by his generals; his military tormentors were now debating whether to have him publicly flogged for his misdeeds or hanged or both. In India, however, the Front had decided to take the former Prime Minister to court on the esoteric charge of *détournement de pouvoir*, which was a polite legalistic way of saying she had subverted the Constitution. Since everyone who had lived in India for the last three years with his eyes open knew she had subverted the Constitution, it did not seem to be a charge that required much proof. Yet the chosen means did not serve the choicest ends: the lawcourts, Ganapathi, with the solitary recent exception of post-Falklands Argentina, are not the place for a people to bring their former rulers to account. Priya Duryodhani and her skilled lawyers (minus Shakuni, who was now loudly asserting his democratic credentials and disavowing the Siege, the ex-Prime Minister and all her works) ran circles of subtlety around the Front's witnesses.

It was all like an elaborate game between teams of unequal strength. Law, of course, rivals cricket as the major national sport of our urban élite. Both litigation and cricket are slow, complex and costly; both involve far more people than need to be active at any given point in the process; both call for skill, strength and guile in varying combinations at different times; both benefit from more breaks in the action than spectators consider necessary; both occur at the expense of, and often disrupt, more productive economic activity; and both frequently meander to conclusions, punctuated by appeals, that satisfy none of the participants. Yet both are dear to Indian hearts and absorb much of the country's energies. The moment the law was chosen as the means to deal with the former Prime Minister, it was clear that the toss had gone Priya Duryodhani's way.

As with cricket, the problem with law is one of popular participation. The lawcourts of India, Ganapathi, are open to the masses, like the doors of a five-star hotel. Priya Duryodhani could afford to command the best in the profession; 'the people', on the other hand, though she was being prosecuted in their name, could not always find a place in the courtroom where she was questioned about her crimes against them. Whatever purpose her trial served, it was not that of popular justice.

The case dragged on and, after the first few sensational revelations, lapsed into unreality. Duryodhani's lawyers so effectively turned it into a showcase for their forensic skills that the issues behind their legalistic hair-splitting were soon forgotten. The fatal turn occurred: people became bored. Their ennui banalized her evil.

The trial was in its fourteenth meandering month when the crisis within the Front, hopelessly riven over conflicts of its own making, came to a head.

The issue that brought the simmering pot of mutual dislike to a boil was ostensibly the government's attitude towards the Untouchables – Gangaji's Harijans, or Children of God. It all started with a sage whom Yudhishtir went to see, an ochre-robed godman whose vocabulary was as out of date as his garments.

Godmen are India's major export of the last two decades, offering manna and mysticism to an assortment of foreign seekers in need of them. Once in a while, however, they also acquire a domestic following, by appealing to the deep-seated reverence in all Indians for spiritual wisdom and inner peace, a reverence rooted in the conditions of Indian life, which make it so difficult for most of us to acquire either. These backyard godmen, unlike the made-for-export variety, are largely content to manifest their sanctity by sanctimoniousness, producing long and barely intelligible discourses into which their listeners can read whatever meaning they wish. (If religion is the opium of the Indian people, Ganapathi, then godmen are God's little chillums.)

The godman whom Yudhishtir approached came into this category, advocating measures either so unexceptionable (regular prayer) or so exceptional (regular consumption of one's own liquid wastes) that his following was confined to a small number of devoted devotees. Indeed, no one might have paid him any attention at all, were it not for the fact that the Prime Minister was discovered one day at one of his speeches. At a speech, in fact, in which the godman carelessly, or unimaginatively, or perversely – it really doesn't matter which – referred to the nation's traditional outcastes as 'Untouchables'.

That was all, mind you. He didn't suggest that they deserved to be where they were, didn't imply they had to be barred from temples or from our daughters' bedrooms; he simply called them 'Untouchables' instead of the euphemism Gangaji had invented in an effort to remove the stigma of that term. And Yudhishtir committed, in the eyes of his most radical critics, the unpardonable sin of neither correcting him nor walking out of his audience.

Now you know as well as I do, Ganapathi, that words are among India's traditional palliatives – we love to conceal our problems by changing their names. It mattered little to the men and women at the bottom of the social heap whether they were referred to by the most notorious of their disabilities or by the fiction of a divine paternity they supposedly shared with everyone else (which was almost as bad, because if *everyone* was a Child of God, why were *they* the only ones branded as such?). But to the professional politicians anxious to score points against my insensitive grandson, Yudhishtir's silence when the term was employed in his hearing meant acquiescence in a collective insult. The government, they declaimed to Priya Duryodhani's enthusiastic endorsement, was anti-Harijan.

Ashwathaman, the Front's radical leader, was foremost in his criticism of the Prime Minister. He could not, in all conscience, he announced, continue to support a government which had thus revealed its casteist cast. Yudhishtir's rivals, scenting his blood on the trail of their own ascent to his throne, agreed.

Suddenly the fragile unity of the Front began to crumble. One legislator declared he would no longer accept the party whip; another demanded that the Front expel its 'closet casteists'. There was open talk of forming a new Front, purged of 'reactionary' elements. A majority of the ruling party's legislators were just waiting, it was said, for a signal to abandon Yudhishtir. The signal had to come from the man whose Uprising had first started them on their ascent to power – Drona.

121

But the new Messiah lay on his sickbed, his liver devastated by the privations of Priya Duryodhani's prisons. Ill, exhausted, bitterly disappointed by the way in which the popular tide of his dreams had dribbled wastefully into the arid sands of sterile conflict, Drona lay torn between loyalty to the government he had created and the son for whom he had, all those years ago, changed his life.

'I can't afford to lose him to the other side,' Yudhishtir said to me. 'I must get him to issue a statement in my favour before Ashwathaman returns from his tour of the southern states and beats me to it.'

'Yama, the god of death, might beat you *both* to it,' I said. My own advancing years had made my imagery even more traditional, at least on the subject of mortality. 'I saw him this morning and felt he wouldn't last till tomorrow. But if he does, Yudhishtir, he is not going to support you against his son.'

'I realize that. And if he adds his voice to Ashwathaman's, I am finished,' Yudhishtir said matter-of-factly. 'The time has come for me to act as our ancestors would have done.' Without responding to my raised eyebrow, the Prime Minister beckoned to his youngest brother. 'Sahadev, I want you to go to Drona's house now and tell him Ashwathaman's plane back to Delhi has crashed.'

I was numbed by his words. 'You can't possibly do this,' I protested as soon as I had recovered my breath.

'Tell him also,' Yudhishtir went on obliviously, 'that I am on my way over to give him the news myself. I shall follow you in about ten minutes. Make sure no one else is with you when you say this, or when I enter.'

'But Yudhishtir,' I expostulated, 'you've never told a lie in your life!'

'And I never will,' my grandson replied piously.

'Drona knows that,' I pointed out. 'And he is bound to ask you for the truth of Sahadev's information.'

'Precisely.' Yudhishtir seemed undisturbed.

'You can't lie to him then! A dying man – your own guru . . .

'Don't worry, VVji,' Yudhishtir said. 'I won't lie.'

I went with him to Drona's house. The old man lay in a darkened room, surrounded by the medicines and equipment that kept him alive. Sahadev was crouched miserably at his bedside; I was shaken to see that the Messiah was weeping.

As we entered, he turned to Yudhishtir with a desperate anxiety even his frailty could not efface. 'He tells me this terrible fate has befallen my son,'

Drona said. 'Tell me, Yudhishtir, is it true? I cannot believe it unless it comes from you. Tell me, is Ashwathaman safe?'

A look of genuine sadness appeared on the Prime Minister's face. 'I am sorry, Dronaji,' Yudhishtir said. 'Ashwathaman is dead.'

Even I believed him then, for Yudhishtir simply did not lie. His honesty was like the brightness of the sun or the wetness of the rain, one of the elements of the natural world: you simply took it for granted.

'Ashwathaman,' he repeated softly, 'is dead.'

A terrible cry rose from Drona's lips. He turned his face away from us, towards the white-plastered wall, his voice drained of all emotion. 'Then I have nothing more to live for.' His eyes closed.

'I am sorry, Drona, to ask you this at this painful time,' the Prime Minister whispered, 'but will you not support the unity of the Front you did so much to create and place in power?'

The Messiah did not look at him. 'Yes,' he whispered. 'Of course.'

I saw the triumph in Yudhishtir's eyes at the same time that I saw the light fade from Drona's. Within minutes, the old guru was gone.

We stood in vigil as the life ebbed away from him, and I felt regret flood my spirit. Throughout his life, during his days of violence and of peace, his years of teaching and of withdrawal, Drona had been one of India's simplest men. 'The new Mahaguru', a Sunday magazine had dubbed him, but he was a flawed Mahaguru, a man whose goodness was not balanced by the shrewdness of the original. He had stood above his peers, a secular saint whose commitment to truth and justice was beyond question. But though his loyalty to the ideals of a democratic and egalitarian India could not be challenged, Drona's abhorrence of power had made him unfit to wield it. He had offered inspiration but not involvement, charisma but not change, hope but no harness. Having abandoned politics when he seemed the likely heir-apparent to Dhritarashtra, he tried to stay above it all after the fall of Dhritarashtra's daughter, and so he let the revolution he had wrought fall into the hands of lesser men who were unworthy of his ideals. Now he was dying, and the nation did not know what it would mourn.

'"J.D.," our modern Messiah, is no more,' Yudhishtir announced outside when it was all over. 'And his last words were a stirring plea for unity amongst us in the Front. It is no secret that he was deeply saddened by the troubles that have affected the government – *his* government, a government he did more than anyone else to make possible. It is sadly true that Dronaji died a deeply disappointed man, but his legacy lives on in the hearts of the Indian people – to whom, in the last analysis, he taught their own strength.' Yudhishtir paused, his voice breaking. 'I plead with all his followers and heirs today – let us not dissipate that strength. On this tragic occasion I shall call on every member of the Front, and in particular on Dronaji's son Ashwathaman, our party's President, to rededicate ourselves to the cause J.D. held so dear.'

'Ashwathaman?' I asked Yudhishtir later when we were alone. 'I thought you told the old man he was dead.' I shook my head in disappointment. 'You, Yudhishtir; you of all people. I believed you could never lie.'

'You believed right, VVji,' Yudhishtir said implacably. 'I didn't lie this time either. When I said Ashwathaman was dead, I was speaking the truth. Before leaving the house I caught a cockroach in the closet, named it Ashwathaman, and crushed it under my prime-ministerial despatch-box. So you see, VVji, I did not lie to Drona. I never said it was his son who had died.'

I stared at him, breathless at his sophistry. 'Your words, Yudhishtir,' I said at last, 'took away the last spark of life from the old man. In effect, they killed him.'

'You are being most unjust, VVji,' Yudhishtir replied. 'He was ill; he was dying. Perhaps his grief hastened his end, but is it not said that the time of our going is determined from our births? I may not have spoken the whole truth, but I spoke no *untruth*, and my words may have helped sustain a greater truth by prompting him to endorse my plea for unity. Would it have been better to allow his tremendous moral authority to have been manipulated by the radical rabble to bring down the government that has restored Indian democracy? I believe, VVji, that I acted righteously, in full pursuit of dharma. Dharma, you know, is a subtle thing.'

'But not as subtle as that, Yudhishtir,' I replied sadly. 'I do not believe you will profit from your deception. Our national motto is *"Satyameva Jayate,"* Truth will Prevail. Not your truth or mine, Yudhishtir; just Truth. A truth too immutable to be uttered only in the letter and violated in the spirit.' I rose, clenching my walking stick so tightly my palm hurt. 'Goodbye, Yudhishtir. You shall not see me again.'

I did not turn to see if my exit had even momentarily shaken his complacency.

 *122*

It did not matter, for of course I was right. Drona's dying benediction achieved no more than his lifetime's crusades. A majority of the Front's MPs left the Prime Minister's emunctory embrace. The government fell; and in the elections that followed, Priya Duryodhani was returned overwhelmingly to power. The still unresolved case against her was discreetly withdrawn. Dharma had turned full circle.

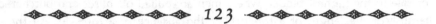 123

What remains to be said, Ganapathi? There is, of course, the question of expectations. This story, like that of our country, is a story of betrayed expectations, yours as much as our characters'. There is no story and too many stories; there are no heroes and too many heroes. What is left out matters almost as much as what is said.

Let me, as so often in our story, digress once more. There is, Ganapathi, a curious parallel. To most foreigners who know nothing of India, the one Indian book they know anything about is the *Kama Sutra*. To them, it is the Great Indian Novelty. The *Kama Sutra* may well be the only Indian book which has been read by more foreigners than Indians. Yet it is for the most part a treatise on the social etiquette of ancient Indian courtship, and those who think of its author Vatsyayana as some sort of fourth-century pornographer must surely be sorely disappointed to go through his careful catalogue of amatory activities, which reads more like a textbook than a thriller. But what a far cry it is from the precision of the *Kama Sutra* to the prudery of contemporary India! It never ceases to amaze me, Ganapathi, that a civilization so capable of sexual candour should be steeped in the ignorance, superstition and prurience that characterize Indian sexual attitudes today. Perhaps the problem is that the *Kama Sutra*'s refined brand of bedroom chivalry cannot go very far in a country of so many women and so few bedrooms.

It is no better with the great stories of our national epics. How far we have travelled from the glory and splendour of our adventurous mythological heroes! The land of Rama, setting out on his glorious crusade against the abductors of his divinely pure wife Sita, the land where truth and honour and valour and dharma were worshipped as the cardinal principles of existence, is now a nation of weak-willed compromisers, of leaders unable to lead, of rampant corruption and endemic faithlessness. Our democrats gamble with democracy; our would-be dictators do not know what to dictate. We soothe ourselves with the lullabies of our ancient history, our remarkable culture, our inspiring mythology. But our present is so depressing that our rulers can only speak of the intermediate future – or the immediate past.

Whatever our ancestors expected of India, Ganapathi, it was not this. It was not a land where dharma and duty have come to mean nothing; where religion is an excuse for conflict rather than a code of conduct; where piety, instead of marking wisdom, masks a crippling lack of imagination. It was not a land where brides are burned in kerosene-soaked kitchens because they have not brought enough dowry with them; where integrity and self-respect are for sale to the highest bidder; where men are pulled off buses and butchered because of the length of a forelock or the absence of a foreskin. All these things that I have avoided mentioning in my story because I preferred to pretend they did not matter.

But they matter, of course, because in our country the mundane is as relevant as the mythical. Our philosophers try to make much of our great Vedic religion by pointing to its spiritualism, its pacifism, its lofty pansophism; and they ignore, or gloss over, its superstitions, its inegalities, its obscurantism. That is quite typical. Indeed one may say it is quite typically Hindu. Hinduism is the religion of over 80 per cent of Indians, and as a way of life it pervades almost all things Indian, bringing to politics, work and social relations the same flexibility of doctrine, reverence for custom and absorptive eclecticism that characterize the religion – as well as the same tendency to respect outworn dogma, worship sacred cows and offer undue deference to gurus. Not to mention its great ability to overlook – or transcend – the inconvenient truth.

I have been, on the whole, a good Hindu in my story. I have portrayed a nation in struggle but omitted its struggles against itself, ignoring the regionalists and autonomists and separatists and secessionists who even today are trying to tear the country apart. To me, Ganapathi, they are of no consequence in the story of India; they seek to diminish something that is far greater than they will ever comprehend. Others will disagree and dismiss my assertion as the naïvety of the terminally nostalgic. They will say that the India of the epic warriors died on its mythological battlefields, and that today's India is a land of adulteration, black-marketing, corruption, communal strife, dowry killings, you know the rest, and that this is the only India that matters. Not my India, where epic battles are fought for great causes, where freedom and democracy are argued over, won, betrayed and lost, but an India where mediocrity reigns, where the greatest cause is the making of money, where dishonesty is the most prevalent art and bribery the most vital skill, where power is an end in itself rather than a means, where the real political issues of the day involve not principles but parochialism. An India where a Priya Duryodhani can be re-elected because seven hundred million people cannot produce anyone better, and where her immortality can be guaranteed by her greatest failure – the alienation of some of the country's most loyal citizens to the point where two of them consider it a greater duty to kill her than protect her, as they were employed to do.

Perhaps they were right. Or perhaps it is simply that I can no longer distinguish between right and wrong, real and unreal. For as I arrived near the end of my telling of this story, Ganapathi, I again began to dream.

I dreamt again of Hastinapur. Not, this time, of the glorious palace of the princely era, resplendent in its prosperity and basking in the warmth of the people's adulation, but of a drab township with squalid streets and peeling walls, with rancid rubbish accumulating in the open spaces of what had been the Bibighar Gardens. In my dream great hot winds blew into the town, filling it with swirling clouds of gritty dust. The sun disappeared from sight. Out of the breath-choking haze emerged, at savage random, flying objects that sprang from the sky and smashed in splinters on the ground, aimlessly mutilating passers-by and pavement-sleepers. In the murky half-light of dawn and dusk, hands outstretched as if groping for direction, roamed a hundred headless figures, the gaping emptiness at their necks suppurating horribly. The sacred river that flowed by the palace backed up in a surging torrent that swept it against nature, returning it toward its source.

I groaned in my sleep as I saw these things, Ganapathi, but my tossing and turning would not drive the images from my fevered brain. Hastinapur crumbled before my eyes. Fierce-toothed rodents scurried through the town, gnawing and nibbling at the stocks of grain, the vegetation, the electrical wiring and the fingers of the maimed street-dwellers. The milk on every stove boiled over, reeking of the odour of charred flesh. Pots and plates developed cracks; white vessels became black in the washing. The purest milk turned watery and ripe mangoes tasted more bitter than gourds. Sacks of rice were found to contain more stones than grain. The most carefully prepared food turned out to be crawling with maggots. Wells turned brackish, roads broke up into rubble, roofs caved in. I was dreaming, Ganapathi, of the worst kind of devastation – that which occurs when nature turns upon itself.

Even the full moon could not be seen on its appointed night. Instead the *koyals*, songbirds once, never stopped crowing; cows brayed like donkeys and whelped mules rather than calves; and jackals howled in the streets as if they belonged to the houses of Hastinapur rather than to the jungles surrounding it.

I could see, even in my sleep, that the process could not be overcome; it could only be escaped from. In the distant hills overlooking Hastinapur loomed the snow-covered top of a gleaming mountain, and from it, a celestial peace on their visages, Gangaji, Dhritarashtra and Pandu smiled and beckoned. From the debris of the town, looking up at that shining light on the mountain, our recent protagonists decided to embark on the ascent.

They had not even begun their march when Krishna fell to the ground, a deep wound oozing in his heel. He clutched his foot, his face contorted in agony. 'I cannot move,' he gasped. Krishna's dark features were sallow with pain. 'I can sit, I can speak, I can give you advice, but I cannot walk on with you. Go without me.'

And so, as the others sorrowfully turned away, Krishna's life oozed into the earth of my dream. And a voice from the mountain-top echoed in my mind: 'He could have prevented all this, but he chose not to act. He remained content with his little fief, giving advice and verse to Arjun, and then went back to his comforts and allowed all this to happen. India has too many Krishnas. His brilliance burned itself out without illuminating the country. He cannot reach the top.'

Leaving him behind, the others set out across rock and ravine, valley and hill, towards the foot of the mountain. A little dog attached itself to them, and trotted beside Yudhishtir. Onward they walked, then upward, till each step seemed unbearably heavy and the thin air rasped in their lungs. Then Draupadi collapsed to the ground.

'Why her?' I asked the faceless voice in my dream.

'Democracy always falters first,' came the echo. 'She can only be sustained by the strength of her husbands. Their weakness is her fatal flaw. She cannot endure to the mountain-top.'

The others walked on. After hours of trudging through the mire of my mind, Sahadev stumbled and fell. In my dream, I no longer needed to ask the question: the unseen voice answered the unspoken query.

'He knew what was right, but did nothing with his knowledge,' it said. 'He stayed outside the country, saw its greatness and its failings in perspective, but did not involve himself in its true struggle for survival. He cannot stride to the mountain-top.'

Nakul was the next to give up.

'He was too willing to serve institutions rather than values. Dharma consists of more than just doing one's duty as narrowly defined by one's immediate job. There is a larger duty, a duty to a greater cause, that Nakul ignored. He will not see the mountain-top.'

When Arjun fell, I remember the shock radiating even through my dream. 'But Arjun — the paragon of virtue, who by the unanimous wish of the people succeeded Priya Duryodhani! How can *he* fall?'

'He believed himself to be perfect,' resonated the reply, 'and allowed others to believe it. But India defeats perfection, as the rainclouds obscure the sun. His arrogance tripped him up when his gaze aimed even beyond the peak. He will never get to the mountain-top.'

They were still some way from the crest when Bhim sank heavily to his knees.

'He protected the Pandavas and the country, but that was not enough. He did not do enough to shield Draupadi Mokrasi from abuse, because he saw himself as only one of her guardians and placed his commitment to his brothers above his commitment to her. He will not stand on the mountain-top.'

Yudhishtir, unflagging, climbed on steadily, alone except for the little dog still trotting by his side. 'Why him?' I asked. 'Yudhishtir, with his priggish morality, his blind insensitivity to others, his willingness to gamble Draupadi away, his self-serving adherence to the letter of honesty rather than its spirit? How can he be allowed to climb on when all the others have fallen?'

The voice seemed surprised by the question. 'But he was true to himself throughout,' it said. 'He was true to dharma.'

And indeed, Yudhishtir at last reached the top of the mountain, and looked around him, seeing the peaks and the valleys below, at a level with the fluffy white clouds that floated past like gossamer from nature's veil.

One of the clouds swooped down upon him in my dream. Upon it was seated a splendid figure of godlike magnificence, wearing a golden crown on his smooth and unwrinkled brow.

'I am Kaalam, the god of Time,' he said with a dazzling smile. 'You have reached the mountain-top, Yudhishtir; your time has come. Mount my chariot with me and let us travel to the court of History.'

'I am greatly honoured,' our hero replied. 'May this dog come with me?'

'No, he may not,' Kaalam said with some distaste. 'History has no place for dogs. Come, we must hurry.'

'I am sorry,' Yudhishtir pursed his lips. 'This dog has been my faithful companion throughout my long ascent. I cannot abandon him now that I have reached the top.'

'Then I shall have to leave without you,' Kaalam said impatiently.

'Leave then, if you must,' Yudhishtir's jaw was set. 'I shall not come without the dog. It would not be dharma to repay devotion in this manner.'

'You must be crazy,' Kaalam exclaimed. 'You wish to turn down a place in history for the sake of a mere dog? A creature associated with unclean things, in whose presence no meal is eaten, no ritual performed? How did the noble and upright Yudhishtir form such a peculiar attachment?'

'I have never forsaken any person or creature who has been faithful to me,' Yudhishtir said. 'I will not start now. Goodbye.'

And as he looked down at the little dog, it transformed itself, in my dream, into the resplendent Dharma, god of justice and righteousness. Yudhishtir's true father.

'You have passed the test, my son,' Dharma proclaimed. 'Come with me to claim History's reward.'

The three of them boarded Kaalam's cloudy chariot and floated serenely to History's court. There Yudhishtir had his first shock: for seated on a golden throne, fanned by nubile attendants, sat his late tormentor, Priya Duryodhani.

'I don't understand,' he stammered when he had caught his breath. 'This tyrant, this destroyer of people and institutions, this persecutor of truth and democracy, seated like this on a golden throne? I do not wish to see her face! Take me to where my brothers are, where Draupadi is.'

'History's judgements are not so easily made, my son,' Dharma replied. 'To some, Duryodhani is a revered figure, a saviour of India, a Joan of Arc burned at the democratic stake by the ignorant and the prejudiced. Abandon your old bitterness here, Yudhishtir. There are no enmities at History's court.'

'Where are my brothers?' Yudhishtir asked stubbornly. 'And my pure and long-suffering wife? Why don't I see them here, where Duryodhani holds court?'

'They are in a separate place, my son,' said Dharma. 'If that is where you wish to go, I shall take you.'

He led Yudhishtir down a rough and pitted pathway, over rubble and broken glass. The pair picked their way through brambles and strings of barbed wire, past rotting vegetation and smouldering pyres. Yudhishtir braved the smoke, the increasing heat, the stench of animal decomposition. Mosquitoes buzzed about his ears. His feet struck rock and sometimes bone. But still, in my dream, he trudged unwaveringly on.

Dharma stopped suddenly. 'Here we are,' he said, though they seemed to have arrived nowhere in particular. The darkness closed in round Yudhishtir like the clammy hands of a cadaver. Despite the intense heat, he shivered.

And then a wail rose around him from the darkness, a cry joined by another and yet another, until Yudhishtir's mind and mine seemed nothing but the echo-chamber for a plaintive, continuous lament. As it went on he could make out the voices begging pitifully for his help – Bhim's, Arjun's, the twins', even Draupadi's . . .

'What is the meaning of this?' he burst out. 'Why are my brothers and my wife here, in this foul blackness, while Duryodhani enjoys the luxuries of posthumous adulation? Have I gone mad, or has the world ceased to mean anything?'

'You are quite sane, my son,' Dharma said calmly. 'And you can prove your sanity by leaving this noxious place with me. I only brought you here because you asked for it. You do not belong here, Yudhishtir.'

'But nor do they!' Yudhishtir expostulated. 'What wrong have they done that they should suffer like this? Go — I shall stay with them, and share their unmerited suffering.'

At these words, the darkness lifted, the filth and the stench disappeared. Yudhishtir's brow was cooled by a gentle breeze and his senses calmed by a fragrant aroma of freshly flowering blossoms, as his eyes opened to a refulgent assembly of personages from our story.

Yes, Ganapathi, they were all there in my dream: gentle Draupadi and genteel Drewpad, boisterous Bhim and blustery Sir Richard, grim Gandhari and grimacing Shikhandin; the Karnistanis and the Kauravas; the British and the brutish; pale Pandu embracing his wives; blind Dhritarashtra and blond Georgina. And they were smiling, and laughing, and clapping. 'You have passed your last test, Yudhishtir!' Dharma proclaimed. 'It was all an illusion, my son. You will no more be condemned to an eternity of misery than Duryodhani will enjoy perpetual contentment. Everyone must have at least a glimpse of the other world; the fortunate man samples hell first, the better to enjoy the taste of paradise that follows. All those you see around you have passed through these portals before; tomorrow you will stand amongst them to greet a new entrant as he comes in. And the illusions will go on.'

'The tests you put me through,' Yudhishtir asked, frowning. 'Has everyone here gone through them?'

'Yes, but very few have passed them as you have,' Dharma said.

'And what were they meant to prove?'

'Prove?' Dharma seemed vaguely puzzled. 'Only the eternal importance of dharma.'

'To what end? If it makes no difference to all these people, who all have their place here . . .'

'*Everyone*,' Dharma said, 'finds his place in history, even those who have failed to observe dharma. But it is essential to recognize virtue and righteousness, and to praise him who, like yourself, has consistently upheld dharma.'

'Why?' Yudhishtir asked.

'What do you mean,' Dharma replied irritably, ' "why"?'

'I mean why?' Yudhishtir replied, addressing everyone gathered before him. 'What purpose has it served? Has my righteousness helped either me, my wife, my family or my country? Does justice prevail in India, or in its history? What has adherence to dharma achieved in our own story?'

'This is sacrilege,' his preceptor breathed. 'If there is one great Indian principle that has been handed down through the ages, it is that of the paramount importance of practising dharma at any price. Life itself is worthless without dharma. Only dharma is eternal.'

'India is eternal,' Yudhishtir said. 'But the dharma appropriate for it at different stages of its evolution has varied. I am sorry, but if there is one thing that is true today, it is that there are no classical verities valid for all time. I believed differently, and have paid the price of being defeated, humiliated, and reduced to irrelevance. It is too late for me to do anything about it: I have had my turn. But for too many generations now we have allowed ourselves to believe India had all the answers, if only it applied them correctly. Now I realize that we don't even know all the questions.'

'What are you saying?' Dharma asked, and Yudhishtir saw to his astonishment that the resplendent deva beside him was changing slowly back into a dog.

'No more certitudes,' he called out desperately to the receding figure. 'Accept doubt and diversity. Let each man live by his own code of conduct, so long as he has one. Derive your standards from the world around you and not from a heritage whose relevance must be constantly tested. Reject equally the sterility of ideologies and the passionate prescriptions of those who think themselves infallible. Uphold decency, worship humanity, affirm the basic values of our people – those which do not change – and leave the rest alone. Admit that there is more than one Truth, more than one Right, more than one dharma . . .'

I woke up to the echo of a vain and frantic barking.

I woke up, Ganapathi, to today's India. To our land of computers and corruption, of myths and politicians and box-wallahs with moulded plastic briefcases. To an India beset with uncertainties, muddling chaotically through to the twenty-first century.

Your eyebrows and nose, Ganapathi, twist themselves into an elephantine question-mark. Have I, you seem to be asking, come to the end of my story? How forgetful you are: it was just the other day that I told you stories never end, they just continue somewhere else. In the hills and the plains, the hearths and the hearts, of India.

But my last dream, Ganapathi, leaves me with a far more severe problem. If it means anything, anything at all, it means that I have told my story so far from a completely mistaken perspective. I have thought about it, Ganapathi, and I realize I have no choice. I must retell it.

I see the look of dismay on your face. I am sorry, Ganapathi. I shall have a word with my friend Brahm tomorrow. In the meantime, let us begin again.

They tell me India is an underdeveloped country . . .

AFTERWORD

Many of the characters, incidents and issues in this novel are based on people and events described in the great epic the *Mahabharata*, a work which remains a perennial source of delight and inspiration to millions in India. I am no Sanskrit scholar and have therefore relied only on a highly subjective reading of a variety of English translations of the epic. I should like to acknowledge, in particular, my debt to the versions of C. Rajagopalachari and P. Lal, respectively the most readable renderings of what scholars call the southern and northern rescensions of the work. The two differ sufficiently in approach, style and narrative content to be complementary, even though they both deal with essential aspects of the same story. I have relied greatly on both of them.

While some scenes in *The Great Indian Novel* are recastings of situations described in translations of the *Mahabharata*, I have taken far too many liberties with the epic to associate any of its translators with my sins. Those readers who wish to delve into the *Mahabharata* itself in search of the sources of my inspiration need look no further than Lal's 'transcreation', Rajagopalachari's episodic saga or Prof. J. A. B. Van Buitenen's scholarly, thorough but incomplete translation for the University of Chicago Press. While this novel was with the publishers I also discovered Jean-Claude Carrière's stage script of the *Mahabharata* in Peter Brooke's most readable translation, and recommend it highly. The responsibility for this entirely fictional version is, of course, mine alone.

A NOTE ON DHARMA

Of the many Indian words and expressions in this book, the meanings of most of which are readily apparent from their context (or from the glossary), the one term it may be necessary to elucidate is *'dharma'*.

Dharma is perhaps unique in being an untranslatable Sanskrit term that is, none the less, cheerfully defined as a normal, unitalicized entry in an English dictionary. The definition offered in *Chambers Twentieth-Century Dictionary* is 'the righteousness that underlies the law; the law'. While this is a definite improvement on the one-word translation offered in many an Indian Sanskrit primer ('religion'), it still does not convey the full range of meaning implicit in the term. 'English has no equivalent for dharma,' writes P. Lal in the Glossary to his 'transcreation' of the *Mahabharata*, in which he defines dharma as 'code of good conduct, pattern of noble living, religious rules and observance'.

My friend Ansar Hussain Khan suggests that *dharma* is most simply defined as 'that by which we live'. Yes — but 'that' embraces a great deal. An idea of the immensity and complexity of the concept of dharma may be conveyed by the fact that, in his superb analytical study of Indian culture and society, *The Speaking Tree*, Richard Lannoy defines dharma in at least nine different ways depending on the context in which he uses the term. The nine (with page references to the Oxford University Press paperback edition in brackets): Moral Law (xvi), spiritual order (142), sacred law (160), salvation ethic (213), totality of social, ethical and spiritual harmony (217), righteousness (218, 325), universal order (229), magico-religious cycle (233), moral, idealistic, spiritual force (294). Lannoy also quotes Betty Heimann's excellent version in her 1937 work *Indian and Western Philosophy: A Study in Contrasts*: 'Dharma is total cosmic responsibility, including God's, a universal justice far more inclusive, wider and profounder than any Western equivalent, such as "duty".'

The reader of *The Great Indian Novel* is invited, upon each encounter with dharma in these pages, to assume that the term is used to mean any, or all, of the above.

Shashi Tharoor

GLOSSARY

(All the words defined are from Sanskrit and/or Hindi, except where otherwise indicated)

aarti – Hindu religious rite involving the ceremonial waving of lighted lamps before the object to be worshipped or honoured

Angrez – Briton (colloquial)

Arthashastra – classic political treatise ascribed to Chanakya (Kautilya), a Machiavellian statesman-philosopher of the fourth century B C

ashram – the hermitage of a spiritual figure and a retreat for his disciples

ayah – nanny

babu – low-level functionary, clerk

Bakr-Id – Muslim festival at which goats are sacrificed

barfi – Indian sweet made of milk, often covered with edible silver foil (*vark*)

bhai – brother

chakra – wheel

chakravarti – universal emperor

chappals – slippers

chaprassi – peon

chela – pupil, acolyte

dal bhaat – rice and lentils (i.e. the basic staple)

darshan – inspiring vision or sight, used to refer to audience granted by king or holy man

dharma – see note opposite

dharna – act of political agitation or demonstration, usually involving the agitators sitting at the door of the authorities concerned until their demands are granted

dharti – earth

dhobi – washerman

dhoti – ankle-length waistcloth, traditional male attire in most parts of India

doodhwala – milkman

durwan – guard, watchman

gurudwara – Sikh temple

Holi — Hindu spring festival marked by the splashing of coloured water

janmabhoomi — motherland

jawan — soldier

-ji — suffix denoting respect

karanavar — a Malayalam word meaning landlord, elder of a joint Kerala family

karma — Hindu cycle of predestined birth and rebirth; destiny

khadi — homespun Indian cotton

kukri — Gurkha knife

kundalini — vital force of cosmic energy embodied in everyone, and pictured as a coiled serpent at the base of the spine

kurta — loose collarless shirt

lathi — bamboo or wooden stave used by Indian policemen

maidan — playing-field

Mathrubhoomi Azhichapadippu — popular weekly journal in Kerala

meghdoot — cloud messenger (from a classic poem by Kalidas in which a cloud is implored to convey tidings of a lost wife)

MLA — Member of the Legislative Assembly (of a state, rather than the national Parliament in Delhi whose members are called MPs)

mofussil — outlying, provincial, rural

moksha — salvation

mullah — Muslim priest

mundu — South Indian *dhoti* (see above)

namaskar, namaste — traditional Hindu greeting, usually with the palms joined

Naxalites, Naxals — violent Maoist revolutionaries, particularly active in Bengal in 1967–71

neta — leader

padayatra — long journey on foot, usually undertaken for social or political purposes through an area affected by calamity

panchayat — village council

pandal — temporary covered structure for outdoor receptions, ceremonies, etc.

patideva — respectful term for husband

patwari — village official

puja — ritual players

Puranas — ancient collections of popular Hindu myths and legends of religious and social significance

razai — quilt

rishi — holy man, sage

sadhu — Hindu holy man

sainik — soldier

sannyasi – Hindu holy man, usually an ascetic

satyagraha – literally 'truth-force', used by Mahatma Gandhi to define his non-violent agitation

satyagrahi – one who undertakes *satyagraha*

saunf – aniseed

Shaitaan – Satan

shama – songbird of the thrush family

shamiana – large tent

shastras – Hindu holy books, especially those laying down laws and precepts

sherwani – traditional North Indian knee-length jacket

Shri – Mr

sloka – verse

subedar – non-commissioned officer

Sudra – member of the lowest Hindu caste

swadeshi – indigenous, i.e. Indian

swaraj – self-rule

Swatantra Sena – (fictional) Independence Army

swayamvara – ceremony in which a noblewoman chooses a husband from amongst assembled suitors

tamasha – fun, spectacle

twice-born – upper-caste Hindu, one who has undergone a 'second birth', i.e. a spiritual one; generally used to refer to Brahmins

veda – one of four principal sacred texts of the Hindus – the *Rig Veda*, the *Yajur Veda*, the *Sama Veda*, and the *Artharva Veda* – composed circa 1500–1200 BC and consisting of sacred Sanskrit hymns

yuddha – war

zamindar – landlord

zenana – women's quarters

zilla – sub-district

zindabad – long live

ACKNOWLEDGEMENTS

I am grateful to Prof. P. Lal for permission to quote from his book, *The Mahabharata of Vyasa*.

My gratitude also goes to Tony Lacey, David Davidar and Julia Sutherland for their valuable editorial guidance; to my agent, Deborah Rogers, for her dedication and perseverance; to my brother-in-law, Dr Chandra Shekhar Mukherji, for his early and repeated encouragement as the work progressed; to my friends Deepa Menon, Margaret Kooijman, Ansar Hussain Khan and Arvind Subramanian, for volunteering to inflict the draft manuscript on themselves and for reading it with affection and insight; to my sisters, Shobha Srinivasan and Smita Menon, for their love, support and hospitality on two continents; to my wife, Tilottama, for bearing with me throughout the difficult evenings and weekends of my writing, and for trying (with only partial success) to get me to approach her own high critical standards; and to my parents, Chandran and Lily Tharoor, for teaching me to aspire, and for sustaining my faith in this book as they have sustained all my writing for so many years.